Someday at Christmas

Lizzie Byron

CORONET

First published in Great Britain in 2020 by Coronet
An Imprint of Hodder & Stoughton
An Hachette UK company

This paperback edition published in 2020

1

A CIP catalogue record for this title is available from the British Library

Paperback ISBN 978 1 529 38489 5
eBook ISBN 978 1 529 38490 1

Typeset in Plantin Light by Palimpsest Book Production Limited,
Falkirk, Stirlingshire

Printed and bound in Great Britain by Clays Ltd, Elcograf S.p.A.

Hodder & Stoughton policy is to use papers that are natural,
renewable and recyclable products and made from wood grown in
sustainable forests. The logging and manufacturing processes
are expected to conform to the environmental regulations
of the country of origin.

Hodder & Stoughton Ltd
Carmelite House
50 Victoria Embankment
London EC4Y 0DZ

www.hodder.co.uk

For everyone who believes in the true wonder of love
and Laura Mercier setting powder

CHRISTMAS EVE

1954

In the seventeen years since Patrick Duke opened the doors to Duke & Sons, the store had survived a war, an exuberant soda fountain that almost flooded the café in the basement and his son Charles's bright idea to distil whisky in a corner of the warehouse. As such, it was fair to say that there was very little that surprised him any more.

One thing that would never cease to amaze him, though, was how many people were nonchalant enough to leave buying their gifts until Christmas Eve. Even Renée Flynn, who visited the store almost every day to purchase table linen for a dinner party she was hosting or to linger in the Scarf Hall, admiring each one with the sort of hushed wonder usually reserved for an art gallery, still left it until an hour before the store closed to rush in.

She swept through the revolving door in her usual whirl of blonde curls and Gaulin perfume, then stopped to pat the snowflakes from her conker-coloured mink coat. When she finally looked up, he took a step forward to greet her.

'Mrs Flynn,' he said brightly, hands behind his back.

She turned her cheek towards the sound of his voice, then immediately softened when she saw it was him. 'Oh,

Mr Duke, thank goodness!' She pressed a gloved hand to her chest. 'You're a sight for sore feet!'

'Please.' He bowed his head. 'Call me Patrick.'

Wide-eyed and wasp-waisted, Renée Flynn was exactly the sort of customer Patrick had imagined when he opened Duke & Sons: a Grace Kelly blonde with exquisite taste and a weakness for Hermès scarves. She used to be a model, or so the gossip on the shop floor went, and after a scandalous affair with a Hollywood star, she had surprised everyone by marrying Adam Flynn, the CEO of Great Capital Bank. Now she was every bit the Ostley housewife, but she still had a mischievous glint in her eye.

'Patrick.' She beamed, immediately back to her playful self as she reached up to squeeze his shoulders with her hands, then kiss him swiftly on each cheek. 'Thank goodness you're still open. I didn't think I'd get here in time. My train from London was delayed because of the snow.' She plucked off her leather gloves with great flourish. 'I took the children to see *The Nutcracker*.'

'How was it?'

'I enjoyed it, but I think they would rather have seen *Jack and the Beanstalk*.'

Patrick chuckled lightly.

'Still. At least they're thrilled at the promise of a white Christmas.'

Her smile was more wistful as she glanced over her shoulder at the snow falling quietly outside. Patrick, too, smiled wistfully at the sight of it and the crowd that had gathered on the pavement outside, little hands and noses pressed to the frosted glass as they gazed at the DUKE & SONS TOYLAND display in the window.

When he turned back to Renée, her gaze was darting around the busy Beauty Hall.

'It's so late,' she said. 'I thought everyone would be at home with their families by now and I could run in and collect Charlotte's locket. But it's busier than when the store reopened last month. Are you having a sale?'

'No.' He chuckled again, but he could see why she thought that, aware of the building chaos. The nearer they got to five o'clock, browsing became snatching and the panic was almost palpable. They'd sold out of Duke & Sons hampers by midday, which never happened. He'd failed to put one aside and his wife would *not* be amused. 'It's our first Christmas since rationing ended. I think people are enjoying being able to buy whatever they please this year.'

'Oh, yes, of course.' Mrs Flynn adjusted the collar of her coat, then lowered her voice. 'I do acknowledge how lucky Adam and I were to be able to eat out most evenings and we had use of the dining hall at the bank, of course, but there's nothing like a home-cooked meal.' She leaned a little closer to him. 'And when I say *home-cooked*, I mean cooked by our housekeeper, Mrs Montgomery, of course. You and Mrs Duke must come over for supper in the New Year. Bring Charles. How old is he now? Eighteen?' The corners of her mouth twitched when Patrick nodded. 'Does he have a sweetheart? If not, I can introduce him to David's niece, Philippa. She's his age and quite lovely.'

Before Patrick could respond, she glanced around the busy Beauty Hall again. 'Speaking of lovely, look at this! Things almost feel normal again.'

'They certainly do.' Patrick turned to the queue of children holding their parents' hands and clutching their neatly written letters as they waited to see Father Christmas. 'The store on Bridge Street was a welcome refuge while we were rebuilding, but it's nice to be home. Especially for Christmas.'

'And it's nice to have you back.' She reached up to squeeze his shoulder again. 'Nowhere does Christmas quite like Duke & Sons.'

'Well, yes.' Patrick's cheeks flushed with pride. 'This is all Charles's doing, though. He loves Christmas. It was his birthday yesterday so he gets everything at once.'

'These are beautiful.' She pointed at the garland of holly edging the Gaulin counter.

'They're more modest than Charles would have liked.'

That was putting it mildly given the *heated discussion* they'd had about them last month.

As it was the first Christmas since Duke & Sons had reopened, Charles was resolute that the store *had* to look exactly as it did that first Christmas in 1937. He was only a year old when it opened, but Charles insisted he remembered it. He couldn't possibly, but Patrick did. He remembered the tree, and the heavy spruce garlands that edged each of the counters in the Beauty Hall and lined the handrail of the carved wooden staircase that twisted up from the middle of the store, circling the floors to stop under the stained-glass dome in the ceiling.

'And the tree is *stunning*,' Mrs Flynn added. 'Better than any I saw in London today.'

The Duke & Sons Christmas tree used to be a tradition in Ostley Spa. Everyone would make a point of coming in to see it. He had missed many, many things about the store when they had decamped to Bridge Street, but watching customers' faces when they walked in and saw the tree was one of the things Patrick had missed most. It didn't matter how cold it was outside or how busy the store was, everyone would stop to stare at it, standing in the middle of the floor, the point of the gold star almost touching the stained-glass dome.

It was good to be home.

'Well.' He plucked the pocket watch from his waistcoat and checked the time. 'If you'd care to join me by the tree, Charles tells me he's arranged something that is sure to get us all in the Christmas spirit.'

'Oh, what is it?'

'It's a surprise.' He extended his arm. 'Shall we find out what it is?'

As they approached the tree, there was a commotion on the staircase and Patrick frowned as a group of men appeared in top hats and black suits with red tartan ties and waistcoats.

'What's this?' Mrs Flynn gasped, but he had no idea.

One of the men tipped his top hat to Patrick, then turned to the others with a smile. That was obviously their cue, because they immediately ran down the stairs towards the tree. They were swiftly followed by a group of women in white shirts and long red tartan taffeta skirts

7

that swished loudly. The gentle murmur of chatter faded as everyone in the Beauty Hall stopped and turned to watch the men and women gather around the Christmas tree with their backs to it, each holding up a lantern with a church candle inside.

The sudden hush was enough to draw the curiosity of the shoppers on the other floors, and Patrick watched a series of heads pop up along the banister as a small girl with cola-coloured ringlets appeared on the staircase. She was wearing a knee-length red tartan taffeta dress and glossy black patent shoes that tapped lightly on the steps as she skipped down them to join the others at the Christmas tree. When she stood in front of them, there was a collective coo as she lifted her chin with a smile. She waited a beat, then took a deep breath, and when she started singing 'Silent Night', Patrick covered his mouth with his hand.

Charles remembered.

Patrick bit down on his bottom lip to stop himself giving in to the rush of emotion charging through him as the little girl sang. And, with that, the whole store was still, as it was only at night, when the doors were locked and it was just him, wandering the shop floor, straightening the perfume bottles and wiping the smudges from the glass countertops with his handkerchief. Quiet in the way it had been that chilly morning in 1940 when he approached Ostley High Street to find that it was barely a street any more. Rather, a layer of smoking rubble with shards of metal sticking up towards the sky, like candles on a birthday cake.

Sky. That was what he remembered most about that morning. An endless, uninterrupted stretch of ash-coloured sky. The sky and Duke & Sons, in the middle of it all, the roof gone and one corner bitten off, but still there. Even the clock above the revolving door remained, although it had stopped at seven twenty, the time the first bomb had dropped the night before.

Patrick Duke was advised to demolish the store and rebuild. He refused, renting temporary premises on Bridge Street so Duke & Sons could keep trading and he could plough every spare penny he had into the repairs. The store had been open for just a few years so it wasn't difficult to reassemble the team who had worked on it originally and could restore it to its former glory. The decorators, who remembered without needing to be told which colours they'd used. The carpenters, who made new counters, relaid the parquet floors and built another staircase that was somehow more beautiful than the one it replaced. The glazing company, who sealed the windows and delivered the stained-glass dome, piece by delicate piece, from Frome, and painstakingly reassembled it the day before the store had reopened last month.

The only thing Patrick hadn't fixed was the clock outside over the revolving door, its hands now stuck for ever at seven twenty.

It had taken fourteen years, and while there had been moments when he wondered if he should stop referring to the store on Bridge Street as temporary, he never did.

When he was a child, Patrick saw a photograph of Le Bon Marché in Paris in his father's newspaper and

9

dreamed of living in a department store like that, of sleeping in a different bed every night and wearing whatever he wanted from the boys' department. The night before Duke & Sons had reopened last month, he had done just that. He had slept in the grand four-poster bed on the top floor and woken to buttery sunlight pouring in through the stained-glass dome, his nod to Le Bon Marché, and for one sweet moment, he'd thought he was in Heaven.

As he listened to the little girl sing, he felt the same way, and when the other carollers joined in, everyone in the store was equally enchanted. Some sang along, but most just stood there, lips parted.

When the carol ended, he joined in with the applause, then turned to find his son next to him.

'Do you remember, Pops?'

'Of course, Charles,' he said, reaching over to ruffle his blond hair.

'Remember what, Patrick?'

He turned to Mrs Flynn, who also had tears in her eyes. 'That first Christmas Eve, after . . .' He coughed to dislodge the knot in his throat. 'I insisted that we check on the store on our way back from midnight mass. Mary, Charles and I picked our way through the rubble and stood right here.' He pointed down at the floor. 'And looked up at the hole in the roof, at the stars and the flat black sky. Just as we did, it started snowing. I remember that Charles,' he glanced at him with a proud smile, 'who was only three at the time—'

'Three and one day,' Charles corrected.

'Three and one day,' Patrick agreed. 'I was carrying Charles, and when he saw the snow, he started singing "Silent Night". It was the first real moment of hope I'd felt since I heard the first bomb drop.'

Renée turned to Charles with a tender smile. 'What a wonderful thing to do for your father!'

'Thank you, Mrs Flynn,' he said graciously, then went to thank the carollers.

When she and Patrick were alone and the chattering in the Beauty Hall resumed, he pushed his shoulders back and said, 'Now, Mrs Flynn, you said something about needing to collect a locket?'

'Oh, yes.' Her blonde curls quivered as she shook her head. 'A last minute Christmas gift for my daughter, Charlotte. I asked for it to be engraved and Henry called earlier to say that it's ready.'

He held out his arm to her. 'May I escort you to the third floor?'

'That would be lovely.' She curled her arm around his and let him lead her to the lifts.

As they passed the Gaulin counter, the woman behind it smiled. She was wearing a neat white shirt and the gold bells hanging from the red tartan bow pinned to it swivelled gently when she greeted them. 'Good afternoon, Mrs Flynn, Mr Duke.'

Renée stopped. 'Molly, darling. Has that lipstick arrived yet?'

'Yes. It came in this morning. Shall I wrap it for you?'

'It's just for me.' She waved her leather gloves at Molly. 'No need to wrap it.

'I'm terrible, I know,' she confessed with an unrepentant smile, her blue eyes shining as she stopped to sniff a perfume before they continued to the lifts. 'Something for me. Something for Charlotte.'

'My favourite kind of Christmas shopping.'

The grand brass doors opened as they approached. Jonathan the lift attendant heaved back the cage, letting everyone out. 'Mrs Flynn. Mr Duke.' He invited them to step in and asked which floor they needed.

'Third, please, Jonathan,' Patrick said. 'The Scarf Hall, Handbags & Accessories, and Jewellery.'

Henry, who managed the Duke & Sons jewellery department, must have heard they were coming because as they ambled towards the cluster of counters, he emerged from his office holding a small black leather case.

'Mrs Flynn, Mr Duke,' he said, arm extended, gesturing to the round table in the middle.

'Henry!' she sang. 'How lovely to see you.'

He and Patrick waited for her to sit, then did the same.

'Always a pleasure, Mrs Flynn,' Henry said, with a smile. 'I hope you're well.'

She put her handbag and gloves on the table. 'Very.'

'Marvellous.' He held up the leather case. 'Would you like to see Charlotte's necklace?'

'Yes!' She clapped as he opened the case and slid it across the table to show her the fine gold chain and heart-shaped locket. She pressed the point of her red lacquered nail to the locket, then admired the freshly engraved *C* in the centre. 'Oh, it's perfect, Henry. Thank you. I know it was a rush, but when I saw it yesterday, I had to have it for her.'

'You're very welcome. If you're happy, I'll get it wrapped for you.'

He returned a few minutes later with a red tartan box tied with a green ribbon.

'Look at that! Like something from a Christmas card.'

Patrick nodded towards the gold bell attached to the ribbon. It tinkled when Mrs Flynn shook the box. 'Charles's idea, I take it? My son and his ideas.'

'I like this one.' She shook the box again. 'And his "Silent Night" surprise.'

Patrick raised an eyebrow.

'Oh, leave him be. He's young. He just wants to make his mark on the place.'

'He's certainly doing that!'

'I know, but the store is called Duke & *Sons*,' she reminded him.

'That's very true, Mrs Flynn,' he agreed with a small smile. 'But lest we forget, this store has survived two wars. Hopefully it can survive my son, as well.'

NOW

Chapter One

There's always a moment, right after Shell hands a client the mirror to show them what she's done, when things can go either way. Either she'll be heralded a genius. Princess of Highlight, Queen of Contouring, ruler of all her blusher-brush touches, or she'll be told she's ruined their life.

Or their day, at least.

Shell isn't trying to ruin anyone's day – quite the opposite, in fact: she wants her clients to leave the ART counter not only feeling beautiful but empowered and brave enough to try purple eyeshadow again – but a reaction like that is easier to deal with.

It's the ones who won't tell her they hate what she's done who are the worst. She knows as soon as they see their reflection in the mirror. Their face falls and they let out a tiny 'Oh,' and Shell knows what's coming: a painful stretch of silence followed by a mumbled, 'Yeah, it's nice . . .' Like when your hairdresser gives you layers you didn't ask for, so you pretend you love it and cry on the bus home.

Luckily, after eleven years, reactions like that are rare.

If there's one thing Shell has learned it's that it's not what her clients *say* they want, it's what they *don't* say. So, someone asking for a 'dewy, natural look' doesn't actually want anything remotely natural. They want two layers of foundation and enough highlighter that their cheekbones can be seen from space. And someone who wants to 'try something different' doesn't want to try anything different. They're just curious to see what a peach blusher looks like instead of their usual pink one.

Like her current client Mia Morris. Mia came in an hour ago asking for 'something witchy' for Halloween. Shell's instinct was to go *in* with a slime-green glitter eyeshadow and a glossy black lip, but this is Ostley, not Shoreditch. And while ART customers are more adventurous than most, it's still a struggle to get them to try something other than a copper eye and a nude lip, so if she used green eyeshadow and black lipstick on a client, they'd flee from the store in hysterics and never come back.

Besides, Shell's been doing Mia's makeup long enough to know that when she says she wants 'something witchy' she means a smoky eye and a red lip. Which is exactly what she's given her.

'I love it!' Mia squeals, jumping out of the chair. She throws her arms around Shell, the pair of them swaying from side to side with such enthusiasm that one of the pink silk roses falls out of Shell's flower crown. When Mia finally lets go, she raises the mirror and looks at her reflection again. 'How did you cover up that hideous spot on my chin, babe? You can't even see it any more. I tried this morning and it ended up looking like a brown clay mountain.'

'Use that cream concealer you got last week,' Shell tells her, as she bends down to pick up the rose, then tosses it onto the counter. 'The thick one in the jar, not the stick you use under your eyes.' Mia nods. 'Do your skincare, put on your primer, then cover the blemish with a concealer brush. Don't worry about being precise, just make sure it's covered, then let the concealer settle for a second, apply your foundation with a sponge, like you usually do, and set your face with some powder. That will hide the blemish without making it cakey.'

Mia nods again, then looks back in the mirror. 'And *how* did you get my eyeliner so neat? I can never do it.'

'Eleven years of experience and a steady hand.' Shell winks.

'Let me see,' Ricky says, from behind the counter, the train on his black-lace cobweb dress swishing behind him as he sashays over to where Mia and Shell are standing. '*Yes*,' he hisses, a hand under Mia's chin, tilting it up to the light. 'Perfection, Shell! This is how batwings should be: black as my heart and sharp enough to kill a man.'

Mia giggles, then turns to the other ART girls watching from behind the counter. 'What do you think?'

Becca and Soph bump into each other in their haste to run out from behind it so they can stand in front of Mia. They've dressed the same for Halloween, the pair of them in matching leopard-print catsuits, black knee-high boots and fluffy leopard-print cat ears. Their hair is the only way you can tell them apart: Soph's as dark and long as Shell's, and Becca's a frothy candy-floss pink that makes her eyes an even more vivid blue.

It's the most animated they've been all day and Shell gets it. She remembers what it was like to be a Saturday girl on the Gaulin counter when she was sixteen and in awe of the makeup artists who were as immaculate as their clients. Back then, the Gaulin girls embodied the sort of old glamour Duke & Sons was renowned for: perfect, radiant skin and red lips that were always curled up into a smile. Women came in because they wanted to look like them, and Shell would stand by, transfixed, as she watched the makeup artists work. It didn't matter how indifferent or impatient the customers were when they approached the counter, they left beaming with a promise to come back soon.

And they always did.

Alexa Price, who was the senior Gaulin adviser back then, had taken Shell under her wing and would allow her to hover next to her while she was working on a client so that Shell could see what she was doing. When Alexa was done and the client had left, Shell would bombard her with questions. How she applied concealer under the client's eyes so it didn't crease. Why she dusted blush on the tops of their cheeks not the apples. Why she used loose powder for setting and not a compact.

Shell had learned more from Alexa than she had on her NVQ. So she understands Becca and Soph's eagerness to do something other than clean brushes. She tries to keep them engaged, but they only work on Saturdays, which is the busiest day on the counter. She usually has back-to-back clients, which doesn't leave time for much more than to show them what she's doing and which brush to use.

'Look at them.' Ricky tips his chin at Becca and Soph, who are suddenly wide-eyed and chattering gleefully. They're utterly *besotted* with Mia. But, then, they're eighteen so, Shell supposes, Mia is who Becca and Soph aspire to be: she earns an obscene amount of money working in recruitment and has thirty thousand Instagram followers. Perfect hair. Perfect teeth. Perfect life with her perfect boyfriend and their perfect cockapoo puppy.

But Shell's been doing Mia's makeup for five years now and knows that her life is far from perfect. Yeah, she's killing it in recruitment, but that's not what she *wants* to do. She studied history of art at university but her mother was diagnosed with MS when she graduated and couldn't work any more so Mia needed to find a job straight away to support her. So that 'perfect' bedroom everyone sees on Instagram, the one with the lights around the mirror and the fluffy white cushions, is actually the same bedroom she's always had because she still lives at home.

As for Instagram, she has so many followers because she's recovering from an eating disorder and is an advocate for body positivity. That's why Mia made a beeline for Shell the first time she walked into Duke & Sons. She approached the counter asking Shell to be on her YouTube channel because, she said, plus-size people needed to see that they didn't have to wear black all the time. It took some persuading, but Shell relented and is now a regular on her channel, the pair of them doing clothing hauls and giving advice on styling while Shell does Mia's makeup.

So, while Mia doesn't care that people dismiss her as the pumpkin-spice-latte-drinking, Ugg-boot-wearing girl who has it all, it pisses Shell off, because she's so much more than that. Plus, she's nice. Really, genuinely nice.

Shell should probably rescue her from Becca and Soph, but Mia seems to find them endearing.

'Where you going tonight, Mia?' Soph asks, then nods at Becca. 'We're going to Hannigans.'

'Number Twenty-Eight.'

'In Church Cabham?'

Mia nods.

'Classy,' Becca and Soph say in unison.

'What's your costume like?' Soph asks, adjusting her cat ears.

'I'm going as a witch, so a long black wig, black dress, fishnets and heels.'

Becca and Soph nod, eyes wide. 'Wow.'

'Wow,' Ricky mouths at Shell, then rolls his.

Given that he's dressed as Sharon Needles – or a Filipino Sharon Needles, he isn't as pale but he has all of her attitude – in the floor-length black-lace cobweb gown and a grey bouffant wig studded with plastic spiders, Shell can't blame him for mocking Mia's lack of effort. Even Shell's made a point of not dressing like a witch again this year and is Frida Kahlo. Her yellow and blue floral maxi dress isn't as dramatic as his, but she's twisted her long black hair into a pile on the top of her head and embellished it with a flower crown of hot-pink silk roses, the space between her eyebrows filled in with strokes of mascara.

Not that most of her clients have known who she's dressed as.

One asked her if she was an Indian flower witch, whatever that is.

'You're the only one who can do my eyeliner, babe,' Mia says, peering at her reflection in the mirror again as she fusses over her fringe with her fingers. 'Mine's always wonky. I think I need that brush you used.' She turns to the counter. 'And that eyeshadow palette.'

Shell reaches for it. 'This one's great because it has loads of neutrals, which are perfect for work, and a few fun colours for when you're going out. I love this one.' Shell rubs the pad of her forefinger over the small square of green eyeshadow that she was hoping to use, then swipes it across the back of her hand. 'It's a bit bright, I know,' she admits, when Mia's eyes widen. 'Use the tip of a cotton bud and just apply a line of it along your lashline. It'll look great with your dark hair and eyes and it really pops on camera.'

She seems to consider it. 'I have a bag that colour, actually.'

'Give it a go. Try the dewy foundation trick I showed you with a nude lip, highlighter and a bit of this. Pair it with a black dress and that bag the next time you go out.' Shell makes the okay sign with her fingers. 'Trust me.'

'Always.' Mia grins. 'Maybe that's a Christmas look we could try on my channel. Speaking of,' she turns to Ricky. 'Shell sent me a link to your girlfriend's Insta and I love it. Denise, right?'

He nods.

'Do you think she'd be up for doing something for my channel? I'm planning my Twelve Days of Christmas content and I'd love to do a video on lingerie. The stuff she finds is always *so cool*.'

'I'm seeing her in a bit so I can ask her what she thinks.'

'Would you? I did something similar last Christmas, a naughty and nice thing, you know? So, like, fuzzy slippers and festive pyjamas as well as sexier stuff. My subscribers loved it, but I'm trying to champion more indie brands and Denise knows way more than I do.'

'She's *obsessed* with lingerie so I'm sure she'd be up for that.'

'Thanks, Ricky. If she is, Shell's got my number, so tell her to get in touch.'

Before he can respond, Soph, in a rare moment of initiative, is behind the counter, putting a new eyeshadow palette and angled liner brush into an ART bag. 'Did you want anything else, Mia?'

'Oh, yes! I'll take the gel liner as well, please.'

'What about the lipstick?' Shell suggests. 'It holds like a grudge, but you may want to freshen it later.'

'Good call!' Mia points at her. 'I'll take the lippie and don't forget to charge me for the lashes you used.'

'Got it.' Soph grabs what Mia needs from the shelves

and rings it up. 'Do you need some lash glue? Those ones are reusable, so if you're careful, you can get a few more wears out of them.'

'It's okay, Soph.' Shell waves a hand at her. 'Just chuck a tube in. Don't charge her.'

'Thank you!' Mia hugs her again, but when she steps back, she gasps and clutches Shell's arm. 'Oh, my God! *Please* tell me I remembered to book in with you next Saturday for my mate's wedding!'

'I'll check the diary,' Becca offers, grabbing it from under the counter. '*Next* Saturday, right?'

Mia nods, looking nervous. 'November the seventh.'

'Yep.' Becca confirms, with a sweet smile. 'You're the first one in at ten thirty.'

'Thank God! Ten thirty is perfect.'

Mia hugs Shell again, then bends down to retrieve her bag. While she pays for her stuff, Shell glances to the revolving door to find that the security guard, Gary, is already standing in front of it as the clock over the lifts chimes five times, announcing, with its usual sombre indifference, that Duke & Sons is closed.

With that, there's a flurry of activity at the other counters in the Beauty Hall as everyone chatters and checks their makeup ahead of the Christmas Changeover meeting. It's starting in ten minutes so, as soon as Soph gives Mia back her credit card and hands over the paper bag of products, Shell puts her hand on the small of Mia's back and gently guides her towards the revolving door, telling her she can't wait to see her next Saturday.

She hurries back to the ART counter to a quiver of

thank-yous around the Beauty Hall as Ricky turns off 'Monster Mash' for the last time this year.

When she gets back to him, he has an eyebrow arched at Becca and Soph. 'No way!'

'What?' Shell asks.

'These two. You won't believe today's gossip.'

'It's not gossip!' Soph insists, all but stamping her foot. 'Becca and I saw it with our own eyes, Shell!'

'Saw what?' she asks, grabbing the mirror Mia was just using and checking her makeup before the Christmas Changeover meeting starts. She's glad she did, because she's crossed the line from glowy to greasy.

'Go on.' Ricky goads, as Shell pulls a fresh tissue from the box on the counter. 'Tell her.'

Shell doesn't look up but recognises Soph's huff. 'When we were at lunch, Becca and I saw Old Mr Duke.'

'Yeah?' Shell mumbles, blotting her forehead carefully so as not to disturb her Frida brow.

'At the Bridge Street Café.' When she still doesn't look up, Soph huffs again. 'Why was he on Bridge Street?'

'Why were *you* on Bridge Street?'

'McDonald's.'

Of course, Shell thinks, as she blots the corners of her nose with the tissue, then takes a brush out of the leather belt around her waist. She goes to find the ART setting powder in her shade so she can reset her face, her foundation starting to separate around her nose and mouth. They're going to the pub after the meeting, so she needs it to last a few more hours.

'Shell!' Soph snaps, clearly put out that she's not paying attention.

She finally looks away from the mirror she's holding, powder brush poised. '*What?*'

'Why was Old Mr Duke in the café on Bridge Street when he *always* has lunch downstairs?'

That's true. He does always have lunch in the café downstairs. He's been known to join the old dears sitting on their own, much to their delight, regaling them with stories about the store.

'Get to the point,' Ricky hisses, obviously as aware of the time as Shell is.

The staff have already started to gather at the foot of the staircase for the meeting, and while there's no sign of Old Mr Duke yet, he's never late.

'He was with this *super*-hot guy,' Soph adds, almost breathless with the drama of it as Shell dips her brush into the powder, then flicks off the excess. 'Like super *super*-hot, Shell. Like the hottest man I've ever seen in real life.'

'And we've met Ovie from *Love Island*,' Becca reminds her.

Shell tries not to laugh as she resumes powdering her nose. 'Maybe that's why they were in the Bridge Street Café, then, because this *super-hot guy* wanted to meet there.'

'Come on.' Shell can't see her, but she knows Soph is rolling her eyes at her. 'Old Mr Duke is, like, a *hundred*. It's rude to make him go all the way to Bridge Street when they could have met here.'

Unless Old Mr Duke didn't want anyone to see them.

The thought arcs through Shell's head, like a stray football through a window. She dismisses it, though, putting the lid back on the loose powder.

Soph takes a step towards her, annoyed that she isn't taking this seriously. 'He was wearing a suit, Shell.'

'Who was wearing a suit? Old Mr Duke?' she asks, as she slides her powder brush back into her belt and tugs out the one for bronzer. 'He always wears a suit, Soph. He probably sleeps in one.'

'*No*, the hot guy.' Apparently, that's his name now. The Hot Guy. 'Who wears a suit on a Saturday, Shell?'

'I don't know. Maybe he was going to a wedding afterwards, or something,' she suggests, swirling the brush in the bronzer, then applying some to her cheeks.

'The hot guy was taking notes, though.'

'That doesn't mean anything,' she tells Soph, reaching into her brush belt for a tube of lash glue.

'Shell!' Soph snaps again, as she watches her apply it to the back of the silk rose.

'What?'

'I'm just saying . . .'

'What? What are you just saying, Soph?'

She's trying not to lose her patience, but the meeting is about to start and they can't be late.

Christmas Changeover is Old Mr Duke's *favourite* staff meeting.

'I'm *saying*,' Soph makes the word sound about a minute long, 'it was a business meeting. You could tell.'

'So?'

'Shell's right,' Ricky says. 'It's probably nothing.'

'Yeah, but what if it's not?' Soph looks between them. 'The store's been quieter than it has been in *years*.'

'*Years?*' Shell laughs. 'How would you know? You've only been working here since June.'

'David from Furniture told me.'

'Well, David from Furniture is wrong. You were here today. You saw how busy it was on the counter.'

'Yeah, the Beauty Hall is busy, but the rest of the store is dead.'

'No, it's not!' Shell laughs again, then hesitates when no one else does. 'Is it?'

When she turns to Ricky to back her up, he's gazing aimlessly across the Beauty Hall.

'Ricky?' He catches himself, and when he looks at her with a sad frown, she reciprocates. 'What?'

'Denise told me that she only had five customers in Lingerie today. *Five*. On a Saturday.'

That makes Shell hesitate for the first time.

'And David told *me*,' Soph tells her, glancing towards the furniture department on the top floor, 'that Old Mr Duke said he's not allowed to place any new orders until they've sold all their existing stock.'

'Yeah, but that's *furniture*. How many five-thousand-pound beds are people in Ostley going to buy?'

'Yeah, but Bella in Handbags & Accessories told *me*,' Becca finally chips in, 'that Mrs Price told *her* that Old Mr Duke's assistant told *her* that Ostley and North East Somerset Council are threatening to take Duke & Sons to court next month because we haven't paid our business rates. We owe, like, twenty-five thousand quid!'

Shell tells herself to ignore the prickle of panic across her scalp.

Ricky seems genuinely worried, though, his whole face tight.

'Come on, Ricky. You're not buying this, are you?'

'We didn't have a summer party this year, did we?'

'Because we couldn't afford it. That's what David said.' Soph jabs a finger at him, then at Shell. 'Plus, Old Mr Duke is what? *Ninety?*'

'He's eighty-three,' Shell corrects, aware it doesn't sound *that* far off now she's said it out loud.

'Okay, he's *eighty-three*. Whatever. He can't keep going much longer, can he?'

'Exactly,' Becca says, with a fierce nod. 'What happens to this place when Old Mr Duke . . . you know?'

She doesn't finish the thought, but she doesn't have to as Shell and Ricky catch one another's eye.

Shell hadn't even thought about that.

Old Mr Duke's always been here.

'Duke & Sons opened in 1937,' Shell reminds them. 'It's not going anywhere and neither is Old Mr Duke. Trust me. I've been working here for *eleven years*. There are always quiet periods. Watch. It'll pick up before Christmas.'

Ricky knows that too, but when he doesn't agree, she feels betrayed.

'I dunno. Henri Bendel in New York was open for, like, a hundred years and they went bust.'

'Wait. So Duke & Sons is going bust now? Just because Old Mr Duke had lunch with a hot guy?'

Shell knows what shop-floor gossip is like, but that's a stretch.

'Even if we aren't going bust,' Soph admits, looking between them, 'Old Mr Duke will need to retire soon and who is he going to pass the store on to? There are no sons, are there?' When they don't respond, she pushes, 'What if that's what Old Mr Duke and the hot guy were talking about?' She looks at Shell when she says, 'About selling Duke & Sons.'

Chapter Two

As they approach the huddle of staff gathered at the foot of the old wooden staircase in the middle of the store, Shell is so distracted by what Soph just said that it takes her a moment or two to register how noisy it is. And not in that idle, pass-the-time-until-the-meeting-starts kind of way. It's louder than that, everyone talking at once.

'Guys! Over here!'

Shell looks up to find Denise waving them over. She's secured a spot by the Clarins counter, which is perfect. Close enough to hear what's going on, but far enough away that they can't be seen so Shell can lean against the counter and ease the pressure on her feet without Old Mr Duke seeing. He's old-fashioned like that. He likes them to stand up straight and smile and say, 'Welcome to Duke & Sons,' even if it's the thirtieth time the customer has heard it.

It's so busy that it takes some effort for them to get to her. Shell can't help but wonder what they must look like. They already stand out at these meetings because the staff in the Beauty Hall are the only ones allowed to deviate from the strict Duke & Sons white shirt, black trousers or skirt policy: they have to wear whatever the brands dictate. Today, however, she, Ricky, Becca and Soph are the only ones who have dressed up for Halloween so they stand out even more, some people actually *staring* as they make their way through the crowd. But then the ART Kids, as everyone calls them, have always been the misfits, like the Goths at the back of the class.

'Hey.' Denise grins when they reach her, then claps. 'You guys look amazing, I'm so jealous!'

She may not have been allowed to dress up, like they have, but Denise always finds a way to manoeuvre the Duke & Sons uniform policy so she looks more like herself. Denise is black so her white shirt is almost *fluorescent* against her rich dark skin and she's matched her heels to the thin leopard-print belt around the waist of her pencil skirt. Her thin black braids are piled into a generous bun on top of her head and, as she insisted when Shell complimented her earlier, are being held up by pins and prayer.

'Great minds,' Denise says, pointing at her belt, then at Becca and Soph.

They give her a twirl and, not to be left out, Ricky does the same, if with more gusto. So much, in fact, that one of the plastic spiders falls out of his wig. She laughs as she watches him, and when he stops, she takes his face in her hands and quickly kisses him on the mouth.

'I missed you today, sweetheart,' she tells him, with a gentle smile.

'Sorry about lunch. It was so busy on the counter, I couldn't get away.'

'Oh, don't worry. It gave me a chance to start my Christmas shopping.'

'Christmas shopping?' Shell blinks at her. 'Den, it isn't even November yet.'

'I know, but some of us,' she juts her chin at her boyfriend, 'can't afford to leave it all until the last minute then put it on Mummy and Daddy's credit card.'

Ricky ignores her, inspecting his black acrylic nails as he tells her about Mia.

Denise seems keen to make her YouTube debut, but is distracted by something more pressing.

'Did you hear the rumour?' she asks eagerly.

So that's what everyone's talking about, Shell thinks, as she looks around the Beauty Hall.

'You two saw Old Mr Duke at the Bridge Street Café, right?' Denise asks Becca and Soph, who nod furiously, clearly thrilled to be at the middle of all the drama. 'He was with some guy in a suit?'

They nod again.

'A *super-hot* guy.' Soph is sure to clarify.

Denise's eyebrow almost disappears into her braids. 'You don't believe it, do you, Shell?'

'Of course not! Every couple of years there's a rumour that Old Mr Duke is going to retire and sell out to some big chain, but he never does.'

'She's right,' Shell hears someone say. It's Bella from Handbags & Accessories. 'My dad plays golf with Kevin Costley, you know, of Costley's.'

Shell knows. Costley's – or Costley's of Ostley, as it's known locally – is a chain of discount stores that seem to be popping up all over Somerset, selling everything from sports socks to garden hoses.

It's the antithesis of Duke & Sons.

'Anyway,' Bella goes on, 'my dad told me that Kevin Costley told him he's been trying to buy Duke & Sons for years because it's the biggest store in Ostley, but Old Mr Duke refuses to sell it to him.'

Shell gestures at her as if to say, *See?*

That seems to appease Denise, but before Shell can reassure her that Duke & Sons isn't going anywhere, the babble in the Beauty Hall dims and Old Mr Duke appears at the top of the wooden staircase. There's a cheer, and when everyone breaks into an unprompted round of applause, Shell joins in, grinning up at him as he waves at them from under the stained-glass dome.

She knows that most people hate their bosses, but she *loves* Charles Duke, or Old Mr Duke, as he's affectionately known on the shop floor. Everyone does. If you include the temps, there must be at least two hundred people who work at Duke & Sons, but he knows everyone's name. He remembers their birthday and when they've been on holiday, and made a point of congratulating Shell with a bunch of flowers when ART used one of her looks in a print campaign last year. He really is the kindest, most gentle soul, and Shell would do anything for him.

When you see Old Mr Duke, the store makes sense. Ostley may be the sort of place people come for the weekend, but once you get past the cobbled streets and pretty Regency buildings, the high street looks like every other high street in every other town. There's a Boots and a Marks & Spencer and three Starbucks. Duke & Sons, however, maintains all of its old-fashioned charm. It's a lighthouse of sparkle and glamour, and Charles Duke is the lighthouse keeper.

Old Mr Duke *loves* Christmas. He used to dress the store himself, but now he's in his eighties, his wife, Philippa, won't let him. He still oversees everything, though. He knows on which branch of the tree each bauble should go, which toys should be in the carriages of the Ferris wheel that sits in the DUKE & SONS TOYLAND display in the window and how far apart the garlands that hang from the staircase should be.

Soph's right: he should have retired by now. He was supposed to, but his son, Michael, passed away suddenly and there was no other son to take over Duke & Sons. He can't pass it on to a stranger, can he? Besides, Old Mr Duke *is* Duke & Sons. He's there to greet her when the store opens and there to say goodnight when it closes. There with coffee and cake for stock take, and he attends *every* meeting.

This one is his favourite, though, because he can't resist talking about Christmas. He's always so excited. It doesn't matter how broke they are or how cold it is outside, his enthusiasm is enough to get everyone else excited about Christmas as well.

'Hello!' Old Mr Duke bellows from the top of the stairs, as he starts to walk down.

'Who is *that*?' Ricky and Denise hiss.

It's then that Shell notices a man beside Old Mr Duke. Ricky and Denise turn to her with matching expectant expressions, clearly hoping that, as she's worked at Duke & Sons longer than them, she'll know who he is. She doesn't. She's never seen him before, panic pinching at her as she wonders if Soph is right.

Still, there's something familiar about the man. He's younger than Old Mr Duke – about Shell's age, in his late twenties or early thirties – and is equally immaculate in a charcoal single-breasted suit and paper-crisp white shirt, the top three buttons open to expose an inverted triangle of pale, pink skin. He's smiling as he helps Old Mr Duke down the stairs and his eyes, big and Bombay Sapphire blue, remind her of someone, but she can't think who.

'It's *him*,' Soph whispers fiercely, elbowing her in the ribs. 'Shell, it's *him*.'

'Him *who*?' Shell mouths, rubbing her side.

'Hot Guy,' she and Becca whisper at once.

Ricky twists around to face Becca and Soph so suddenly that he almost hits Shell in the face with his bouffant wig.

'That's him?' he says, through his teeth. '*That*'s who you saw in the Bridge Street Café earlier?'

They nod.

'You said he was hot, but fuck me running,' Denise whispers, with a hint of *How dare he?* as though she's furious with him for being so good-looking. 'I want to punch him in the face then kiss it.'

Soph looks unreasonably proud of herself. 'I told you.'

'That mouth.' Ricky presses his hand to his forehead. 'I've never seen a white man with a mouth like that.'

'I *know*,' Denise agrees.

'And those cheekbones.'

'I *know*.'

'Some ART Silver Factory highlighter and he could guide ships into shore.'

'Okay. Calm down,' Shell tells them, under her breath. 'He's not *that* good-looking.'

'Not *that* good-looking? Are you blind?' Ricky tries to lower his voice and fails. 'Look at him.'

All four of them stare at her as though she's lost her mind, their lips parted.

Okay. Yes, he's good-looking. Actually, he's not good-looking, he's *handsome*. Handsome in that old Hollywood way. Young, pale and lean with broad shoulders and a sharp jaw that she can imagine Joan Crawford slapping. If you googled 'handsome', he'd be the first result, no doubt accompanied by a photo of him with his artfully untidy blond hair, his full pink mouth pursed as if deep in thought about how to solve the global-warming crisis with just a hint of *I could ruin you if you let me*.

'He's not my type,' Shell tells them, with a shrug that makes Ricky groan.

'I forgot. Unless they're wearing black skinny jeans and a Joy Division T-shirt, you're not interested.'

Denise covers her mouth with her hand to stop herself giggling.

Shell knows who they're referring to.

Nick Wallace.

The mere thought of him makes her smile in the loose, clumsy way she does whenever she thinks of him. She compares everyone she meets to Nick. He was her first crush, and while he never knew it at the time, ten years later she's immediately besotted if she meets someone who doesn't wash his hair every day and likes Bon Iver.

When she looks back at the staircase to avoid their gaze, she realises that the man with Old Mr Duke is resolutely the opposite of that. Stiff as the collar of his white shirt but with a slight swagger that tells her he'd rather sip champagne in a rooftop bar somewhere than drink beer from a plastic cup while dancing to Robyn.

But when Shell looks around, everyone else is equally enamoured. They're watching as he navigates the stairs with a lightness – a grace – he is far too tall to command, his hand cupping Old Mr Duke's elbow. Even the Gaulin girls are in a flutter, blushing and whispering furiously to one another.

Finally, they reach the bottom of the stairs.

'Hello!' Old Mr Duke bellows again, fine lines fanning from the corners of his blue eyes when everyone in the Beauty Hall cheers again, prompting him to smile brightly. 'How are we all? Excited about Christmas?'

He says it – *Christmas* – like a magician might say *Abracadabra*. Like an incantation. Like if he says it *just right*, there will be a puff of smoke and glitter and the Christmas tree will appear in the middle of the store.

'You're probably wondering who this handsome chap beside me is.'

'We sure are,' Ricky says, with a wiggle.

Shell is, too, but for very different reasons as she thinks about what Soph said.

'This,' Old Mr Duke smiles proudly, his chest out as they all hold their breath, 'is my grandson, Callum.'

There's another cheer – of relief this time – and the muscles in Shell's shoulders finally unclench.

He isn't selling Duke & Sons.

She knew he'd never sell Duke & Sons.

'Grandson?' Denise whispers. 'Did you know Old Mr Duke had a grandson?'

'I knew his son, Michael, *you know*,' Ricky raises his eyebrows and whispers back, 'but I didn't know he had a kid. Did you, Shell?'

She's as surprised as they are.

Michael passed away long before she started at Duke & Sons. But that's all she knows. As much as they love to gossip on the shop floor, trading stories about who's shagging whom is one thing, but talking about Old Mr Duke losing his only child is something else entirely. She doesn't even know how he died, just that it was sudden, and that there were so many flowers on the pavement outside the revolving door that people were stepping over them for weeks.

Only a handful of staff have worked at Duke & Sons longer than Shell and they're so loyal to Old Mr Duke that they would never discuss his personal life on the shop floor. Not that she's asked. He's such a private man and he's been so good to her, giving Shell her job back after that miserable year at university studying law, of all things. She'd never want him to think she's gossiping about him.

'Thank you.' Callum bows his head and raises his hand to wave, which prompts another loud cheer.

This one is more fervent, though, thanks to Denise and Ricky, who *WOO-HOO* shamelessly.

'I know most of you are yet to meet Callum,' Old Mr Duke says, 'but some of you remember how he used to run up and down the stairs and steal the jelly beans from the sweetshop we used to have on the children's floor.'

'Thanks for that, Pops.' Callum blushes and Shell hears Becca and Soph groan next to her.

'That was twenty-five years ago, though.' Old Mr Duke pats Callum playfully on the back, then turns to wink at Mrs Price from Haberdashery. 'Even if some of you don't look old enough to remember that far back.'

Mrs Price chuckles. She's a small woman with neat white curls she has set every Monday morning before the store opens, and a face as soft and pink as Shell's grandmother's favourite armchair. That's all they know her as, Mrs Price. No one knows how old she is, just that she's been working at Duke & Sons *for ever*.

Old Mr Duke's chest puffs up even more. 'He grew up in California and graduated from Harvard, the first Duke to go to university!' He waits for the *ooooh*s to subside then turns to Mrs Price again, with a wicked smile. 'Bet he can't calculate the price of twelve and a half metres of Duke Palmeral Velvet off the top of his head, though.'

Mrs Price doesn't miss a beat. 'One thousand five hundred pounds.'

They all laugh and Old Mr Duke is thrilled, clapping Callum on the back again. 'After graduating from Harvard, he travelled around the world for a while, then got his MBA from Stanford.'

There are more *ooooh*s and Callum smiles, but is clearly mortified.

'Then he betrayed us all and worked for Henri Bendel in New York. Boo! Hiss!' The staff reciprocate, much to Old Mr Duke's delight. 'Before starting his own luxury fashion brand which he just sold to LVMH.'

'LVMH?' Soph asks over the chorus of *aaaahs*.

'Louis Vuitton Moët Hennessy,' Ricky tells her.

He doesn't need to say any more than that. Her face is alight as Old Mr Duke turns to Callum, his eyes wet.

'I can't tell you how happy I am that he's home. So, please,' he turns back to the assembled staff, his arms out, 'join me in giving a warm Duke & Sons welcome to my grandson, Callum Duke!'

He claps and they join in, albeit less enthusiastically as they wonder what's going on.

Old Mr Duke smiles, but there are no crinkles around his eyes this time. No cheeky chuckle and slap on the back. He just nods, his eyes wet. 'Callum is taking over Duke & Sons when I retire.'

Chapter Three

R etire.
 The relief that Old Mr Duke isn't selling the store
is immediately replaced by a different kind of panic as
the word – *retire* – buzzes around the Beauty Hall, like a
wasp looking for an open window. Everyone starts whispering sharply, their feet shuffling on the polished parquet
floor. Some of the staff don't even bother to lower their
voices, as they wait for an explanation.

There isn't one, though, so after a few minutes, they
stop asking what's going on and then it's quiet in a way
Shell has never heard before. Even when the store is
closed and it's just her, restocking the counter and cleaning
her makeup brushes for the next day, it's not this quiet.
She can still hear the squeak of Gary's shoes, the keys
on his hip jangling with each step. And she can hear
Anna, the cleaner, humming happily somewhere above
her as she starts on the top floor and works her way
down.

The five of them look at each other, unsure what to
do. The other staff are doing the same, clearly waiting for
a cue. Do they cheer? Clap? Congratulate him? Is this
good news? It doesn't feel like good news. Shell can't

imagine coming into the store in the morning and not seeing Old Mr Duke in his three-piece suit, wandering around the Beauty Hall, straightening the perfume bottles and adjusting the white roses in the vase on the Gaulin counter.

'I can't believe he's retiring,' Ricky leans in to whisper. 'What's he going to do all day? Play golf?'

'He'll be bored within a week,' Shell scoffs, going for playful but landing just shy of sour.

'He's not sick, is he?' Denise murmurs, her forehead creased with concern. 'What if he's dying or something?'

'Don't even say that out loud,' Shell warns. 'Don't put that into the universe, Den.'

'He's always said that the only way he'd leave Duke & Sons is if they carried him out in a box,' Ricky reminds her.

That hadn't even occurred to Shell.

Old Mr Duke can't die.

Oh, my God.

What if he's dying?

The thought coils like a snake in the pit of her stomach as she gazes at him standing at the foot of the staircase. He looks like he always does, his blue eyes bright and his cheeks apple skin red, his wild white eyebrows, which Ricky is always threatening to pluck, sticking up in all directions. Yeah, he walks with a cane now and his hip is bothering him more than it used to, but he still chuckles in the cheeky way he does when he walks onto the shop floor to find Ricky singing into his bronzer brush or when one of the Gaulin girls sees a mouse and shrieks.

'He can't retire,' Shell says firmly. 'He *can't*. There's no Duke & Sons without Old Mr Duke.'

'Don't worry.' Old Mr Duke holds up his hands as Shell looks around at the staff, at their closed, concerned expressions, and wonders if she's the only one trying not to cry. 'I'm not retiring just yet. You can't get rid of me that easily!'

He laughs, then waits for them to reciprocate, but they don't this time.

So he puts one hand on top of the other over his heart. 'I'll still be here, I promise. I want to give Callum time to get to know you all and the store, so for the next year, he'll be our creative director. He's got lots of exciting plans to bring Duke & Sons into the next century.'

But he doesn't sound excited at the prospect, Shell notes.

If anything, he sounds defeated.

'So you'll still be in charge, then?' Shell hears someone ask, but can't see who it is.

Old Mr Duke nods, the white pom-pom on the end of his Santa hat bobbing. 'Nothing is changing in that sense. I'll still be responsible for the day-to-day running of the store for the next year until I retire and Callum takes over as CEO. But you know what I'm like, David,' he says, and Shell realises that it's David from Furniture. 'I'll never be able to let go of Duke & Sons.'

Callum visibly stiffens at that. He catches himself quickly, smiling smoothly, but the five look at one another, Ricky's eyebrows rising at the hint of some possible Duke Drama.

Old Mr Duke turns to Callum. 'My grandson has lots of ideas that he's excited to implement, and once you hear them, I'll think you'll be excited as well. So I'm going to hand over to him, because you know how I feel about change. I'm still mourning the loss of the Fur Department, after all.'

He laughs, but the staff don't as the mood in the Beauty Hall shifts again at the mention of that word.

Change.

'Okay.' Old Mr Duke claps. 'I'll see you all tomorrow for Christmas Changeover and stock take.'

Callum hands him his cane and, with that, Old Mr Duke totters off.

Everyone turns to watch him go, like children in the playground on their first day of school, as he pushes through the revolving door and disappears into the grim, drizzly evening. When he's gone, they turn back to eye Callum warily.

'I don't want you guys to worry,' he says, with a smile, but he's obviously as anxious as they are. His voice is as deep as Shell expected, but he has this weird English/American hybrid accent that is deeply annoying.

You guys.

'Grandfather is fine. He's fit as a fiddle!' Callum says, prompting a collective sigh of relief.

Shell hears Denise let go of a breath and turns to her as she mouths, *Thank God.*

'Thank goodness for that,' Louise Larson from the Gaulin counter pipes up, batting her eyelashes at him.

Callum looks across the Beauty Hall at her, immediately

falling for her saccharine smile. She may look innocent – all blue eyes, pink cheeks and big blonde curls, like something from a Botticelli painting – but Louise is a demon.

'But my grandfather is eighty-five next year,' Callum goes on. 'He should have retired twenty years ago but . . .'

When he trails off, the mood in the Beauty Hall softens as they finish the thought in their heads.

. . . *my father died.*

Callum starts again with a smile that goes nowhere. 'Next year is going to be an exciting one for Duke & Sons. As my grandfather said, we're going to be making some much-needed changes.'

The atmosphere in the Beauty Hall immediately stiffens again at *much-needed.*

'All of this will be a lot to take in, but don't worry,' he says again, and Shell wishes he'd stop telling them not to worry because it's doing nothing to reassure her that she shouldn't. 'I'll put all of this on our new staff intranet, which,' he holds up a finger, 'is the first of the changes. It's where you'll now be able to choose your shifts, book time off and check your payslips.'

Shell hears someone huff grumpily and realises that it's Old Mr Duke's PA, Gladys.

That's her job.

Or, at least, it used to be.

'A new staff intranet that,' he adds cheerily, seemingly oblivious that most of the staff are staring at him with their arms crossed and their heads tilted, 'you'll be able to access on the Duke & Sons Wi-Fi.' He laughs lightly.

'I know,' he says, even though no one has actually acknowledged what he said. 'About time, right?'

Silence.

This is excruciating, Shell thinks, her top lip sweating.

But Callum persists, his smile almost manic now. 'So you won't need to punch in and out on that archaic machine in the break room any more because you'll have new tablets!'

He waits for the applause, as though he's Oprah and he's just told everyone that they're getting a new car.

You get a tablet!

And you get a tablet!

But they continue to stare at him, their gaze narrowing. Even Shell's suspicious.

Why do they need tablets?

What's Mrs Price going to do with a tablet? She still insists on giving out handwritten receipts.

'So when you get in for your shift,' Callum explains, 'all you have to do is log into your tablet and the system will make a note of it and send the info to Payroll.'

Becca and Soph look at one another, their eyes wide.

Okay. Maybe the tablet thing isn't such a bad idea, Shell concedes, trying not to laugh. Hopefully they'll be on time now.

'The tablets are also going to replace the tills,' Callum goes on, slightly hysterical now, like a secondhand-car salesman trying to flog them a clapped-out Ford Fiesta. 'The tills are going and you'll be able to do everything from your tablet. You can ring customers up, issue returns, replenish stock and order items from our website, which is where this is all leading,' he says, clearly proud of himself. 'The website is getting a complete overhaul.'

He pauses, still waiting for a reaction, but he doesn't get one, everyone even more sceptical now.

'We actually made the switch last year,' he says, with a quick flick of his wrist. 'More Duke & Sons customers are shopping online than coming into the store, thanks, in part, to ART.' Shell tenses at that, unsure where he's going. 'We've seen a pattern with customers reordering the same ART products again and again. Things like foundations and concealers they've purchased before so don't need to come in store to get colour-matched for.'

That makes sense, but Shell is still deeply suspicious.

'It's also because Shell and Ricky,' Callum goes on, as they blink at one another, stunned that he knows their names, 'encourage customers to go to our website if an item is out of stock, which is brilliant and exactly what I want you all to be doing from now on. Otherwise we lose that business to one of our competitors.'

Shell's cheeks flush at the compliment, but there are murmurs of discontent from the rest of the staff.

When she glances at the Gaulin girls, they're staring at her, arms crossed tightly.

'So, going forward,' Callum continues, his smile more careful now and Shell wonders what he's about to say, 'we'll be making some changes to the store in the hope of attracting more brands like ART. Young, aspirational brands that are exclusive to Duke & Sons so customers won't have to travel into London for them.'

There's another murmur of discontent that goes on for a beat longer than is comfortable.

'We'll be starting in the Beauty Hall,' he says, and Shell hears a sharp intake of breath from the Gaulin girls.

Even Ricky stands up straight, his chin up as he eyes Callum over the assembled heads.

'ART are so happy with the way the team have performed,' he tries to sound upbeat, but it's like throwing a tennis ball into a pond, 'that they've decided to increase their presence at Duke & Sons!'

He pauses again for a round of applause that doesn't come, just a slightly apologetic *Yay!* from Becca and Soph.

'They're thrilled with Shell, in particular, who, in the last four years, has turned ART from a display stand in the corner of the store to a vibrant, busy counter. Our online sales are up by *three hundred* per cent and ART are so impressed with her #HeART campaign, they're implementing the hashtag across all their social media.'

There's a cheer from Ricky, Denise, Becca and Soph, and the rest of the staff join in, albeit tepidly.

Before Shell can catch her breath, Callum continues, clearly buoyed by the reaction. 'We've hired an incredible merchandising company, who will be transforming the store into a Christmas wonderland overnight, and while they're doing that, it's the perfect opportunity to make some changes to the Beauty Hall.'

'What kind of changes?' Louise asks, the words snapping off her tongue.

'We'll be swapping the ART and Gaulin counters over.'

There's a tense stretch of silence, then the Gaulin girls

explode, talking over one another, all at once. Becca and Soph turn to Shell, Ricky and Denise, their mouths open, not even trying to hide how amused they are.

'Excuse me?' Louise raises her voice over the other girls. They hush immediately. 'You can't just *move* the Gaulin counter, Mr Duke! It's been at the front of the store since Duke & Sons opened in 1937!'

'One does not simply . . . move the Gaulin counter,' mutters Ricky, forcing a snigger from Denise, which she hastily turns into a cough.

'Well—'

'Does your grandfather know about this?' Louise interrupts.

'He does.'

Louise is clearly flustered by that, but recovers. 'And he's happy with it?'

'He is.'

Shell exchanges a look with Ricky and they raise their eyebrows at one another.

'The ART counter needs more space,' Callum says, as though it really is as simple as that.

Louise doesn't seem to think so, though. 'This is *out-rageous!*'

It starts a ripple effect through the Beauty Hall, the word repeated over and over. Emboldened by the staff's reaction, Louise stands up straight, her hands on her hips.

'I'm all for change, but Duke & Sons isn't Superdrug. Women come here because they expect *glamour.*' Her blonde curls rise then fall, as she turns her head to glare at the ART crew. 'Not Little Mix and black lipstick.'

Shell doesn't know why she has to act like an outraged middle-aged woman demanding to speak to the manager just because she works for Gaulin.

She's two years younger than Shell.

'I happen to be rather fond of Little Mix, actually,' Callum says.

Louise glares at him, and while she may be tiny, it's enough to make his cheeks flush as he realises that his attempt to lighten the mood has failed miserably.

'Anyway . . .' his voice falters, aware that Louise is staring at him, her hands still on her hips '. . . overnight, we'll be swapping the Gaulin and ART counters . . .' this prompts a snort from Louise, which he ignores '. . . in the hope it will bring in new customers who are as happy to shop online as they are in store.'

'Online? So your plan is to replace us with computers?' Shell hears someone ask as the mood tenses again.

Callum shakes his head. 'Not at all, Daniel.'

'*David*,' he corrects, and Shell realises it's David from Furniture again.

'*David*,' Callum continues, if a little less confidently. 'We're going to be offering Click and Collect for free to encourage customers to come into the store to pick up their orders, and while they're here, they'll purchase something else. So, for example,' he says, gesturing towards where the ART crew are standing, 'if someone comes in to collect a foundation, Shell or Ricky can upsell them an eyeshadow palette.'

'Upsell?' Ricky mouths, and Shell shakes her head.

Upselling is not something Old Mr Duke has ever

encouraged. He doesn't want the customers to feel harassed or, he insists, they won't come back.

'Don't worry,' Callum says *again*, 'I know we're heading into our busiest time of year, so we won't implement any of these changes until February. Plus, you'll be given full training so don't worry.'

That's two don't worries, Shell notes.

It does nothing to reassure David, of course. 'Tell me, Mr Duke. How is someone going to Click and Collect an armoire?'

'It depends how strong they are.' Callum chuckles. David doesn't so he tries again. 'Click and Collect will be for smaller items. When customers come in store to collect them, we hope they'll make an impulse purchase.'

'What's all of this in aid of?' someone asks, but, again, Shell can't see who it is.

'It's the future!' Callum says, like he's Elon bloody Musk.

Shell feels a bit sorry for him. He's clearly trying, and everything he's suggested is nothing a department store like this shouldn't have already, but that's the problem: he's trying *too hard*. If he 'calmed down and spoke to the staff as people, not an audience for his TED Talk, he might get a better response. All of these 'exciting new changes', and no one's bothered to ask *them* how they think the store can be improved, yet they're the ones on the shop floor, dealing with customers every day.

Predictably, no one looks impressed and Callum must know he's lost the room, because he doesn't bother to try to sugar-coat it as he says, 'And we'll be opening on Sundays from the new year.'

That prompts the biggest reaction. Everyone gasps.

'No way,' Ricky says, not even bothering to lower his voice. 'I am *not* working on a Sunday.'

'Don't worry,' Callum says *again*, and Shell puts her head into her hands to stop herself screaming. 'It's entirely up to you guys if you want to work on Sundays, but I hear some of you are looking for extra hours.'

'What if we're not?' Ricky asks, before Shell can stop him.

'That's fine,' he says, with a stiff smile. 'Obviously you guys get first refusal, then we'll offer the hours to the Christmas temps who want to stay on in the new year. If we need more staff, we'll hire them.'

Ricky doesn't let it go, though, much to Shell's horror. 'So you're hiring *more* staff, not letting them go?'

There's another sharp flurry of whispers as everyone waits for Callum to answer.

He doesn't flinch. 'We're not letting anyone go at this stage.'

It's the worst thing he could have said because everyone starts talking over each other again.

'*At this stage?*' Shell hears someone ask. 'What does that mean?'

'It means . . .' Callum pauses to lick his lips as he chooses his next words carefully '. . . it means that if these changes are a success there's no reason why Duke & Sons shouldn't continue to thrive for another eighty-three years.'

'And if they aren't successful?' David from Furniture asks.

Callum doesn't answer the question. 'There's no reason why they shouldn't be. I have faith in you all.'

It does nothing to appease them: they all fire more questions at him.

'Hang on, everyone. Hang on!' David raises his arms, immediately regaining control. 'I just want a straight answer from Mr Duke and I think you all do, too.' He turns to face Callum. 'Are any of us going to lose our jobs?'

There's an uneasy silence before he answers, the Beauty Hall suddenly so quiet that Shell hears a bus roll by on the street outside.

Finally, Callum shakes his head. 'Not if we see a significant increase in revenue in the new year.'

'And if we don't?' David pushes. 'What then?'

Callum just smiles. 'I sincerely hope it doesn't come to that.'

Chapter Four

Louise storms off in a blur of blonde curls and Gaulin perfume, her heels clacking purposefully on the polished parquet floor. The other Gaulin girls hesitate, clearly keen to hear what else Callum has to say, but when she stops to glare at them, they scamper after her out of the Beauty Hall towards the back of house.

'Shit,' Ricky mutters, another plastic spider falling out of his wig. 'I can't lose this job, Shell! Where am *I* going to work?' He gestures at his costume. 'I know it's Halloween, but this is just a Wednesday for me.'

'You'll be fine.' Denise tells him, but it isn't with her usual affection for her boyfriend's soap-opera theatrics. There's a hint of bitterness that makes the tips of Shell's ears burn. 'He singled you two out as the saviours of Duke & Sons.'

She says it so sharply – *the saviours of Duke & Sons* – that even Ricky notices.

'What's that supposed to mean?'

'It *means*,' she says tightly, 'that you two will be fine. It's the rest of us who have to worry.'

'You'll be fine, too, babe,' Ricky tells her, reaching for her hand and bringing it up to his mouth to kiss it, leaving a smear of black lipstick. 'You're so good. You could sell underwear to a Victoria's Secret model.'

She softens. 'I know, but I don't have anyone to sell *to*.'

'What do you mean?' Shell asks, with a frown.

'Duke & Sons is on its arse, Shell. I mean, look at this place.' Denise throws her hands up. 'It's massive. It must cost a fortune to maintain. I don't know how they've managed to keep it open for so long, given that we have *no* customers. If it wasn't for ART, this place would have gone bust three years ago. That's what all of this is about, right?' She looks at them in turn. 'All these *exciting* new changes. Old Mr Duke has no choice.'

'No.' Soph shakes her head, then looks at Becca, who does the same. 'Duke & Sons has been around *for ever*.'

'Exactly,' Shell says. 'We've been open for eighty-three years.' When Ricky doesn't back her up, she knows he's thinking about Bendel's again. 'I know it's been quieter over the last few years. But it can't be *that* bad, can it? Plus, tourists *love* this place. You should have seen the queue for the café earlier.'

'Yeah, they come in to have a cream tea and take photos, but they don't actually *buy* anything, do they? Maybe a tin of shortbread or a fridge magnet, but that's it.' Denise heaves a defeated sigh. 'And the locals can't afford to shop here any more. The days of the Ostley housewives in mink coats buying Hermès scarves are long gone. People want to shop in Zara and H&M, or they order everything from ASOS without even having to leave the house.'

'That's true,' Soph murmurs, looking at Becca who is clearly anxious.

'I mean,' Denise gestures at Ricky, 'you didn't buy that dress here, did you, babe?'

He laughs at the thought. 'Yeah, Duke & Sons don't really do this look.'

'And what is that look?' Shell asks, trying to lighten the mood.

'The mistress who turns up at the funeral, even though the family asked her not to.'

Shell laughs, but Denise doesn't, turning to her this time. 'And I know you didn't buy that here, either.'

'It's not my fault.' Shell tries not to sound defensive as she smoothes her hands down her dress. 'My options are limited. Nowhere on the high street stocks my size.'

'Fair enough. Still. *No one* our age shops in Duke & Sons, do they?'

'I guess not,' Shell concedes.

'If I didn't work here, where would I work?' Denise exhales sharply and presses a hand to her forehead. 'Seriously. What are my options? The bra department at Marks & Spencer?'

'Babe, breathe,' Ricky tells her, taking a deep breath in through his nose and letting it out through his mouth.

Denise doesn't copy him. 'What am I going to do? I can't lose this job. I mean, we've been looking at flats and—' She gasps, her brown eyes wide. 'We have to pay for Mykonos at the end of January!'

'It's okay,' he says, but she ignores him, hand still pressed to her forehead as she tries to catch her breath.

'Why did I buy that ridiculous Fendi bikini? I know it was in the sale, but still . . .'

'It's okay.' Shell tries this time as Denise's breathing shallows and beads of sweat bubble up along her hairline, like a string of pearls. Shell waits for her to look at her, then adds, 'No one is losing their job, okay?'

'You aren't,' Denise sobs. 'I don't sell enough to cover my wages. How can they keep me on?'

'Listen,' Shell says softly, suddenly aware that Becca and Soph have huddled closer so they're now on either side of her. She slings an arm around each of their waists and pulls them to her. 'All of you. I know his delivery wasn't great, bless him. But everything Callum just said is true. We need to drag Duke & Sons into the next century. We've been saying it for ages, haven't we?' she reminds Denise. 'We know that the customers who shop here are . . .' she stops to think of a polite way of saying it '. . . of a *certain generation*.' She hears Ricky chuckle, but doesn't let her gaze waver from Denise's. 'So, to attract the next generation, we need to stock brands that appeal to them, right? American tan stockings and Roger & Gallet soaps aren't going to cut it any more.' Ricky chuckles again, louder this time. 'Like Savage X Fenty. Imagine if we got a brand like that!'

Denise takes her hand away from her forehead, her eyes bright again. 'That would be amazing.'

'Right?' Shell smiles, as she watches Denise's breathing begin to settle. 'So talk to Callum—'

'Yeah, right,' she interrupts. 'Like he'd listen to me.'

'Why not? If he really wants Duke & Sons to survive, he'll listen,' Shell tells her, and Denise believes that.

'Getting cool new brands is all good for us, but what

about this lot?' Ricky says, under his breath, pointing his grey bouffant wig towards Mrs Price, who is talking to Old Mr Duke's PA, Gladys.

The Beauty Hall is almost empty now, and the staff who have stayed are huddled in small groups, deep in conversation. Jennifer from Shoes has her hand on Robin from Little Duke's shoulder, her head bowed. When Shell sees that Robin is crying softly, her hands pressed to her stomach, she remembers that Robin has just found out she's pregnant and suddenly feels sick.

Ricky's right. Most of the staff are either retired or have young families: they work at Duke & Sons because it's local and the hours suit them. No one's there because they want a career. Shell, Ricky and Denise, maybe, but the rest just want a quiet life. To come in, sell some cashmere socks, and go home again. And there's nothing wrong with that. They work to earn enough to pay their bills each month and that's all they care about. Besides, there's no commission. No bonuses or bottles of champagne for the person who makes the most sales that week.

Shell hopes Callum Duke remembers that when he's rolling out all of his changes.

'Thanks, everyone,' he says then, and she jumps.

She'd forgotten he was there.

She turns to find him standing at the foot of the staircase and feels a pinch of admiration. Given that most of the staff have left and the rest are ignoring him in favour of whatever conversation they're having about what he's just told them, she's surprised he's still there. She thought he would be hiding in Old Mr Duke's office by now.

'Great. Brilliant. Thanks,' Callum says, as the staff who are left disperse, heading through the Beauty Hall towards the back to get their stuff. 'Lovely to meet you all. Very much looking forward to working with you.'

Mrs Price gives him a withering stare that punctures his sarcasm.

'Good evening, Mrs Price,' he says, contrite, his cheeks pink. 'See you tomorrow.'

'I don't work Sundays,' she tells him, then plods off to where Gladys is waiting for her.

'Bollocks,' Shell mutters, under her breath, as they pass the ART counter on their way out to join the others in the pub.

Ricky must be thinking the same thing because he dumps his coat on the counter with a heavy sigh.

Denise frowns at him as she tugs hers on. 'What?'

Becca and Soph seem equally confused, but when they realise why Shell and Ricky have stopped, they tilt their heads and whine, '*No!* Can't we do it tomorrow?'

'We're moving counters,' Ricky reminds them, with a wicked smirk. 'We have to do it now.'

Denise's frown deepens. 'Do *what* now?'

Shell closes her eyes and lets out a pained groan. 'Pack up the counter.'

'What – *now*?' Denise gasps, looking at her, then at the clock over the lifts. 'It's almost six.'

'Please, *Shell*.' Soph stamps her foot, her dark curls bouncing. 'Please don't make us do it now.'

'Yeah, Shell, *please*,' Becca begs, her hands pressed together. 'Can't we do it tomorrow? It's gonna take *ages*.'

Shell's about to tell them not to worry, she'll do it, when Ricky grins at them. 'No, it won't,' he promises. 'There's five of us. If we all do a bit, we'll be out of here in fifteen minutes.'

Soph holds her arm out to the Gaulin counter. 'They're not doing it. Why do we have to?'

'I don't want to be here, either,' he tells them, hands on his hips. 'I'd rather be in the Anchor with everyone else, but it's better to do it now or this merchandising company that Callum has hired to decorate the store will just shove everything into random boxes and it'll take *for ever* to sort out tomorrow.'

'What would you rather?' Shell tries. 'To stay fifteen minutes later now or two hours later tomorrow?'

Soph scowls at her. '*Neither.*'

'Plus, it will make stock check tomorrow *much* quicker.' Shell smiles sweetly. 'So we won't be here as long.'

'That's true,' Becca admits reluctantly. 'I don't want to spend my whole Sunday at work.'

Soph is utterly horrified. '*Et tu*, Duncan.'

'Right!' Shell claps her hands, ignoring Soph, who has slung her coat and bag on the Clinique counter and is fake-sobbing. 'I'll go out back and grab some boxes. Denise.' Shell points at her as she shrugs off her coat. 'If you take down the Halloween decorations, you guys can do the shelves while I cash up.'

'Good plan.' Ricky holds up his index finger to Becca and Soph. 'If we do it logically, all the foundations and concealers in one box, all the blush and bronzer in another, and so on, tomorrow we can just take everything out of the boxes, count them so we know how much we've got, and put them straight on the shelves.'

'Why can't we count them now?' Becca asks. 'That way we don't have to do it tomorrow.'

Ricky blinks at her, clearly as startled as Shell. Not just that she's made a sensible suggestion, but that she was actually paying enough attention to make it. But that's Becca: you think she's not listening, but then she says something to make you realise that she was all along.

'I mean, yeah.' He holds out his palms. 'That would be brilliant and I wish we could, but we have to note everything on the brand inventory forms and we won't get them from Gladys until tomorrow morning.'

Becca huffs. 'Fine.'

Before Shell goes to the back of house to get some boxes, Shell grabs her phone from her bag and takes one last photo of the counter. It's the only one in the Beauty Hall decked out for Halloween, and while Shell went for a more tasteful interpretation this year – no fake blood and zombies, rather rose-gold skulls, candles and a pile of pumpkins that she had great fun painting white and splattering with different colours – the Gaulin girls still complained that it was tacky. ART loved it, though, reposting her photo on their Insta, saying, 'If you've got it, haunt it.'

When she returns with the boxes, Ricky, Becca and Soph are helping Denise with the decorations. They've gathered up the skulls dotted around the counter, blown out the candles and now seem to be taking great pleasure in picking off the black wax that has pooled on the glass beneath. She takes another photo of the pile of paint-spattered pumpkins and posts it to the Duke & Sons account with 'There's only 365 days left till next Halloween!'

Seventeen minutes later – Soph made sure to set the timer on her phone – they're done. The only thing left on the counter is the float, which Soph glares at, her gaze narrowing.

'It's okay.' Shell tries not to laugh. 'You guys go. I'll take this out to the safe and catch you up.'

'You sure?' Denise asks, as she puts her coat on again. 'We can wait.'

'It's fine,' she tells her, reaching for the float. 'You guys grab a table. I'll be, like, ten minutes max.'

The back of house is actually a long corridor with a labyrinth of rooms behind a concealed door at the back of the Beauty Hall. Like Narnia but with more cardboard boxes. It has all the usual stuff you'd expect to find in a department store: a supply cupboard filled with loo roll and mouldy mops, the break room with a wall of lockers, and the safe, which is outside Old Mr Duke's office, behind Gladys's desk.

'You robbing us, Frida?' Shell hears someone say and looks away from the safe to find Callum leaning against the doorframe of Old Mr Duke's office with his arms crossed. When their gaze meets, he smiles slowly, his eyes almost neon blue in the dim light.

'Sorry, Mr Duke,' she says, putting the float inside the safe and heaving the door shut. 'I didn't know anyone was still here.'

He presses his hand to his chest. 'Callum, please. There's only one Mr Duke.' He winks at her, which should make her skin crawl, but there's something about the way he does it that reminds her of Old Mr Duke. Like he's trying to put her at ease rather than leer at her.

'Alright. Callum.' She thumbs over her shoulder. 'I'm done, so I'm going to head off.'

He straightens and, just like that, he's back to the stiffly formal Callum Duke. 'Would you mind if I escorted you out, Shell? There's something I need to discuss with you.'

She stiffens herself, but tries to hide it with a shrug. 'Of course.'

'I was going to tell you this tomorrow,' he says briskly, his chin up and his shoulders back as they walk in step down the corridor, 'but as it's just the two of us, it's probably best we discuss it now.'

'Okay,' she says carefully, as he shuts the door to the supply cupboard then gestures at her to go ahead of him as they walk around a pile of cardboard boxes dotted with red FRAGILE stickers.

He obviously senses her apprehension because he says, 'Don't worry,' in the way he did at the meeting. It did nothing to reassure her then and it doesn't now as they pass through the concealed door back into the Beauty Hall.

'It's good news, Shell,' he adds, turning to her with a smile that she's sure is supposed to reassure her, too, but does nothing of the sort. She tries to smile back, but can't quite manage it as she struggles to keep up with him while he strides toward the ART counter.

All she can think is, *What else is he changing and what does that have to do with me?*

'Oh.' He stops so suddenly she almost walks straight into the back of him. But before she can ask him what's wrong, he spins around to face her. 'You've packed up the counter already. The Changeover crew would have done that.'

'I know, but they'll just put everything in one box and it'll take ages to sort out.'

He nods, clearly impressed, then gestures at the Gaulin counter. 'They didn't think to do the same?'

Shell almost laughs at the thought of Louise and the girls staying late to do something like that, but resists and smiles sweetly instead. 'Well, at least the counter will be clean and ready for them when they do.'

'So you're pretty much done, then? You'll be in and out tomorrow.'

'I wish. We still need to unpack all ART's Christmas stock and decorate the counter.'

'I liked what you did for Halloween. I can't wait to see what ART has planned for Christmas.'

Her cheeks warm at the compliment. 'It's safe to say that it will be very different from the rest of the store.'

'What do you mean?'

'Don't get me wrong, the store always looks *beautiful* at Christmas. It's just that ART prefers something more . . .' she hesitates, trying to think of a way of saying it that doesn't sound rude '. . . modern.'

Callum's eyes brighten. 'I think you'll be surprised this year.'

'Yeah?'

He waggles his eyebrows, clearly excited about whatever he has planned. Shell just hopes he's cleared whatever it is with Old Mr Duke. She's about to grab her coat off the counter when she glances up at the ART logo. 'Oh, crap.'

'What's wrong?'

She points at the shelf of decorative paint cans and brushes. 'We forgot to pack those.'

'Don't worry.' He waves his hand at her. 'I can help with that. Have you got a box?'

'No.' She lets go of her coat and sets off for the back of house. 'I'll grab one.'

'I'll go. I've just remembered, I have something for you in the office.'

He returns a few moments later with a cardboard box, a feather duster and a white and black paper bag with rope handles. He puts the bag on the floor at their feet, the duster on the counter, then hands her the empty box.

'Here. Allow me,' he says, stepping behind the counter, reaching up for one of the paint cans and passing it to Shell. 'I checked your figures, and I have to say I'm very grateful that we don't pay you commission.'

Shell fills with pride as she puts the paint can and brushes into the box.

'I must confess,' he reaches up for the next one on the shelf, 'before I worked at Bendel's, I had no idea how beloved makeup is. A couple of years, we stocked a range by a beauty *influencer*,' he says it like it isn't a real word,

67

'and so many people turned up for the launch, they had to shut down Fifth Avenue.' He hands her the paint can. 'I've never seen anything like it. The police were *furious*.'

Shell knows exactly what he's talking about: she saw it on Instagram. 'Jeffree Star? How quickly did it sell out?'

'Immediately! We couldn't keep it in stock.'

She puts the paint can into the box with the others. 'Wild, isn't it?'

'Actually, Jeffree kind of reminded me of Ricky.'

'There's only one Ricky,' she tells him.

'Oh, I'm sure of that.' He laughs to himself, reaching for the last paint can. 'As much as I was looking forward to seeing my grandparents again, after living in Brooklyn for the last three years, I wasn't relishing the prospect of moving back to Ostley.'

'Whatever do you mean, Mr Duke?' Shell says, feigning shock. 'I'll have you know that Ostley is the Brooklyn of Somerset.'

'Clearly.' He smiles. 'I had no idea it had a drag scene, though.'

'To be fair, Ricky *is* Ostley's drag scene. Or he's Ostley's only bisexual drag queen, at least.'

He laughs again. 'Does he have a stage name?'

'Andy Whorehol.'

Callum stares at her, momentarily stunned, then says, 'Well. Okay, then.'

'He's performing tonight, if you're curious.'

He seems to consider it as he reaches for the feather duster. 'Are you going?'

As she watches him sweep the empty shelf, Shell feels

another pinch of admiration. When she saw him saun-tering down the staircase with Old Mr Duke earlier, she didn't think he'd be the type to get his hands dirty.

'I can't,' she says, closing the cardboard box and putting it on the floor with the others. 'It's Halloween so I prom-ised my little brothers and sisters I'd be home to see them in their costumes before they go to bed.'

He turns back to her, feather duster poised. 'You have little brothers and sisters? How old?'

'Patrick and Arun are five. Kitty and Sim are eight.'

'Wait.' He blinks at her. '*Two* sets of twins?'

'Yep. My parents are unreasonably proud of themselves. My mother for the sheer efficiency of it all, *boom, boom, done*. And my father because he seems to think it's proof of his extraordinary virility.'

'That's quite an age gap, though.'

'I know,' she tells him, as he resumes dusting. 'I'm not saying I was an accident, but I was an accident.'

'How old were they when they had you?'

'Sixteen.'

He turns back to her and pulls a face as if to say, *Yikes*. 'That is young.'

'I couldn't imagine having a kid at sixteen. I'd have an eleven-year-old.' She pretends to shudder at the thought. 'Still. My mum doesn't regret it. She had me, and when I started school, she went to uni, got settled in her career. Then, when she and my dad were ready, they started a family.'

'What does she do?' he asks, moving down to the next empty shelf, even though she's dusted it already.

'She's a social worker.'

'And your father?' he asks, using a fingernail to pick at something on the shelf. 'What does he do?'

'He's a gardener.'

Callum spins around to face her. 'Do you think he could sort mine out? I just bought a house on Ostley Crescent that I'm doing up. The garden has loads of potential, but I have no idea where to start.'

'Of course. I don't have one of his cards on me, but I'll bring one in tomorrow.'

'Thanks. I'm good with a feather duster,' he holds it up to her, 'but I'm useless with weeding.'

Ostley Crescent? Surely that would be a little stuffy for Callum. It's beautiful – a neat crescent of Regency houses on a hill that overlooks the city – but she'd have assumed he'd opt for a glossy penthouse.

'I'm trying to restore it to how it would have looked when my great-grandfather bought it in 1855,' he goes on, returning to the dusting. 'But, you know, with a wine fridge and a steam shower.'

'Sounds nice.'

'Do you live in Ostley, Shell?'

'Yep,' she says, with a small sigh, as she imagines living somewhere like Brooklyn. 'All my life.'

'That's no bad thing. Look at my grandfather. There's something to be said for putting down roots.'

'True.'

'Do you still live at home?' he asks, dusting the last shelf with surprising enthusiasm.

'Yep.'

'What's that like?'

'Loud.'

He chuckles, but before she can tell him she loves it, he steps back and peers at the counter.

'I think we're done.'

Shell comes to stand next to him, her arms crossed. 'Good work, Mr Duke. Do you need a job?'

He turns to smile at her, his blue eyes so bright that she has to look away.

'I'd better get to the pub before Ricky and Denise start on the shots.'

'We didn't have our discussion, did we?' Callum reminds her, laying the duster on the counter. He tugs at the cuff of his white shirt, and when he smiles sharply, just like that, he's back to the stiffly formal Callum Duke.

'Oh, yes.' She reaches for her coat and puts it on. 'Of course.'

'As I said in the meeting earlier, ART are very happy with the work you've done. So happy, in fact, that,' he pauses for dramatic effect, 'they're promoting you to a brand ambassador.'

'*Promoting* me?' Shell yelps with delight.

'Yes.' He reaches inside his jacket to pull out a white envelope. '*This*,' he hands it to her with a firm nod, 'is a letter from ART confirming it and details your pay rise.'

She tries not to yelp again. 'Pay rise?'

'It's effective as of tomorrow.'

'Wow,' she says, staring down at the envelope in her hands.

'There are also details of an ambassador/influencer trip in February that ART would like you to attend.'

'A trip? Where to? London?'

'A bit further than that. Mexico.'

'*Mexico?*' Shell tells herself not to yell and fails. 'But my passport's expired!'

'You'd better renew it, then!'

'Why Mexico?' Not that Shell's complaining, of course.

'It's to promote their Mayan range. It should be fun. Think white beaches and blue sea.' He tips his chin up at her. 'You should go to Frida Kahlo's house while you're there. It's stunning.'

'La Casa Azul? Are you kidding? I'd love to!'

He's so genuinely pleased for her that she has to look down at the envelope again.

'Oh, and ART sent you this as well, Shell.' Callum reaches for the bag he left at their feet earlier when he came back with the box.

Shell clocks the Gucci logo immediately and her heart starts to beat very, very slowly.

'What's that?' she asks, when he hands it to her, too scared to look directly at it.

'It's for you.' Callum holds it up. 'From ART to say thank you for all your hard work.'

'It's Gucci,' she whispers, like the bag can hear her.

He leans towards her and whispers back, 'Yes, it is.'

'Can I open it?'

'I wish you would. I'm desperate to see what's inside.'

She puts the envelope on the counter next to her and takes the paper bag from him. It's heavy, she realises, undoing the black ribbon securing it, then reaching inside to find a black box. It's tied with black ribbon as well, but this ribbon is thicker and knotted into a bow in the centre. She glances at Callum, her smile a little wider now as she tugs it, releasing the bow and opening the box to reveal a white dust bag with GUCCI in the centre. Shell undoes the strings carefully and pulls out a hot-pink suede bag.

'Oh, my God,' she murmurs, running her hand over the quilting. 'It's beautiful.'

'It is, isn't it?' Callum says softly, watching as she traces the Gucci logo with the tip of her finger. 'I haven't known you long, Shell, but I think they chose wisely. That colour is perfect for you.'

'I can't believe it,' she breathes, unable to take her eyes from it. It's a Gucci bag.

'As I said in the Christmas Changeover meeting . . .' He trails off and when she looks up at him, his eyes are closed. 'Sorry,' he says, when he opens them again, pretending to shudder. 'I just had a flashback.'

She tries not to laugh.

'I think it went well, don't you?'

'Oh, yeah.' She slips the bag carefully back into the dust bag.

'I definitely won David Fox over, I know that for sure.'

'Don't you mean Daniel?'

He throws his head back and laughs, and when he looks at her, all trace of his sharpness is gone and she sees that he has the same fine lines fanning from the corners of his eyes that Old Mr Duke has when he smiles.

'Oh, God.' He puts his head into his hands and groans. When he stops, he takes them away.

'See, I knew his name was David. I don't know why I said Daniel. It was like some sort of fever dream. I could hear myself talking and I kept telling myself, *Shut up about the tablets, Callum. They don't care about the bloody tablets.*'

Shell laughs at that, but it's more a splutter as he looks at her, his forehead creased.

'*Jesus.* Everyone must think I'm an utter asshole.'

Before she can tell him not to be so hard on himself, they hear someone banging on the revolving door to get in and look over, as the security guard, Gary, strides towards them, to see who it is. It's Louise Larson, Shell sees, as she sweeps in, blonde curls bouncing with each step as she stomps over to where she and Callum are standing.

'Mr Duke,' she says, with a small sob. 'Can I speak with you, please?'

Shell tries not to groan at the performance. Her timid voice and trembling chin, a single, perfect tear rolling down her perfectly pink cheek. This isn't the fierce, belligerent Louise she's worked with for years. She suddenly seems as fragile as a china doll, like she'd smash into pieces if you raised your voice to her.

Callum falls for it immediately. 'Of course, Louise,' he says gently, taking a step towards her.

Remembered *her* name, didn't he?

Chapter Five

'Shell!' Denise calls, when she walks into the pub, waving her over.

The Anchor is always busy, but it's Saturday night so it takes Shell a while to get to where Ricky and Denise are sitting. A year ago, they would *never* have hung out in the Anchor, but then a young couple took it over and transformed it into a warm, welcoming place brewing its own beer and old albums spinning on a record player behind the bar. As Shell passes on her way to her friends, she glances at the sleeve propped on top of the record player to find that it's a South African Synth-Disco album called *Boogie Breakdown*. It's a welcome relief from listening to 'Monster Mash' and 'Thriller' all day.

'Emma not here yet?' Shell asks, when she finally gets to their table.

They're sitting by the fireplace, of course, because Denise is always cold. Shell would usually object because she's always hot, but she's only staying for one so there's no point in making a fuss. Besides, it's so pretty, the warm light from the candles on the mantelpiece, which are always there – not just in honour of Halloween – flickering against the walls and weeping white wax onto the cast-iron surround, like spilled paint.

'Where have you been?' Denise hisses, taking her bag and coat off the chair next to her so Shell can sit down. Before she can, though, she's on her feet. 'Drink?' she asks, snatching her wallet off the table.

She's about to head to the bar when Ricky gasps, 'Is that Gucci?'

Denise freezes and turns on her heels to face the table again. 'Is what Gucci?'

'It is!' He points at the white and black paper bag hanging from Shell's wrist. 'It's Gucci!'

'Shell!' Denise looks down at the bag, then up at her. 'You can't just *buy something* from Gucci without telling me. What did you wear to Gucci?' She points at her feet. 'Tell me you didn't wear those DMs to Gucci!'

'I didn't *go* to Gucci. It's a gift.'

'Who from?' Ricky and Denise ask in unison.

'ART.' Shell holds her arms out and squeals, the paper bag swinging from her wrist. 'I got a promotion!'

'What?' Denise screams, launching herself at her and hugging her so tightly, it knocks the air right out of her.

When she lets go, Ricky is on his feet as well, pulling her into his arms. 'You star!'

'Promoted to what?' Denise asks, reaching for her arm and squeezing it.

'Brand ambassador.'

'What does that mean?'

'I'm not sure,' Shell admits. 'But it's more money and they're sending me to Mexico!'

Denise yelps. 'Mexico?'

Ricky reaches for her other arm, squeezing it almost as hard as Denise is. 'Are you serious?'

'In the New Year. It's an influencer trip to promote their new Mayan range.'

Denise points at the bag. 'So that's from them?'

'Yeah.' Shell holds it up to her. 'To say thank you for all my hard work.'

'Um.' Ricky lets go of her arm to cross his. 'I work hard as well.'

'Babe, you fell asleep in the break room yesterday,' Denise reminds him.

When she goes to take the bag from Shell, he gasps, 'Don't!'

She and Shell freeze, turning to him to find that he's glaring at Denise.

'Wait!' He bends down, reaching into the pocket of his black fake fur coat, which is hanging on the back of his chair, and producing a small bottle of hand sanitiser. 'Don't you dare touch whatever's in there with bare hands.'

Shell waits for Denise to tell him to stop being so dramatic, but she takes the bottle from him. 'Yes!' she says, flipping the cap open and squeezing some into the palm of her hand, then gives it back to him. She rubs her hands together with such vigour you'd think she was about to perform surgery. When she's satisfied that they're dry, she reaches for the paper bag again, her eyes wide.

'Don't put it on the table!' Ricky warns, using some of the hand sanitiser as well. 'It's filthy.'

He oversees as Denise does as she's told, carefully

handing him each piece as she unwraps it – the paper bag, the box, the ribbon, the dust bag – to reveal the hot-pink suede handbag.

She holds it up, her hands and the gold chain straps trembling. 'Holy shit, Shell.'

'Oh, God,' Ricky murmurs, and he looks faint. 'It's the Marmont shoulder bag.'

Denise doesn't look any steadier. 'The small?'

'No.' He presses the back of his hand to his forehead. 'The medium.'

Denise shows Shell the bag, her eyes *huge*. 'Babe, it's the Marmont shoulder bag.'

'Isn't it beautiful?' Shell says, barely able to contain her glee.

'Isn't what beautiful?' Emma asks, suddenly at her side. Then she sees the bag and gasps. 'Is that Gucci?'

She reaches for it, but Ricky stops her. 'No!' He slaps her hand away. 'Absolutely not. You're too clumsy for Gucci, Russo.'

She's clearly appalled, but it's true.

Must be hereditary, Shell thinks, as she remembers how many bottles of foundation Soph dropped today.

She loves them dearly, but the Russo sisters are a liability.

'Rude,' Emma tuts, unwinding her yellow scarf from around her neck. There's a crackle of static as it catches in her tangle of dark curls, Emma tugging it off with such fury she snuffs out one of the candles on the fireplace. 'Shell, what are you doing buying a Gucci bag? Your mum is going to kill you *dead* if you come home with *that*!'

'Oh, I didn't buy it. Like *I* can afford a Gucci bag.'

'I was gonna say.' Emma unbuttons her coat.

'It's a present. From ART,' Shell says, watching as Ricky supervises Denise, telling her to be careful as she slips the handbag back into the dust bag. 'They've promoted me to brand ambassador.'

'No way!' Emma screeches, trying – and failing – to hug her with her coat still half on and off. Shell helps her and as soon as her arms are free, she leaps on her, almost knocking Shell off her feet. 'Congratulations!'

'Thanks!' Shell says into her hair. It's twice the size, thanks to the rain.

'What's a brand ambassador?' Emma asks when she steps back.

'We don't know,' Denise tells her, putting the dust bag back into the box. 'But they're sending her to Mexico.'

'Mexico?' Emma gasps, punching Shell's shoulder. 'But your passport is out of date!'

'I know. I'm going have to do something about that.'

'That's amazing.' Emma kisses her cheek. 'We need to celebrate! Wine?'

With that, she's gone, disappearing into the huddle of people waiting to be served at the bar. As Shell watches them, patiently waiting their turn, she's suddenly very grateful that Ricky and Denise managed to secure a table, even if it is by the fireplace. She cannot stand up a moment longer, and is unsure how she's going to manage the twenty-minute walk home without some Kendal Mint Cake and one of those foil blankets they give you at the end of a marathon.

A few minutes later Emma returns with a bottle of white wine and three bags of crisps, gripped between her teeth. As soon as Shell tugs them out, she begins talking, demanding to know what else she missed. So they fill her in on the meeting, about Old Mr Duke retiring and Callum, as Shell opens the crisps and puts them in the middle of the table.

'I literally *just* saw Soph at home and she didn't say a word about any of this.' She reaches for a crisp. 'She and Becca are too busy getting ready to go to the Halloween party at Hannigans tonight.'

Shell groans. 'Oh, God. Hannigans.'

'Hannigans was *the* club when we were fifteen because they didn't check IDs,' Emma tells Denise.

'Every town had a Hannigans.' Denise pretends to cringe. 'In Birmingham, my mates and I used to go to a place called Oscars that had a big plastic Oscar statue outside that all the lads would take it in turns to hump when they were leaving. Every Sunday morning there would be a different bra around its neck.'

Ricky looks appalled as he reaches for his glass.

'Babe,' Emma turns to Shell, 'remember when you broke the heel off your shoe running to the dance-floor?'

'How could I forget? We were in the queue for the loos and we heard the intro to "Back That Azz Up" and we just started running. My heel snapped right off. I almost broke my ankle.'

Emma throws back her head and laughs. 'You had to walk home barefoot.'

'Good thing it was summer.'

'Hey,' Denise says. 'Do you reckon Callum Duke would ever go to Hannigans?'

Ricky shakes his head so hard that another plastic spider falls out of his wig. 'Absolutely not!'

'So,' Emma says, a glint in her eye, 'how hot is this Callum? Ostley hot or actual hot?'

'*Actual* hot,' Denise confirms.

'Chris Evans in an Aran jumper hot,' Ricky adds.

'His mouth is *obscene*,' Denise chimes in.

'I just want to suck on his bottom lip,' Ricky tells her, with a dreamy sigh.

'Really?' Emma raises her eyebrows, biting down on the crisp. When Shell doesn't join in, she turns to her. 'You're being unusually quiet. This Callum too pretty for you, then?'

Ricky points his wine glass at Emma. 'You know it.'

'He's just too . . .' Shell sighs and reaches for a crisp. '. . . I don't know . . .'

'Clean?' Denise offers.

Ricky snorts. 'Well dressed?'

'Okay. Fine. He's too pretty for me. He's got that whole blond-haired, blue-eyed, cartoon-Disney-prince thing going on and it doesn't do anything for me.' Shell pops the crisp into her mouth.

Emma tuts. 'So he's no Nick Wallace, then?'

'You've met the infamous Nick Wallace, haven't you, Em?' Denise asks.

'I haven't, actually. That was when we were living in Manchester so I wasn't here for the whole Nick Wallace saga. But I heard all about it, of course.'

'It was hardly a *saga*,' Shell scoffs.

'So do you believe they were just friends, Em?' Ricky pushes, with an eager grin.

'Shell says nothing happened and I believe her.'

'Thank you.' Shell sticks her tongue out at Ricky.

'But she was still out of her mind in love with him.'

'Excuse me.' Shell puts her glass on the table in front of her. 'I wasn't in love with him.'

Emma gives her a thumbs-up as if to say, *Yeah. Sure.*

'I wasn't. We were just friends.'

Ricky and Denise give her a similar look.

Shell huffs, glancing around the pub as she finishes her wine. It's then that she realises she recognises most of the faces: clusters of her colleagues are dotted around the pub. The warehouse staff are at the long table by the doors out to the beer garden in their navy blue sweatshirts and trousers. David Fox is sitting in one of the battered leather chairs by the other fireplace, holding court at the table opposite theirs. He's gesticulating wildly, his greying hair sticking up from where he keeps stopping to push his hand through it, and she wonders what he's saying, if he's planning some sort of protest. A mass walk-out in opposition of the changes.

The guys from Shoes are sitting around a table in the middle of the pub, with Bella from Handbags & Accessories, knocking back prosecco. But it isn't with their usual Saturday night gusto. No one's talking, and when Shell notices her smudged mascara, she remembers that Bella's getting married in the summer and suddenly feels like crying herself.

All these people with weddings and mortgages and holidays to Mykonos to pay for and they don't even know if they'll have a job much longer.

And what about Old Mr Duke? What's it going to do to him if he has to close the doors to Duke & Sons?

Then she remembers what Denise said after the meeting and something in her catches light. 'Den, you're right.'

'Right about what?' she asks, when Shell leans across the round table.

'We have to do something about this.'

'About what?' Emma asks, reaching for the bottle of wine and refilling their glasses. 'Nick Wallace?'

'No. Duke & Sons. If the store is in trouble, we have to do something about it.'

'Us?' Ricky snorts. Denise seems equally sceptical.

'Yes. *Us.*' She gesticulates wildly at the space between them. 'We always sit here after work, moaning about the brands we should be stocking and the events we could be doing, so let's do it.'

Denise frowns at her. 'Do what, Shell?'

Emma tries to tuck one of her long curls behind her ear, but it won't comply. 'Yeah, do what?'

'Tell Callum our ideas.'

From their expressions, Ricky and Denise clearly think she's lost it.

'No. Listen,' Shell insists, suddenly so fired up that she almost knocks over her wine glass. '*Listen.* Why is Callum here? Think about it.' She taps her temple with a finger. 'He was living in New York. Why *on earth* would he come back to Ostley? Unless his grandfather needed him to.'

They're obviously not convinced, but Shell can see their suspicion softening somewhat.

'Old Mr Duke obviously *knows* something needs to change but, as he says all the time, he hates change, so he's brought Callum back from the US to do it for him. I mean –' Shell stops to gulp some wine '– you said it yourself. We can't keep going the way we are, can we?'

'She's right,' Emma chips in. 'I mean, I love Ostley, but if you go to Taunton or Yeovil or Church Cabham, they have all the same shops. The only thing that makes our high street different is Duke & Sons, but it's for old dears and tourists.'

'Exactly!' Shell says, putting her glass down. 'It's so frustrating because people *love* Duke & Sons, but no one our age shops there because why buy a Burberry dress from us when they can get one in Zara for, like, thirty quid? But *that*'s the problem,' she says, her hands balled into fists now. 'Everyone ends up shopping in Zara so everyone is wearing the same polka-dot dress. If they want something different, they either have to get it online or go into London, but *why*? Duke & Sons should be where they go for something different. That's why ART's doing so well – because we're the only store between here and London where you can buy it.'

Ricky and Denise are listening more intently now.

'We need to stock more brands like ART. Cool, aspirational brands that are affordable as well. And, yeah, I get that Duke & Sons prides itself on glamour, but there has to be a mid-point between the brands we stock and what they sell on the high street. *That*'s our sweet spot.'

Shell jabs the table with a finger, then snatches up her glass. 'Affordable luxury. People around here might not be willing to drop a couple of grand on a Burberry dress, at least not regularly, but they'd spend two hundred, for sure, if it was different and well-made, and it made them feel special.'

'God,' Emma mutters. 'Do you know how many times I pass someone in the street and think, '*I'll have that.*'

'Plus, people our age are really starting to think about how and where their clothes are made.' Ricky looks around the table. 'They'd rather pay a bit more for something if they know it will last.'

'Right!' Emma exclaims. 'I'm so sick of buying stuff and it fading after two washes.'

'Yeah, like this.' Denise tugs on the collar of her white shirt. 'This is The Kooples. It cost ten times as much as the ones I bought for work from Primark, but I've had it for *years* and it still looks brand new.'

'Exactly!' Shell says, fired up all over again. 'If Duke & Sons is going to survive another eighty-three years we need new blood. Customers like *us.*' She gestures at the four of them so enthusiastically, she spills her wine. Not that she notices because she's trying to keep up with her brain as it barrels on without her. 'And we want something different from what's on the high street, but something we can afford.'

She gestures at Denise, who doesn't look convinced. 'We've been saying that for years.'

'That's my point!' Shell doesn't mean to raise her voice and tells herself to calm down as the people sitting at the next table stare at her. 'We've been saying that for years *to each other*. Now we need to tell Callum.'

Denise and Ricky burst out laughing.

'What?' Shell asks, trying not to sound defensive and failing. She thinks it's a great plan.

'He's not going to listen to *us*, Shell.' Denise takes another sip of wine.

'Why not?' Emma frowns. 'I thought you said he was nice.'

'No, we said he was *hot*,' Ricky corrects.

'*I'm* saying he's nice,' Shell confirms.

Ricky raises an eyebrow. 'And how would you know he's nice, Shell Smith?'

'Because I just talked to him.'

That gets their attention.

'When?' Ricky asks, with mock indignation that she didn't tell him.

'Just now.' Shell shrugs. 'When I was putting the float in the safe.'

'Is *that* why it took you so long?' Denise asks, with a mischievous smile.

Shell ignores her. 'He knows his stuff. He told me that Ricky reminds him of Jeffree Star.'

He's horrified. 'How does *Callum Duke* know who Jeffree Star is?'

'Because when he worked for Bendel's they stocked Jeffree Star Cosmetics.'

Ricky mutters into his wine, clearly unamused at being compared to Jeffree Star.

'I'm telling you,' Shell insists. 'Callum *will* listen to

us. He *needs* us. He can't turn the store around by himself.'

'Okay.' Denise still doesn't sound sure, but asks, 'So what's the plan?'

'Talk to Callum tomorrow, during stock check. Tell him your ideas for Lingerie.' Shell holds a hand up to her when she starts to object. 'He's not scary, I promise, Den. Just be honest with him and he'll listen.'

Ricky points his wine glass at Denise. 'Tell him about that brand you saw on Instagram.'

'As for us . . .' Shell turns to Ricky, who pulls a face. He was obviously hoping he'd be able to get away without actually having to do anything. '. . . you tell him your idea to charge clients for makeovers.' He rolls his eyes and Shell raises a finger. 'It's a good idea! You're right. We should charge them. People take the piss. They come in just before the store's closing, asking to "try a foundation" and we know they want us to do their face before they go out.'

'That's true,' he admits, with a scowl. 'And they don't even buy anything.'

'We could charge, what?' She shrugs. 'Twenty quid? That's *cheap* for a full face of glam for prom or whatever. They can redeem it against an ART product, which you *know* they will, so they feel like they're getting their money's worth.'

Ricky shakes his head. 'We should charge forty. Then they'd have to buy at least two products.'

'See?' Shell says. '*This* is what I'm talking about!'

'And now you've got the bigger stand,' Denise says,

noticeably more enthused than when Shell first suggested it, 'you can get a cute little table and one of those mirrors with the light-bulbs around it. Make them feel special.'

'So it's decided?' Shell says, holding her glass up. 'We're doing this?'

Denise and Ricky glance at each other again, then nod.

'To saving Duke & Sons!' Shell cheers.

Denise clinks her glass with Shell's. 'To saving Duke & Sons!'

'I know I don't work there but . . .' Emma joins in '. . . to saving Duke & Sons!'

Ricky raises his glass with a moody sigh. 'To saving Duke & Sons! Let's hope it doesn't turn out like it did for Leslie Knope when she tried to save that video shop.'

God, I hope not. Shell finishes her wine.

Chapter Six

They're still plotting when Shell checks her phone to find that it's nine fifteen. 'Oh, no!' she mutters. Her little brothers and sisters should have gone to bed over an hour ago.

Hopefully, with all the sugar they've consumed after trick or treating, they're refusing.

'Stay,' Denise pleads, holding up the bottle of wine she's just bought. 'Have one more.'

'I can't. I promised them I'd be home in time to see them in their Halloween costumes.'

'You coming to my show at Mirage tonight?' Ricky asks, as Denise refills his glass.

'Next time, I promise.' Shell presses her palms together and holds them up, then snatches her coat off the back of her chair and grabs her handbag and the Gucci bag. 'I'll see you tomorrow morning for stock check, though, okay?'

He groans. 'Can't wait.'

'Text me when you get in,' Emma tells her, blowing her a kiss.

'Bye. Bye. Bye,' Shell says, blowing kisses back as she hurries off.

Then she's gone, rushing out of the pub and straight into a guy who is smoking on the pavement outside.

'Sorry!' she says.

'I'm not,' he tells her, with a slow smile as he looks her up and down. '*Hola, wapa!*'

Whopper?

Shell is so stunned that she glares at him, her lips parted.

'Oh, no!' he says, holding his hands up, beer spilling out of his pint glass and down his knuckles as he does. 'I'm not calling you fat.' He looks her up and down again, licking his lips this time. 'I don't mind it, actually.'

Is that supposed to be a compliment? Shell asks herself, as she continues to glare at him.

'*Wapa* means beautiful in Spanish.' He nods at her costume. 'Frida Kahlo, right?'

Oh.

Okay.

If it was any other night, she might have asked herself if this was their meet-cute. After all, it's almost perfect, isn't it? Her crashing into him in the rain and thinking he was calling her fat when he was actually calling her beautiful. To be fair, he's not bad-looking. He reminds her of Michael B. Jordan, tall with broad shoulders and a smile cheeky enough that if it wasn't *lashing down* she might have stayed and flirted a little.

But she scurries off, trying to get her leopard-print coat on without having to put the Gucci bag on the pavement. The rain's so heavy now that the silk flowers in her hair must be wilting as she roots through her handbag for her umbrella before hustling up the street.

As she approaches Duke & Sons, the merchandising team have arrived to decorate the store for Christmas. Callum is on the pavement, his back to her, the shoulders of his charcoal suit almost black and his blond hair flattened by the rain. She stops on the other side of the street for a moment, watching as he directs the men unloading a huge gingerbread house complete with a white-frosted roof edged with fake gum drops from the back of one of the trucks.

Old Mr Duke will not like that, she thinks, as she carries on, turning onto the road that leads to her house.

She's so focused on getting home that she doesn't hear someone say her name until they shout it.

'Shell Smith? Is that you?' they say, squinting at her across the street.

It's so dark that she does the same, then steps back because it can't be.

It looks like . . .

'Nick?' she gasps, unable to disguise her delight as he waits for a car to pass, then crosses the street.

'It is you!' he says, throwing his arms around her and pulling her into a huge hug.

She's sure it's just nostalgia, but he smells like Body Shop banana shampoo and oil paint, just like he did all those years ago when it was just the two of them in the art room, cleaning the brushes and discussing pointillism.

The shock of it makes Shell poke him with her umbrella when they finally step apart.

'I'm sorry!' she gasps again, covering her mouth with her other hand.

'No worries.' He grins, dipping his head to join her under the umbrella. She raises her arm so he can fit. 'Shell, you look *amazing*. A ray of sunshine on a miserable evening.'

'Oh, thanks. You look well.' More than well. He looks just as she remembers.

It comes back to her in such a rush that she feels lightheaded. His eyes, big and brown with the *Mona Lisa* inscrutability that makes him appear to be smirking even when he isn't. His hair, longer now, thick dark waves, the ends of which hang in curls around the nape of his neck. His jaw, which she still wants to trace with the tip of her finger, softened with stubble now so that it draws more attention to his mouth.

He's all in black – as always – the collar of his leather jacket turned up as though that will somehow protect him from the downpour. She sneaks a look lower to find that he's wearing black skinny jeans and tries not to laugh as she sees his DMs, like the ones she's wearing, except hers are hot-pink.

She can't believe that Nick Wallace is right there, gazing at her as if she's the only thing he can see.

'I'm so glad I bumped into you, Shell.'

'Yeah?' She smiles hopefully.

'I've been trying to get hold of you. You deleted your Facebook.'

'I know. I saw this documentary on Netflix and it scared the crap out of me. Besides,' she nudges him with her elbow, 'I thought you hated Facebook.'

'I do, but I wanted to invite you to some reunion drinks in the Anchor next Saturday.'

'I was just in there, actually.'

'Nice.' He nods. 'Anyway, I hope you can make it. It should be fun. Just the usual crew.'

She has no idea who *the usual crew* are, but she doesn't care as long as he's there.

'Please come.' He reaches down for her hand, and when he squeezes it, the warmth of his skin against hers is enough to make her breath catch in her throat. She hopes the rain is too loud for him to hear. 'I'd love to catch up.'

'Of course,' she says, a little dizzy at the promise of it. 'What time?'

'I don't know. What? Six?'

'Six works.' She nods. 'I'll see you in there.'

'Excellent,' he says, kissing her cheek quickly.

Then he's gone, and as Shell watches him walk away, she wills him to look back. Before he gets to the corner he stops, and when he turns, her heart almost leaps clean out of her chest as his mouth thins into a smile.

Now that, she thinks, *was a meet cute.*

Or a re-meet cute in their case.

Chapter Seven

As soon as Nick's out of sight, Shell closes her umbrella and finds a tree to shelter under so she can call Emma.

'You'll never guess who I just saw,' Shell says, as soon as Emma answers.

Emma doesn't hesitate. 'Not Nick Wallace.'

'*Yes*, Nick! Wallace!'

'Shut up!' Emma's voice gets further away. 'Shell just saw Nick Wallace.'

Then she can hear Ricky and Denise talking at once.

Emma shushes them. 'Hold on. Let me ask.' She must bring her phone to her ear again because her voice is back to being too loud, which is nothing to do with the din at the Anchor. That's just Emma. 'When? Where?'

'Just now as I was walking home.'

'How did he look?'

'Good.' Shell feels the corners of her mouth lifting. 'The same.'

'Why's he back?'

'I don't know. I didn't ask.'

'How long's he back for?'

'I don't know! I didn't ask!'

'So what *did* he say, then?'

'Not much.' She tries to sound casual, not like her heart is beating so hard that it's about to break through her ribcage and launch itself into the road to be run over by a minicab. 'Just that it was good to see me and that I should come to some college reunion drinks he's trying to sort out.'

'When?'

'Saturday.'

'I thought we were going to see the new Bond film on Saturday.'

Shell tries not to whine. 'Can we go on Friday instead? I'll pay,' she says, before Emma can object. She mumbles something Shell can't quite hear over the buzz of the Anchor so she adds, 'Popcorn and ice cream as well.'

'Fine.' Emma sighs dramatically. 'Just promise me one thing, okay?'

'I won't eat all your peanut M&Ms, I promise.'

'No, not that. Although you'd better not,' she warns. 'Just promise me that you'll take it slow this time.'

'Em, it's just a drink with some people I went to college with.'

'It's never *just* anything with you two.'

'What's that supposed to mean?' Shell huddles closer to the trunk of the tree to avoid the rain, the sheer, dizzying joy at seeing Nick again wilting like the silk flowers in her hair.

'Shell, you're like magnets. As soon as you get within a few feet of one another, you become inseparable.'

Her heart flutters. It's true. Wherever they were – the

95

pub, a party, a festival – it would always end up being just the two of them at the end of the night, huddled in a corner, talking and laughing as though they were the only ones there.

Like tonight. Nick doesn't have her new number and she doesn't have his, yet they still found one another. So if she'd stayed at the Anchor for one, like she intended, or if he had left home five minutes earlier, they would never have seen each other.

But they did.

'I don't want you to get hurt again, babe,' Emma says, so suddenly it winds her.

It takes Shell a second or two to recover before she says, 'I won't. I promise.'

'Just take it slow this time, okay?'

'Take it slow,' Shell repeats, with a nod.

When she finally makes it home and walks through the front door, she almost trips on Sim's scooter, which has fallen on its side. She props it against the wall with the other three, then picks up Arun's blue padded coat, somehow managing to hang it by its hood on one of the already full hooks. She takes off her DMs and finds another spot for her coat, the fake fur so wet as she hangs it up that she doubts it will be dry by morning.

It's suspiciously quiet, Shell notes, as she walks around the scooters. She can hear the television as she heads down the hall towards the living room and the splosh of the washing-machine in the kitchen, but that's it. No shrieking. No crying. No roar as her little brothers and sisters realise she's home and charge towards her, all at once, to show her their Halloween haul or to complain about some unforgivable misdemeanour the other has perpetrated.

She stands in the doorway to the living room to find that it's dark except for the light from the television. Her parents are fast asleep on the sofa, curled into one another under a blanket, her father's head tipped back, his mouth open, her mother's cheek on his chest. They're watching – or were watching – one of those grim crime dramas her father likes so much.

They look so content that she daren't go over and turn off the television in case she disturbs them, so she slinks upstairs to bed. The door to the boys' room is ajar and she pushes it, standing there for a moment, taking in the chaos. There are clothes abandoned on the floor, no doubt belonging to Arun who has to change at least three times a day for reasons known only to him, unlike Patrick who would spend all day in his underpants, if he was allowed.

Their night light is on, illuminating the army of Lego ninjas lined up on the bedside table, poised to pounce at the first sign of danger. On the carpet beneath, there are two orange plastic pumpkins containing what's left of their trick-or-treat bounty, and Shell feels a fresh stab of guilt at missing them in their costumes.

Hopefully her parents took lots of photos.

They're getting so big, all trace of their chubby-cheek babyishness gone, so she likes watching them sleep because it's the only time she can still see it. Like her sisters, her brothers aren't identical, but they could be as they snore sweetly, thick eyelashes fluttering. Patrick's bare foot is sticking out from under his Spiderman duvet, toes twitching as he sleeps, and Arun has kicked off his Ninjago. She wonders what he was dreaming about when he did it.

This used to be Shell's room, but when her parents found out they were pregnant again – with another set of twins, no less – they had to convert the loft. It looks completely different now, but it still has the same energy. The itchy sort of happiness she remembers so fondly. All those Christmas Eves she lay awake, waiting to hear Santa, and the raucous Friday nights when she and Emma were kids and couldn't sleep because they'd eaten too much ice cream then insisted her father tell them a ghost story before they went to bed.

Her little brothers don't have that issue, though. They sleep like the dead, as her mother says, so she knows she won't wake them when she steps into the room. Still, she carefully picks her way through the piles of clothes and abandoned toys on her way to Arun's bed. She takes his duvet off the floor, kissing his warm forehead before she covers him with it. Patrick stirs when she goes over to his bed and gently tucks his foot back under his duvet, but he doesn't wake up, just murmurs something to her that only he understands.

Shell leaves the door ajar and crosses the hall to her sisters' room. It's even more untidy, if that's possible. A stew of clothes and shoes and, again, an orange plastic pumpkin on the floor by each of their beds. Now they're eight, the girls are too old for night lights, they insist, but the white fairy lights around the metal frames of their headboards twinkle gently against the purple and pink unicorn wallpaper they fought over so furiously when their room was redecorated last year. Kitty wanted purple and Sim wanted pink, and neither would budge, to the point at which they refused to share a room any more. Their mother was about to paint the whole thing white and be done with it when their father, always the peace-maker, found a wallpaper online that was the perfect mix between the two.

'Shell?' Kitty murmurs, lifting her head off the pillow.

'It's okay,' she whispers, padding over to her bed and sitting on the edge. 'It's okay,' she says again, stroking the mess of dark curls as Kitty lets her head drop back to the pillow. 'Go back to sleep.'

Then Sim is awake as well. 'Shell?'

'Sorry.' She winces, goes to her bed and does the same. 'Did I wake you?'

Sim says something incoherent, batting her eyelashes, then opens them to look at her with a fierce frown. 'Where were you? We waited up for you. I wanted you to see our princess dresses.'

'I'm sorry, Sim. I had to work.'

'You're *always* at work.'

'I know.' Shell feels wretched. 'But I'm not next Monday. Why don't we go to the cinema after school?'

'Yeah?' Sim perks up at that. 'Can we?'

'Can we?' Kitty asks as well, sitting up in bed, suddenly awake again.

'Of course.' She turns her knees so that she's facing Kitty as well. 'What do you want to see?'

'Can we see that new Christmas film?' Sim's eyes light up. 'The one with the dragon and the snowman?'

'A dragon and a snowman?' Shell frowns. 'That's a weird combination.'

'They're best friends,' Kitty says, like she should know.

'Every time the dragon laughs he melts the snowman's head.' Sim giggles, covering her mouth with her hand.

Kitty does the same. 'And the dragon has to make him a new one out of snow.'

They're both giggling now and Shell can't help joining in. 'Sure. That sounds fun.'

'Yay!' they cheer.

She presses a finger to her lips. 'You'll wake your brothers.'

'Shell,' Sim says, trying to lower her voice, but she's obviously too excited to do so. 'Tell us the story.'

'Yeah,' Kitty says, her hands fisted in her purple chenille blanket. 'Tell us the story.'

'Which one?' Shell teases, even though she knows full well which story.

'The one about the sisters who find the magic lipstick,' they say together.

Shell had made it up for them when they were tiny, but they haven't asked her to tell it for months. It's comforting to know that, while they're too old for night lights, they're not too old for their big sister's stories.

'Okay,' Shell says, waiting for them to stop giggling and lie down. 'Once upon a time, in a town called Ostley, there were two fearless girls called Kitty and Sim, who find a magic lipstick . . .'

By the time Kitty and Sim fall asleep again, Shell is halfway there herself, the sound of their snoring and the murmur from the television downstairs making the climb up the narrow wooden stairs to her room feel like a Herculean task. She knows she should shower so she doesn't have to in the morning, but now she's back in the warm embrace of her room, she doesn't want to do anything to disturb the rare moment of stillness.

Shell was twenty-one when her parents found out they were expecting Patrick and Arun and she was sure that was it: they were going to ask her to move out. As much as she loved working at Duke & Sons, she was hardly raking it in, so it was a big relief when they said they were using the money her father had inherited from his grandmother to convert the loft into another bedroom.

With hindsight, maybe she should have moved out because, six years later, she's still here. She knows it's a bit weird, but she loves living at home. She loves watching her little brothers and sisters grow up. And even though her parents apologised for banishing her to the attic, Shell *loves* her room. It's just far enough away from the pandemonium of the rest of the house, the running and crying and lost shoes, to feel like an escape, yet close enough that she's never lonely.

It's not, she knows, but it feels like a studio flat. She

has her own bathroom, so she can take as much time as she likes in the shower without someone banging on the door, and it's big enough for a double bed, a wardrobe and a dressing-table to do her makeup. There's even space for a small mustard yellow sofa: she'd sacrificed her latte every morning for a year to pay for it. Her parents were so proud that they bought her two cushions to go with it, both black with cartoon-print leaves and Frida Kahlo (of course) in a red dress holding a monkey.

Shell Smith doesn't have much to show for her twenty-seven years on earth. She dropped out of uni after a year and has been unable to maintain a relationship for much longer than that. She doesn't even have an up-to-date passport. But at least she has this: a room of her own. And while *technically* it's not hers, it feels like it is, with its deep turquoise walls and bright yellow floral sheets, which are not unlike the dress she's wearing, now she thinks about it.

One wall is dedicated to prints by her favourite artists – Frida Kahlo (of course), Georgia O'Keeffe, Basquiat, Yayoi Kusama – mixed with photos she's taken over the years. Her brothers dressed as ninjas last Halloween. Her sisters on their eighth birthday, Kitty in purple and Sim in pink. She, Ricky and Denise at last year's Duke & Sons Christmas party, holding up glasses of champagne, the three of them laughing about something, she can't remember what. She and Emma on the beach in Blackpool, Emma's hair *everywhere*, the pair of them in matching red bikinis. That was the summer Shell had decided she wasn't going back to uni for her second year.

Looking around the room, it feels strange to say that somewhere with so much colour is calming, but it is.

It's her port in a Smith Storm.

Shell has a strict bedtime routine that she has more or less perfected over the years. It begins with her playing *Kind of Blue* on low, even though Nick would laugh if she told him, and ask when she graduated from Miley Cyrus to Miles Davis. Then she lights the ludicrously expensive fig candle that, even with her Duke & Sons discount, was still ludicrously expensive.

It concludes with her favourite part: taking off her makeup.

Shell may deviate from the other steps – she may play Laura Marling instead of Miles Davis, if she's in the mood, or neglect to light her candle if it's nearing pay day and it's running low – but she never skips this one. It's the same every night: eye-makeup remover, first cleanse, second cleanse, toner and serum, finished off with eye cream and a ten-minute massage with facial oil. Emma mocks her mercilessly for it every time they go away, but it doesn't matter how tipsy she is or how bad a day she's had, it's the only thing that calms her down before bed.

Half an hour later, the bathroom smells of roses and her bedroom smells of figs. As she tugs on her red and pink heart-print pyjamas, she should be ready to land, face first, in bed, but her whole body is still *humming* from seeing Nick. She could turn off the light and try, but she knows that she won't be able to sleep, so when she glances at her laptop, she thinks she might as well distract herself with the project for her online marketing course.

It's not due for another two weeks, but that doesn't mean anything. When she counts the days in her head, she doesn't have that long at all. She doesn't have tomorrow off, like she usually does, because of stock check, but if she can squeeze in a couple of hours next week after work and works all day Sunday, she should get it done. She just needs to come up with an excuse in case her parents ask her why she's holed up in her room on her only day off.

This would be *so* much easier if she could just tell them she's doing the course, but after that miserable year at university, she doesn't want them to get their hopes up in case she abandons this one as well. Not that she has any intention of doing so, but when she signed up for it, she had no idea that working full-time and doing the course on the side would be so hard. But if she and Mia Morris are going to start their app that hooks up influencers with photographers and freelance makeup artists, Shell is going to need to know how to do more than contour. Mia's boyfriend, Johnny, is doing all the technical app-y stuff and Mia is going to be the face of it, so Shell offered to handle the marketing. Coming up with ideas and promotions to lure new clients to the ART counter is one of her favourite things about working at Duke & Sons, even if she's got by so far on charm and sheer enthusiasm.

Hence the course.

Plus, it's fun, she reminds herself, as she trudges over to the sofa to grab her laptop. Not as much fun as doing people's makeup all day, but way more than learning about the sovereignty of Parliament, as she had at university. At least with this course, she actually understands what she's asked to read and can see how it applies to what she and Mia want to do with the app. Which is kind of the point of doing it, she thinks, as she sits cross-legged on her bed and waits for her laptop to fire up.

As soon as it does, she finds the email from her tutor and opens it.

Write a Creative Brief for a digital marketing agency on behalf of a traditional high street brand seeking to increase its online presence with the purpose of attracting new customers who may not have heard of them.

As she looks at the list and reads each thing she has to do – *Marketing Objective, Context, Communications Challenge, Audience, Cultural Insight, Core Desire, Brand Idea, Stimulus, Reasons to Believe, Response, Measures of Success, Mandatories, Budget, Deliverables and Timings* – she presses her hand to her forehead and groans.

This is definitely not something she can bang out in a few hours, is it?

Shell hasn't even decided what high street brand she's going to choose yet. Her first thought was Costley's, because they have no online presence, which she thought would be interesting. But as she's looking at the list, her desire to do it on a brand as dull as Costley's is waning.

Something occurs to her then and she sits a little straighter, cursing herself for not thinking of it sooner.

Duke & Sons.

While it isn't strictly a *traditional high street brand*, it is in Ostley. Plus, she *knows* Duke & Sons. She's worked there for eleven years. She knows the customers, knows the challenges, and certainly has reason to believe that it has the potential to turn things around. Besides, isn't that *exactly* what Callum is trying to do?

Drag Duke & Sons into the digital age.

She feels a flutter of excitement as she realises that *this* is what she can do to help the store. She can write a creative brief, research some digital marketing agencies that can implement it and present it to Callum.

With that she's typing. The next thing she knows it's almost one o'clock. She's itching to keep going and considers it, but between Christmas Changeover and stock check, tomorrow is going to be a demanding day of moving things, cleaning and broken nails, so she'll need as much energy as she can summon. Five hours' sleep certainly isn't enough, but it will have to do.

Chapter Eight

It feels like her eyes have been closed for all of ten minutes before her alarm goes off. Shell checks her phone three times to make sure it's right, furious to discover that it is as she hauls herself out of bed.

She's not often up first. Usually, she doesn't need to set an alarm because she's woken by four pairs of little feet charging down the stairs and the smell of burned toast. But, then, it's six o'clock on a Sunday morning, which is obscenely early, even for her little brothers and sisters. So she showers and gets ready as quietly as she can, lest she incur the wrath of her mother for waking them.

She keeps it simple, opting for black jeans and a black wool jumper, which is uncharacteristically basic for her, but there's no point in putting on anything more glamorous if all she's going to be doing is heaving boxes around all day. Transferring everything from her usual handbag into her Gucci one puts a spring in her step, though. She'd vowed to use it only on special occasions. Going to work on a Sunday for stock check certainly isn't that, but it's *so pretty*.

She hangs it on her shoulder, admiring it in the mirror

one last time before she heads out, remembering to grab the Christmas decorations she's bought for the counter. She hisses at the plastic bags, hoping the rustle doesn't wake anyone up as she creeps downstairs. She sits on the last step and puts on her DMs, then grabs her still damp coat from its hook. Mercifully, it's stopped raining, but she remembers to take her umbrella from the porch as she heads out, closing the front door behind her as carefully as she can.

As much as she loves her new bag, it keeps slipping off her shoulder, which would be a pain in the arse at the best of times. Given that she's carrying four plastic bags heavy with baubles, candy canes and two fake wreaths, and having to stop every few steps to tug the gold chain straps back onto her shoulder, it's making the walk to Duke & Sons twice as long.

By the time she finally turns the corner onto Ostley High Street, her arms ache. Thankfully, she can see Gary standing outside the store, having a smoke, and smiles at him, glad she won't have to go through the warehouse. He grins back, not in the least surprised that she's arriving for work an hour earlier than everyone else. He takes one more drag from his cigarette, then flicks it into the street as she approaches.

'You didn't have to do that, Gary,' she tells him. 'I'm not going to grass you up.'

'I know you wouldn't, Shell.' He smiles again, warmer this time. 'I thought you needed help.'

Gary is one of her favourite people at Duke & Sons. He's big and bald with a laugh you can hear throughout the store. He has this Phil Mitchell energy that scares people who don't know him, which is perfect for a security guard, she supposes. But Shell's worked with him long enough to know that he's actually a big softie. 'Bless you, Gary,' she says, when he takes the bags from her. 'You're a star.'

Shell follows him through the revolving doors into the store, then stops. 'What the . . .' She gasps as she turns in a circle to look at the Beauty Hall.

Gary stops as well, raising his eyebrows. 'I know. Old Mr Duke is going to do his nut.'

What has Callum done?

The Beauty Hall looks *nothing* like it usually does at Christmas. There are no garlands. No red tartan bows. No thin crystal vases at the end of each counter filled with velvety red roses, berries and pine cones.

'Where's the tree?' Shell gasps again, when she realises it's not there, standing proudly in the middle of the store, so tall that the point of the gold star almost touches the stained-glass dome.

Gary gestures at the red-and-white-striped hot-air balloon hanging from the ceiling, with what looks like a family of polar bears standing in its basket, a mother, father and two little ones, peering over the edge. Shell stares at it for a moment, then turns and pushes through the revolving door, running out onto the pavement.

She lets go of a breath when she sees the Ferris wheel turning steadily in the window surrounded by a wintry scene. Except the sign over it doesn't say DUKE & SONS TOYLAND: TOY has been replaced with BEAUTY, and instead of a toy in each carriage, there's a different product from the Beauty Hall. Bottles of perfume. Jars of moisturiser. ART makeup brushes.

The Ferris wheel is on a bed of snow, like it is every year, but is flanked on either side by Christmas trees – a big one with a smaller one in front of it – their branches white. And there's no cheerful scene. No snowmen. No ice rink. No tiny plastic children throwing snowballs. Rather, large red-and-white-striped candy canes standing in clusters. Even the backdrop is different, the black velvet curtain replaced by a white wall with LET IT GLOW in red glitter.

Shell runs to the window on the other side of the revolving door to find the large gingerbread house she saw the men unloading from the truck last night. It, too, is sitting on a thick drift of snow, and is surrounded by more Christmas trees and glass jars of various shapes and sizes, some plain, others ribbed and filled with sweets – jelly beans and marshmallows and Smarties – each lid topped with a gold star.

It's so bright that Shell has to step back to take it all in. There are more sweets dotted around the window, handfuls of massive red-and-white-swirled lollipops sticking out of the snow and gingerbread men in Santa hats. But when she sees that next to the house there's a red glitter letterbox with a letter addressed to Santa sticking out, ready to be posted, she can't help but smile as she imagines the twins' faces when they see it.

When she pushes through the revolving door back into the store, she notices that it even smells different. There's no spruce and cinnamon and orange mixed with the other scents of the Beauty Hall. It smells weird, sweet but cold somehow. Peppermint, she identifies, no doubt due to all the candy canes dotted around.

They're everywhere, rows of small ones hanging from red ribbon around each of the counters and large plastic ones standing in threes, in the corners of the shop floor. The crystal vases at the end of each counter are still there, but instead of flowers, they're each filled with something different. More candy canes on the Gaulin counter, baubles – white with red stripes in one, red with white dots in another – and the one on the ART counter is stuffed with smaller versions of the swirled lollipops in the gingerbread window.

It's *a lot* of red and white.

Red and white lights.

Red and white Christmas stockings.

Red-and-white-striped bows.

But every now and then there's a welcome pop of green from the wreaths and the one modest Christmas tree in the Beauty Hall (it's actually *huge*, but modest compared to the sixty-foot one they usually have). The tree is next to the ART counter, which is now in pride of place at the entrance to the store, the tree decorated with everything in the vases – the candy canes, the baubles, the lollipops – bringing the whole space together.

Now that Shell takes a step back and looks at it, she likes it.

Really likes it.

Yeah, it's different – the antithesis of the Duke & Sons traditional glamorous Christmas – but it's *fun*. Every time

Shell looks around, she notices something else. The stools at each of the counters have been replaced with red and white toadstools and the two huge polar bears by the staircase – no doubt waiting for the hot-air balloon to land – are wearing matching knitted jumpers that say, MERRY CHRISTMAS, YA FILTHY ANIMALS.

It's young and fresh and exactly what Duke & Sons needs if it's trying to update its image.

Old Mr Duke is going to *hate* it.

'I thought you guys were done?' Shell hears someone say as she emerges from the back of house into the Beauty Hall.

She stops, lowering the massive box she's holding to find Callum in front of her, frowning.

He looks far too pristine for eight thirty on a Sunday morning, his shoes polished and his blond hair deftly treading the line between coiffed and artfully untidy, a look Shell suspects took some time to achieve. His suit – another single-breasted number similar to the charcoal one he was wearing yesterday but in black – looks brand new, like he's just cut the tags off it and slipped it on. It's fitted, but not tight, another white shirt beneath it that, again, like yesterday, is paper crisp and unbuttoned just enough to reveal an inverted triangle of pale skin.

Plus, he smells good.

Much nicer than she smells after battling with boxes.

'Shell?' he says, his forehead smoothing when he real-ises it's her.

She peers at him over the box. 'Hey, Mr Duke.'

'Call me Callum, please,' he tells her again, taking it from her. 'I'm sorry, Shell. I didn't recognise you out of costume. I thought you were one of the merchandising team we hired to decorate the store.'

'No worries,' she tells him, deciding to take advantage of his help and heading through the concealed door into the back of house to grab another box.

When she returns, he looks genuinely conflicted, no doubt trying to work out how he's going to carry that one as well. She doesn't need him to, though, and marches over to the ART counter.

'Shell,' he says, when he catches up with her. 'What on earth are you doing here so early? You didn't need to be in until nine.'

'I know. I got in at eight. I wanted to get a head start.'

'You got in at *eight*?' Callum asks, as she puts the box she's carrying on the floor, then turns to take his and puts it on top of the other. 'How did you even get in?'

'Gary was here.'

'Who's Gary?'

'The security guard.'

'Oh.' He flushes, clearly embarrassed that he didn't remember his name.

'Even if he wasn't, I have a key.'

'You have a key to the store?'

'Yeah,' she says, grabbing a pair of scissors from the counter. 'I'm either the first in or the last out so Old Mr Duke . . .' it's her turn to blush as she looks up at Callum '. . . I mean *your grandfather* . . .'

He waves her off with a smile. 'I know everyone calls him Old Mr Duke. I like it. It's sweet.'

'Okay.' She avoids eye contact as she opens the flaps of the cardboard box and riffles through it to see what's inside. 'Old Mr Duke gave me a key after I got locked in for, like, the fourth time.'

'You've been locked in the store *four* times?' he says, but she just hmms, too distracted by what's in the box.

It's the new ART lipsticks. The boxes are usually glossy white and splattered with paint, but for Christmas this year, they're matte white with red foil stripes. She holds one up to Callum with a smile to show him how perfectly they go with his candy-cane theme, then opens it to find the tube is red, with Sparkle written along it in a swirly white font. There are four new shades, she discovers. After Sparkle – an obnoxious glittery pink – she finds Cheer, an inoffensive nude, then Joy, a classic red, and finally Magic, which looks like the perfect balance of pink and purple.

Like Kitty and Sim.

'What?' Callum asks, when she smiles and shakes her head.

'Nothing.' She shows it to him. 'It's just that I've been telling Kitty and Sim this bedtime story since they were little about these sisters who find a magic lipstick and have to save a prince.'

'*They* have to save the prince?' he asks, taking the lipstick from her and looking at it.

'Of course. Why not?'

Callum hands it back.

'So they have to free the prince from the tower,' she goes on, looking down at the word 'Magic' written on the lipstick with another smile. 'Before an evil gargoyle takes over the kingdom.'

'That's lovely.'

'Yeah,' Shell says to herself, putting the lipstick back into its thin box.

'So?' He smiles eagerly, gesturing at the decorations. 'What do you think?'

'Oh.' She straightens. 'It's cool.'

'*Cool?*'

That clearly wasn't the response he was hoping for.

'I like it,' she assures him. 'It's young and cool and a bit quirky.'

Callum looks around and nods.

When he turns back to her, she says, 'Wanna see something funny?'

'Always.'

She bends down to reach into one of the plastic bags of decorations she brought with her to dress the counter and pulls out a box of candy canes she got at the pound shop last week.

'No way!' He beams, taking them from her.

She reaches in again and pulls out a white bauble she'd painted with red stripes a few days earlier.

'Did you do this?' he asks, handing her back the candy canes.

She nods. 'Red and white, eh? Great minds.'

'So,' he says, when she turns back, gesturing around the Beauty Hall. 'You really do like it?'

'I do.'

'Do you think my grandfather will?'

'Oh, no,' Shell says. 'He's going to hate it.'

He looks stricken. 'What am I going to do?'

'Unless you have a sixty-foot Norwegian spruce hiding somewhere, there's not much you can do.'

He thumbs over his shoulder. 'I'm going to hide in my office.'

Shell nods. 'Good call.'

Chapter Nine

Callum has been pacing back and forth by the revolving door for the last ten minutes.

Everyone is here now, the Beauty Hall buzzing as they inspect the decorations. Even Becca and Soph were on time. Sulking and hung-over, but on time. Ricky wasn't long behind them – barefaced and equally hung-over – approaching the ART counter with a groan and a promise never to go drinking with Emma again.

Still, at least he'd brought Shell a latte.

He looks awful, bless him, his topknot sagging and a pair of sunglasses perched on his nose. He only got home a few hours ago, apparently, so Shell makes him put on some blush, then sits him on a toadstool while they wait for Old Mr Duke to arrive. She's done everything already – given the counter and shelves a good scrub, unpacked everything they put into boxes last night as well as the new Christmas stock – so all he, Becca and Soph have to do is the fun stuff. She gets the girls to finish the tree and sort out the stands with ART's *Time to Sleigh* posters while Ricky starts decorating one of the wreaths she bought with the ART Christmas lipsticks. He has to secure them to the wreath with florist's wire, which he seems to be managing between long sips of coffee.

The clock over the lifts chimes nine times and everyone looks up. Callum stops pacing, his hands behind his back as he faces the revolving door. Sure enough, a few seconds later, it turns and there he is.

Old Mr Duke.

Silence settles over the Beauty Hall as they wait for his reaction. Even Shell holds her breath as she listens to the steady tap of his cane on the parquet floor before he stops a few steps in front of the ART counter. Callum stands by his side, his lips parted as he follows Old Mr Duke's gaze around the store, taking in every detail. He stares at the red-and-white-striped hot-air balloon hanging from the ceiling where the tree should be, a deep crease forming between his white eyebrows, and it's suddenly so quiet that Shell's sure she can hear Callum's heart beating.

Old Mr Duke nods and that's it.

He doesn't say a word.

He glances around at the counters, and the look on his face is enough to make everyone jump and pretend to be busy, the Beauty Hall buzzing once more, a blur of dusting and furious whispering.

Shell should probably do the same, but she can't stop looking at Callum, who is crestfallen. So crestfallen that Shell doesn't notice that Old Mr Duke is walking towards the ART counter until he's in front of her with a massive bouquet of hot pink roses. She has no idea where he got them from, but then she sees Gladys standing behind him in her neat navy wool coat, and wonders if she's been there the whole time.

'Shell.' Old Mr Duke beams, handing her the flowers. 'Congratulations on your promotion.'

'Oh.' She reaches across the counter to take the bouquet. 'They're beautiful, Mr Duke. Thank you.'

He reaches for her other hand and squeezes it, still beaming. 'I'm very proud of you, Miss Smith.'

She blushes, but when he lets go and steps back, she looks at Callum again and panics. 'So?'

Old Mr Duke frowns. 'So, Shell?'

She gestures at the Beauty Hall. 'What do you think?'

Callum's eyes widen, as if to say, *WHAT ARE YOU DOING?*

What *is* she doing?

'Well.' Old Mr Duke clears his throat. 'It's certainly very different, isn't it?'

'It's *not* that different,' Shell shrugs as Callum watches her, clearly wary of where she's going with this. Not that even she knows. 'The Ferris wheel is in the window, of course, and I love the gingerbread house in the other one.'

'Hmm,' Old Mr Duke murmurs, his whole face tight.

'It reminds me of the one we used to have in Little Duke's every Christmas.'

His blue eyes brighten. 'Oh, yes. That's right. In the corner.'

'And do you remember when we used to have the post-box in the entrance?' He turns to where it used to stand, as though it's still there. 'So the kids could post their letters to Santa. Well,' she adds, with a sad sigh, 'until everyone started posting their rubbish and chewing gum into it and we had to get rid of it.'

'Oh, yes.'

When his shoulders slump, Callum glares at her again.

She catches herself, grasping for a happier memory. 'And the lollipops!' she says a little too loudly, pointing at the vase of them on the ART counter. 'You gave me one of those the first time I came in here to see Santa.'

His eyes light up again. 'You remember that?'

'Of course, Mr Duke. It's one of my earliest memories!'

'Oh.' He chuckles warmly. 'How lovely that you remember it, Shell.'

She smiles as she looks around the Beauty Hall. 'It's like a tribute to *all* the Duke & Sons Christmases.'

It's then she notices that Callum has embellished his suit jacket with a red tartan pocket square, exactly like the one in Old Mr Duke's suit pocket. He nervously adjusts it, and when Old Mr Duke sees him do it, he smiles. 'Yes, I suppose it is, Shell.'

'Did you see?' When she points at the front of the ART counter, he glances down at the red and white stockings. There are four. SHELL. RICKY. BECCA. SOPH. She gestures at the other counters. 'We all have one.'

'You do?' Old Mr Duke looks at her, then at his grandson. 'What a thoughtful gesture, Callum.'

Callum blushes at the compliment, then strides over to the tree to which Becca and Soph have been adding an ART touch. 'Did you see that Shell's little brothers and sisters helped paint the baubles, Pops?'

'No,' he says, trotting over to it and peering at them. 'Would you look at these, Callum?'

Callum gestures underneath them. 'Each one is signed by the artist.'

Old Mr Duke takes a bauble off the tree and turns it so he can read the bottom. 'Arun Smith!' He spins on his heels to face Shell with a huge smile. 'He's a veritable Jackson Pollock! You must be very proud.'

She points at the tree. 'They each did one, actually.'

'Let me see,' he says. Callum helps him find one of each and Old Mr Duke reads the name aloud. First Kitty, then Patrick and, finally, Sim. 'Can I keep these?'

'Of course. They did loads. They had so much fun.'

He holds the baubles to his chest with a deep sigh. 'I'm going to hang them on mine once I put it up.'

'You mean, your Christmas tree isn't already up, Mr Duke?'

He chuckles again, holding a finger up to her. 'December the first, and not a moment before, Miss Smith.'

'Duly noted.'

'Thank you, Shell.' He tips his head at her. 'You tell those little artists to come and see me soon, okay?'

She tips her head back. 'I will, Mr Duke.'

'And Mr O'Neill.' He turns to Ricky this time. 'I think you should go back to bed.'

'Thank you, Mr Duke,' he whimpers, pushing his sunglasses back up his nose.

'Right, Callum!' Old Mr Duke sings, clapping him on the back. 'Show me the rest of these decorations!'

'Of course, Pops. This way.' He holds his arm out, but

before he follows Old Mr Duke through the Beauty Hall, Callum looks over his shoulder at Shell and mouths, *Thank you.*

By the time Ricky has finished decorating the wreath, everyone in the Beauty Hall is done and putting their coats on.

'That's really cool, actually,' Soph says, as she watches Shell hang it.

'Thanks.' Shell grins. 'It's infinitely Instagramable, don't you think?'

Denise appears from nowhere, dumping Shell's coat and Gucci bag on the counter.

'Hey,' Shell scowls, 'I gave you the combination for my locker in case of emergencies!'

'This is an emergency!' Denise tells her, her dark eyes wide. 'Pub! Now!'

As soon as they get into the Anchor, Denise points at the table they sat at last night, the one by the fire, and heads to the bar. It's the only one that's free so Shell can't object, shrugging off her coat and sitting down.

'Do you think that guy over there kind of looks like me?' Ricky asks, as he sits in the chair opposite hers.

She looks across the pub to the man at the table in the corner by the window. 'I guess.'

He has the same milky tea-coloured skin and dark eyes, but other than that, Shell can't see the resemblance.

Ricky tilts his head at him, the skin between his perfectly plucked eyebrows creasing. 'Maybe it's my dad.'

'Didn't your parents adopt you when they were working in the Philippines? Why would he be in the Anchor?'

'Maybe he's come looking for me. Maybe he's here to rescue me from all this.'

'All *what*?' Shell scoffs, when he sighs dramatically. 'You live in a massive house on Ostley Crescent where your parents treat you like a king.' Now he scoffs, turning his cheek away. 'Ricky, you're *twenty-four* and you called me the last time you were home alone to help you find what was beeping in the kitchen because you'd never turned the dishwasher off. Plus,' she adds, before he can interrupt, 'your job is *literally* playing with makeup all day.'

He gives another theatrical sigh and finally takes off his sunglasses. 'I guess.'

'Okay,' Denise says, out of breath as she rushes back from the bar.

When Ricky sees the bottle of white wine and the three glasses she's holding, he pretends to heave. 'Babe, I can't. I can still taste the tequila from last night.'

'Fine,' she says, sitting down and throwing her wallet onto the table. 'Shell and I will drink it, then.'

'No. No.' He reaches for a glass and holds it out. 'I'll have a little one. '

'Den, what's going on?' Shell asks, as Denise fills their glasses. 'What's the emergency?'

'You'll never guess what.'

'What?'

'Oh my God, Shell. You'll never guess,' Denise says again.

'What?' Ricky joins in.

Denise pauses for dramatic effect, then leans forward. 'I spoke to Callum.'

They do the same.

'You did?' Shell asks. 'About what we were saying last night?'

She nods.

'Well. Come on, then,' Ricky says. 'Don't leave us hanging. What did he say?'

'Shell, thank you!' She reaches out to clasp her hand. 'I'm so glad you made me talk to him.'

'What did he say?'

'Okay.' Denise lets go, then closes her eyes and sucks in a deep breath, which she exhales slowly through her nose. When she opens her eyes again, she says, 'Before I start, let me get this off my chest, because I have the utmost respect for Callum Duke and I'm honestly not trying to objectify him in any way.'

Ricky and Shell wait as she takes another deep breath and eases it out with a sigh. 'That man is *so hot.*'

Ricky doesn't hesitate. 'So hot. Every time I see him, "Love Man" by Otis Redding starts playing in my head.'

'His arse in the suit he's wearing today . . .' Denise pretends to fan herself.

'God help me. It was all I could do not to bite it.'

'Can you *imagine* the power throuple we'd make?'

'I have!' Ricky looks at Shell. 'Sorry, Shell.'

She blinks at him. 'When were *we* a throuple?'

'Okay. Stop.' Denise waves her hands at them. 'Enough objectifying Callum Duke. I feel bad.'

Shell is even more bewildered. 'I didn't even—'

'So,' Denise goes on as though she hasn't said anything, 'I spoke to him.'

Shell lets it go, reaching for her glass of wine. 'What did he say?'

'You were right. He was *so* nice.'

'I told you!'

'Did you know that his first job out of college was as a buyer for Anthropologie?'

Shell shakes her head.

'He's been all over the world.' Denise gesticulates wildly. 'Like, *everywhere.*'

So that's why he was in Mexico, Shell realises.

'Then he did womenswear merchandising for Bendel's, but he didn't leave there to come here, like Old Mr Duke said. He actually left in 2017 to start Hannah Banana, that high-end sustainable, zero-waste fashion brand.'

'I know Hannah Banana!' Shell points at her. 'It's one of the few places that stocks over a size eighteen!'

'Hannah Banana is his mum's nickname, or something. Anyway, he just sold it to LVMH for millions.'

Ricky presses a hand to his chest. '*Millions?*'

'He's planning to plough it all into Duke & Sons, so if it goes bust, he'll lose *everything.*'

'Wow.' Shell looks between them. 'No pressure, then.' She wondered who had paid for all the new Christmas decorations. And the new website. And the tablets.

'Anyway,' Denise stops to gulp some wine, 'we were

in his office for ages after Old Mr Duke went home, talking about my ideas for Lingerie, and he really *listened* to everything I had to say.'

Shell grins. 'I'm so pleased, Den.'

'That's not the best bit.' She's bouncing up and down in her chair, like the twins do when they're having chicken nuggets for tea. 'He's going to book meetings with the brands I suggested and asked if I wanted to go with him.'

Ricky and Shell gasp.

'It gets better! He says that going to him showed *great initiative*. Me!' She points at herself and laughs, eyebrows raised. 'Denise Varina-Williams. I have initiative. Who knew?'

'Actually,' Ricky interjects, '*technically*, Shell was the one who told you to go to Callum so she has initiative.'

She and Denise glare at him and he goes back to sipping his wine.

'Then he asked me if I'd ever considered becoming a buyer! *A buyer!*'

'Shut up!' Ricky hisses.

Shell waves a hand at her. 'Did you tell him that's what you studied at the London College of Fashion?'

'Yeah. I mean, he wanted to know what I was doing here, working in the Lingerie department of Duke & Sons, not buying it for Selfridges, or something.' She shrugs sadly, her mood dipping. 'So I told him about my dad.'

Ricky and Shell glance at one another, then back at Denise.

'I told him a lot of stuff, actually,' she says, almost to herself as she tucks one of her thin braids back into her bun. 'About my dad. About moving here from Birmingham after I graduated from uni because they were trialling that leukemia stem-cell therapy at Ostley Royal Infirmary. About how, you know . . .' She shrugs. 'It didn't work.'

Ricky reaches for her hand, bringing it up to his mouth and pressing a kiss to it.

'I told him stuff no one at work knows. Only you guys.'

Shell realises something then. 'He's really easy to talk to, isn't he?'

'Yes!' Denise agrees. 'On the shop floor he's all super-smooth, New York guy so I thought he'd be all cold and professional, but when you talk to him, one on one, he's nice. Like *really* nice. He told me about his dad. He was only six when he died.' She casts a look around the pub, then lowers her voice. 'He had this heart thing he didn't know about, then one day, he was carrying a box into the Beauty Hall and . . .' She clicks her fingers. 'Just like that.'

'Bloody hell,' Ricky mutters, looking at Shell, who is equally horrified.

'His mum's American. That's why he grew up there because she wanted to move back after, you know . . .'

They know.

'Callum really misses her and is trying to get her to move here, but she won't.' Denise tips her chin at Shell. 'Did you know that she's, like, a shit-hot doctor?' Shell shakes her head. 'She's a surgeon. Cardio-something.'

'Cardiothoracic,' Ricky says. '*What?*' he asks when they stare at him. 'I watch *Grey's*!'

'Anyway,' Denise goes on, 'there's something about him. I mean, yeah, he's hot, but, I don't know, he has this *energy.* This . . .' She stops to think about the right word. 'He's just really gentle and kind, and every time I look at him, I see Old Mr Duke at that age. I don't know.' She sighs. 'Maybe it's bullshit, but, like with Old Mr Duke, I really do believe he cares about Duke & Sons and about us, you know?'

They nod.

Denise reaches for her wine glass and takes a sip, the glint returning to her eyes. 'When I told him I have a degree in fashion buying and merchandising, he said he had *no idea* and that it would be a shame to waste it because I clearly have huge promise! *Me!*' She points at herself again. 'I have promise!'

'Den, that's amazing!' Shell can feel herself welling up, her chest aching with pride.

'Between us, he says that he's not very happy with the buying team. He says they need a kick up the arse. So he's going to train me up as a womenswear buyer!'

'Shut. Up.' Shell puts her glass down, a tear escaping from the corner of her eye.

Denise reaches across the table for her hand again, squeezing it as Shell swats away the tear with the other.

'Thank you.' There are tears in Denise's eyes now as well. 'Seriously, Shell. If it wasn't for you, I would never have spoken to him. Yesterday I thought I was losing my job and today I have a whole new career.'

Ricky interrupts with a pointed sigh.

'What?' they ask, as he takes a long sip of wine.

He sighs again. 'Just wondering what my career would be like if I actually gave a shit.'

'You're Ostley's only bisexual drag queen, don't forget,' Denise reminds him, holding up her glass and winking at him across the table. 'You're already breaking boundaries, babe.'

'True.' He closes his eyes and nods solemnly. 'True.'

Chapter Ten

Shell gets home to the smell of roast potatoes and is so happy she almost cries again.

'Shell!' she hears a voice holler, and Arun is charging towards her down the hallway.

He throws his arms around her legs, squeezes tightly, then steps back and thrusts a piece of paper at her. 'Look!' he says, peering at her from under his thick eyelashes.

'What's this?' Shell asks, stroking his hair.

'I drawed Mum!'

'Did you?' She studies the piece of paper, then has to swallow a gasp.

He's drawn their mother as a witch.

Mercifully, she doesn't need to respond as he snatches the drawing back and flies into the living room as her sisters come running down the stairs so quickly that she holds her breath, sure they're going to fall.

They don't, though, and come barrelling towards her, grabbing a hand each.

'Shell! Come and see what we made!' they tell her, dragging her into the kitchen.

Her father is at the stove, dancing to Beyoncé – actually, it's more a wiggle – stirring something in a saucepan.

'Shell!' he says, when he sees her. 'Just in time! Dinner's almost ready.'

'Shell, look!' her sisters say, pulling her to the counter. 'We made an apple plait!'

'Wow!' she says, eyes wide, as she regards the baking tray. It's not the neatest plait and is struggling to restrain the slices of apples that are trying to escape. 'Did you do this all by yourselves?'

'Daddy peeled and sliced the apples, but we did everything else,' Sim says, with a proud smile.

'We plaited it like you taught us,' Kitty tells her, equally proud.

'It's perfect!' Shell leans down to kiss the top of their heads. 'I can't wait to taste it!'

Kitty lifts her little chin. 'Daddy's making custard to go with it.'

He holds up the saucepan he's stirring – *Yeah, I am!*

'Shell!' Her mother is in the kitchen doorway, holding a basket of washing. She puts it down on the floor in front of the washing-machine and points to Shell's feet. 'Shoes!' But before she can apologise and tell her she didn't have a chance to take off her DMs before Kitty and Sim dragged her into the kitchen to see their apple plait, her mother points at her shoulder this time. 'Bag!' She strides over, grabbing Shell's handbag. 'Is this *Gucci*? How can you afford a Gucci bag?'

'I can't,' Shell says, slipping the straps off her shoulder when she lets go. 'It was a present.'

That makes her mother even more suspicious. 'Who from?'

'ART. To thank me for all my hard work.' Shell grins, doing a happy little dance and adding, 'They've promoted me to brand ambassador!'

'Shell!' Her father spills the custard as he drops the saucepan onto the stove and pulls her into a hug.

'My turn, Shaun! My turn!' her mother tells him, shooing him away. As soon as he lets go, she kisses Shell's cheek and hugs her while Kitty and Sim squeal.

Shell isn't sure they know why they're squealing, but they hug her waist.

When her mother steps back, her eyes are wet as she takes Shell's face in her hands. 'My little shining star!'

Only Eleanor Smith can go from furious to overjoyed in the space of three seconds.

Shell has often asked herself how her parents ever got together. They seem to exist in exact opposition to each other. Her mother is from a huge Indian family, who are always talking over one another, while her father is an only child who grew up in a tiny, chilly terrace house near Leeds. While her mother throws her feelings around shamelessly, he's a quiet, gentle man, who would rather keep the peace then say how he really feels.

Her mother is a Picasso, basically, and he's a muted Monet, pale and blond and toothpick thin. Her mother is much like Shell, the pair of them all soft curves and big hips with small, round faces and full cheeks, their skin the same warm nutty brown that makes her father look even paler. And she's fearless. Catcher of spiders and protector from playground bullies. Her father is fierce in an entirely different way. He's the one Shell goes to if she needs advice because he knows when she should apologise. And he doesn't tell the boys to stop crying and man up when they fall off their scooters, or tell the girls they're being hysterical when they're upset, just sits them down and listens to whatever injustice they think has been done to them.

Shell always thought it was an opposites-attract thing with her parents, but now she's older, she can see that they're the perfect foil for each other. They balance one another out. Where her mother is unpredictable, he's steady, and where he's scared of everything – heights and dogs and the twins falling off the slide at the park – she forces him to try new things. He didn't even know what okra was before they met, let alone tried it. He'd never eaten a mango with his bare hands or been on a plane for longer than three hours. And her mother had never done anything she didn't want to do. Never gone for a walk just for the sake of going for a walk or out for dinner with another couple when her father could cook something better at home.

Maybe they're a pointillist painting. A series of seemingly unrelated dots that make no sense up close. You have to stand back and see her parents for what they really are: in perfect harmony.

But what her mother lacks in tact, she makes up for with affection. She may tell Shell off first and ask questions later, but she's equally quick to let her know she loves her. She'll tell her in the biscuit aisle at the supermarket or when Shell's in the kitchen, waiting for the kettle to boil. Those are the things she loves about her mother. Yeah, Shell and her father have their private jokes and secret smiles across the dinner table, but her mother makes her try on clothes she'd never consider and have another jilabei when one of her aunties makes a comment' about how she'll never find a husband if she doesn't lose weight.

'We're so proud of you, darling,' Shaun says softly, rubbing her back.

Eleanor frowns. 'What is a brand ambassador, by the way?'

'No idea,' Shell admits. 'But it's an extra three quid an hour and they're sending me to Mexico.'

'Mexico!' Her mother grabs the tops of her arms and shakes her.

'I know!'

'When? You need to renew your passport!'

Shaun checks on the custard. 'Don't worry, darling. We can sort it out.'

'Right!' Her mother kisses her cheek again, then claps her hands together. 'This calls for a celebration! Let me nip to the offie and get the finest bottle of prosecco they sell for under twenty quid! Or *maybe* . . .' Eleanor twirls around to face Shell again, her dark eyes alight with mischief '. . . I should get tequila in honour of Mexico!'

'Don't even think about it,' her father warns, without looking away from the custard. 'It's a Sunday night.'

Eleanor pulls a face at his turned back, then heads out of the kitchen in search of prosecco.

★

After dinner, Shell loads the dishwasher, then retreats to her room to work on the creative brief for Duke & Sons. She can hear the kids bickering downstairs, no doubt over what to watch for the hour of television they're allowed before bed, so she puts on her Sufjan Stevens playlist, which always calms her down, and opens her laptop.

She's halfway through an online article about the importance of search engine optimisation when there's a knock on the door and she panics, slamming her laptop shut as though she's looking at porn.

'Hello?' she says, turning to snatch the magazine off her bedside table, pretending to be engrossed.

'Can I come in?' Eleanor asks, but she already is, kicking the door shut behind her and walking towards her, trying not to spill the glass of red wine she's holding. 'I managed to secure you a piece of apple plait,' she says, with a grin, holding up the bowl in her other hand as Shell turns down the music. 'It's mostly custard, though.'

'No complaints here,' Shell tells her, taking the bowl.

'And this,' Eleanor holds up the glass, 'is for me.'

Shell pats the edge of the bed and she sits down.

'What ya reading?' she asks when she does, nodding at the magazine.

'About how to make your Christmas makeup *sparkle*.' Shell holds up the magazine, her eyebrows raised.

Her mother does the same. 'What is the secret?'

'Highlighter, mostly.'

Eleanor chuckles and sips her wine.

'How was your day?' Shell asks, tossing the magazine aside and digging into the custard.

Eleanor closes her eyes and exhales. 'Awful.'

'Why? What happened?'

'I met Robert for coffee this morning.'

'On a Sunday?'

'It couldn't wait until tomorrow, apparently.'

'How come?' Shell asks, going in for another spoonful of custard.

'He's leaving and wanted to tell me before he hands his notice in tomorrow.'

Shell almost chokes on a piece of apple. 'What?'

Eleanor nods.

'Why? I thought he loved working at the community centre?'

'I did too. But apparently not. Apparently he's been doing a part-time degree at Ostley Spa University in psychology and early childhood studies for the last four and a half years.'

'*Four and a half years?*'

'Can you believe it? I had no idea! Why didn't he tell me?'

Shell glances at her laptop on the bed between them, immediately weak with guilt that she hasn't told her about the online marketing course she's doing. But then she remembers how she came home from uni with a bag of books she'd never open again and two suitcases of dirty clothes and she never wants to disappoint her parents like that again.

'He just graduated with a first, no less,' her mother

goes on, with a heavy sigh. 'So he's moving to London to work for a charity that supports trans and gender-diverse young people and their families.'

'That's amazing.'

'It *is* amazing,' she agrees. 'But how on earth am I going to replace him? *Hey! Come work for Royal United Hospitals Ostley NHS Foundation Trust! It's super-stressful and you'll go home crying every night because you're dealing with teenagers who have had the most miserable lives imaginable while earning less than you would if you worked in McDonald's!*'

Shell tries not to laugh. 'Speaking of leaving, you were asleep by the time I got home last night so I couldn't tell you—'

'Tell me what?' Eleanor reaches over to slap her arm before Shell can actually tell her.

'You'll never guess who's retiring.'

'Who?'

'Old Mr Duke.'

'No!' Her mother recoils. 'He can't! What's he going to do? Play golf? He'll hate it. When?'

'Not for another year, he says.'

'So who's going to take over the store?'

'His grandson.'

'Grandson?' She frowns, then her eyebrows shoot up. 'Oh, my God. Callum!'

'You remember him?'

'Barely. He must have been, what, six, seven, when Michael died?'

'You remember Michael as well?'

'Of course.' Eleanor stops to take a sip of wine. 'Everyone *loved* Michael. Poor Old Mr Duke.' She presses her hand to her chest. 'I don't think you ever get over something like that. You're not supposed to outlive your kids. And it didn't help that a couple of weeks after it happened Michael's wife moved back to California because she couldn't bear to be here without him and took Callum with her.' Eleanor shakes her head. 'Poor Old Mr Duke. He lost his son *and* his grandson within a couple of months. I mean,' she clarifies, holding up her hand to Shell, 'he didn't *lose* Callum, of course, but it must have felt that way.'

'Do you remember him?' Shell asks, her heart sore thinking about Old Mr Duke.

'Not really. Before you started working there, the only time we ever went into Duke & Sons was at Christmas. I only saw him in there once, I think.' Eleanor's eyebrows meet as she tries to recall when. 'It was Christmas. You were tiny. You must have been two. No.' She holds up a finger. '*Three*, because you were wearing that black velvet coat, the Victorian swingy one. Oh.' She balls her free hand into a fist and squeals. 'You looked like a doll.'

Shell remembers that coat. It was her favourite. If she could find it in her size, she'd wear it now. 'I remember that day,' she says, with a slow smile. 'Old Mr Duke gave me a lollipop.'

'Yes, he did! Your father and I took you in to see Santa and there they all were, ready to greet us as we came in. Three generations of Dukes. Old Mr Duke, Michael and Callum. They were all wearing the same thing.' She giggles at the memory. 'Black suits with white shirts and red tartan ties with matching pocket squares. Even Callum!'

'How old was Callum?'

'I think he's, like, three years older than you, so he must have been about six.'

Something occurs to Shell then. 'Wait. Did we meet?'

'Yes!' Eleanor laughs. 'Callum shook your hand and said, "Welcome to Duke & Sons."'

Shell has to put the bowl down and cover her mouth with her hands to stop herself shrieking.

'It was so cute. You wished him a happy Christmas.'

'No way. That's so funny.'

'And to think he'd end up being your future boss and we didn't even know it.'

'He's not my boss for another year,' Shell is quick to clarify. 'But still.'

'Hey!' She slaps Shell's arm again. 'Guess who I just saw coming out of the offie.'

'Nick Wallace?'

'Yes! How did you know?'

'I bumped into him last night.'

Her mother tilts her head, an eyebrow arched. 'So *that*'s why you didn't make it home last night.'

'I did make it home.' Shell pulls Patrick's 'actually' face. 'You'd know that if you hadn't fallen asleep on the sofa at ten o'clock on a Saturday night.'

'Hey!' She points her wine glass at her eldest daughter. 'I spent yesterday keeping four children under eight occupied while your father worked on that garden in Church Cabham.'

'Fair enough.'

'So is he *back* back? Or just home for the weekend?'

'No idea. We didn't talk for long.'

'So you're not going to see him, then?'

There's a hopeful tone to her voice that Shell ignores. 'He invited me for a drink on Saturday.'

'What? Like a date?'

'No! Just some college reunion thing he's organising.'

'Are you planning to go?'

Shell notes her mother's careful tone and it makes the back of her neck *burn*. 'Yeah. Course.'

Eleanor doesn't say anything, clearly choosing her next words carefully, which isn't like her at all.

'Don't,' Shell says. 'Whatever you're going to say, Emma's already said it.'

'Did she tell you to be careful? Because I think you should be careful.'

'Yes,' Shell mutters, shovelling the last of the custard into her mouth.

'Well, she's right. What he did to you was awful.'

Shell looks up from the bowl with a fierce frown. 'What did he do to me?'

Her mother raises her eyebrows as if to say, *Oh, come on.*

'What, Mum? What did he do to me?'

'He strung you along for two years, Shell. He made you think it was all in your head. That you were *just friends* when he must have known how you felt about him.'

Shell feels the finger quotes for *just friends* like a cricket bat to the chest.

The shock of it is so dizzying that she doesn't have the strength to deny it. 'Thanks, Mum.'

'I'm not trying to be cruel, darling.' She presses her hand to the mattress between them. 'It's just that, sometimes, we look back on these things years later and remember them more fondly than they deserve.'

Shell can't look at her and stares into the empty bowl.

But her mother won't let it go. 'The only way you could get over him was by letting him go to Central Saint Martins while you literally went in the opposite direction, as far away as you could.'

Shell puts the bowl on the bed between them. 'And why did I end up at the University of Aberdeen, Mother?'

'Okay.' Eleanor finishes her wine. 'I am partially to blame for making you do law, not letting you go to Central Saint Martins with *him*, like you wanted.'

Shell notes the *him*.

'I should never have let your grandmother talk me into insisting you do a proper degree, whatever that is.'

'Medicine. Engineering.' Shell counts off each thing on her fingers. 'Accounting or law.'

'True. Your options were quite limited.'

Shell scoffs as if to say, *Ya think?* 'I only chose law because it didn't require maths.'

'I'm sorry.' Eleanor reaches out for Shell's hand and holds it. 'I really am. But you were their do-over after I got knocked up at sixteen and disgraced the family. You were their One True Hope. The Shah that would go to uni and make something of your life. *I'm sorry*. I should *never* have let them put that pressure on you.'

Shell can't look at her.

'Even so,' Eleanor says, under her breath.

That gets Shell's attention. 'Even so?'

'Well.' Eleanor throws up her hands. 'You didn't have to go to Aberdeen, did you? You had loads of offers. You could have gone to UEL or Kingston or Middlesex, but *he* was in London, wasn't he?'

Shell notes the *he*.

'Mum, it's been *nine years*.'

'I know,' she concedes. 'And people change. I just think you should be careful. I know what you're like when you're with him. You'll fall back into it and won't even notice.'

'Mum, it's just a drink!'

Eleanor arches an eyebrow at her. 'It's never *just* anything when it comes to Nick Wallace.'

Chapter Eleven

Shell can't sleep after her conversation with her mother. At least she has the chance to finish her project, so she can go to the pub after work tonight with Ricky, Denise and a clear conscience.

She rereads the email to her tutor, then hits send and heads downstairs as the kids are leaving for school.

'But, Daaaaaad . . .' Arun whines, as he sits on the bottom step, tugging on his yellow Fireman Sam wellies.

Her father doesn't let him finish, waiting by the front door. 'Arun, I told you, the pavements are too slippery.'

Ah, Shell realises. The great Why Can't I Ride My Scooter to School in the Rain? debate.

'Morning, Shell!' Her father sees her waiting on the stairs for Arun to get up.

'Morning, Dad. You okay?'

'Yeah. Yeah. Good,' he mutters, fishing through the hooks by the door to find the twins' coats.

'Mum at work already?'

'Yeah. She couldn't sleep, so she went in early.'

'Is she still fretting about Robert leaving?' she asks.

'Yeah. I keep telling her it'll be okay, but you know what she's like.'

Shell certainly does.

'It's lashing down, you know.' He gestures at her leopard-print coat as he finds Arun's blue padded one. 'You need to get yourself something waterproof.' He winks. 'Maybe ART can buy you a Gucci raincoat.'

'Yeah, but, Dad,' Arun tries again, still sulking on the bottom step about the scooter.

Shaun ignores him, holding out his coat to him, then tipping his head back and yelling, 'Patrick! Sim! Kitty!'

Patrick is the first to appear, emerging from the kitchen with a piece of toast. He already has strawberry jam on his Ostley Primary sweatshirt and it's not even eight thirty.

Then Sim and Kitty charge down the stairs, dark curls everywhere. Luckily, Arun stomps off to take his coat in time for Shell to get out of the way before they run into the back of her.

'Daddy! Daddy!' Sim says, in such a hurry, she jumps off the last step. 'I can't find my book bag!'

He holds it up. 'Come on. Come on. Come on. We're going to be late.'

'Daddy! Can we get a dog?' Kitty asks, as she stuffs her feet into her purple glitter wellies.

'Yeah, Daddy, can we get a dog?' Sim adds, as she puts on her pink ones.

He's not listening, though, too busy handing out coats and book bags as he opens the front door. He presses his hand to the top of each of their heads as he ushers them out into the rain – one, two, three, four – then turns to Shell, who is still standing at the bottom of the stairs. 'See you later, sweetheart! Have a good day at work.'

Then the house is quiet in a way it rarely is.

Shell walks into the living room to turn off the television and stands there for a moment, soaking up the silence as she asks herself if this is what it would be like to live alone.

Calm.

Quiet.

Just her.

She finished the creative brief for Duke & Sons at three, but she still couldn't sleep and stayed up until gone four, looking at flats. She does it every few months, then realises she can't afford it.

It's her own fault. Surely that was the point of living at home. So she could save up for a place of her own. But, according to her bank statements, once she's paid her phone bill and the meagre amount she gives her parents in 'rent', the rest of her money goes on ASOS orders and lattes, which explains why she can barely stretch to a studio over a kebab shop.

But she *loves* living at home. She loves their clamorous Sunday roasts, each of them fighting over the best potato. And she loves coming in from work to be greeted by the twins shrieking like they haven't seen her for three weeks as they tumble towards her, like a pack of puppies.

Soon they'll be teenagers, who refuse to leave their rooms, and she wants to cherish every bright, loud moment with them before they become monosyllabic and don't want to be seen with her because she embarrasses them.

What's wrong with that?

Why does she have to move out?

Because she's twenty-seven?

I still feel seventeen, she thinks.

Maybe that's the problem.

When she goes into the kitchen, she sees her travel cup by the kettle, a banana next to it on top of what look like some forms. Passport renewal forms her father's printed off, she realises, pressing her hand to her chest.

There's a hot-pink Post-it note stuck to them: *Don't drink the water! Dad xx*

Shell thinks of the two of them on the sofa last night, watching *Gilmore Girls* while her mother was in the bath, laughing helplessly over Lane and Zack's disastrous honeymoon to Mexico.

Maybe she won't move out *just* yet.

Chapter Twelve

*D*ad *wasn't exaggerating, was he?* Shell thinks, as she opens the front door and steps back as a gust of wind blows a leaf into her face. She peels it off her cheek and grimaces at the driving rain, wondering how she's going to manage the twenty-minute walk to work without looking like a witch who's crawled out of the sea. Not that she objects to resembling a sea witch – that would make a cool Halloween costume for next year – but she was going for a glowy just-got-back-from-a-month-travelling-around-Thailand look today so that will not do.

She takes a deep breath, opens her umbrella and steps out into it. She doesn't need to shut the door as the wind does it for her, pushing her down the path, then blowing her umbrella inside out with such force that she squeals.

It's broken, she realises, as she tries to put it up again, the wind whipping her hair across her face. It clings to her cheek and she whimpers. She's already bedraggled, and she hasn't even got to the end of the path yet. She can feel her fringe sticking to her forehead and wonders if her mascara is running as she steps onto the pavement. The metal spokes of her brolly are bent beyond repair, though, one of them piercing the orange and turquoise leopard-print fabric. 'Brilliant,' she mutters, cursing it, but as she's about to run back into the house to find another, a car pulls up in front of her and she jumps back before it splashes her.

The passenger window comes down and she hears someone say her name.

She stoops to see who it is and her heart does this weird jumpy thing in her chest.

'Nick.'

'Shell!'

'Well,' she says, looking at the glossy black Mini Cooper. 'You've traded up from Scrappy!'

He laughs at the nickname they gave his first car because it was a feisty orange Fiesta, the same colour as the flowers on the Mystery Machine. The deep dimples that she's wanted to stick her finger in so many times appear in his cheeks as he says, 'Oh, Scrappy. She's gone to the great scrapyard in the sky now.'

'Whence she came.'

'Come on.' He pats the passenger seat. 'You getting in?'

'It's all right.' She nods up the road. 'I'm not going far. Just to the high street.'

'That's okay. Get in.' He pats the seat again. 'It's filthy out there. Come on.'

Shell doesn't have the arse for a Mini Cooper, so it's an effort, but she gets in as gracefully as she can.

'Here,' he says, taking the travel cup from her so she can put on her seatbelt.

If Nick drives anything like he did when he was seventeen, she's going to need it.

'Thank you,' she says, as he hands it to her with a warm smile. 'You saved me.'

'Any time,' he says, his dark eyes settling on hers for a moment longer than is comfortable.

When he licks his lips and sweeps his hair off his face with a hand, Shell can feel herself melting. She stares at the raindrops chasing one another down the windscreen, sure that if he keeps looking at her like that, in a few moments all that will be left of her is a puddle on the passenger seat.

'You still live at home then?' he asks.

'Oh. Yeah. I mean I'm looking for somewhere . . .'

'Don't bother,' he tells her, as he pulls away. 'Stay at home for as long you can. Do you know how much rent I pay for a one-bed in London?' He whistles. 'It's criminal.'

'You're still in London?' she asks, hoping she's not dripping too much on the fancy leather seat.

He nods. 'Hackney.'

Shell tries not to laugh. Of course he lives in Hackney. 'So what brings you back to Ostley?' she asks, trying not to stare, but she really, *really* wants to touch his hair.

He just shrugs. 'Mum died.'

Shell almost drops her travel cup. 'Shit.' She didn't mean to say it out loud, and covers her mouth with her other hand. When she takes it away, she balls it into a fist and winces. 'I'm sorry.'

'It's okay. She had breast cancer. By the time they caught it, she was too far gone.'

'Nick, I'm sorry.'

'It's okay,' he says again, even though it isn't. 'I'm back to sort out the house. Think I might sell it, but . . .'

He pulls over to let a car pass and Shell knows what he's thinking. He's an only child. His father left when he was five, so it was just him and his mother. Now she's gone, the house is the only thing he has left.

'God, Nick.' She shakes her head. 'I'm so, so sorry.'

He reaches over for her hand and squeezes it. Her heart does that jumpy thing again, the heat of his palm against hers making every bit of her warm as she squeezes his hand. Then it's so quiet in the car that all she can hear is the relentless tappity-tap-tap of the rain on the roof.

He lets go of her hand when the car passes. 'Work have been great about it,' he says, continuing, then slowing as they approach a zebra crossing. He stops to check that no one is about to step out, then carries on. 'They told me to take as much time as I need. My MD thinks I should get away. Go travelling or something. I don't know.' He shrugs again. 'I don't know how going to Cambodia will help. I just think I need to feel it, you know?' He turns his head to look at her again. 'Let it hurt until it doesn't.'

She reaches for his hand this time.

'Anyway,' he says, threading his fingers through hers. He doesn't let go, just keeps holding her hand as they join the procession of traffic waiting to turn onto Ostley High Street. 'Can we talk about something else?'

'Sure.' She has no idea what to say after that, so goes for the safest option. 'What do you do now?'

'I'm an art and creative director for an agency in Shoreditch.'

'A *director*? Already?'

He bites down on a smile and, just like that, they're in college again, driving around, 'Kool Thing' by Sonic Youth blaring, the pair of them waiting to do the clicky bit with their tongues.

The memory of it makes her heart feel brand new. 'Do you enjoy it?'

'Yeah. Yeah, I do, actually.'

He must realise they're going to be stuck there for a while because he lets go of the steering wheel, but before he does, she notices that he still does that thing where he drives with his left arm out straight, fingers curled around the top of the steering wheel. She can't say why she finds it so sexy. Maybe it's because his black jumper is tugged up to reveal the length of his forearm. He has a sharply drawn sleeve of tattoos now. Big, loose art-nouveau lilies and leaves and, in the middle of it all, a woman with black hair on tiptoe, back arched, her gown curling around her, like waves.

'Hey,' he says. 'Remember that Saturday job you had when we were in college? The one at Duke's.' She nods, her ears burning as she realises that nothing has changed since he last saw her.

She's still living at home.

Still working at Duke & Sons.

'That makeup brand you used to work for, ART, is one of my clients.'

'Yeah?'

'We did a print campaign for them last year.'

'One of those looks was mine, actually,' she admits sheepishly.

'Yours?'

'I still work for ART. I dropped out of uni.'

'I heard. I don't know why you did law, Shell. You should have come to Central Saint Martins with me. You should have done art. You're so talented.'

She thinks about what her life would have been like if she'd had the guts to stand up to her grandparents, not chased a career that she didn't even want because it was steady.

Safe.

Maybe if she'd gone to art school with Nick, they'd be living in a converted loft in Hackney now, their canvases leaning against the walls. Or maybe they'd have a house they'd be doing up, room by room. Somewhere with a garden where her father would plant tulips that would appear in the spring. Teardrops of red and yellow that she'd smile at while she was doing the washing-up.

But she catches herself.

Who cares that I'm not living in Hackney?

She hadn't even *thought* about living in Hackney until Nick said he was living there.

I'm doing it again. Doing exactly what her mother and Emma told her not to.

Five minutes alone in a car with Nick and she's tumbling back down the rabbit hole.

'Uni's not all it's cracked up to be,' he says sourly, head falling against the headrest. 'At least you're not thousands of pounds in debt.'

True.

'So who cares as long as you're doing something creative, right?'

Right.

'So what do you do for ART? It must be pretty cool
if you did a look for a print campaign.'

Shell shrugs. 'I still work on the ART counter at Duke's.'

She hears the *still* and curses herself.

'Oh.' Nick nods. 'Oh. Okay. That's cool.'

When she looks at the Gucci bag in her lap, something
kicks at her, and she lifts her chin. 'It *is* cool, actually. I
love my job and I'm really good at it,' she tells him,
without hesitating this time.

No shrug.

No *still*.

Only *I am*.

The corners of his mouth twitch and she knows what
he's thinking.

There she is.

When they turn onto the high street, Shell sees Duke &
Sons ahead, lit up like a lighthouse in the rain. He pulls
up outside and there's a painful moment of silence when
he just looks at her and she catches herself holding her
breath because it's him – it's him and it's them – and, as
always with Nick, she has no idea what he's going to say.

'Listen, Shell,' he says, turning off the engine and
twisting in his seat to face her. 'Thank you.'

She blinks at him. 'For what?'

'For not changing.' He smiles, big and bright. 'For being true to yourself. Do you know how hard that is?'

She does, actually.

'I'm so glad I bumped into you,' he says, and she believes him. 'I've missed *this* so much.' He gestures at the space between them, the dimples sinking into his cheeks again as his smile turns into a grin. 'This. *Us*. Driving around in my car, talking. *God*.' He puts his hand in his dark hair and fists it. 'I feel seventeen again.'

And he looks it, his cheeks pink and his dark eyes bright, like he's three beers in and trying to persuade Shell to bunk off college tomorrow so they can drive to London to see some band that's playing at the Garage.

Shell arches an eyebrow. 'Is that a good thing?'

He lets his hand drop back into his lap and leans in, his voice lower. 'A very good thing.'

Her heart goes from an unsteady canter to a gallop, so suddenly that he must be able to hear it.

'And I'm glad you didn't cut your hair.' He reaches over to turn one of her loose waves around his finger. The shock makes her scalp shiver, and she shivers again as he leans closer, close enough to press his mouth to her cheek, then breathe into her ear, 'I've missed you, Princess Jasmine.'

He leans back again, just far enough that he can see her face, his lips parted.

It's like he's waiting for something, but she doesn't know what, so waits as well.

He reaches for her this time, warm hands cupping her cheeks. She barely has a chance to catch her breath before he tilts his face and they're kissing, slow and soft. He runs his tongue along her bottom lip and she complies, hearing him groan into her mouth as their tongues touch. Her fingers tighten around her travel cup as if to check that it's still there, that this is real, because they're kissing. Not a quick peck goodbye, but actually *kissing*.

She's in Nick Wallace's car, kissing Nick Wallace.

How many times did she imagine this when they were at college? When they were driving around, taking turns to play songs to one another? She would will him to look at her – really *look* at her – but he never did.

Now he sees, though.

Now he sees.

But before she's composed herself enough to kiss him back, it's over.

She overthought it, like she always does, and now she's missed it.

The moment's gone.

He lets out a long breath, hands still on her face. 'I've been wanting to do that since I saw you on Friday.'

'Yeah?' She blinks groggily as she remembers the two of them under her umbrella in the rain.

'Actually,' he adds, tucking her hair behind her ears. 'I've been wanting to do that for ten years.'

'Do it again,' Shell hears herself say.

Then they're kissing again, quick and breathless. The sort of kiss she'd dreamed about when he dropped her home and she'd stand outside her house, watching Scrappy stutter off, waiting for the sound of his music to fade.

It was *this*. Exactly this. A frantic, smudged-lipstick, hands-fisted-in-hair sort of kiss that makes her want to tell him to drive and keep driving, see where they end up.

But he pulls back and laughs.

'Wow.' He presses his forehead to hers. 'Why didn't I do that when we were seventeen?'

Why didn't you? 'I don't know,' she says instead, curling the fingers of her left hand around his wrist to feel his pulse.

He pulls back to look at her, his eyes black now and his mouth an obscene shade of pink.

She must look the same, hair everywhere, lipstick kissed clean away.

'I know it's been nine years since I last saw you, Shell, but I can't wait till Saturday.'

She suddenly can't either.

'I'll pick you up after work, yeah?'

She nods.

'What time?'

'Six?'

Their noses knock together in their haste to kiss goodbye and she giggles against his mouth.

'Go,' he tells her, with a groan. 'Go before I tell you to quit your job and run off to Cambodia with me.'

Shell does as she's told, but as she's about to open the car door, he reaches for her hand.

She turns back as he presses his lips to her knuckles. 'Six, yeah?'

Shell's legs are so weak that she doesn't know how she

manages to get out of the car, but she does, and stands on the pavement, her whole body tingling as she watches Nick pull away. She doesn't even notice that it's still raining until she turns and walks straight into someone carrying a black golf umbrella.

It's Callum.

'Shell.' He smiles, then nods at Nick's Mini Cooper as it disappears up Ostley High Street. 'Who was that?'

'Oh? Er, just a friend,' she says, pressing her fingers to her lips and running towards the revolving door.

Chapter Thirteen

Thank God I'm early. Shell runs into the supply cupboard, closing the door behind her. It reeks of bleach and mouldy mops, but she doesn't care. It's the only place she can tell Emma without anyone overhearing.

And she *has* to tell Emma.

Her hands are shaking as she takes her phone out of her bag to check the time. Usually, she'd be on the shop floor by now, reading the updates and sales-target emails that Gladys prints out and leaves on each counter. But between her sleepless night and all the car snogging with Nick, she has only nineteen minutes before the morning meeting starts. She should probably wait until lunch, but she can't wait *four hours*.

She may well have exploded by then.

Please don't be in a meeting, Shell pleads, fingers tapping at the screen of her phone. *Please don't be in a meeting.*

To her delight, Emma answers on the second ring.

'I just kissed Nick!' Shell yells into the phone before she's even said hello.

There's a long beat of silence then a furious hiss. 'You did *what*?'

'I just kissed Nick! Nick Wallace!'

'When?'

'Just now.'

'Shell, it's not even nine fifteen. How have you kissed someone already?'

She tries not to shriek and fails. 'Not just someone, *Nick Wallace!*'

'So the whole taking-it-slow thing is going well, then?'

Shell laughs, but before she can tell her what happened, she's interrupted by Emma's satnav: *At the roundabout, take the first exit onto New Road.*

'Are you in the car? Where are you going?'

'I'm taking some Carrara marble samples to this *hideous* woman in Marlborough. She's so rude. I can't stand her, but I have to be nice to her because she's spending an obscene amount of money redoing her kitchen.'

'How obscene?'

'A hundred grand.'

'One hundred thousand pounds on a kitchen?'

'She's having an antique Aga delivered tomorrow. I hope it doesn't work,' she mutters, under her breath.

'One hundred thousand pounds, Emma?'

'I know! You could buy a studio flat in Lowbridge for that!'

'Who wants to live in Lowbridge, though?'

'True,' she says, then shouts. 'Oi! You prick!'

'You okay, Em? Be careful.'

'I'm fine. Just some dickhead cutting in front of me at the roundabout. *Get off your phone!*'

'You're on your phone, Em.'

159

'Yeah, but I'm on hands-free,' she says indignantly. 'Anyway. Sorry! Nick Wallace. Tell me.'

Shell squeals. 'So, I was leaving the house this morning. It's lashing down.'

'I know,' Emma growls. 'I'm wearing suede heels. Pray for me.'

'Oh, *God*. Good luck. Anyway, so my umbrella breaks and who pulls up?'

'Your knight in skinny jeans!'

Shell detects the note of sourness and ignores it. 'He offers me a lift to work and we talk and. . .'

'You kiss.'

She was hoping for more of a build-up – to tease Emma a little – but, yes, that was essentially what happened.

'Did you kiss him, Shell? Or did he kiss you?'

'He kissed me, of course,' she says, with a smug smile, doing a twirl and almost putting her foot in a bucket.

When she recovers she laughs, waiting for Emma to shriek and demand to know what it was like.

If Nick is a good kisser.

If it was worth the wait.

But she doesn't say anything.

Then all Shell can hear are cars swishing by in the rain. 'Em, you still there?'

'Yeah. Yeah,' she says at last. 'I just don't get it.'

'Get what?'

'It doesn't make any sense.'

'*What* doesn't make any sense?' she asks, cheeks burning.

'He dicked you around for two years, then five minutes alone in a car with you and he pounces.'

Her whole face burns now. 'He didn't dick me around.'

'He did.' Emma doesn't try to soften the blow. 'He acted like your boyfriend but didn't want to be.'

'That's not what happened, Emma. You weren't even here.'

'Hmm.'

'And even if he did do that, it's been *nine years* since I last saw him. People change.'

'Hmm.'

Shell balls her free hand into a fist. 'Plus, his mother just died.'

She was hoping that would earn Nick some sympathy, but Emma says, 'Oh, that explains it!'

'Explains *what*?'

'He's grieving, Shell. He's looking for a bit of comfort.'

'Don't say it like that,' she says, furious. 'Like I'm a comfort blanket, or something.'

'That's not a bad thing. You were there for him in college and he obviously needs you again.'

She can hear Emma's shrug, even through the phone, and Shell wipes away a tear.

A few minutes ago, she'd felt on top of the world, and now she feels under it.

'I've got to go,' she murmurs, utterly deflated. 'The morning meeting is about to start.'

'Don't be like that, Shell.'

'Like what?'

'Look. I know I'm being a mardy cow, but I don't want you to get hurt again.'

'I won't.'

Emma starts to say something, then thinks better of it. 'I'll call you later, okay?'

Shell hangs up without saying goodbye.

When Shell walks into the break room, Ricky turns to her, his hands on his hips.

'Where have you been?' he hisses. 'I was about to send out a search party. The meeting starts in five minutes.'

She holds up her phone. 'I was talking to Emma.'

'Tell her I want my pink wig back.' He points at her then blinks. 'I just had a flashback to walking out of Mirage on Saturday night with her wearing it.'

When she doesn't laugh, just walks over to her locker and opens it, he frowns. 'You okay, babe?' he asks, grabbing the latte he's bought her from the table in the middle of the room.

He saunters over, waiting for Shell to put her travel cup into her locker before handing it to her. She feels bad to be wasting the coffee her father made her – which she didn't get a chance to drink, thanks to Nick and all the kissing – but if Ricky's got her a double shot gingerbread latte, and she really hopes he has, she needs it.

He has, she discovers as she takes a long sip. 'God, I really need this,' she says, handing it back to him so she can unbutton her coat. 'Thank you.'

His frown deepens. 'What happened with Emma? Did you two have a row, or something?'

When she looks up to tell him – about Nick and Emma, murderer of joy and deliverer of Carrara marble samples and advice Shell didn't ask for – she notices that Louise Larson is by her locker. Shell glares across the break room at her, as if to ask, *Can I help you?* Louise just smiles, making no effort to hide the fact that she's listening.

'I'll tell you later,' she says, under her breath, shouldering off her bag.

'That's nice,' Louise says, as she watches Shell put it into her locker. 'Is it Gucci?'

'Yes,' Ricky tells her, when Shell ignores her. 'It's from ART. Shell's been promoted.'

He pretends to flick his hair, even though he's wearing the topknot today, exposing the shaved underneath. She sees that there are still drops of rain in it so his dramatics were uncalled for, as usual, because he must just have got in.

'Yes, Callum said,' Louise says, her blue eyes alight with mischief. 'Congratulations, Shell.'

It sounds surprisingly genuine, which is most unlike Louise. She's the queen of making comments that sound like compliments, but half an hour later, you're, like, *Hang on.* Kind of like getting a raspberry seed stuck in your teeth: they shouldn't bother you as much as they do, but they'll distract you for the rest of the day if you let them.

When Shell shrugs off her coat to reveal her ART Christmas uniform, which consists of a black T-shirt with *Nice* in silver cursive crystals, Louise presses a hand to her chest, like a damsel in an old horror film.

That's more like it. Shell hangs her coat in her locker. With that, Louise is back to her sour self, her whole face tight as Ricky holds up Shell's coffee cup and cocks his hip at her. He's in full glam: glossy gold eyeshadow, an equally glossy red lip and his signature thick lashes that he bats at Louise as he smiles sweetly. It should be in direct opposition to his quite sombre outfit – he's channelling David Rose from *Schitt's Creek* today, in a black skirt/trouser combo and biker boots – but when he shows Louise his ART T-shirt, which is exactly the same as Shell's but with *Naughty* in cursive red crystals, it goes perfectly.

'Wow.' The corners of Louise's mouth are twitching. 'How festive.'

'I know it's not a tartan bow and a bell,' Ricky tells her, 'but our clients will love it.'

'Yes. Well,' Louise says, her smile a little stiffer. 'Gaulin clients prefer something a little less . . .' she waves her hand at him as he and Shell arch their eyebrows at her, waiting for what she's about to say '. . . *flamboyant.*'

They both know what that's code for, but before either of them can say anything, Camilla, one of the Gaulin girls, opens the door to the break room and sticks her head in. 'The morning meeting's about to start.'

'Shoot,' Shell hisses, slamming her locker shut and taking the coffee from Ricky.

As much as it pains her not to savour it, she's not allowed to have it on the shop floor, so she gulps it down as quickly as she can, then tosses the empty cup into the bin by the door, vowing to sort out her hair and reapply her lipstick when she gets to the ART counter as she and Ricky hurry out.

They get into the Beauty Hall and behind the counter a moment before Callum strides in.

Even though Old Mr Duke isn't retiring yet, Callum has resumed the role of wishing them well when the store opens and thanking them when it closes. Most of the staff are still wary of him, of course – and his motives – but showing his face on the shop floor every day and making an effort to ask them how they are, rather than hiding in his office, is slowly winning them over.

'Morning, ladies,' he says, then gives Ricky a small bow. 'Good morning, Mr O'Neill.'

Ricky giggles and waves at him, hips wiggling.

Today Callum is head to toe in black. An impeccably tailored black suit that makes his shoulders look broader and his legs longer, and a black shirt that's open at the collar, as always.

'Murder me,' Ricky says, out of the corner of his mouth.

'I hope you're all well on this grim Monday morning.' Callum rubs his hands together, pretending to shiver. 'If there was ever a day that Ostley could do with a little of that Duke & Sons sparkle, it's today.'

There's a titter of agreement, which makes Callum smile as he resumes the morning admin. Who's off sick. What deliveries they're expecting. Their targets. Another push about upselling that prompts Louise Larson to remind Callum that Old Mr Duke doesn't like customers to feel harassed. This time, she's sweetness and light, her delicate chin up and her eyelashes fluttering. Not at all like she was in the Christmas Changeover meeting on

Saturday. Callum laps it up, of course, thanking her for being so conscientious about the 'customer experience', as he puts it.

'Have a good one, guys.' Callum beams when the clock over the lifts chimes ten times.

There's a smattering of applause as he turns to Gary, gesturing at him to unlock the revolving door.

Ricky's clearly forgotten that Shell wanted to tell him about her conversation with Emma, his gaze narrowing as he watches Callum glide from counter to counter, saying good morning to each of the girls.

'Do you think he's bi as well? I think he is,' he says, asking and answering the question as he secures his leather brush belt around his waist without taking his eyes off Callum. 'No straight man dresses that well.'

Shell just shrugs. 'I don't know.' And she doesn't care, still stinging from what Emma said about her being Nick's comfort blanket.

Callum stops at the Gaulin counter, his smile more playful as he says something to make them erupt into giggles, Louise's blonde curls rippling with delight as she slaps his arm.

Ricky and Shell turn to each other and pretend to fall about laughing.

'Oh, you!' Ricky slaps her arm.

'No, you!' She slaps him back, laughing maniacally.

'What's so funny, guys?' Callum asks, suddenly in front of the counter.

'Nothing,' they say, turning to face him and standing to attention.

'Okay.' Callum nods, then looks between them. 'Well, you guys have a brilliant day.'

'Actually,' Shell says, before he turns to walk away, 'Ricky wanted to talk to you.'

Ricky looks bewildered. 'I do?'

'He does?' Callum looks equally bewildered.

'Yeah. He has some ideas about the counter, don't you, Ricky?'

'Really?' Callum brightens, but when he drags his front teeth up his bottom lip, Ricky quivers.

'Yeah.' Shell nudges him because he's obviously forgotten how to speak. 'Tell Callum what you told me on Saturday night.'

'Um,' he splutters, looking desperately at her. 'What did I say?'

'About charging for makeovers, remember?'

'Yes!' he says, too loudly, as he turns back to Callum, who seems more confused than curious now. 'Makeovers. Customers always come in, usually before we close on a Friday and a Saturday, wanting to *test*,' he emphasises the word with his fingers, 'a foundation when, really, they want us to do their makeup before they go out.'

Callum looks impressed. 'That's quite clever, actually.'

'It is, but they rarely buy anything. Maybe a lipstick, but that's it. It's a complete waste of time. So,' he's finding his stride now, 'why don't we offer it as a service? Come into Duke & Sons and we'll give you a full face of glam for your first date or prom or whatever. You can have it all. Whatever you want, but you have to pay forty pounds, which is cheap. Hiring a MUA would cost *way* more.'

Callum doesn't look convinced. 'Do you really think people would pay forty pounds for that, though?'

Ricky doesn't hesitate. 'Yes.' He smirks. 'Because we're the best. But if they don't want to, who cares? If they've got the cheek to come in here and expect us to do their makeup for free, without having the decency to buy something, we don't need them. Those customers waste our time and our products.'

'True,' Callum concedes, if a little startled by Ricky's honesty.

'But, if they're willing to pay it, they can redeem the forty pounds against ART products. They'll definitely buy at least two so they feel like they're getting their money's worth.'

'Brilliant.' Callum grins. 'What a brilliant idea, Ricky.' He pretends to doff his cap at him.

'I've already emailed ART,' Shell adds proudly. 'They love the idea and, if you agree, they're going to send us a table with one of those mirrors with the lights around it. You know, to make the clients feel special.'

'And we should open a brow bar,' Ricky suggests, clearly on a roll. 'It wouldn't take up much space.' He shrugs, like it's no big deal, but Shell knows he cares more than he's letting on. 'We'd just need a chair, a mirror and a brow tech, so it wouldn't cost much to set up. Plus, at twenty quid a pop, it would pay for itself by lunch.'

A groove appears between Callum's eyebrows as he considers it.

'And a nail bar,' Ricky goes on, obviously buoyed by the fact that Callum is actually listening to him. 'There's only one decent place in Ostley and it's booked up for *weeks*. Or there's the nail shops on Bridge Street, which are great, but they're like a production line. In, out. In, out. It's not very luxe, is it?' He waits for Callum to nod, then goes on, 'Plus, you can't book an appointment, you have to just sit there and wait, which is a nightmare, especially if you're on your lunch break or you need to pick your kids up from school, or something. We could put it in the window.' Callum's head turns, following Ricky's finger as he points a sharp black nail towards the gingerbread house. 'So people can see it when they walk past and hopefully come in. We could set up the brow bar next to it.'

'That's the perfect spot, actually. We wouldn't lose any of the shop floor.'

'Exactly. We can offer appointments or walk-ins during the week when it's less busy.'

Two women come through the revolving door and when Callum sees them heading their way, he presses his hand to the counter. 'Why don't we go for lunch later and discuss?'

'Okay.'

'Shall we say one?'

'I'll check my diary.' Ricky sighs, looking at his nails.

'Well, be sure to let me know!' Callum laughs as he strides off.

As soon as he does, Shell nudges Ricky. 'See? I told you he'd listen.'

'Whatever.' But she can see that he's fighting a smile.

*

It's the busiest Monday they've had in years.

Word has got out about the new Christmas decorations and everyone in Ostley seems to be coming in to see them. For the most part, it's positive, kids hugging the polar bears in Christmas jumpers at the foot of the wooden staircase, and gaggles of schoolgirls stopping to take photos of the lipstick wreath that Ricky made on Sunday when he was hung-over. ART loves it so much that Shell and Ricky have done three more since then – one with eyeshadow, one with blush and one with a combination of the three – which, according to the schoolgirls, are *sick*.

The Duke & Sons regulars are less enthused, wandering around with upturned noses and sour faces as they ask where the tree is. One woman even demands to see the manager. Louise offers to get him, running off, blonde curls bouncing. Shell has never seen Louise run before and chuckles as she hears her heels tapping on the parquet floors as she hurries through the Beauty Hall and out into the back to fetch Callum.

They return a few minutes later, Callum sweeping towards the woman, arm outstretched, and introducing himself. She's not interested, though, and proceeds to yell at him for a solid ten minutes, asking him what polar bears and hot-air balloons have to do with Christmas. She doesn't give him a chance to respond, though, lecturing him on how Duke & Sons is a family store and the new decorations are an attack on Christmas.

To his credit, Callum takes it on the chin, then offers her a lollipop from the ART counter, with a gracious smile, which the woman refuses as she stalks away, muttering to herself.

That's how it goes for the rest of the day, a weird mix of excitement and bewilderment from everyone who comes in. It's so busy that Shell almost wishes Becca and Soph were there, having to juggle serving customers and a consultation with a bride who is getting married on New Year's Eve while Ricky is at lunch with Callum. When Ricky finally returns, beaming and bouncing, from their conversation, all Shell wants to do is sit in the break room for an hour and stare at the wall, but then she remembers her date with Nick that evening.

'Arse,' she mutters, looking down at her ART *Nice* T-shirt.

While he'd no doubt find it amusing, it's not exactly the impression she was hoping to make.

So she grabs her coat and bag from her locker and rushes home. It's finally stopped raining – *thank God* – and no one's in – *thank God* – so she can run up to her room without being called upon to mediate an argument between Kitty and Sim or explain to her mother why she's home at two twenty on a Monday afternoon.

She already knows what she's going to wear and snatches her yellow and black Dalmatian-print playsuit from her wardrobe – and her orange leopard-print maxi dress just in case there's a horrible wardrobe malfunction and the zip on her playsuit breaks, or something – then grabs her makeup bag and runs back down the stairs.

She checks the time on the microwave in the kitchen to find it's two twenty-six, which gives her enough time to get back to the store with ten minutes to spare. That's enough to grab a sandwich from the café downstairs, but she won't have time to eat it. So she raids the cupboards, finding a breakfast bar and taking a banana from the fruit bowl on the table before unhooking a canvas tote bag from the back of the door and stuffing everything into it.

Shell doesn't like eating in the street, but she should be safe to eat the banana without anyone tutting, so she forces it down as she heads back to Duke & Sons, her DMs squeaking on the still wet pavement. It starts raining again as she turns onto the high street and she shrieks, running the rest of the way before her hair doubles in size.

According to her phone, she pushes through the revolving door at two forty-eight, which gives her twelve whole minutes to hang up her playsuit and dress so they don't crease, and slump at the table before she has to go back onto the shop floor. She's only just sat down and opened the breakfast bar when she hears someone say, 'Healthy,' and looks up to find Louise Larson in the doorway, her nose wrinkled as though someone's asked if her dress is from Primark.

Shell ignores her, pretending to be absorbed in something on her phone as Louise saunters over to the table and sits opposite her without having to pull the chair out. She has one of those reusable water bottles – a rose-gold one, of course, unlike Shell's which is turquoise with cartoon red chillies – and opens it with great flourish as Shell tenses, readying herself for what she's about to say.

'I feel great,' she says, with a happy sigh. 'This juice cleanse is giving me so much energy.'

Shell tells herself not to take the bait. She's used to Louise's comments about how 'brave' she is to be wearing whatever she's wearing that day and she never acknowledges the leaflets for the local Slim and Win meetings that Louise leaves on the table in the break room, but Shell finds herself sitting up a little straighter in spite of herself.

'I wish I could eat something like that,' Louise sighs again, 'but I have a wedding dress to fit into!'

Shell can't imagine wanting to get married at twenty-five.

She can't even imagine getting married at twenty-seven.

'Hmm,' she mutters, taking a bite out of the breakfast bar. She's not sure how surviving on whatever is in that water bottle is any healthier than what she's eating, but that's Louise. When she's not juice cleansing, she seems to live on energy drinks and chewing gum, so while she may have an enviable figure, she's hardly healthy.

But she looks it, which is all that matters, isn't it?

Shell knows not to let Louise get to her. Most of the time, she couldn't give a shit what people think about the way she looks. She used to. When she was at college, she hid under long black skirts and baggy black jumpers, but she realised that it doesn't matter what she wears: people like Louise will only ever see her as a fat girl.

So she decided that she might as well wear what makes her happy, picking out her clothes each morning with the same joy she'd experienced as a kid and that was all they were, clothes. Now she wears what she likes: dresses that make her want to stop and twirl in the street and T-shirts that expose the tops of her arms. And if she wants to pair lime green eyeshadow with orange lipstick she will, thank you very much, because it looks great.

So while Louise Larson is hard to ignore sometimes, Shell refuses to let her digs puncture the self-esteem she's spent the last few years so carefully cultivating. If Louise wants to attach her value to the way she looks, because she thinks that being fat is the worst thing she can be, so be it. But Shell knows there are much worse things and would rather be a better friend and a better daughter and a better sister. She'd rather live as loudly and as fearlessly as she can and take up as much space as she wants, because she deserves to.

It took her far too long to realise that, but now she does.

So enough, Shell thinks, checking her phone. She still has another six minutes before her lunchbreak is over, but the joy of sitting down is not enough to endure making polite – or impolite, in this case – conversation with Louise Larson. So she finishes the breakfast bar, throws the wrapper into the bin and heads back to the shop floor to find Ricky at the counter, singing along to 'Do They Know It's Christmas?' as he tidies the foundation bottles.

It's not really a singalong Christmas song, but he looks so happy that she leaves him to it.

The rest of the day is lost to customers coming in to look at the decorations and wanting to try the new ART Deco the Halls eyeshadow palette. Ricky is desperate to play with it as well so Shell lets him experiment on her because she's willing to try something more ambitious than their clients. But, as much as she loves the Liberty purple eyeshadow look he's given her, it clashes horribly with the yellow playsuit she wants to wear.

'What?' Ricky asks, as she inspects her reflection in the mirror.

'Nothing,' she lies, fussing over her fringe with her fingers.

Thankfully, she doesn't need to elaborate as the clock over the lifts chimes five times and Denise is at the counter with Ricky's leather jacket asking if she wants to go to the Anchor with them.

'Come on,' she tells Shell. 'We need to discuss Ricky's lunch with Callum.'

'We've already discussed it.' Shell grins, pinching his cheeks. 'I'm so proud of my sweet boy.'

'Get off,' Ricky hisses, but he's clearly thrilled, his dark eyes gleaming.

'Come anyway,' Denise tells her.

'I can't,' Shell says, feeling a sharp stab of guilt at not telling them she's meeting Nick.

They'll probably be thrilled, but after her conversation with Emma, she doesn't want to take the risk in case they bombard her with questions and dampen the fresh flush of excitement she feels about seeing him in an hour.

Is it a date?

Are you seeing him, then?

Is he staying in Ostley or are you going to do the long-distance thing?

Maybe they aren't Ricky and Denise's questions. Maybe they're hers.

Either way, she doesn't know the answer to any of them so, until she does, maybe she shouldn't tell them.

Not that she gets a chance as Callum walks into the Beauty Hall.

'Thanks, guys. You've been awesome today,' he tells them, with a smile. 'Take care. Have a good evening.'

Ricky and Denise are instantly distracted, standing straighter as Callum strides towards the ART counter. Just before he gets to them, though, Louise steps into his path, looking up at him with a smooth smile. 'Mr Duke,' she says, batting her eyelashes at him.

He presses his hand to his chest. 'Call me Callum, please.'

'Callum.' She giggles delicately, tilting her head at him. 'I heard you went to lunch with Ricky today to discuss ideas for the ART counter.'

'Yes.' He nods. 'Yes, I did.'

'Well.' She takes a step closer to him. 'I have some ideas that I'd love to share with you.'

'I bet she does,' Denise says, under her breath.

Ricky covers his mouth with a hand to conceal a snigger, but Shell isn't listening, wishing Louise would take Callum – and her little performance – elsewhere so she can get ready to meet Nick.

As if on cue, Louise takes Callum by the arm and leads him through the Beauty Hall towards the back of house. Denise's eyebrow jerks up as she does, but Ricky doesn't seem bothered as he refreshes his lipstick.

'So, you coming to the Anchor, Shell?' he asks, pouting at himself in the mirror.

'I can't. I—'

'Taco Tuesday!' Denise points at her. 'You'd better get home before your dad eats all the guac.'

Wow, Shell thinks. *Am I really* that *predictable?*

'Babe.' Ricky frowns at her. 'It's Monday.'

'Oh, yeah.' Denise shakes her head. 'It's been a long day.'

'So what is it, then?' he asks, putting the lipstick back with the others. 'You filming with Mia tonight?'

The lie is out of Shell's mouth before she can stop it. 'Yeah.'

Ricky just shrugs. 'Okay. Cool. See you tomorrow.'

Forty-five minutes later, Shell has cashed up, tidied the counter, cleaned her makeup brushes, changed into her playsuit and is now struggling with a false eyelash that *will not stick*, no matter how many times she bargains with it. She wishes Ricky was here. It's much easier to apply lashes on someone else.

After a few minutes, it relents and she pulls her coat on and grabs her Gucci bag off the counter.

She takes a deep breath, shaking at the thought of Nick outside waiting for her and heads towards the revolving door. She's halfway there, when she hears someone behind her say, 'Still here?'

She turns, the soles of her hot pink DMs squeaking on the polished floor as she does, to find it's Callum.

'Wow,' he says, slowing when he sees her.

Shell freezes. 'What?'

'You changed,' he says, stopping in front of her and nodding at her playsuit.

'Yeah.' She looks down at it, then tugs her coat closed, wrapping her arms around her chest. 'I'm going to the pub and I don't want anyone to think I'm too nice and push in front of me at the bar.'

'Where are you off to?'

'Nowhere. I'm just meeting Ricky and Denise in the Anchor for a drink,' she lies again.

She dismisses it this time, though, telling herself she's just being professional. Callum doesn't need to know about her love life.

He gestures at the revolving doors. 'May I escort you out?'

Shell hesitates. God. Why did she have to lie? If Nick's there – and she *really* hopes he is – Callum will know she's not meeting Ricky and Denise. She considers making an excuse about forgetting something, but he is already guiding her towards the door.

She pushes through it and there he is, Nick Wallace, leaning back against his car with his arms crossed.

He stands up and smiles when he sees her, quickly closing the distance between them.

'Hey,' he says, taking her face in his hands, his fingers cold against her hot cheeks as he kisses her.

When he steps back, he has a smear of her lipstick on his chin, like she's branded him.

Mine, Shell thinks, as she reaches up and wipes it away with the pad of her thumb.

'Oh, hey,' Nick says, clearing his throat. 'I didn't see you there, man.'

Callum extends his hand and introduces himself. 'Pleasure to meet you . . . ?'

'Nick.' He fills in the gap. 'Nick Wallace.'

They stand there, shaking hands, for a moment longer than is comfortable.

They're both in black, but they couldn't be more different. Callum is immaculate in a long wool coat, his eyes almost fluorescent blue in the dark. Whereas Nick is in a battered leather jacket and a knitted beanie, the ends of his dark hair curling. The knees of his jeans are grey with age and the cuffs of his jumper, which are sticking out from the sleeves of his jacket, are frayed.

She thumbs at Callum when they finally stop shaking hands. 'Nick, this is Callum Duke.'

'Oh.' He stands a little straighter when he clocks Callum's surname. 'Okay. Cool.'

'So, where are you guys off to?' Callum asks, with a polite smile.

Shell senses an opportunity to atone for her lie, but before she can tell him that they're off to meet Ricky and Denise, Nick says, 'I thought we could try that new Thai tapas place.'

'The one in Church Cabham?' Callum asks and Nick nods. 'I went last night, actually. It's nice. I'd give the Pad Thai a miss, but the beef Massaman curry and roti is . . .' He grins and makes the okay sign with his fingers.

'I'm vegan,' Nick says.

Of course he's vegan, Shell thinks, trying not to laugh.

'Oh, well, roti and jasmine rice it is.'

She does laugh then, covering her mouth with her hand.

'It was a pleasure to meet you, Nick.' Callum holds out his hand and he shakes it again. 'Have a good night.' He turns to Shell with a wicked smirk. 'And I'll see you tomorrow, Shell. Have fun with Ricky and Denise.'

He waits long enough to see her wince, then strides away.

Nick lowers his voice as Callum strides away. 'What happened to the old guy?'

'Old Mr Duke? He's still around. Callum's his grandson.'

'I didn't know he had a grandson.'

'He moved back to the States when his father died.'

'God. I remember Mum telling me about that. That was, what? Twenty years ago?'

'Twenty-five.'

'So he's been in the States since then?'

'He came back to go to Oxford, then did his MBA at Stanford.'

'Really,' Nick says to himself, as he watches Callum disappear up the high street.

'He travelled for a bit, then worked for Anthropologie. Then he was at Bendel's in New York for a couple of years before he started a luxury sustainable zero-waste fashion brand.'

Nick raises his eyebrows. 'Hannah Banana?'

'Yes! He just sold it to LVMH for an *obscene* amount of money, apparently.'

'What are you? Callumpedia?' Nick laughs, but there's

something about the way he says it that makes Shell's shoulders tense.

'No.' She smoothes her hands down her hair, avoiding his gaze. 'I just thought you were curious.'

'Yeah, but I don't need his life story, do I?' he mutters, opening the car door for her.

Chapter Fourteen

Callum was right: the roti is lush.

Dinner is weird, though. Shell doesn't know what it is, if it was bumping into Callum or the nine years since they last saw each other, but they need to find their groove again. Whatever it is, Nick hasn't said much, just sipped his beer and picked at his tofu Pad Thai, which she's sure he ordered to prove Callum wrong. He was right about that as well. Shell could tell from the first mouthful Nick took that it was horrible.

He hasn't touched it since.

'So,' he says finally, finishing his beer, 'what's it like working with such a hottie?'

So it is about Callum.

Shell pretends to plead ignorance as she dips a piece of roti into her beef Massaman curry. 'Huh?'

'Callum Duke.' He doesn't look at her. 'I wondered why you were still at Duke & Sons after all this time.'

She ignores the jibe. 'He only started on Saturday.' Nick doesn't look convinced, though, so she adds, 'Besides. I never see him. He's always in his office.'

Shell doesn't know why she lies, but it works, because Nick softens.

'I'm not worried.' Something tells her that he's lying this time.

'You shouldn't be.'

'I know. He's not your type.'

'Oh, yeah? How do you know what my type is?'

His dark eyes flash. 'He's too prim and proper for you.'

'Yeah?'

'Yeah. He's too perfect for you. You like 'em a little rough round the edges. A little bit broken.'

'I do?' Shell makes a show of licking her lips, and with that, they're the only ones in the restaurant. When he watches her do it, his eyes go from brown to black, and she almost laughs. It's strange, the two of them flirting shamelessly. She's so used to holding back when she's with him – not touching his hair, not dipping her finger into his dimples, not saying anything to disturb their safe little bubble – that this is all new to her.

Now Nick licks his lips. 'Shall we get out of here?'

Shell nods.

Before they leave, Shell makes a point of retreating to the bathroom to check her makeup and gargle some of the travel-sized mouthwash she remembered to put in her bag. Callum was right, the beef Massaman curry was *amazing* but riddled with garlic so pops some gum into her mouth for safety.

She can see Nick watching her as she returns to their table, a lascivious smile on his face.

'What?' she asks, as she grabs her coat from the back of her chair.

His smile sharpens to a smirk as he looks up at her from where he's sitting. 'Nothing.'

'*What?*'

'You.'

'Me?'

'Yeah, *you*.' His pupils are black again. 'I know I said you haven't changed, but you have.'

She frowns at him. 'I have?'

'Yeah. You have this energy now. This *confidence*. It's really sexy.'

'Stop it.'

'No. Look.' He casts a glance around the restaurant. 'Everyone is staring at you.'

'I think this playsuit has something to do with that.'

'That's what I mean.' He raises his hand to her. 'You would never have worn that when we were at college, but look at you, in *yellow*, no less. With red lipstick that I fully intend to kiss off in about three minutes.'

'Nick. *Stop.*' She giggles, buttoning her coat because she can't look at him, her cheeks flushing.

'No, you stop, Shell.' He stands up and leans over to press his mouth to her ear. 'You're so fucking *hot*.'

She slaps his arm and giggles again as his breath makes her shiver.

'You are,' he insists, his voice a growl now. 'You were always pretty, but now you're sexy too.'

She doesn't know what to say to that, so in an effort not to giggle like a teenager again, she points at the plastic takeaway tub on the table next to them. 'What's that?'

'Some Pad Thai for sexy Callum.' He steps back, with an unrepentant smirk.

She swats him, but he just laughs, grabbing her hand and leading her out of the restaurant.

'Come here,' he says, as soon as they're out of the door, pulling her to him. He lets go of her hand to cup her face, fingers pressing into her cheeks. His other arm curls around her waist, sweeping her off her feet in the middle of the street, kissing her in front of the restaurant window for everyone to see.

He does it again when they get to his car, pushing her against it and pinning her to it as he kisses her with an urgency that makes her reach for the front of his leather jacket and fist her hands in it.

He kisses her again before he starts the engine, then at each red light, then when he parks outside her house. And each time it's a little deeper – a little more demanding – as though he's testing her. Waiting to see what she'll do. If she'll stop him and push him off or meet him halfway. When she does, he tries to pull her onto his lap, but there's no room. So he tries to crawl into her lap, but there's no room for that, either, and he sighs into her neck.

'Why did I have to get a Mini?' he whines, and she laughs, tugging off his beanie so she can stroke his hair.

Then they're kissing again, his hand slipping under her coat to grab her hip. When he does, she can feel herself falling and squeals against his mouth as the passenger seat drops back and she's suddenly horizontal.

'Oh, my God,' he gasps. 'I didn't do that on purpose, I swear. I must have hit the thing.'

'Smooth, Wallace.' She laughs as he helps her up.

'Jesus. This was much easier in Scrappy, wasn't it?' he says, adjusting the lever on the seat.

Not with me, she thinks, the back of her neck burning.

He leans in again, but she thumbs at the house. 'I'd better go.'

If he realises what he's said, he doesn't acknowledge it, just tilts his head at her and grins. 'Hey. You free tomorrow night? I thought I could go for the KO.'

He looks so cute that Shell can't help but laugh, what he just said forgotten as she kisses him quickly. 'I'll wear a helmet, just in case.'

As she reaches for the door handle, he holds up a finger and pouts. She sighs theatrically and leans in as he does. It starts off chaste – a swift kiss goodnight – but it soon melts into something more fierce, his hands around her neck as he kisses her until she's shivering so much, he must be able to feel it.

'Come back to mine,' he breathes, mouth on her neck now, and – *Oh, God* – she wants to.

But she's supposed to be taking this slow, isn't she?

'I'll see you tomorrow, okay?' she promises, as he lifts his thick eyelashes to look at her.

For a moment, she thinks he isn't going to let go of her, but he does.

'Tomorrow,' he says, pressing a kiss to her hand.

★

As soon as she walks through the front door, her mother emerges from the living room.

'Shell Damini Smith,' Eleanor hisses, beckoning her into the living room.

'What?' Shell asks, when she does, stopping in front of her with her arms crossed.

'Was *that* Nick Wallace?'

Shell gasps and points at the living-room window. 'Were you watching?'

'No. I was looking at the moon. It's so pretty tonight.'

Shell's gaze narrows as if to say, *Sure you were, Mum*.

'Listen,' Eleanor says, obviously trying to keep her voice down so she doesn't wake the kids. 'Was it Nick?'

Her arms are still crossed. 'Yes, Mum.'

'You were *snogging*.'

Snogging? What is she? Thirteen?

'I can't have this conversation with you, Mother.' Shell closes her eyes, mortified.

'Well, you'd better. Or I'm telling your grandmother that you're kissing boys in cars.'

Shell doesn't know what to say to that so she sighs petulantly. 'I'm tired. I'm going to bed.'

When she turns to walk out of the living room, her mother reaches for the sleeve of her coat.

'What?' Shell stops and turns to face her again.

Eleanor frowns sadly. 'Is it true that his mother just died?'

'How did you know that?'

'Mrs Cross at number eleven told me.'

Shell crosses her arms again.

When she doesn't say anything, the groove between Eleanor's dark eyebrows deepens. 'Shell, he's grieving.'

Here we go again.

'Just be careful, okay?' her mother warns.

Eleanor waits for Shell to meet her gaze. 'Just make sure he's not using you to break his fall.'

Chapter Fifteen

'Morning, Shell. Nice evening?' Gary asks, when she pushes through the revolving door the next morning.

She holds up her travel cup. 'Put it this way, Gary, this is my second.'

'I hear ya.' He holds up his own mug of coffee.

Shell glances around the empty Beauty Hall as she heads for the break room, inhaling the soothing smell of peppermint. This is her favourite time of the day, when it's just her and she can drink her coffee and do all the things she won't have time to do when the store is open. Clean the glass counter and replenish the cotton buds, make sure that everything – every foundation, lipstick and brush – is in its place. She pats the polar bears at the foot of the staircase on the head, then walks towards the back of house.

As she heads for the break room, she sees Callum further down the corridor walking to Old Mr Duke's office and calls to him. 'Morning, Callum.'

He stops and turns to her, his smile easier when he sees that it's her approaching. He's wearing a petrol blue suit today. He always wears either black or grey so she can't help but smile at the rare flash of colour.

She dreads to think how Ricky and Denise will react when they see him in it.

'Good morning, Shell,' he says, tugging at the cuffs of his white shirt.

'I have something for you.' She reaches into her canvas tote bag and pulls out the takeaway tub, handing it to him with a mischievous smirk. 'Got you some tofu Pad Thai from that place in Church Cabham.'

'Gee, thanks,' he says grimly, holding it up to assess the contents. 'Bet the tofu really enhances the flavour.'

She wrinkles her nose. 'Oh, yeah.'

'Did you at least try the curry and roti?'

'Yeah. It was.' She holds up her hand, making the okay sign with her fingers.

'I told you. I'd never lead you astray.'

'Thanks for warning me about the garlic, though!'

He laughs in a way that makes her wonder if he did it on purpose, then does that thing where he drags his front teeth up his bottom lip and peers at her from under his eyelashes.

It's like he's waiting for her to say something, but she doesn't know what.

When she doesn't say whatever he's waiting for her to say, he points the tub at her. 'Have a good day!'

'You too,' she tells him, heading into the break room.

'So you went to the new Thai place?' Louise says, as soon as she walks in.

Shell jumps, so stunned to see her there early that she almost drops her travel cup.

'Third wheeling it with Ricky and Denise again, were you?' she asks, with a sharp smile.

Shell takes a deep breath, ignoring the dig as she heads to her locker. 'Good morning to you, too.'

'The Pad Thai is awful,' she pushes, when Shell doesn't bite back. She's trying to sound casual, but Shell knows she's calculated the weight of each word. 'But the beef Massaman curry and roti is . . .' Her smile is even sharper as she makes the okay sign with her fingers and Shell stares at her.

'How do you know about that?'

'I went on Sunday night,' she says, with an elegant shrug.

There's something she isn't saying, though, which isn't like Louise at all.

Shell waits, but Louise just looks at her as if to say, *Come on,* like she's waiting for her to catch up.

It takes a moment, but then there it is: *Didn't Callum go on Sunday night?*

Before Shell can ask, though, Louise is gone and she's left wondering why it bothers her so much.

'Isn't Louise engaged?' Shell says, staring at the Gaulin counter as they wait for the nine-thirty meeting to start.

Louise is floating around, curls rippling, eyes sparkling, like there's champagne in her water bottle this morning, not some God-awful kale concoction. She laughs at something Camilla says, then sprays her with a perfume bottle, as if Camilla's a badly behaved cat.

'Louise Larson?' Ricky asks, without looking away from the mirror as he adjusts one of his fake lashes.

'Yeah. Isn't that why she's doing that juice cleanse? To fit into her wedding dress.'

'Who cares?'

He's right, she shouldn't care, but she didn't think Callum was like that.

Shell crosses her arms, gaze narrowing at Louise. 'She went for dinner with Callum.'

That gets Ricky's attention. He spins on his heels to face her, grabbing her arm. 'Louise went where with *who*?'

Shell forces herself to look away from the Gaulin counter and turns her cheek back to Ricky, who is equal parts appalled and thrilled at the prospect of some gossip.

'Callum and Louise went for dinner on Sunday night, after stock check.'

'How do you know?'

'Louise told me earlier.'

'She *told* you that she went for dinner with Callum on Sunday night?'

'Not *explicitly*,' she admits. 'But she *implied* it.'

Ricky's shoulders sink. 'Oh,' he says, sounding deflated. 'What?'

'Listen. You know I love a tasty bit of gossip.' He holds his hands up. 'But even if Louise isn't engaged, Callum's still senior management, so I wouldn't repeat that, if I were you. It's not fair if you don't know, like, *for sure*. That's the sort of rumour that ruins careers.'

She feels a pinch of shame. 'You're the first person I've told.'

'Good! I should always be the first person you tell these things. If you get receipts, then *happy days*.' He throws up his hands theatrically. 'I'll make sure everyone in a ten-mile radius knows.'

'Sincere apologies for being late, guys,' Callum says, suddenly in the Beauty Hall. 'My previous morning meetings went on much longer than I'd anticipated.'

'That's okay, Callum,' Louise says, with a well-practised smile, tilting her head at him.

'Anyway.' The smile he bats back isn't as open. 'It's almost ten o'clock, so I'll keep it brief, I promise. I've put a note about this on the staff intranet, but not all of you read it, so I'm going from floor to floor, to let everyone know that for the next few Sundays, while we're closed, we'll be making some small cosmetic changes. Nothing you're likely to notice. Just some repainting here and there and some minor repairs to the floors.'

He's clearly waiting for someone to object, but when no one does, he goes on. 'We're also going to be taking new shots of the store for the website and doing some filming for a Duke & Sons YouTube channel we're hoping to launch in the new year. If I can get my grandfather to understand what YouTube is, of course.'

There's a gracious titter.

'So, from this weekend until the one before Christmas, a crew will be coming in to set up after we close on a Saturday so they can film on the Sunday. It's not going to affect you guys in any way, but I thought I'd let you know in case you pass and see people in the store and wonder what's going on.'

He pauses again, clearly convinced that someone will object to that and ask what on earth they're filming for a YouTube channel for *seven* Sundays in a row. Shell's curious, but no one else seems bothered.

Even Ricky, his gaze wandering around the Beauty Hall, his arms crossed.

Callum nods. 'Okay, then. Thanks, guys. Have a good day.'

Shell seethes quietly over the Louise thing for the rest of the day. But then Nick picks her up after work, and as soon as he kisses her, it's forgotten.

Last night, over dinner, she mentioned that they're showing *The Godfather* at the Rex. Emma won't go with her because she says it's too violent and Nick remembered her complaining about it and booked tickets, insisting Shell get whatever she wants from the pick-and-mix stand.

And that's how it goes for the rest of the week.

On Wednesday night, they go to the Depot to see an Irish band Shell has never heard of. They're great, though, and it's like they're seventeen again, the pair of them dancing until they're laughing and sweaty and spilling their beer.

On Thursday night, they were supposed to go to a party at his mate's house, but stop at a pub for a drink first and end up staying, playing pool, then winning a bottle of champagne in the quiz, which they share as he walks her home. They stop to kiss under each streetlight, Nick admitting that he googled their winning answer on his phone with an unrepentant laugh as she insists they take the champagne back, even though they've finished it.

On Friday night, he wants to go to a club night at a former police station, but as she's about to agree, she remembers that she's going to see the new Bond film with Emma. Luckily, Emma's been so busy going back and forth to Marlborough to work on the kitchen refit that she hasn't registered Shell's absence this week. So, when they meet at the cinema, Emma starts talking as soon as she hugs her hello and doesn't stop, only to order the popcorn and ice cream Shell promised her.

She's still complaining when they find their seats, telling Shell about how the refit will take twice as long because the client's insisted they re-lay the parquet floor: she wants double herringbone now, not single. Emma's still whinging when the trailers start and Shell can't wait any longer. So as soon as Emma stops to shove a handful of popcorn in her mouth, Shell says it.

'I've been seeing Nick.'

Emma almost chokes, a piece of popcorn arcing across the head of the person sitting in front of them.

'Sorry.' Shell winces when they turn to tut at them, patting Emma's back.

When she recovers she stares at Shell, her dark eyes wide. 'You're *what?*'

She says it so loudly that someone behind them shushes her.

'Talk during the trailers is acceptable,' Emma says, over

her shoulder, with a scowl, then turns back to Shell. 'Are you going to tell me what's going on before the film starts and I get kicked out for yelling at you?'

'I've been seeing Nick,' Shell says again, her nose wrinkling. *Don't get mad.*

But she does, popcorn spilling out of her box as she twists around in her seat to face her. 'I know you kissed, but I didn't know you were seeing each other. When?'

'Every night this week?'

'*Every night?*' Someone shushes her again and she ignores them. 'Are you kidding me?'

Shell shakes her head sheepishly.

'Why didn't you tell me?' she asks, as though it isn't obvious from the fact that she looks about ready to hurl the tub of popcorn at Shell. 'I thought you were meant to be taking it slow.'

That's true, but when Emma arches an eyebrow at her, something kicks at Shell. 'Dan Harper. Jason Crossley.' She counts off each one on her fingers. 'Ravi Singh. Luke Maxwell.'

'What do *they* have to do with anything?' Emma asks, her eyebrow even higher.

'I told you.' She jabs her ice cream at her. '*Every time.* I told you, but you never listened.'

'So?'

'So? I told you, Em, and you didn't listen, and when it inevitably went wrong, I never said I told you so. Not once. Because we're best friends and that's the deal. And, no, I don't know why Nick wants me now when he didn't want me then, but he does and I'm happy and I'm not saying you have to be happy for me as well, but you're my best friend, so that's the deal. That's what you signed up for.'

Emma's quiet for so long that Shell's sure she's going to call her an idiot and storm out.

But she doesn't.

She just nods. 'Okay.'

Shell nods back. 'Okay.'

By the time Duke & Sons closes the next evening, Shell is exhausted.

Happy exhausted.

Her heart fluttering at the thought of seeing Nick again in an hour.

'What's wrong with you?' Ricky asks, as Gary strides over to stand by the revolving door.

With that, the Beauty Hall is humming as everyone starts chatting about what they're up to tonight.

'Have fun at Hannigans,' Shell tells Becca and Soph, as they hurry out giggling, their coats already on.

They wave, but when Shell waves back, Ricky elbows her.

'Ow!' She winces. 'What was that for?'

'I asked you a question.'

'What?'

'What's wrong with you?'

'What do you mean?'

'You've been acting weird all day.'

'Have I?'

'Like now. You're cleaning your brushes, Shell. What's to be so happy about?'

'Nothing.' She swirls her bronzer brush into a folded-up piece of tissue and smiles. 'Just life.'

'Stop it!' Ricky snatches the brush from her and points it at her. 'You're freaking me out!'

'Who's freaking you out?' Denise asks, suddenly on the other side of the counter with Ricky's coat.

Today, her mandatory Duke & Sons white shirt is buttoned to the collar and teamed with a black tie. With her braids down, black cigarette trousers and leather jacket, Denise looks like she should be fronting an all-girl punk band.

'Shell!' Ricky tells her. 'She's being *weird*.'

'There's nothing's up with me,' Shell insists, the corners of her mouth betraying her.

'You're seeing someone.' Denise gasps, then turns to Ricky. 'She's seeing someone.'

Ricky glares at her, teeth bared. 'First of all, *how dare you*?' He jabs the brush at the space between them. 'And second of all, if you don't tell me who it is right now, I'm going to pull out all of your eyelashes.'

'It's not Callum, is it?' Denise asks, eyes wide.

That makes Ricky even more annoyed. 'It'd better not be Callum! I mean . . .' he stops to shrug at Denise then tilt his head at Shell '. . . congratulations if it is, but I'll never speak to you again.'

'Of course it's not Callum,' she shout-whispers.

'Who is it, then?' Denise pushes. 'Who's making you smile so much?'

'Yeah.' Ricky elbows her in the side. 'Spill, Smith!'

Shell dips her head and lowers her voice. 'Remember Nick Wallace?'

'Oh, my God.' Denise reaches over the counter to slap Ricky's arm. 'She bumped into him on Saturday night!'

'Yes!' Ricky points the powder brush at her, then at Shell. 'You called to tell Emma when we were in the pub!'

Denise slaps him again. 'How did we forget that?'

'Because Emma got us *completely wasted* that night?'

Denise winces. 'We're terrible friends.'

'No, you're not!' Shell waves a hand at her.

'So?' Ricky says, motioning at her with the powder brush to go on.

Shell tries to be cool, but can't stop herself grinning. 'We've been out four times this week.'

'*Four* times?' Ricky barks. '*That*'s why you haven't been coming to the pub after work!'

Denise looks betrayed. 'You said it was because you were working on that thing for your marketing course.'

'I know.' Shell feels awful. 'But I didn't want to say anything until I was sure.'

Denise softens, her dark eyes lighting up. 'So you're sure?'

'I guess. Things have been going great. He's kind and funny and keeps telling me that I'm hot.'

'Too right!' Ricky says, pulling a face at her as if to say, *As he should.*

'Yes! Yes! Yes!' Denise jumps up and down, clapping, her braids swinging back and forth. 'It's so romantic!' She stops to clasp her hands together and hold them to her chest with a long, dreamy sigh. 'It's like a movie! Your first love coming home from the big city for the first time since you left college, and you fall in love all over again.'

Ricky taps Shell on the nose with the powder brush, then grins. 'I'm so happy for you, Shell!'

It's the first time anyone has been and the relief brings tears to Shell's eyes. 'Thanks, guys.'

'When can we meet him?' Ricky points the brush at her again. 'Wait. It's Saturday, right? Isn't tonight your college reunion thing?'

'Yes!' Denise starts clapping again. 'Yes! In the Anchor?'

'About that,' Shell says carefully. She tries to smile, but it's more of a wince. 'I was going to ask you a favour.'

Denise stops clapping, her tone noticeably cooler. 'You don't want us to go to the Anchor tonight.'

'But we always go to the Anchor after work.' Ricky looks confused. 'Always.'

'I know.' Shell presses her hands together and holds them up. 'But *please*. Can you *please* not go tonight?'

He gapes at her, his lips parted.

'Just this once? *Please*, Ricky.'

'Why? Are you ashamed of us or something?'

'No!' Shell says, mortified that he would think that. 'God, no! Of course not! It's just that this thing with Nick is new so I don't know how to introduce him yet. Plus, all our old college friends will be there and that's going to be awkward. They're probably going to tease us about how they always said we were together and now we are and I guess . . .' She stops to suck in a breath and fan herself with her hand. 'I guess I'm just a bit overwhelmed and I can't take it if you're mad at me as well.'

'Shell,' Denise says softly, coming behind the counter to stroke her back, 'of course we're not mad at you. Why would we be mad at you?'

'For not telling you about Nick before now.'

'To be fair,' Ricky admits, 'we didn't tell you we were together for, like, a month.'

'Exactly!' Denise points at him. 'So who are we to get mad at you?'

'Well, Emma's mad at me.'

'She's not mad at you.' Ricky waves the powder brush at her. 'She's worried about you.'

'You spoke to her about this?'

'No! Of course not. But I know Emma well enough to see that she's not mad at you.'

Denise strokes Shell's back again. 'She just doesn't want you to get hurt.'

'Yeah, but what if I don't get hurt?' Shell looks between them. 'What if this is it? What if Nick really has changed? Wouldn't you want him to give me a chance if it was the other way round?'

'True,' Ricky concedes with a nod. 'I mean, we've all had that ex who dicked us around and wouldn't commit. I mean, that's the dream, isn't it? That they realise what a fool they were and come back to sweep us off our feet.'

Denise points at him. 'Now, *that*'s a movie!'

Chapter Sixteen

Shell kind of wishes she'd let Ricky and Denise come to the pub because Nick is on top form. Charming and funny and holding court with his stories about college, showing them all the scars and tattoos to prove it.

He doesn't leave her side all night, arm slung around her shoulders. It's all *Shell and I* this and *Shell and I* that, and every time someone mentions a bar or restaurant they've been to, he kisses her and says, *Let's go there.*

It's the most perfect evening that concludes with him insisting on walking her home, even though everyone else is going on to Hannigans, the pair of them giggling and holding hands like a couple of teenagers as they leave the pub.

When they turn onto the high street, Shell sees the glow of Duke & Sons ahead. There are three huge trucks parked outside and the Beauty Hall is teeming with people, Callum in the middle of it all, talking to a guy in a headset. Even from the other side of the street, she can see how stressed he is, his jaw clenched as the guy tells him something.

'What's going on in there?' Nick asks, gesturing across the road at the store.

'Callum's hired a production company to film some stuff for YouTube, apparently.'

'Who's he hired?' Nick chuckles as they stroll past. 'Martin Scorsese?'

She wouldn't be surprised.

Seriously, though, it does seem very professional for a YouTube video. There are lights and monitors and massive white screens, most of the people inside walking around in red T-shirts with CREW written across the front in white. When a man passes the window pushing the sort of camera you'd usually see on a film set, she almost laughs.

No wonder Callum looks so stressed.

She doesn't care, though, immediately distracted as Nick suggests they go away for the weekend.

They talk about it for the rest of the walk home, excitedly batting suggestions back and forth.

Ice skating at the Rockefeller Center.

Weihnachtspunsch at a Christmas market in Vienna.

New Year's Eve in Reykjavík.

'Let's go everywhere,' he tells her, when they finally stop outside her house, then kisses her clean off her feet.

Is this it? Shell wonders, as she falls asleep that night. *Is this what it feels like to be sure?*

And that's how it goes, the pair of them inseparable.

Nick always answers his phone when she calls, always texts back. He double texts. Triple texts. Tells her that he misses her. He's the first person she speaks to when she's in the warm embrace of her bed, listening to the twins thundering down the stairs. And he's the last person she speaks to at night, when she's weak and groggy and it feels like she's walking around and around the edge of a swimming pool, and if she makes one misstep, she'll fall in.

Before she knows it, it's December and the air is whispering with the promise of Christmas. There's a wreath on every door and a tree in every window, and she gets it then, why Old Mr Duke loves this time of year so much.

It's nothing but sparkle and magic and joy.

Shell doesn't know how she does it, but she's spent the last month juggling it all: work, Nick, her family, her friends, her online marketing course, filming with Mia. She even found time to go to London for ART's 2021 showcase yesterday, which was at a painfully cool gallery with no name in Spitalfields.

Nick insisted on going with her, amusing himself with buying records while she was at the showcase, before meeting her on Brick Lane for a curry. He got so wasted on Kingfisher beer that she had to drive his Mini Cooper back to Ostley, which was *terrifying*, given that she hadn't been behind a wheel since she took her driving test last year.

She was furious with him but, luckily, it was after midnight so the roads were clear, and when he passed out in the passenger seat, he looked so adorable that she couldn't stay mad at him.

Besides, she can't.

It's his birthday today: 5 December.

I'm an almost Christmas baby, he keeps saying, and she lets him, even though it's nowhere near.

Shell doesn't know what it is. Maybe it's because it's

the first Saturday of December so listening to Mariah Carey's 'All I Want For Christmas Is You' all day at the counter feels more appropriate this week than it did last. Even Becca and Soph haven't complained about it, dancing with Ricky every time he got his bronzer brush out to give his client a show.

Whatever the reason, she finds herself texting Emma at lunch: *Nick's having some birthday drinks in the Anchor tonight. Fancy coming?*

She replies immediately. *What time?*

After six?

See you in there xx

She waits until the store has closed and Denise is at the counter to do the same. 'Nick's having some birthday drinks in the Anchor tonight—'

'Yes!' Ricky doesn't let her finish, turning to Denise with his hands up. 'Okay. This is it.'

'Let's do this!' Denise high-fives him over the counter, then asks Shell, 'What about Emma?'

'I've already texted her.'

'How do I look?' Ricky snatches the magnifying-mirror off the counter. 'Do I look shiny?'

'You look lovely,' Shell tells him, then thumbs over her shoulder. 'I'm gonna change.'

She returns a few minutes later to whoops and cheers from Ricky and Denise.

He's doing her makeup and turns to Shell with a shimmy. 'Hello, legs!'

Denise points at Shell's black playsuit. 'Is that real leather?'

'Of course not!' she scoffs.

'I like it.' He points the crease brush he's holding at her. 'Very rock and roll.'

'It's so weird seeing you in black, though,' Denise says, as Shell dumps her stuff on the counter.

'Weird?' Shell stares at Ricky's ART uniform. 'I wear black every day.'

'Yeah, only for work. You always look so colourful when you go out.'

Shell studies her reflection in the mirror behind the counter. 'Don't you like it?'

'No, I do!' Denise assures her. 'Of course I do. I love it. What is it? A dress?'

'It's a playsuit.'

Ricky turns back to finish Denise's eyeshadow. 'Shell loves a playsuit.'

'Oh, yeah. I love nothing more than getting naked in a pub toilet.'

She hears someone clear their throat and turns to find Callum standing behind her.

'Good evening, Shell . . .'

'Callum,' she says, saying a little prayer that he didn't hear what she just said. Judging by the way the corners of his mouth are twitching, he obviously did.

'Hey, Callum,' Ricky and Denise say, clearly trying not to laugh as they wave at him.

He lets himself smile now. 'Where are you guys off to this evening?'

'Oh, just to the pub,' Shell says casually.

'It's Shell's boyfriend's birthday,' Ricky tells him.

'Oh, yes. Nick.' He says *Nick* like he says *influencer*. Like it isn't a real word.

Shell turns back to Ricky and Denise to find them glaring at her, no doubt wondering how Callum knows about him. 'We were just leaving. Weren't we, guys?'

'No need to hurry,' Callum tells her, as she raises her eyebrows at Ricky and Denise, motioning to them to wrap it up. 'I was just checking to see if the team had arrived to set up for tomorrow.'

'We'll get out of your way,' she says, ushering Ricky and Denise out of the store.

Emma meets them outside the Anchor and jumps on Shell as they approach, kissing her cheek.

'This is it, guys!' She holds her gloved hands up at Ricky and Denise.

The three of them high-five and Shell *really* hopes Nick didn't see that. 'Can you guys just be cool for once?'

'I *am* cool.' Ricky looks appalled. 'I hung out with Dua Lipa at London Pride last year.'

'You didn't *hang out* with Dua Lipa,' Denise reminds him. 'You gave her a chewing gum.'

Emma points at him. 'She didn't even ask for it. You just gave it to her, like a toilet attendant.'

'Still!' he barks. 'Have *you* given Dua Lipa chewing gum? No, Emma Russo, you have not.'

'Can you stop saying Dua Lipa!' Shell presses her hand to her forehead. 'I'm really stressed out!'

'Don't be stressed,' Emma soothes, hand on her back, guiding her to the door. 'We'll be good, I promise.'

They push through it, tumbling in and stopping in the middle of the pub.

'Where is he?' Ricky asks, scanning the bar with the focus of a heat-seeking missile.

'Found him,' Denise says. 'Dirty hair and skinny jeans one o'clock.'

Shell looks up to see who she's pointing at and, to her horror, it's Nick. 'Be nice,' she says, through her teeth, as they march her over.

'Hey, Nick,' Shell says, when they stop in front of him, which prompts a chorus of *Hey, Nick* behind her.

'Hey, guys!' he says, recoiling slightly at being confronted by all four of them at once.

Emma doesn't wait to be introduced and sticks her hand out. 'I'm Emma. Emma Russo.'

Then they introduce themselves to him, all at once, Nick shaking their hands, clearly terrified.

Terrified and tipsy.

She doesn't know how long he's been here, but she's guessing that bottle of Peroni in his hand isn't the first.

'So lovely to meet you all at last,' he says, with a crisp smile.

Shell notes the *at last* and ignores it as she steps forward to kiss him on the mouth. 'Happy birthday, babe!'

He hugs her a little too tightly, nose in her hair, then lets go.

When she steps back, he thumbs at the bar. 'Do you guys want a drink?'

'Don't you dare!' Emma holds her finger up to him. 'It's your birthday.' She gets her purse out of her bag and says to the others, behind her. 'Why don't you guys find a table and I'll get them in?'

The pub's so busy that they have to sit in the beer garden. If it was any other cold night, they would have had one, standing by the fireplace, then left.

They certainly would not sit in the beer garden with the smokers, especially in December.

But they can't – it's Nick's birthday – so they huddle around a table, under a gas lamp that is somehow so hot that it's burning Shell's scalp, but not warming her anywhere else, and sip their wine.

Nick's friend arrived when Emma was at the bar, so he went to say hello and they haven't seen him since. The Peroni Emma got him is still sitting untouched on the table between them.

'He'll be out in a minute,' Shell says, trying not to look at it.

But an hour later they're on their second bottle of wine and there's still no sign of him. Shell can feel the veneer of politeness slipping as they exhaust all avenues of small-talk that don't lead to Nick. Work. Christmas. The guy at the table next to theirs who kind of looks like Tom Hardy but isn't, no matter what Emma says.

Even Shell is struggling, so cold now that she isn't

shivering any more, she's straight up shuddering. 'He'll be out in a minute, I'm sure,' she says, aiming for nonchalant and landing just shy of desperate.

They keep sipping their wine.

Ricky and Denise do, at least.

Emma just glares at Nick through the glass doors into the pub. 'Likes a drink, doesn't he?'

'Em,' Denise says through her teeth.

'What?' She shrugs.

With that, Emma stops trying.

Shell feels the shift immediately.

'Do you know how many shots he's knocked back while we've been sitting here?'

Shell's too hot then, her whole face burning. 'It's his birthday, Em.'

'There's always something, isn't there?' Emma won't look at her, only ahead at Nick laughing in the pub.

So Shell looks at Ricky and Denise, waiting for them to back her up, but they don't.

'They agree with me,' Emma says tartly. 'We've discussed it.'

Shell stares at them, her eyes wide. 'You've discussed it?'

Denise shoots Emma a look.

'So? What?' Shell looks around the table. 'You think Nick has a drinking problem?'

'Of course not!' Denise insists. 'But you have to admit, everything you do revolves around booze.'

'Oh, *come on*.' Shell throws her hands up. 'We all like a drink.'

'Not every night has to be a bender, Shell,' Denise says quietly.

She feels it like a slap. 'What's *that* supposed to mean?'

'It *means*,' Ricky joins in, 'that it's affecting your work, Shell. You were late this morning.'

'For the first time in eleven years,' she reminds him.

'Exactly! You're never late. But since you started seeing Nick, you've been getting to work later and later until this morning you turned up with your hair still wet from the shower!'

Shell snatches her wine glass off the table.

'And you weren't wearing any makeup!' he adds. 'I almost called the police!'

'Ricky, stop it. You're being melodramatic.'

'Am I?' He presses his hands to his chest and leans forward. '*Am I?* You're going out drinking *every night* until two, three in the morning and it's catching up with you. You're not used to it.'

'We don't drink *every time* we go out.'

'Don't you?' Denise taps in then, obviously sensing that Ricky's about to lose his temper. 'Have you ever gone out with Nick and done something that didn't involve booze?'

'Of course we have!'

'Really?' Denise tilts her head at her. 'Whatever you guys do, you don't *always* end up in the pub?'

They don't.

Do they?

'If it's something that involves drinking, like going to a gig or to that pub quiz you two go to at the George on

Thursday nights where you *always* cheat,' Denise goes on, holding up her wine glass to stop Shell denying it, 'then Nick is all over it. But if it's taking the twins to the cinema or coming ice skating with us, he's not interested.'

'That is *not* true, Denise.'

'It is.' Ricky backs her up, his white wig bobbing as he points across the table at her.

'So what are you saying? That Nick can't be with me unless he's wasted?'

'No!' Denise looks mortified. 'We're just worried about him.'

'And you,' Ricky adds, with a frown.

'You're being suspiciously quiet!' Shell turns to glare at Emma. 'Given you started all this!'

She softens, her shoulders falling as she tilts her head at Shell. 'I'm sorry, but you know how I feel about him.'

'I certainly do. You've made it painfully clear that you hate him.'

'I don't hate him. I don't even know him. At least, not the Nick you know. I only know this Nick.'

'And who is *this Nick*?'

'The Nick who's just lost his mum and is out of his mind with grief.'

'Where are you going?' Emma asks, when Shell stands up and snatches the bottle of Peroni off the table.

'I'm going to check on my alcoholic boyfriend.'

She can hear them calling after her as she storms into the pub, but doesn't look back.

Chapter Seventeen

'There she is!' Nick holds out his arms with an unfocused smile. 'Where've you been?'

'Where've I been?' Shell asks, but he's not listening as he pulls her into a huge hug, nuzzling her neck.

He reeks of whisky and weed, which she didn't even know he still smoked, but that explains why he keeps disappearing. She knows it's his birthday, but why tonight? Why did he have to revert to being a sloppy, surly teenage dirtbag tonight?

He reaches around to squeeze her arse, then slap it, and that's enough.

She shoves the bottle of Peroni at him. Luckily, it's so cold outside that it hasn't gone warm.

'I've been waiting for *you* in the beer garden for the last hour.'

'Oh. Sorry,' he says, but he doesn't sound sorry at all. 'But I didn't want to disturb you.'

'Disturb me?'

'Yeah, not when you were with your friends.'

Wait, Shell thinks. *Is* he *mad at* me?

'You put everyone else before me, even on my birthday. Don't you want to spend time with me?'

'Of course I want to spend time with you, Nick. I—'

'No, you don't,' he interrupts, with a petulant huff. 'All you want to do is hang out with your precious friends.'

If he's trying to piss her off, it's working.

'You haven't spoken to me since you got here.' He huffs again. 'You've just been with them all night.'

'Nick.' She stops to take a deep breath, trying to keep cool as she points to the door out to the beer garden. 'You told me that you'd come and find me when you'd said hello to your mate. Who,' she holds up a finger before he can interrupt again then jabs it at her chest, 'you didn't introduce *me* to, did you?'

'Oh. What?' He holds his arms out. 'So I'm not allowed to hang out with my friends now?'

Shell balls her hands into fists and holds them up to him. 'Nick, you just said—'

'You know what?' He waves her away. 'Forget it, Shell. Just go.'

She stares at him, completely disoriented.

'Just go, Shell. You don't want to be here, do you? So you may as well go,' he tells her, pointing the bottle of beer towards the door out to the street, the hum of chatter noticeably dimmer as everyone in the pub stares at them.

Or maybe it's that Nick is shouting now, so he's all she can hear.

'I mean,' he adds, with a sniff and a sneer, 'you never have time for me, so why would you tonight?'

'Never have time for you?' Shell tries not to raise her

214

voice as well. 'Nick, I've seen you *four nights* this week.'

'I didn't see you last weekend, though, did I?'

'You did!' Shell says, her fists balled so tightly now she can feel her nails cutting into the palms of her hands. 'I was working on Saturday, then we had a drink before Soph's birthday, which you were invited to, by the way,' she reminds him, 'but you didn't want to come because you said you didn't want to go to Hannigans with a load of teenagers, remember? Then we had a roast in that pub in Church Cabham on Sunday.'

'I didn't see you that night, though, did I?'

'Because I promised to take the twins to the cinema, which *again* you were invited to, but you hate Pixar.' *Who hates Pixar films?* she almost says, but bites her tongue as another thought skids through her head. *Because he can't drink his way through a Pixar film. Not in front of my little brothers and sisters, anyway.* She tries to bat it away, but it takes hold, sinking in deeper, like a splinter.

'Well.' He sweeps his hair out of his face with his hand then fists it. 'You never call me.'

'Nick. I *literally* speak to you seventeen times a day.'

'Not during the day, you don't.'

'I *always* call you when I'm on break.'

'Fucking work,' he mutters, under his breath. 'All you do is work.'

'Okay. Fair enough.' She can't very well argue with that. 'Six days a week is a lot.'

He pulls a face at her. 'You'd think you were a fucking paediatric surgeon the way you go on, Shell, but you literally mess about with lipstick all day.'

Everything around her swirls so suddenly that he swims out of focus for a second or two.

'Oh don't look at me, like that, Shell! It's hardly a career, is it? Working on a makeup counter for minimum wage.'

She hears him call after her as she heads back towards the doors to the beer garden. She doesn't know how, though: her legs are so unsteady she feels like she's under water, everything blurry and out of reach.

'Shell!' he barks, following her out. 'Where are you going?'

She doesn't answer – can't answer, can't speak, can't catch her breath – her hands trembling when she gets to where she was sitting with Emma, Ricky and Denise and grabs her bag from the table.

'Shell!' he barks again, when she doesn't respond. 'Are you leaving?'

She can hear her friends asking the same thing, but all she can manage is, 'I have to go.'

'What? *Now?*'

She can't look at him, pulling away when he reaches for the sleeve of her coat.

'Where you going?' He snorts. 'Got some sort of lipstick emergency?'

He laughs – not at his joke, but at *her* – and there's a collective gasp from the table.

With that, something finally gives way and she lifts her chin to look him in the eye. 'Fuck you, Nick.'

There's another collective gasp as everyone in the beer garden turns to look at them this time.

'Good girl!' she hears Emma say, as Shell charges away.

'Shell!' Emma calls, heels slapping loudly on the pavement behind her.

She stops and turns to face her. 'I don't want to talk about it, Em.'

Emma stops and does the same, as though Shell's a cornered cat who'll swipe at her if she gets too close.

'Okay,' Emma says carefully. 'We don't have to talk about it. We can get a curry, or something.'

She smiles, and Shell wishes she'd stop being so nice and just say, *I told you so.* Shell knows she wants to. 'I'm fine, Em.'

'No, you're not.'

'I just need a minute.'

Shell needs more than a minute. She needs to go back in time to Halloween and leave the Anchor ten minutes earlier so she didn't see Nick that night in the rain. If she had, he would have remained her infuriating adorable friend who never loved her back and whom she thinks about when she listens to Miles Davis.

'I'll come with you.' Emma thumbs over her shoulder at the pub. 'Just let me grab my stuff.'

'No.' She tugs her bag back onto her shoulder. 'I need to be on my own for a bit.'

'Shell, wait.' Emma grabs the sleeve of her coat as Shell tries to leave. When she turns back to look at her, Emma smiles again, but it's much sadder this time as she clutches Shell's arm. 'We don't have to talk about it, I promise, but I can't let you leave without reminding you how much I love you. Ricky and Denise as well.'

Shell can't look at her, shrugging her off and crossing her arms.

'We weren't trying to attack you earlier. I swear, Shell. We're just worried.'

'Well, you were right.' She unfolds her arms. 'He's an arsehole.'

'I don't think he is, actually.'

Then it's so quiet that she can hear 'Fairytale of New York' playing in the pub. It's the only Christmas song Nick can abide, and when she wonders if he's in there, singing along, Shell suddenly feels very, very sad.

'He needs time,' Emma continues. 'You have to give him the time and space to work his way through this, through his grief.'

'And in the meantime?' she asks, her chin trembling. 'What about me? About *us*?'

Emma doesn't say anything, but she doesn't have to because Shell knows.

She knows.

Chapter Eighteen

S hell doesn't know where she's going, just that she needs to go. She promises to text Emma later, then heads through Ostley Square, past the big lit-up Christmas tree, towards the high street. She walks until she sees the light of Duke & Sons ahead of her.

Before she knows it, she's there, on the pavement outside the revolving door, the clock over it permanently at seven twenty and the bright windows either side, the Ferris wheel turning steadily on the left and the ginger-bread house, with its white frosted roof and fake gum drops, on the right.

She's safe now.

'Excuse me, love,' a man says, slipping past her to push through the revolving door. He's carrying a coil of thick black cables and her heart sinks.

She forgot the production crew were setting up for tomorrow and curses. She'd hoped to have the store to herself, desperate for the stillness of it. The peace. The glossy floors and clean glass counters. The old staircase that groans with each step and the rolls and rolls of fabric, standing to attention in Haberdashery.

She needs that right now. To soak up the silence as she

wanders from floor to floor, fingers trailing along the silk scarves in the Scarf Hall and the solid, steady sideboards in Furniture so she can gather her strength before she has to go home and pretend that nothing's wrong.

But when she walks in, it's chaos. There are people – strangers – everywhere.

'Shell,' she hears someone say, and Callum, in his neat grey suit, is in front of her.

'Hey.'

'Are you okay?' he asks.

No, she almost says, but doesn't have to when he frowns.

He reaches for her, hands cupping her elbows. 'Are you crying?'

'No,' she says.

But she is.

Callum leads her to Old Mr Duke's office.

His office now, she supposes, but it will always be Old Mr Duke's.

He takes her coat, then gestures at the high-backed brown leather chair behind the desk. 'Would you like to sit in the big chair?' he asks, with a warm smile.

It's the only thing that remains from Old Mr Duke's original office, the one that used to be on the top floor. He'd stopped using it by the time Shell started working at Duke & Sons, but she's seen photos of it, of the grand wood-panelled walls and the large desk sitting on the larger rug.

This office is infinitely less glamorous. It's grim. It's as grey as a prison cell, the opposite of the welcoming warmth of the store. Shell feels very sad at the thought of Old Mr Duke sitting here at the Formica desk with nothing to look at but a row of metal filing cabinets topped with catalogues and a miserable spider plant.

Her pleather playsuit rubs comically against Old Mr Duke's chair as Shell sits on it. Callum has the grace not to comment on it, though, as he hangs her coat, grabs a less glamorous folding chair from beside the water-cooler and sets it down at the end of the desk, to her left. He unbuttons his suit jacket and sits, crossing his legs neatly.

'Would you like to talk about it?' he asks, when she doesn't say anything.

She can't.

He doesn't want to hear about her mess of a love life.

Besides, she's just been promoted, hasn't she? Shell wants him to think she deserved it, that she's focused and professional and an excellent ambassador for both ART and the store. She wants him to look at her and think she has it together.

'I'm okay,' she says, with a sob, resting her elbows on the desk. 'I just need a minute.'

Pull yourself together, Smith, she tells herself. *Don't do this.*

She digs the heels of her palms into her eyes to stop the tears making their escape, but it's too late, her shoulders shaking as it all spills out of her in a miserable, uncontainable rush.

'Shell,' he says gently, so gently that it's even harder to stop crying.

'Don't be nice to me,' she sobs. 'Please don't be nice to me.'

He waits for her to finish, and when she looks up, he tugs the handkerchief from his jacket pocket. 'Thanks,' she says, with another sob, taking it from him.

'Open the bottom drawer on the right,' he says, when her breathing begins to settle.

Shell does so, to find a green glass bottle. She takes it out, glancing at the label before she hands it to him. It's Scottish, she thinks – whisky, she thinks – but it says *46.2% vol.*, which is all that matters.

'There should be a couple of glasses in there as well,' he tells her.

She finds two heavy crystal tumblers.

'What happened?' he asks, as Shell puts them on the desk between them.

She can't look at him. 'Please don't be nice to me,' she says again.

'I'm not being nice, I'm being nosy.'

She actually manages a chuckle as she catches another tear with the silk handkerchief.

'It's nothing.' She sniffs, wiping her nose. 'It's stupid.'

'Stupid *haha* or stupid you need a lawyer?'

She laughs again.

'Look, Shell, just tell me so I can decide whether or not it's worth wasting this *very nice* bottle of whisky on it.' When she doesn't say anything, just blows her nose in his silk handkerchief, he grimaces. 'That's Hermès, by the way.'

She squeaks, her lips parted in horror.

'It's fine.' He waves her hand away when she tries to give it back. 'Keep it.'

Nice, Shell.

He probably only offered it to her because he thought she'd use it to dab the corners of her eyes delicately.

He doesn't seem bothered, though. 'Now. Am I pouring this or what?'

'I don't know.'

'Is it Nick?'

She nods glumly.

He puts the bottle down. 'This is an Ardbeg nineteen-year-old Traigh Bhan. I'm not wasting it on a vegan.'

'I think we broke up,' she finally admits.

The relief when she finally says it out loud – to him, of all people – startles her.

Callum raises his eyebrows, then pours some of the whisky into one of the glasses. 'Fine.'

She snatches it as he pours for himself, knocks it back in one, then immediately regrets it as it tries to come back up. *Oh, no,* she thinks, as she clamps her eyes shut, trying to keep it down. She waits a beat and, mercifully, it works. When she's satisfied that she's not going to vomit all over the desk, she opens her eyes again. 'That's not bad, actually. More, please.'

'Try to sip it this time,' he warns, as he refills her glass. 'Or you could just down it in one like a two-for-one sambuca in Wetherspoons,' he mutters, as he watches her knock it back.

'Okay.' He takes the glass from her and puts the cork stopper back into the bottle. 'That's your lot.'

It's enough, though: her whole body feels warm and loose and noticeably less heartachy.

'Nick said all I do is mess around with lipstick for minimum wage.'

'Excuse me?'

Callum looks so horrified that it makes her feel better. Like maybe she didn't overreact after all. 'I officially give up,' she tells him. 'I've spent the last nine years convinced he was the one.'

'Come, come now, Shell Smith. You can't let one vegan put you off.'

'You don't understand. Nick was the last in a long, *long* line of hopeless relationships. There was Zack. He was my university boyfriend, even though I was only there a year. He was in a band.'

'Of course he was.' Callum is swirling his whisky around in his glass.

'Then when I came home from uni, there was Dylan, the poet.'

'A poet?' Callum's face goes pink from trying not to laugh.

'We broke up because he went to Goa to Eat, Pray, Love it and never came back.'

Callum gives in to it then, laughing, loud and bright. 'I'm sorry.' He holds his hand up when he looks at her again, tears in his eyes. 'I'm so sorry.'

'It's fine! Laugh it up, Duke! But this is my actual life.'

'I'm sorry.' He tries not to laugh again and fails.

'Then, last summer, I decided to give online dating a go. Are you ready for this?'

'I'm ready,' he says, clearly trying to keep a straight face.

'Because I don't think you are.'

Callum nods. 'I'm ready, Shell Smith.'

'Well, first, there was Louis. He turned out to be someone Ricky knows from the drag circuit who was only using me for my ART discount. Then there was Johan, the mortician, who wanted to do *my* makeup.'

Callum snorts and tries to style it out as a cough, covering his mouth with his fist.

'After that, I decided to lie on my profile and say that I worked in finance. And that's when I met Jonathan.' Shell pretends to swoon. 'Jonathan took me to Pizza Express and asked me why I was on Tinder if I have a fiancé.'

It takes Callum a moment, but when he makes the connection, he actually howls.

'And he still went out with you?'

Shell tilts her head at him with a proud smile. 'And he still went out with me!'

'Je-sus.' Callum laughs, the sound enough to make Shell laugh as well.

'So you can see why I thought I was on to a winner with Nick, then?'

'Did you meet him on Tinder as well?'

'Oh, no. We've known each other since college, but we were just friends.'

He waits for Shell to elaborate.

'Seriously. Nothing happened. But that's the thing, Callum.' She points at him. 'That's the thing, isn't it? The thrill for me was in the anticipation. The waiting. *Does he like me? Doesn't he like me?*' Her shoulders slump. 'But we got together and *look*! It all went to shit within a month.'

'You can do *much* better, Shell Smith,' he tells her, taking another sip of whisky.

She warms at that, then immediately feels awful.

'It's not his fault.'

'It's not?'

'His mother just died.'

Callum raises his eyebrows. 'Oh.'

She waits for Callum to agree with her, but when he doesn't, just looks into the glass in his hand, she wonders if he's thinking about his father. Then she remembers what Emma said outside the Anchor about how you never really get over losing a parent. The expression on Callum's face confirms that she's right and she feels even worse.

'I need to give him time, don't I?' Shell says.

Callum is still gazing into the glass at what's left of his whisky. 'I think you probably do.'

So what now? *Do I wait?* Shell thinks. *How long does it take to get over your mum dying?*

'How long did it take you to get over your dad dying?' Shell hears herself say it and almost runs out of the office.

Did she really just say that out loud?

'Oh, God. I'm sorry, Callum. I'm sorry. I'm sorry.' She covers her face with her hands again.

'It's okay. Come on,' he says, reaching over to tug them away. 'Let me see,' he says, pretending to think about it. 'It was twenty-five years in June, so I'm thinking I should be over it by . . .' he stops to count on his fingers '. . . two o'clock next Wednesday.'

She shuts her eyes and exhales through her nose. 'I'm sorry.'

'Stop saying sorry.'

'I'm an idiot.'

'You're not an idiot.'

'I am. I'm a big, drunk idiot.'

'You're not a big, drunk idiot,' he says, then tilts his head from side to side. 'I mean, you *are* drunk, but I am partially to blame for that for plying you with three-hundred-pound whisky.'

'Three hundred *what now*?' Shell gapes at him. 'You spent *three hundred pounds* on whisky? Thank God you're pretty, Callum Duke, because you do not have one *lick* of sense.'

She waits for him to laugh, but he doesn't.

'What?' she asks.

Then he smiles. 'You think I'm pretty?'

She tries not to blush and fails miserably, her whole face *burning*.

The office door opens then and a man in a red CREW T-shirt sweeps in. 'Mr Duke. Have you seen Mike?'

Callum turns to frown at him. 'No, what's wrong?'

'There's been a bit of an incident.'

Chapter Nineteen

'Jesus Christ,' Callum mutters, holding out his arm to stop Shell going any further when they follow the guy out into the Beauty Hall.

Callum looks up, his jaw clenched, so she does the same and gasps.

There it is, the red-and-white-striped hot-air balloon that was hanging in the middle of the store by the wooden staircase, now tipping precariously on its side with one fewer polar bear.

And with that, Shell goes from tipsy and lightheaded to suddenly, painfully sober.

Callum turns to the guy, who immediately takes two steps back. '*How* did this happen?'

'The thing came off the hook.'

The thing being one of the four long wires securing the hot-air balloon to the banisters on the second floor. It's now only secured by three, hence the polar bear tragedy. When Shell looks down, she sees one of the babies on its back on the floor, its little legs in the air.

'Right!' Callum raises his hands. 'I want everyone out of here *right now* in case this thing falls.'

They all stop what they're doing, some lifting their headsets as they turn towards the sound of his voice.

'*Now!*' he bellows, when they don't move, clapping his hands together. 'Come on!'

They all jump, then scamper away, the Beauty Hall a blur.

As soon as the area clears, Shell sees her: the woman sitting on the bottom step of the staircase.

She's not that much older than she is – late twenties, maybe in her early thirties – with hair parted in the middle to reveal a sweet, heart-shaped face.

A sweet, heart-shaped face that betrays she's in *a lot* of pain.

'Oh, no,' Shell murmurs, running over to her.

Then Callum is there, crouching in front of the woman with a fierce frown. 'Are you okay?'

She's clutching her shoulder, her forehead creased as she looks at the baby polar bear. 'I jumped out of the way just in time,' she says, then laughs. 'What a way to go, eh? Death by polar bear.'

She laughs again, but Callum doesn't. He looks like he's about to be sick.

'Where does it hurt?' he asks, hands hovering as if he wants to touch her, but is too scared to do so.

'My shoulder.'

'Just your shoulder?'

She nods.

'Okay,' Callum says, his cheeks pink again. 'Just breathe, okay?'

Before Shell can ask herself who she is, she hears someone calling across the Beauty Hall.

'Hazel!' She looks back as a man in a creased black suit jacket with a *Jaws* T-shirt underneath runs towards them. 'Hazel! Someone get the medic!'

'I'm fine, Mike,' the woman tells him, when he squats in front of her next to Callum. 'It's nothing.'

He puts his hand on her knee. 'What happened?'

'I almost got killed by a polar bear.' She laughs, still clutching her shoulder.

'It's my fault.' Callum presses his hand to his forehead and Shell's sure he's going to be sick this time.

'No, it's ours,' Mike admits sheepishly. 'We hit it with a boom mic earlier.' He looks up to where the hot-air balloon is clinging by three of the four wires. 'I thought it was okay but we must have knocked one of the wires loose.'

Callum is visibly relieved as Mike turns back to Hazel. 'You're not even supposed to be here tonight. You're not due on set until tomorrow morning.'

'I know. But it's such an early call that I thought I'd come in tonight and get set up so I'm ready to go in the morning.' She shakes her head. 'This is what I get for being organised.'

'What were you doing back here? Your station is in the front of the store by the window.'

'Being nosy,' she admits, with a naughty smile. 'I haven't been here since I was a kid.'

Mike looks relieved that she's lucid enough to remember that. 'Has anything changed?'

'There are no more sweets in the kids' department, which sucks.'

'I miss them as well,' Callum admits. 'Especially the jelly beans.'

'Mike!' Shell hears someone call as a tall man in a dark green uniform approaches.

'Greg, thank God!' Mike says, when he sees him, standing up to clasp his shoulder.

'What happened?' Greg asks, with a deep frown.

Mike points up at the hot-air balloon, then down at the baby polar bear.

It's obviously explanation enough, because Greg squats next to Callum.

'Hi, Hazel. I'm Greg, the paramedic for the production,' he says, putting the bag he's holding on the floor beside him. 'Is it your shoulder? Can you tell me again what happened?'

Callum stands up to let Greg do his thing and walks over to Shell. 'Can we . . .' He trails off, nodding towards the concealed door to the back of house.

As soon as they're through it, and in the long, dim corridor, he lets out a heavy sigh.

'Shell, I have to tell you something.'

She immediately stiffens. 'What?'

'The bottle of whisky.'

She nods.

'It was a gift,' Callum's gaze dips away from hers, 'from Kevin Costley.'

'Kevin Costley of Costley's of Ostley?'

It's quite a mouthful. How she gets it out without

laughing, she doesn't know, but Callum looks so concerned that it suddenly isn't funny.

'Why did Kevin Costley give you a three-hundred-pound bottle of whisky?'

Callum hesitates, then says, 'He's trying to woo me.'

'Oh,' Shell says, trying to be super-calm and casual. 'I didn't know you were, you know . . . woo-able?'

Ricky was right.

It takes Callum a second, but when he realises what she's saying, he laughs.

'No!' He relaxes at that, laughing again. 'I meant woo me in a strictly professional sense.'

'Why is he trying to woo you?' she asks, but he doesn't have to say because she already knows.

'He knows we're in trouble,' he finally admits.

Shell stiffens again.

'He's been trying to buy this place for *years*,' Callum says, 'but my grandfather won't sell. Now I'm here, I think Mr Costley assumes I'll be an easy touch.'

Are you? Shell thinks.

'I'd never sell this place, though,' he says, reading her mind. 'And I certainly wouldn't sell it to someone like Kevin Costley. The man is vile.'

The unfettered disgust on his face leaves her in no doubt that he's telling the truth.

'Is the store really in that much trouble, Callum?'

'Yes. *No*,' he adds, when Shell's eyes widen. 'The store's broke, but I'm not, so as long as I have anything to do with it, we'll be fine.' He stops to exhale and pinch the bridge of his nose with his fingers. He looks exhausted.

'The trouble is, my grandfather doesn't want me spending all my money on the store.'

Shell's confused. 'So why did he ask for your help?'

'I think he thought we could chuck fifty grand at the place and everything would be okay.'

'So what's it going to take, then?'

'Most, if not all, of what I made when I sold Hannah Banana.'

Shell has to lean against the wall so she doesn't fall over.

Callum does the same, his arms crossed. 'I don't care, though. It's just money. I can make more. This place, though, doesn't have many more chances, which is why I lied.'

'Lied about what?'

'About the filming.' He pauses and he looks ill again. 'It's not for YouTube. It's a movie.'

Shell goes from confused to delighted. 'A movie?'

'Yeah. One of those cheesy Christmas ones. Mike's the director.'

'First of all.' She pushes back from the wall to stand up. 'Those Christmas films are not *cheesy*. Well,' she concedes, tilting her head from side to side, 'they are, but that's part of their charm.'

Callum doesn't seem convinced.

'And second of all, that's amazing! What's it about?'

'The usual.' He makes a show of rolling his eyes. 'The girl from the big city has to move back home when her PR firm goes bust and gets a job at the makeup counter of the local department store. Her fiancé ends things with her, but just when she thinks all is lost, she bumps into her high-school boyfriend and they fall in love all over again.'

'Yes!' Shell clasps her hands to her chest, sighing dreamily. 'Denise is going to love it!'

'You can't tell her!' he yelps.

'Don't worry. Denise isn't going to tell anyone.'

'Just her boyfriend, Ricky.'

True.

'No one can find out about this, Shell.'

'But why?'

'Because if my grandfather finds out, he will actually kill me dead.'

'But it's great publicity for the store.'

'*I know*. Plus, they're paying us a *fortune* to use it.'

Shell's eyes widen. *Oh, really?*

'Which is great,' he adds. 'Because that's money we can invest back into the store.'

'So why don't you tell Old Mr Duke, then? That's what he wants, right? For you not to use your own money.'

'Listen,' he says, 'I know my grandfather. Once the film is done and he sees Duke & Sons on the telly, he'll be *thrilled*. But if I told him now, he'd demand to be across what's going on and will spend the entire time stressing that something's going to happen to the store . . . and, well, he's not wrong, is he?'

When he raises his right hand at the door out to the Beauty Hall, Shell tries not to laugh.

'So, we just need to make it from now until the Sunday before Christmas without *this lot* wrecking the place.'

'Don't worry,' Shell assures him. 'They know what

they're doing. These companies film in all kinds of locations. Museums. Stately homes.'

He raises an eyebrow as if to say, *Are you sure?*

'They've been using this place to film for, what, a month?'

Callum nods.

'Well, every Monday morning I come in and you would never even know they'd been here.'

'Yeah, because I'm the one running around peeling gaffer tape off the floor.'

'Either way, it's working, right? As long as they leave the hot-air balloon alone you might get away with it.'

He groans and covers his face with a hand. 'How am I going to fix that at ten o'clock on a Saturday night?'

'Balloon's fixed,' Mike says, pushing open the door and stopping half in, half out. 'Sorry about that, Cal.'

Callum looks so relieved, Shell's sure he's going to cry. 'Thank you.'

'No worries. It's the least we can do, given we broke it. Anyway.' He slaps the doorframe. 'We're going to call it a day. Hazel's okay. Greg thinks she's just dislocated her shoulder, so I've sent the crew home so he and I can take her to A and E to get it checked out.'

Callum nods, visibly relieved about that as well.

'Trouble is,' Mike continues, 'where am I going to find another makeup artist at eight hours' notice?'

'Actually . . .' Callum smiles smoothly, then looks at Shell. '. . . I may be able to help you with that, Mike.'

Chapter Twenty

Shell is already awake and googling *film and TV MUA kit* by the time her alarm goes off at four thirty. Given how little she's slept and how much she drank the night before, she should be horribly hung-over, but even though her hands are shaking, it's not because she's hung-over.

It's because she's scared.

Good scared.

Because, as of today, she's the key makeup artist on a film.

It's something she daydreamed about when she was doing her NVQ. It's what everyone on her course daydreamed of – working in film and television and having the chance to do something fun. Experiment with prosthetics and airbrushing and the colours in her eyeshadow palettes most clients avoid. She'd walk home from college every Wednesday night, imagining herself on set, coordinating looks with Hair and Wardrobe and being called on to blot shiny foreheads and reapply lipstick between takes.

She gets to Duke & Sons early, assuming she'd be one of the first there so she can take a moment to catch her breath before she has to pretend to know what she's doing.

But it's even busier than it was the night before. Everyone's talking at once and pointing around the Beauty Hall, the lights so bright she has to blink a few times to get her eyes to adjust as she heads to the break room to dump her stuff.

Callum is already in there and back in black.

It's quite a contrast with her orange and turquoise leopard-print maxi dress.

He's sitting at the wooden table in the middle of the room, scrolling through his phone. It's strange to see him in there – Shell doesn't think she ever has – among the dented lockers and unwashed mugs. He doesn't fit, like a black cat sitting in the middle of a building site.

'Morning, Callum,' she says brightly, as she walks to her locker and puts her empty travel cup inside.

'Shell Smith. How's your head?' he says, without looking up from his phone.

'Fine,' she says, shouldering off her bag then hanging up her coat. 'How are you?'

'Good, thanks.'

He finally looks up and her stomach clenches like a fist as she waits for him to say something about the night before. To ask how she is or if she's heard from Nick.

He doesn't, though. They just look at one another across the break room for a beat longer than is comfortable before he nods at the paper coffee cup on the table in front of him.

'Is that a latte?' she asks, but she can smell the ginger-bread syrup.

'Triple shot. I thought you'd need it.'

'I've only had three hours' sleep,' she admits.

'*Three?*'

'I don't really do the sleep thing.'

'How do you even function on three hours' sleep?'

'Caffeine and regret, mostly.'

He chuckles then gestures at the brown paper bag on the table. 'Got you that as well.'

'What is it?'

'A cinnamon swirl.'

'Oh, my God. Thank you.'

A banana is just not going to cut it this morning.

'What are you doing?' he asks, when she picks up the bag and bites into the cinnamon swirl.

She looks up to find him staring at her, horrified.

'What?' she asks, around a mouthful of pastry.

'You just *bit* into it.'

'How else am I supposed to eat it?'

'It's a cinnamon swirl, Shell,' he tells her, as though that isn't obvious. 'You're supposed to unwind it, not bite into it, like some sort of savage.' She takes another massive bite to spite him and he huffs out a disgusted sigh. 'I suppose this is the moment I'll look back on one day and say, *I should have known she was a serial killer.*'

She tries not to choke as she laughs.

'*Anyway,*' he says, standing up and rebuttoning his suit jacket. 'Let me tell you this while it's just us.'

'What?' she asks, the paper bag crackling loudly as her fingers curl around it.

'It's nothing bad. I'd just rather not say it on the shop floor.'

'Okay.' She takes a nerve-steadying gulp of coffee. 'Tell me.'

'I wanted to give you an update. Mike called last night to let me know that Hazel has dislocated her shoulder. She won't be able to return to filming so he needs to know if you can commit to taking her place.'

Shell nods. 'Of course!'

'Excellent. It's only the next three Sundays, but do let me know now if that isn't possible.'

'The only Sunday I can't do is the last one, December the twentieth, because I promised I'd help my mother at the community centre. She's doing a toy drive for Christmas.'

'I wouldn't dream of asking you to. Will you be gone the whole day?'

'Just a few hours.'

'Oh, I'm sure we can work something out, then.'

'Maybe Ricky can cover until I get here.'

'Excellent idea.' He starts walking out of the break room. 'Now. Mike says that you should invoice him, but I can help you with that, if you need me to.'

He opens the door, and when he realises she hasn't followed, he stops.

'Wait.' She blinks at him, stunned. 'I'm getting *paid* for this?'

When he grasps that she's being serious, he laughs.

'Shell. You're *the key makeup artist*. You're being paid four hundred pounds a day.'

'What?' She tries not to yell and fails. 'Did you just say four hundred pounds *a day*?'

'Not bad for messing around with lipstick, right?'

Then he's gone and Shell has to run to catch up, falling into step with him as they head down the corridor.

'Just so you know.' He waits for her to walk around a stack of cardboard boxes, then does the same. 'They're not filming *all* of the movie here, just the scenes where the main character, Katherine, is at work on the counter. They're filming the rest of it on a set in London. So.' He stops to push a clothing rail against the wall so they can pass. 'Another MUA called Aggy will be working on the other cast members and the extras, because Mike wants you to focus on the lead.'

'Who's playing her?' Shell can't help but ask, suddenly silly with excitement. 'Is it Keira Knightley?'

'Yes, it's Keira Knightley. Keira Knightley is in Ostley filming a made-for-TV Christmas movie.'

She pulls a face then stuffs the last of the cinnamon swirl into her mouth and screws up the bag in her fist.

'I can't remember her name. Veronica, I think. Anyway, she's not a diva.' He stops when they get to the door that leads into the Beauty Hall and looks at her in a way that makes her wonder if she is a diva. 'But this is her first film, so she's quite nervous and needs some hand-holding,' he says, as he pushes through the door.

Shell follows him. 'I can do that.'

'I know you can. I have every faith.' He looks over his shoulder at her, with a bright smile, then heads to the front of the Beauty Hall by the window with the *LET IT GLOW* Ferris wheel. 'This is your station.'

He stops in front of a table with a mirror surrounded by light-bulbs, like the one they got for the ART counter, except *much* bigger. It's covered with black cloth and it looks like Hazel managed to set everything up before she decided to go for a wander around the store last night. There's a black cape draped over the director's chair and everything is in neat rows, like it was in the videos on YouTube earlier – foundations, concealers, lipsticks, pots of brushes and cotton buds, even skincare.

Shell can see at a glance that she has everything she needs.

Callum reaches to pick up a folder from the seat of the director's chair. 'Hazel left you this.'

She puts down her coffee cup and the balled-up paper bag and takes it. 'What is it?'

When Shell opens it and sees the first photograph, she gasps and slams it shut again.

'It's Verity Appleton!' She whacks his arm with the folder. 'Why didn't you tell me it was her?'

'First of all, *ow*.' He makes a show of rubbing his arm. 'Second of all, who is Verity Appleton?'

'She hosts *that show*. You know? The one on ITV.' He obviously doesn't. '*Last Date*. Where people go for one last date with their ex to try to find out what went wrong.'

'I've never heard of it.'

'It's total trash. I *love* it.'

'Okay,' he says, blinking at her. 'Well, this is her first acting gig, which is why she's so nervous.'

She opens the folder again to find a series of Polaroids of each of the looks she has to do on Verity. They're catalogued, scene by scene, along with a list of the products Hazel used, which, Shell is assuming, are on the table ready to go. All she has to do is replicate them. Clients come to the ART counter all the time with photos on their phones of red carpet looks so it should be a doddle.

'This is amazing. I can't believe how organised Hazel is.'

'She had to be. The production schedule is *very tight*,' Callum reminds her. 'There's not a lot of time so, and I know you will, if someone asks you to do something, make sure you do it as quickly and as professionally as possible.'

'Of course,' she says, leafing through the folder.

'Here we go,' he says, clapping his hands together.

Shell looks up to find Verity Appleton sauntering towards them. She's much smaller than Shell expected, and she's cut her long dark hair so it's now a wavy bob that sways when she walks. She doesn't look like she does on *Last Date*. There's no fake tan and pink lip gloss. No floaty dress and heels. Instead, she's in jeans and white Converse and is swamped in a massive black jumper. But then she smiles, her green eyes flashing, and there she is.

'You must be Shell,' she says, holding her hand out to her. 'I'm Verity. Lovely to meet you.'

Here we go, Shell thinks, taking a deep breath, then shaking her hand.

Shell doesn't know who's more nervous, her or Verity, but they swiftly bond over their shared terror at being on a film set for the first time and their love of ART Degas Dancers blush. By the end of the day, they're swapping numbers, Shell promising to take her to Ricky's *Christmas Cabaret with Wreath Witherspoon* next Saturday.

While she's cleaning the brushes and packing up her station, she glances at the clock over the lifts as it chimes six. When she turns back, she jumps. Callum's next to her.

'So, how was your first day?'

'Good!' she tells him, when she recovers.

'Mike and Verity are *very happy* with you,' he says, with a proud smile.

'Really?' Her cheeks warm at the compliment. 'She's *so nice.*'

It's still only just past six o'clock. The twins were so disappointed when she said she couldn't go bowling with them this afternoon, so she considers heading to the alley to surprise them. But it's a school night, isn't it? By the time she's traipsed over to Lowbridge on the bus, they'll probably be getting ready to come home.

'Do you need a ride?' Callum asks, when she slips the last brush into its leather roll.

'Nah. I'll walk. The fresh air will do me good.'

He laughs and nods at the window. 'Have you looked outside recently?'

'No. Why? Is it raining?'

'It's *biblical.*'

'No.' She groans, remembering that she hasn't bought a new umbrella yet. 'Is that okay?'

'Of course,' he says. 'As long as you don't judge me for singing along to Carly Rae Jepsen.'

★

Callum's is the only car parked behind the warehouse, and as they trot towards it in the rain, she slows.

'Is this your car?' she asks, somewhat surprised that he drives a . . . She doesn't know what it is. Just that it's small and silver and, she suspects, much older than it looks. She thought he'd drive a kitted-out Range Rover or a Porsche or something, but now he's standing next to it, she can see that it's perfect for him. 'Very James Bond.'

'Well spotted.' He salutes her with two fingers before opening the passenger door for her. 'It's a 1963 Aston Martin DB5, like the one in *Goldfinger*.'

What is it with these boys and their tiny cars? she thinks, trying to maintain her dignity as she climbs in.

'Bond fan?' she asks, when Callum runs around the front of the car and jumps into the driver's seat.

'Not at all,' he says, his blond hair flattened by the downpour. 'It's my grandfather's. He isn't a fan either, to be honest. He bought it the year before *Goldfinger* came out, actually. It was one of the first off the lot.'

'How come you have it?'

'My grandmother won't let him drive it any more, and he said it's a shame to let it sit in the garage. I don't usually drive into work. I prefer to walk, but I knew it was going to rain this evening.'

That explains why she hasn't seen it, she thinks, as Callum checks the rear-view mirror. Shell takes the opportunity to glance around the car. It's exquisite. As sleek inside as it is out. And *spotless*. No spare change by the gear stick, no half-drunk bottles of water wedged into the pockets on the doors. Plus, it smells like him. Of worn leather and that aftershave he wears.

Callum puts the key into the ignition and it starts with a thrilling *growl*.

'Sorry,' she mutters, when she hears her phone ringing. She almost drops it when she realises it's Nick.

'The vegan?' Callum asks, as she shoves it into her bag and secures the gold clasp.

'I'll call him when I get in,' she says, watching the wipers sweep back and forth.

'Do you want to talk about it?' he asks carefully, but she shakes her head.

Chapter Twenty-One

It's still lashing down when Callum pulls up outside her house. Only the hall light is on so her family aren't back from bowling yet, which means Shell can surprise them. She'll turn on the heating and tidy up, unload the dishwasher and take whatever needs folding out of the dryer so her parents can chill when they get in.

But as she's about to thank Callum for the lift, she sees someone huddled under the porch.

'Shit,' she mutters.

'What?' Callum asks. When she doesn't respond, he turns to see what she's looking at. 'Oh.'

'Oh,' she agrees, looking at Nick on the porch, clutching a bunch of flowers.

God knows how long he's been standing there. He's *drenched*, his dark hair sticking to his cheeks. As he steps out to glance up the street with a frustrated frown, she realises he can't see her sitting in Callum's car.

Why is he here?

To apologise, she assumes, given the roses, but for what?

For breaking up with her in the middle of the pub?

For shouting at her?

For what he said about her job?

'You're never going to find out if you don't speak to him,' Callum says, turning the engine off. 'Or we could go back to the store, eat all the candy canes and jump on the beds.'

Tempting as that is, she can't just leave Nick there, in the rain.

So she reaches for the door handle, then turns to Callum before she opens it. 'Thanks.'

He lifts his head off the headrest to look at her. 'For what?'

'Just thanks,' she tells him, as she climbs out.

She runs up the path. Nick is so happy to see her that as soon as he steps aside for her to join him on the door-step her heart betrays her. She hates how it recognises him, bouncing up and down in her chest, like a dog that's been home alone all day, the moment it registers the nearness of him.

She doesn't know who that man in the Anchor last night was but *this* is Nick. *Her* Nick. The Nick she used to tear around Ostley with. The Nick who takes two sugars in his tea and insists that the yellow M&Ms taste better than the others.

'Hey, you,' he says, with a grin, and it's perfect.

The rain.

Him on her doorstep, holding flowers.

She wants to go back and tell poor, sweet seventeen-year-old Shell that it's worth it.

That it all works out.

The funny thing is, if she made him watch this film, he'd laugh at this bit. Say how clichéd it is. How cheesy.

But she'd just kiss his cheek and say that there's nothing cheesy about a happy ending.

'Come in,' Shell tells him, when she finds her keys. 'You must be freezing.'

Her hands are shaking so much that her keys rattle as she opens the front door. Then they're in and Nick waits, dripping on the doormat, as he watches Shell hang her bag on the end of the banister then take off her coat with a theatrical shiver.

When he sees her bend down to unlace her hot pink DMs and kick them, he does the same, leaving his on the doormat.

Then he thrusts the flowers at her. 'These are for you.'

She actually giggles when she takes them from him. 'Thank you.'

They are as close as Nick Wallace will ever get to holding a boom box over his head.

'My family will be home any minute so we'd better . . .' Shell thumbs over her shoulder to the kitchen.

'I've never been to your house before,' he says, following her in as she turns on the light.

He's right. He hasn't.

'It's *exactly* how I imagined,' he says, blinking raindrops down his cheeks as he looks around the kitchen. The sloppy, cheerful paintings on the fridge. Her mother's Lionel Richie *Hello? Is it tea you're looking for?* mug on the counter by the sink, still half full, a crescent of pink lipstick on the rim. Patrick's Spiderman in the fruit bowl.

'Yeah?' she asks, putting the roses on the counter next to the kettle.

'Yeah. It's so warm and bright.'

He doesn't say, *Not like my house*, but Shell still hears it.

Her heart hurts for a different reason then and she wants to pull him to her. Press her face into his neck and hold him. Tell him that it will be okay. He'll get through it. She'll help him get through it because Emma's wrong.

He doesn't need time, he just needs her.

'Just like you,' he adds, with a smile that makes her heart spin.

'Tea?' she asks, gesturing at him to sit at the table.

He does, then pats it with his hand. 'Come here, babe. I want to talk to you before they get home.'

Shell sits in the chair opposite his. Their knees graze under the table, which makes her heart spin again, as she moves the fake potted poinsettia out of the way so she can see him properly.

Nick grins at her. 'Hey, you.'

'Hey, you.' She grins back.

'Where were you today?' he asks, as he peels off his leather jacket.

It doesn't even occur to Shell to lie. 'Work.'

The word lands like a brick on the table between them.

Perhaps she should have lied, Shell wonders, as she watches the muscles in his jaw clench. It makes her tense up as well, and it's as though someone has turned the light off.

Nick leans back in the chair. 'I thought Duke's was shut on a Sunday,' he says, before she has a chance to change the subject.

'It is,' Shell says, and she hates how small her voice sounds. 'I was working on something else.'

She wants to tell him. Gush about the film and Verity Appleton and the money she's decided to put towards moving in with Ricky and Denise in the new year. But the look he's giving her says, *More work?*

'Nick—'

'Listen, Shell,' he interrupts.

She waits for him to gather his thoughts, give her the big speech he's no doubt practised.

But he just shakes his head.

'I don't know what to say, Shell.'

That's it.

No *I'm sorry, Shell*.

No *Forgive me, Shell*.

No *It's always been you, Shell*.

He lifts his shoulder and lets it drop again. 'I don't even remember what I said last night. I was blotto.' He sniffs, wiping his nose with the cuff of his jumper. 'But it must have been bad.'

His gaze darts around the kitchen – settling on everything but Shell – and she gets it.

He wants this to be over.

This conversation.

This apology.

He just wants it to be over.

'Listen, Shell.' He leans forward again to rest his forearms on the table. 'Let's just draw a line under this, okay? Forget last night ever happened and start again. Go back to kissing in my car and eating bad Pad Thai.'

No, she thinks. *That isn't enough.*

While she doesn't need a teary, fervent apology, she expected *something*. For him to kiss her and tell her not to worry, that he'll be fine as long as he has her. But he just sits there, hunched in the chair, and he looks exhausted. Not hung-over, but *exhausted*.

He's always been thin, but without his long hair to hide behind, Shell can see how sharp his cheeks are – how hollow – the skin beneath his eyes bruised black, like he hasn't slept for weeks.

He's not right, Shell realises.

She was too close before, so close that there was no space between them at all times, but now she can see him and he looks defeated. The fire's gone, that curious spark that used to be behind his eyes that makes her worry what he's going to say next.

Shell knows then that this is bigger than her.

Nick needs help.

And for the first time since he kissed her in his car that morning outside Duke & Sons, she isn't sure if he wants her – wants this – or if it's just preferable to being on his own.

'It's okay,' she says softly, reaching across the table for his hand. His palm is as clammy as a bar of soap. When he finally lifts his chin to meet her gaze, his forehead is so creased, she wants to smooth away the lines with her fingers. 'It's okay. You just need time.'

Shell waits for him to nod, but he doesn't. He just blinks at her. 'Time for what?'

'Time to get through this.' She squeezes his hand, his

knuckles hard against hers. 'I looked it up last night, and there are five stages of grief, apparently. The first is denial, then anger—'

'Anger?' He pulls his hand away so suddenly that hers drops to the table with a thud. 'You think I said what I said last night because I'm angry about Mum dying?'

'I mean,' she says, her voice too small again, 'what else could it be?'

'It couldn't possibly be anything to do with you, could it, Shell? You're perfect, aren't you?'

'I'm not perfect. I—'

'Forgive me for not taking life advice from someone who has never left home.' He laughs bitterly. 'I mean, you've never lost *anything*, have you, Shell? Nothing. Not even a fucking cat.'

'I lost you,' Shell says, before she can stop herself.

That makes him falter, his cheeks pinker as he shifts in the chair again.

'And why was that?' he asks, when he recovers. 'You ghosted me and fucked off to Aberdeen.'

'And why was *that*?' she counters.

He doesn't say anything, just looks down at Sim's *Frozen* placemat.

'You knew I had feelings for you,' Shell finally says out loud, the words fighting their way up through her chest and onto her tongue. 'You knew and you just pretended that we were friends.'

'We were friends,' he says, but he doesn't look at her.

'No, we weren't.'

He doesn't deny it this time, just fists his right hand in his hair.

'Why, Nick?' she asks at last. 'Why now and not then?'

For one horrible moment she thinks he's not going to tell her, that he's going to say she's mad, that it's all in her head. But then he lifts his chin to look at her.

'Because I was seventeen and stupid,' he says, no doubt assuming that will be enough.

For seventeen-year-old Shell, it probably would have been, but now it's not.

Maybe some things have changed, then.

'Didn't you fancy me, Nick? Was that it?'

'Of course I fancied you! Have you looked in a mirror recently? You're stunning!'

Her cheeks warm and she curses herself.

'What do you want me to say?' He takes his hand out of his hair. ' That I was scared.'

'Scared of what?'

'That I'd fuck it up!'

He looks startled, like he hadn't even thought that until he'd said it out loud.

'You meant so much to me,' he goes on, after a moment or two, giving into whatever he's been holding back all these years and just saying it. 'Like, *everything*, Shell. You were the *only* person who ever just let me be me. I was safe when I was with you. I couldn't lose that, Shell. I *can't.*'

It's exactly what she's waited nine years to hear.

So why isn't it enough? she asks herself, her heart notably calmer. 'Because I'm your comfort blanket.'

253

'Yeah.' He laughs at the analogy. 'I suppose you were. You were my whole world. And I was scared that if we got together I'd fuck it up – and *look*! It only took a month.'

Shell would laugh if it wasn't so painful.

She should leave it at that, she knows. But then he looks at her, his shoulders dipped and his bottom lip bitten pink, and he looks seventeen again.

'Maybe we work better as friends, Nick.'

He doesn't hesitate. 'No. No. Don't say that.'

'I think you really need a friend right now.'

The chair scrapes loudly as he pushes it back and stands up. 'I don't want to be friends.'

But before Shell can say anything else, he's gone.

Chapter Twenty-Two

Shell follows Nick, of course, out into the rain and down the path to press her palm to the door of his car so he can't open it. She insists that he come back inside and talk, but he shakes his head so furiously that raindrops spill off his jaw.

So she lets him go because what else can she do?

Just give him time, Emma keeps telling her.

So Shell keeps herself busy.

She makes sure she has something to do every night. On Monday, Emma, Denise and Ricky take her to the new noodle place on Bridge Street, and they talk about everything but Nick. On Tuesday, it's Taco Tuesday, of course, followed by *Gilmore Girls* on the sofa with her father while her mother reads in the bath. On Wednesday after work, she picks up her sisters from band practice, their princess and unicorn phase now forgotten in favour of DMs and Nirvana T-shirts, much to Shell's delight. She films with Mia on Thursday. On Friday, she and Emma take the twins ice skating. Tonight is Ricky's *Christmas Cabaret with Wreath Witherspoon* and Verity's come with her, bringing the house down when Ricky pulls her onstage to do 'Baby, It's Cold Outside'.

Still, Shell's had her moments. Usually, when it's just her, wandering around her room at night, listening to music. That's when her resolve weakens and she'll reach for her phone, sending him another text to remind him that she's thinking of him and that she's there when he's ready.

Until then, there's this: listening to her brothers laughing in the bath every night and her sisters pestering their father about getting a dog every morning. Sitting in the Anchor after work, mediating while Ricky and Denise bicker over which is funnier: the British version of *The Office* or the American. Callum striding around the Beauty Hall, making sure there are no more polar-bear casualties, while she runs lines with Verity.

It turns out that Verity Appleton couldn't be further from a diva. She's bright and funny, and insists on making Shell dance with her to 'Shake It Off' by Taylor Swift before she does her first scene of the day. They text constantly now, Verity keeping her up to date with the gossip on set (Mike is hooking up with the paramedic, Greg, which Shell would never have suspected).

Working on the film has confirmed that *this* is what Shell wants to do. Mike has already asked if she wants to work on his next project, which starts filming in Paris – Paris! – in the new year. Shell *never* thought she'd consider leaving Duke & Sons, but when she mentions it to Callum, he says that if ART is cool with it, he doesn't see why she can't take a couple of months off to work on the film.

And with that, the new year rolls out from her feet like a red carpet.

'What about the ART trip to Mexico?' her mother asks, when Shell tells her about Paris.

Eleanor and Shaun are up *way* past their bedtime. When she got home from Ricky's cabaret, Shell went into the kitchen to grab a glass of water and found them sitting at the table. Apparently, they'd stayed up to watch a film, but really they wanted to know how her night out with Verity Appleton had been.

Now they're sipping red wine and picking at the cheese they were supposed to be saving for Christmas.

'That's not until March,' Shell reminds her mother, reaching for a cracker. 'I'll be done by then.'

'Paris, *then* Mexico?' Her father raises his eyebrows. 'Not bad, eh?'

'I know, right?' Shell forces a smile. 'Good thing I sent those passport renewal forms off last week.'

Eleanor nods. 'I know you're gutted, darling, but it's probably best things didn't work out with Nick. You might have thought twice about going to Paris if it meant you'd be apart for a couple of months.'

'I guess.'

'Never put your life on hold for a boy,' her father warns, pointing his wine glass at her.

Eleanor thumbs at him. 'Says the dude who got me knocked up at sixteen.'

'Learn from us, Shell,' he tells her, kissing her mother's cheek.

Eleanor giggles and they look so happy. *Twenty-eight years*, Shell thinks as she watches them. *Twenty-eight years, and look how happy they still make each other.*

Her mother looks up then. 'Oh, hey.'

Shell turns in her chair to find Sim standing in the doorway, dark curls everywhere, one pyjama leg up, the other down. 'What's up, Sim?'

She rubs her eyes. 'I thought I heard Santa.'

'Oh, no, baby girl,' Shell says, with a soft smile. 'He's not coming for another two weeks.'

'Thirteen more sleeps,' Sim reminds her, pointing at the four Advent calendars lined up on the windowsill.

'Come on,' Shell says, standing up and reaching for her hand. 'Let's get one of those sleeps out of the way.'

Sim complies, still rubbing her eyes with her other hand as Shell leads her upstairs.

Kitty lifts her head off the pillow when they walk into the bedroom.

'Was it Santa?' she asks, clearly curious but too lazy to come downstairs and find out for herself.

Sim shakes her head glumly and climbs back into bed.

Kitty groans, letting her head fall back onto the pillow. 'Told you.'

'Thirteen more sleeps,' Shell reminds them, looking around at the mess.

'Wait, Shell,' Sim calls, when she turns to leave. 'Tell us the story about the magic lipstick.'

The next day on set, Verity is more excitable than usual because Shell's finally relented and agreed that she can come with her to the Anchor tonight after they wrap to join Emma, Ricky and Denise for a drink. It's not that

Shell doesn't want her to come, it's just that she'll never forgive herself if she's the reason Old Mr Duke finds out about the filming.

So they've come up with the ridiculous idea of passing Verity off as her cousin if anyone recognises her.

'Don't worry, Shell,' Verity assures her, stopping to adjust the *hideous* Christmas jumper they're making her wear in this scene. 'I can handle some locals asking me why I'm in Ostley.'

Before she can tell her that it's an awful idea, Callum is by her side and Shell jumps.

He's in black again, in a suit so tightly fitted that the film's other MUA, Aggy, said that it was enough to, and Shell quotes, *flood her basement.*

'Jesus,' she hisses at him. 'What are you? A ninja.'

Mercifully, he didn't hear what they're talking about, too distracted by the crew setting up outside.

'What's *that*?' he says, under his breath, tugging her away from Verity.

After the hot-air balloon incident, Shell dreads to think. 'What's *what*?'

'What are they doing outside?'

'Setting up for the last scene.'

'I know they're setting up for the last scene, but what's *that*?'

He jabs his finger in the direction of the piece of equipment two guys are pushing along the pavement.

'It's a snow machine.' Shell grins. She's been waiting for this all day. She knows it's not real, but it's going to look *so pretty*.

'A snow machine?' He blinks at her, his cheeks pink. 'As in a machine that generates *snow*?'

'Yeah,' she says, wondering what's wrong with that.

'So they're just going to be spraying snow outside the store at three o'clock on a Sunday afternoon?'

Shell shrugs. 'I'm sure they'll clear it up.'

'I don't care about that,' he says, lowering his voice. 'It's not very inconspicuous, is it?'

It takes her a moment, and when she realises what he's getting at, her eyes widen. 'Oh.'

'Exactly. *Oh*.' He presses his hand to his forehead. 'I'm dead,' he mutters. '*Dead*. Someone is going to walk past, see what's going on and tell my grandfather. How am I going to explain *snow*, Shell?'

'You can tell him that you were taking photos for the Duke & Sons Christmas card, or something.'

'It's December the thirteenth, Shell. We sent out the Duke & Sons Christmas card two weeks ago.'

'I've got it!' She points at him. 'It's the Ostley Primary Carol Concert in the square tomorrow night.'

'Okay.' He arches an eyebrow suspiciously.

'Let's do a Winter Wonderland thing outside the store! We can use the store Santa and borrow the snow machine to make it look like it's snowing. Can you imagine?' She bounces up and down. 'It'll be *magical*. *The First Annual Duke & Sons White Christmas*. Your grandfather will *love* it, and the best bit is, we won't even need to publicise it because everyone's coming to the concert anyway. It's a town tradition.'

Callum considers it. 'I can ask the school if they mind

moving the concert from the square to outside the store. It would be great publicity and the kids would look so cute singing in the snow.'

'So cute!' Shell presses her hands to her chest, thinking about the twins in their bobble hats and mittens. 'And if anyone sees the snow today, we can say we were testing the machine to see if it worked.'

'You, Shell Smith,' he reaches into the pocket of his jacket for his phone, 'are a *genius*!'

She blows on her nails and polishes them on her jumper. 'I try.'

'Right.' He checks his watch. 'We have twenty-six hours and forty-eight minutes.'

She salutes him and stands to attention. 'Copy that, Captain Christmas.'

Chapter Twenty-Three

Shell honestly doesn't know how they do it, but twenty-six hours and forty-eight minutes later, the pavement outside Duke & Sons is thick with snow. Luckily, the council always closes the road for the carol concert so they get to go to town, covering it, too, so everything is white. It looks so real that people have been stopping by all afternoon, taking selfies and having snowball fights. Callum considers stopping them because they're *ruining the aesthetic*, apparently, but they're so happy that Shell tells him to leave them be, reminding him that they can add more if they need to.

After a lengthy conversation with someone called Beatrice and the promise of a makeover, the local garden centre gives in to Shell and donates a cluster of spruce trees that are now standing on either side of the revolving door, their branches heavy with snow. And the stall she helped the team from the café downstairs set up in front of the *LET IT GLOW* window, to sell coffee, hot chocolate, mulled wine and the mince pies Callum drove to every supermarket in a five-mile radius to procure, is already doing a roaring trade and the concert hasn't even started yet.

'We did it!' Callum says, suddenly by her side as she

stands outside, gazing up at Duke & Sons. When he smiles, she wonders if he's thinking the same thing, if this is what the store looked like in its day.

The jewel of Ostley High Street.

Shell hears the twins before she sees them, and then they're tearing towards her, bobble hats bobbing.

'Shell!' they yell, throwing themselves at her and hugging whichever limb they're closest to.

'What do you think, guys?' she asks, as the four begin jumping up and down, kicking the snow.

The response is indecipherable, but she knows it's good.

'So these are my little brothers and sisters,' she tells Callum, as they shriek with delight.

'Wow,' he says, watching them, his smile wider now. 'They're adorable.'

'I'll ask you again in an hour,' she says, then waves when she sees her parents approaching. 'Hey!'

'Shell, this is amazing!' her mother gushes, hugging her tightly. 'It looks so real!'

'The store looks how it used to when you were a kid,' her father says, doing the same.

When they step apart, she gestures at Callum. 'Mum. Dad. This is Callum Duke.'

Her mother's eyebrows twitch up for just a second before she catches herself and smiles. 'Hello, Callum.'

'Mrs Smith.' He leans down to kiss her on both cheeks.

Her face is a little pinker when Callum steps back. 'Please, call me Eleanor.'

'Eleanor.' He holds out his hand to Shell's father. 'Mr Smith.'

'Shaun.' They shake.

Callum blinks at them a few times, his lips parted as he makes the connection.

'Shaun.' Her father points at himself, then at her mother. 'Eleanor.' Finally, he points at her. 'Shell.'

'What can I say? We were sixteen and thought a combination of our names was so *progressive* and third-wave feminism.' Her mother giggles. 'Plus she was conceived on a beach in Ibiza so it was either Shell or Pacha.'

'What?' Shell squeaks, wondering how much wine her mother had had before she left the house.

Conceived *where* in Ibiza?

'Holiday romance,' Eleanor explains. 'I was only there for two weeks. I never thought I'd see him again.'

Shaun nods. 'I locked that shit *down*.'

'Okay!' Shell holds her hands up. 'No more wine for you guys.'

Callum seems thoroughly amused, though. 'So from two weeks to . . .'

'Twenty-eight years.' Her father fills the gap.

Her mother pulls Shell aside. 'Look, I know this is a kids' thing, but *please* tell me there's alcohol.' She closes her eyes and rubs her temples with her fingers. 'If I have to hear "Silent Night" one more time, I'm going to need a drink.'

Shell laughs, waving at the stall in front of the *LET IT GLOW* window. 'There's mulled wine.'

Eleanor looks to the sky. 'Thank God.'

'Do you guys want one?' Shaun asks, already on it.

Callum thanks him and shakes his head, but Shell mouths, *Coffee*, and her father winks.

'Get me two!' Eleanor calls after him, then turns back to them with a smile. 'So, Callum.' She looks him up and down, taking in his blond hair, which is wilting slightly in the damp air, and his black wool coat that is unbuttoned to reveal his white shirt and neat navy suit. There's nothing lascivious about it, though. It's more gentle curiosity about the Callum her eldest daughter keeps talking about. 'Did Shell tell you that you two met when you were kids?'

'Mum!' She covers her face with her hands and groans. 'I forgot about that.'

'No!' Callum looks at her, then at Eleanor, his blue eyes wide. 'When was this?'

'Shell was three so you must have been five or six, I reckon.'

'No way!' Callum seems genuinely tickled. 'Where did we meet? Here?'

Eleanor nods. 'Shaun and I brought Shell in to meet Santa and there you were. You, your father and your grandfather, all in your suits and red tartan ties with matching pocket squares.'

'God, I remember that!' he exclaims.

'You shook Shell's hand and said, "Welcome to Duke & Sons."'

'I did?' He presses his hands to his stomach and laughs.

'And Shell wished you a happy Christmas.'

'You did?' He turns to her with a slow smile. 'Well, happy Christmas to you too, Shell Smith.' He nudges her with his hip.

She nudges him back, but before he does it again, he's distracted by something over her shoulder. 'Excuse me, ladies,' he says, heading over to greet a photographer from the local paper.

When Shell turns to her mother again, she's shaking her head. 'What?'

Eleanor just laughs. 'Nothing.'

Just before six o'clock, the guest of honour arrives.

Old Mr Duke.

There's a huge cheer and he waves gleefully, his other arm through Callum's as they walk towards the store, his cane leaving small circles in the fake snow beneath their feet.

'Hello, everyone!' He waves again. 'Callum! What is this?' he asks, clearly delighted when he sees the scene.

'It's the first annual Duke & Sons White Christmas, Pops.'

The high street would usually be clogged with traffic at this time, so it's uncharacteristically quiet as Shell runs over to join her friends. Ricky and Denise are loving it, wearing matching white fake-fur coats and hats and trying not to spill mulled wine on them.

'If I could just have everyone's attention for a moment,' Callum says, raising his left arm, the other curled protectively around Old Mr Duke. The crowd immediately hushes, everyone turning towards him. Callum smiles brightly. 'If you know my grandfather, then you know how much he *loves* Christmas.'

There's a collective chuckle as Old Mr Duke takes a bow.

'And if you know my grandfather, you'll have also heard the story of that Christmas Eve when he was three.'

Shell, Ricky and Denise exchange glances.

Callum starts to tell the story, but everyone knows it because Old Mr Duke tells it every Christmas Eve. How Duke & Sons was bombed in the Blitz and his parents took him to the battered store after midnight mass. They stood on the spot under where the stained-glass dome used to be. Old Mr Duke had just turned three – three and one day – and was in his father's arms as they looked up at the black sky. Just as they did, so the story goes, it started to snow and when the first flake landed on Old Mr Duke's nose he started singing 'Silent Night'.

'So,' Callum says, smiling at his grandfather, 'in honour of that night.'

That must be their cue, because the children begin 'Silent Night'.

It isn't a pitch-perfect rendition, but what they lack in skill, they make up for in enthusiasm, and Old Mr Duke is immediately weeping. Then everyone is crying. Even Becca and Soph, phones forgotten as they lean into one another as they sway from side to side, holding up their candles.

When Shell looks at her parents, they're crying as well. Crying and singing along as they hold up their phones. She can't help but look at Old Mr Duke again. He's still weeping as he leans into Callum, head on his shoulder as he gently pats Callum's arm. She turns to Callum then, but he's already looking at her. *Thank you*, he mouths, when their eyes meet.

'God, I'm *starving*,' Denise announces, as they head back into the break room to grab their stuff.

'My parents are in Amsterdam until the weekend,' Ricky says, inspecting his freshly painted red-and-white-striped candy-cane nails. 'We could meet Emma in the Anchor for one, then head back to mine and order a pizza or something. It's on me if one of you can show me how to use the washing-machine. I'm down to my last pair of pants.'

'Curry.' Denise checks her lipstick in the mirror on the door of her locker. 'I need lamb korma.'

'Not the place by the station, though.' Shell pulls a face as they head out of the break room. 'It's too greasy.'

They're still bickering about where in Ostley does the best curry – a conversation they seem to have at least once a week – as they push through the revolving door and out onto the pavement.

Shell stops to thank the guys who have the unenviable task of clearing up the snow when she hears someone say, 'Callum's already thanked them.'

They turn to find Louise in front of the window with the gingerbread house, smoking a cigarette.

'Third wheeling it again, I see.' When they ignore her, her smile sharpens. 'Going to the Anchor? I'd go, but I'm waiting for Callum.'

It's the first time she's been so blatant about it and it's

definitely the first time she's been so blatant about it in front of Ricky and Denise.

It bothers Shell more than it should.

It's not the smug look on Louise's face as she waves her cigarette around, eyes alight with mischief, it's that it doesn't make sense. Maybe if it was some guy she'd met at the pub, who didn't know – or care – that she was engaged, but *Callum*? Earnest Callum, who has a smile for everyone and gave each of her brothers and sisters a candy cane to congratulate them on their performance before her parents took them home.

That's what bothers her, Shell realises then.

It's that she thought she knew him, but she obviously doesn't.

Ricky and Denise don't look like they believe Louise, though.

Louise must know that because she adds, 'I'm just waiting for him to pick me up. You can't miss his car.' She glances up and down the high street, which has been reopened now the carol concert is over. 'He drives a silver Aston Martin. Just like the one in *Goldfinger*.'

'Yeah, we know.' Ricky rolls his eyes.

'I've been in it, remember?' Denise reminds her, with a tight smile.

That's true, Shell thinks, the muscles in her shoulders relaxing.

Everyone at Duke & Sons knows about Callum's car. Mostly thanks to Denise, who wouldn't shut up about it after he'd driven them to London for the meetings he'd arranged with the brands she suggested they stock. They've been back to London three times since and each time Denise has come into work the next day *gushing* about how sexy the car is.

When that doesn't elicit the response Louise was hoping for, she takes a drag on her cigarette, then turns to look up the high street. 'Is that him?'

Shell tenses all over again as she turns to see if it is, unsure how she'll react if Callum pulls up and tries to make polite conversation before Louise gets in.

It's just a cab, though, which rolls past them, its light on.

'He'll be here in a sec.' Louise drops her cigarette to the pavement, then steps on it. 'He just texted to say he's dropped Old Mr Duke home.'

Ricky tilts his head at Louise as if to say, *Sure*.

'We'll probably just head to his place.'

'Where does Callum live?' Shell asks, trying to catch her out.

Louise doesn't flinch, though. 'One of those old houses on Ostley Crescent.' She reaches into her bag, pulling out a bottle of Gaulin perfume. 'He's restoring it.' She looks Shell in the eye before she tips her head back, spraying liberally. 'But, you know, with a wine fridge and a steam shower.'

The shock of it knocks the air right out of her.

Denise looks equally uneasy.

Callum must have told her about that as well.

Then Louise delivers her final shot, tossing the bottle back into her bag and pulling out a paint chart. 'I'm helping him pick a colour for the bedroom,' she says, with a vicious smirk. 'Callum says, if we're going to be spending so much time in there, I may as well have a say on what it looks like.'

'Classy, Louise,' Ricky says, but it's all Shell can do not to puke on the fake snow.

As soon as they turn off the high street, Denise and Ricky are talking at once.

'Louise and Callum?' Denise is utterly horrified. 'Louise and Callum?'

'Isn't she engaged?' Shell says.

Denise has obviously forgotten about that because she looks even more horrified as she fusses over her braids, gathering them over her shoulder. 'I didn't think he was like that.'

'Me, either. He seems so . . .'

'Decent,' Denise says, when Shell trails off. 'I'm not gonna lie, I'm disappointed.'

'Me, too.'

'I mean, of all the people he could have shagged at Duke & Sons, why Louise Larson?'

'I know she's vile, but she is gorgeous,' Shell is pained to admit. 'You have to give her that. She's got that whole Betty Draper thing going on that most men *love*.'

'Yeah, but . . .' Denise screws up her nose '. . . can you imagine how vanilla their kids would be?'

'Come on!' Ricky intervenes. 'There's *no way* they're shagging.'

'I don't know,' Shell says, as they carry on towards the Anchor. 'Everything Louise just said was true.'

Denise nods at Ricky. 'Callum told me all that stuff as well.'

'Exactly.' Ricky stops to adjust his fur hat. 'If he told you two, he could have told Louise as well. That doesn't mean they're together.'

'That's true,' Denise concedes.

'And even if they are *you know* . . .' Ricky stops when they get to the Christmas tree in the middle of the square to mock-shudder '. . . I doubt it's serious enough for Louise to be picking out paint colours.'

'Why would she lie, though?' Shell asks, wondering what that could possibly achieve.

It's nothing to be proud of, cheating on your fiancé.

'To wind us up,' Ricky says, as if it isn't obvious.

Maybe, Shell thinks, as they cross the square towards the Anchor. *But that's pretty dangerous.*

This is the sort of rumour that ends careers.

And engagements, if nothing else.

'I don't even care any more,' Denise mutters, as she looks around the pub for Emma. 'Our Callum crush was fun while it lasted, but it's too icky for me if Louise is involved. She can have him.'

'*Your* Callum crush,' Shell reminds them.

Ricky ignores her. 'I agree, babe. It's time to unstan.'

'I've already moved on.' Denise adjusts her hoop earring. 'I'm all about the new warehouse guy now.'

Shell frowns. 'What new warehouse guy?'

Ricky grabs her arm. 'You haven't seen him yet? He started last week! He's *super*-hot.'

'What the hell?' Denise scowls when she sees that there's nowhere to sit. 'It's a Monday night.'

Shell shrugs. 'Everyone must have come in here after the carol concert.'

'I hope Emma managed to get a table,' Denise says, as she gives the busy pub one last scan.

'I didn't,' says Emma, appearing from nowhere, coat still on.

Denise huffs. 'We're going to have to stand outside, then.'

'Not in the beer garden, *please*.' Emma's forehead creases. 'I went home last Saturday smelling like Pat Butcher.'

'Let's stand in the square, by the tree!' Ricky suggests, with a grin. 'It'll be festive.'

'Good idea, babe. You fill Shell and Emma in on Liam while I go to the bar. I'll see you out there.'

'Who's Liam?' Emma asks, as they head back outside.

'The new warehouse guy.' Ricky flicks his red hair and bats his eyelashes. 'He's dreamy.'

Emma perks up. 'How dreamy?'

'He's Australian and looks like Chris Hemsworth.'

Emma's eyebrows shoot up. 'Don't lie!'

Ricky waggles his as they stop in front of the Christmas tree. 'And he likes Shell.'

'What?' Emma's jaw drops.

Ricky nudges her with his hip. 'He asked Den if you were single.'

'Me?' Shell exclaims. 'Are you sure he was talking about me?'

'There's only one hot girl with a fringe on the ART counter.'

I'm a hot girl with a fringe?

Who knew?

'Hold on. Before we go any further, we need to set the mood.' Ricky reaches into his coat pocket, pulling out his phone. The tip of his tongue pokes out from the corner of his mouth and Shell wonders what he's up to as he scrolls through it. But then she hears the familiar opening of 'All I Want For Christmas Is You' and groans.

'Aren't you sick of that song yet? We play it, like, eight times a day on the counter.'

'Sick of Mariah?' Ricky looks alarmed. 'Never!'

He starts dancing and when Emma joins in, Shell can't help herself.

'Are we having a party?' Denise asks, as she emerges from the pub.

Ricky gives her a little wiggle as she approaches. 'Always!'

'Good thing I got some mulled wine. Quick.' She holds out the glasses to them. 'They're hot!'

They each take one, then clink and give a cheer.

'Ricky, did you tell Shell and Emma about Liam?'

He nods proudly.

'Did you tell her that he asked me if Shell was single?'

'What did you say?' Shell asks, with a frown.

'That you were, of course.'

'Denise!'

'What? He's cute! I'll introduce you to him at the Christmas party tomorrow night.'

'He started last week and he's already checking out the staff?'

'So?' Emma winks.

'Yeah, but I only just broke up with Nick, like, a week ago.'

'You wanted to know what would happen if you got together and now you do. It's time to move on,' Emma says, with a sad smile.

'Harsh but fair, Russo,' Ricky says.

'Come on, Shell. It's the Christmas party,' Denise assures her. 'Say hello. Flirt a bit.'

'That's true,' Emma says. 'Just meet him and see if you fancy him.'

'You never know.' Ricky jerks a thumb at the Christmas tree. 'You guys might have great chemis-tree!'

Shell glares at him.

'Yeah!' Emma joins in with a filthy cackle. 'Do something to get yourself on the Naughty List!'

'Stop it,' Shell warns.

'Jingle his bells,' Denise pauses for full impact, 'and go all the way!'

'Okay.' Shell holds her hand up, trying not to laugh. 'That's enough now.'

'One more! One more!' Ricky pleads, jumping up and down, almost spilling his mulled wine.

'Fine.' She groans.

He pantomime-winks at her. 'Maybe you can let him down your chimney on Christmas Eve.'

Shell closes her eyes. 'I think we should see other people.'

Chapter Twenty-Four

Shell gets home as her parents are heading up to bed.

'Hey.' Her mother stops at the bottom of the stairs, then yawns greedily.

'Hey,' she says back, easing the door shut and lowering her voice so she doesn't wake the twins. 'You alright?'

'Tonight was so much fun, darling.' Her eyes are tired but her smile is bright. 'I'm so proud of you.'

Her cheeks warm. 'I'll remind you of that next time I forget to take the bins out.'

'Shell,' her father whispers, emerging from the kitchen with a hot-water bottle. He hands it to her mother, then thumbs back at the kitchen with an excited smile. 'Something arrived for you.'

'What?' she asks, but he doesn't say, just winks at her, then heads upstairs with Eleanor.

Shell hangs up her bag and coat, takes off her boots and heads into the kitchen. As soon as she turns on the light, she sees a huge bouquet of white flowers sitting on the table. She can smell them from the doorway and skips over to pick them up and press her nose into them. They smell *amazing*, of freshly cut roses mixed with pine and eucalyptus, and it's unsettlingly familiar, but she can't quite think where she knows the scent from.

They look just as pretty as they smell. Fat, creamy roses and smaller, whiter ones with long sprigs of greenery and clusters of blue-grey berries. Then she sees them, dotted among the rest, white anemones.

Her favourites.

Her heart hiccups as she puts the bouquet back on the table and tears into the card.

But they're not from Nick.

They're from Callum: *Thank you for your help today. Take tomorrow off and rest up for the Christmas party. Can't wait to see your dance moves! CD*

Shell catches herself smiling as she reaches for the bouquet and smells them again.

As soon as she does, her stomach turns as it finally occurs to her what they smell like.

I know that smell, she thinks, tossing them onto the table and striding over to the bin to throw the card away.

Gaulin Winter White.

Louise Larson's perfume.

Shell's still fuming about it when she pads into the kitchen the next morning in last year's Christmas pyjamas. She doesn't look at the flowers, only at her mother, who is by the counter pushing down on the cafetière.

'Morning, darling,' she says, without looking up.

'Morning,' Shell says, with a huff, leaning against the counter with her arms crossed.

If her mum notices, she doesn't say anything. 'You're up late this morning.'

'Callum gave me the day off to thank me for my help yesterday.'

'That's nice. Those from him as well?' Eleanor asks, admiring the flowers.

'Yeah. How did you know?'

'They're very Callum,' she says, taking the lid off her travel cup. 'Classic. Like a little black dress.'

Shell huffs again.

'Why haven't you put them in water yet?'

'I will in a sec,' she mumbles, opening the cupboard by their heads to grab a mug.

'Shell, I have, like, *four minutes* before I have to leave for work,' she says, as she fills her travel cup with some of the coffee from the cafetière. 'So if something's bothering you, tell me now or for ever hold your peace.'

'Fine.' Shell stops to check the twins aren't nearby. 'I found out last night that Callum's shagging Louise.'

'What?' She misses the travel cup, spilling coffee over the counter. She curses under her breath then trots to the sink to grab a cloth. When she returns, she glares at Shell. 'Are you serious?'

She nods.

'Vile Louise from Gaulin?'

'The one and only,' Shell says, grabbing the cafetière and pouring what's left into her mug.

'He isn't,' Eleanor hisses, trying to not raise her voice. 'He wouldn't.'

'Well, he is.'

'Are you sure?'

'Louise told me, Ricky and Denise yesterday,' Shell says, as she heads to the fridge to get the milk. She hands the bottle to her mother, who is still standing by the kettle. 'And she's engaged.'

Her mother almost spills the milk this time, but manages to stop herself in time. 'Engaged?'

'Yep.' Shell takes the bottle from her and pours some into her mug. 'She's getting married next summer.'

'No!'

'Yes.'

'No!'

'Oh, yes. You should have seen Louise yesterday when she told us. She was all but swaggering.'

'Why would she tell you that? Cheating on your fiancé is nothing to be proud of.'

'Apparently it is if it's Callum Duke you're cheating on him with. She's acting like she's won the lottery, or something. She actually showed us a paint chart, Mum, because she's picking out colours for his bedroom.'

Eleanor gives Shell her best *I'm not angry, I'm just disappointed* face. 'Shame on Callum!'

Shell picks up the milk and walks over to put it back into the fridge.

'He doesn't seem the type, Shell,' she says, as Shell returns to where her mother is standing.

'They're *all* the type, Mum,' she mutters, sipping her coffee.

*

Shell's glad Callum gave her the day off because she honestly doesn't trust herself not to say something to him about Louise. *At least it will be easy to avoid him tonight,* she thinks, as she heads up to her room when the kids have gone to school. Hopefully, she'll have calmed down by then and this feeling will have passed.

Until then, she spends the rest of the day lounging about the house, like a contented cat.

Shell can't remember the last time she just sat around doing nothing. In the evening, maybe, when her feet ache from standing up all day. Then she doesn't feel guilty about sitting on the sofa with her parents, bickering over who the murderer is in whatever crime drama her father is making them watch. (Her mother is *always* right. It's slightly worrying.) But when she has a day off, it's usually for a reason. She has to go into London for an ART showcase about their new range of primers. Or she has to work on an assignment for her course.

But she never does this.

Does *nothing.*

It's *so* self-indulgent, but she gives in to it. She doesn't even shower and stays in her pyjamas, drinking coffee and eating toast while she watches makeup tutorials on YouTube. She looks up the production company and finds one of their films on Netflix. A sunny story about a woman Shell's age who inherits a vineyard in Provence from a long-lost great-aunt. She knows nothing about wine – of course! – but the deal is she *has* to keep it for a year before she can sell it. She can't let it go to ruin or it will be worth nothing, so she hires a hopelessly handsome – of course! – vineyard manager and, together, they keep it going. Soon it's thriving and at the end of the film, she's faced with a dilemma: sell for millions to the big bad global brand that just wants the vineyard for its name so it can put it on cheap bottles of plonk or stay with the handsome vineyard manager and make beautiful wine.

She stays – of course – which Shell knew she would, but that's what makes such films so comforting. The joy isn't in predicting the happy ending. It's in knowing that it's coming.

Shell's still on the sofa when her father and the twins barrel in from school whinging which must mean it's raining *again*. They're beside themselves when they charge into the living room to find her there, jumping on her and regaling her with the day's various victories and triumphs.

They're so excited to have her home, the five of them huddled together on the sofa under a blanket as she mediates over what to watch, that she considers not going to the Christmas party and staying with them. But then her mother gets in and, after listening to the collective *Mum, you'll never guess what happened today*, Eleanor takes the remote from the arm of the sofa and turns off the television.

'Homework,' she says, kissing each of the twins on the head as they traipse off to the kitchen, grumbling.

Then her mother looks down at her. 'Party.'

'I'm not going.' Shell pulls a face. 'I can't be arsed to traipse to Church Cabham on the bus in the rain.'

'Get a cab.'

'That'll cost a fortune.'

'What about Ricky and Denise? Can't you share one?'

'Yeah, but they'll be getting ready to leave soon. Ricky's DJing so they're going early to set up.'

'Fine. I'll give you a lift,' her mother tells her, not giving her back the remote when Shell reaches for it. 'Now come on. Get in the shower, contour, or whatever the hell it is that you do to your face that takes three hours, then put that new dress on. You can't sneak an ASOS bag past me, Shell Smith.' She points the remote at her, when Shell tries to deny all knowledge of a new dress. 'You're going to this Christmas party. It's been a week since Nick left. It's time to have some fun.'

Purple and green should never be seen, Shell says to herself, as she tries to recreate the Liberty purple-eyeshadow look Ricky did for her last month. She puts her own spin on it, of course. She uses less blue and more pink, and smears some gold across each eyelid with the pad of her index finger to bring out the slight shimmer in her green dress.

She's greeted by a barrage of whoops and cheers as she comes down the stairs with her shoes hanging from her fingers. She'd never usually wear something one-shouldered – there's yet to be a strapless bra invented that can comfortably contain her breasts for more than two hours – and she's sure it's too short, but when she showed it to Verity on Sunday, Verity snatched her phone off her and pressed the ADD TO BAG button before Shell could stop her.

'Thanks, guys,' she says, putting her shoes down and stepping into them, one at a time.

'Come on,' her mother says, coat already on, car keys in hand. 'Let's get you to the ball.'

Every year, the Duke & Sons Christmas party is held in the store. It usually consists of warm wine and crisps in the Beauty Hall on the twenty-third for Old Mr Duke's birthday, with everyone piling into the Anchor afterwards.

That's still the plan this year, but in honour of Old Mr Duke's last Christmas as CEO, Callum also wanted to do something special. So they're having dinner at a super-posh country hotel in Church Cabham. The sort of place couples dream of getting married, with a rose garden and a wide green rolling lawn outside, stripped floorboards and roaring fires within.

Tonight, it looks fit for a Christmas card, Shell thinks, as she walks towards the door, white lights twinkling in the trees. All it needs is a thick layer of snow on the thatched roof and it would be perfect.

When she gets inside she follows the sound of 'I Wish It Could Be Christmas Everyday' into what she's guessing is usually the restaurant but has been taken over by Duke & Sons staff in their party best.

'Shell!' she hears Denise call from the bar, but before she can get to her, someone steps into her path.

'Shell!' Callum grins, as she takes a step back.

He's in a black tuxedo and looks *devastating*, which she hates herself for noticing.

'Wow!' He blinks furiously. 'That is some dress.'

'Thanks,' she mutters, tugging it down.

He hands her a saucer of champagne, his smile smoother now. That's obviously what he's doing, his charming Callum Duke thing and greeting staff as they arrive.

'I'll get you a tequila later,' he tells her, when she takes it. 'We can toast your trip to Mexico.'

Before Shell can politely decline because her, plus Callum, plus tequila is a terrible idea that will no doubt conclude with her asking him how he can shag someone who is engaged, she's aware of someone watching them.

It's Louise, of course.

She's standing by the French windows out to the garden, a champagne saucer poised and her eyebrow raised as if to say, *He's mine.*

'Have fun tonight,' she tells Callum, with a cool smile, then struts off to find Denise.

Louise doesn't touch her food, but demurely sips at saucer after saucer of champagne at dinner until she's had one too many and goes from laughing politely to full on *shrieking*.

It's funny at first, but by the time the Christmas pudding is served, she's a mess. Her lipstick is smudged and the pashmina that was draped around her shoulders during dinner is now in a puddle on the floor. It's not funny any more as she heckles Old Mr Duke's speech, much to the horror of everyone at the other tables. Callum has had enough and asks one of the waiters for a glass of water then saunters over to where she's sitting and crouches next to her chair.

Shell doesn't know what he says to her, but it's enough to shut Louise up for the remainder of Old Mr Duke's speech. She even cheers and claps gracefully when he raises his champagne glass and thanks them for all their hard work this year.

Old Mr Duke stays for Christmas pudding but, by nine o'clock, he's flagging.

As soon as Callum puts him into a cab, all hell breaks loose. The tables are removed and the cheery, festive songs give way to the Spice Girls as Ricky takes to the decks in full Judy Christmas Garland drag.

Then the shots come out.

Denise is the first to initiate it, of course. She's dressed in a sleeveless floor-length yellow gown that makes her dark skin look gilded in gold, her box braids gathered into a bun on top of her head. *She should be on a red carpet*, Shell thinks, *not knocking back shots in a country hotel in Church Cabham.*

Two shots later, Denise finally introduces her to the infamous Liam from the warehouse, who, it turns out, is just as hot as advertised and does look remarkably like Chris Hemsworth. He's tanned and solid with blond hair bleached blonder by the sun and his blue eyes all but disappear when he smiles.

He's sweet and kind of shy, which Shell wasn't expecting, given that he's a single man in possession of a face like Chris Hemsworth's. So he's not much of a talker. Or maybe he doesn't *want* to talk, Shell realises, because another two shots later, she finds herself outside with him.

He leads her to the darkest part of the garden, then pins her to a wall, kissing her with such ferocity that she feels like she's knocked back another shot. Maybe her friends are on to something after all. Shell doesn't know whether it's the tequila or Liam's aftershave that smells like he should be in a forest, splitting logs with his bare hands, but she's into it.

This will do, thank you very much.

So why he's pulling away, she doesn't know.

'What's wrong?' she asks, as he jumps back, looking guilty, as though they've been caught snogging behind the bike sheds. Then she turns to see what he's looking at and almost falls off her heels.

It's Callum, clearly as embarrassed as Liam, a cigar between his fingers.

'Sorry.' He holds up the cigar. 'I was just looking for somewhere to smoke this.'

'Sorry, Mr Duke,' Liam mutters, then mutters something else Shell thinks is *See you inside* and he's gone.

Wait for me, she almost calls after him, but it's too late. Callum is walking towards her, then stops in front of her with a curious smile.

'Shell Smith.'

'Callum,' she says, going to tug the straps of her bag back onto her shoulder, but it isn't there.

'I didn't know you and Liam were, *you know*.'

'We *weren't*. Not until about fifteen minutes ago.'

Callum seems amused by that, his smile more playful now as he leans against the wall and crosses his arms. 'I'll have to check our policy on inter-staff relationships.'

So you have a policy, then? Or doesn't it apply to you? she thinks, but bites her tongue so hard, she can taste blood.

Or maybe that's tequila.

'I didn't know you smoked,' she says instead, nodding at the cigar in his hand.

He looks down at it as if he'd forgotten it was there. 'I don't, actually. It's a gag gift from my grandfather.' He brings the cigar up to his mouth, bobbing it up and down in time with his eyebrows and laughing, lightening the mood so she doesn't feel so mortally embarrassed about being caught snogging some guy from the warehouse.

It works, because then Shell's laughing. And, just like that, it's forgotten – Liam, Louise, all of it – as they fall into the gentle back and forth that comes so easily to them.

'It was my great-grandfather Patrick's thing, apparently,' Callum says, when he stops playing with the cigar. 'Pops says that every night, as soon as the store closed, he'd go up to his office and smoke one at his desk. He'd have a cigar, drink a whisky, then check each floor on his way down the stairs and go home for supper.'

'Will you be keeping up the tradition when you become CEO next year?'

'The whisky, maybe,' he says, with a light laugh.

When Shell laughs too, he peers at her from under his eyelashes, his eyes brilliant blue. 'So. Liam, huh?'

Shell's cheeks sting again as he looks at her for a beat longer than is comfortable.

'Yeah,' she mutters, bringing her hand up to her mouth, suddenly aware that her lipstick must be smudged.

'What happened to the vegan?'

'I haven't heard from him since that night you gave me a lift home,' she admits, avoiding eye contact as he leans a little closer. So close that she can smell him and it's making her head spin.

Or, again, maybe that's the tequila.

'I'm sorry,' Callum says, and she believes him.

'It's fine,' she says. 'I suggested the friend thing, but he wasn't interested.'

'Just give him time, Shell. He'll be back when he's ready. And in the meantime,' he says, even closer now, 'there's Liam.'

Or maybe it's her leaning in this time, like a flower turning towards the sun.

'I guess. He's sweet.'

'Is that what you're looking for, Shell?' Callum stops to lick his lips. 'Sweet?'

'I'd settle for uncomplicated right now.'

'I hear that,' he says, raising his eyebrows.

When he does, something nips at her. *He's thinking about Louise, isn't he?*

'I'm going to head back inside. I'm freezing.' She hugs herself, and when she pretends to shiver, Callum doesn't hesitate, pushing away from the wall.

'Don't,' she says, as he starts to take off his jacket.

She doesn't mean to say it so sharply, but it's enough to make his hands still.

'What's wrong?' he asks, with a frown.

'Nothing.'

She goes to walk around him, but he steps to the side to stop her.

Shell has to jump back so they don't collide.

His frown deepens. 'Shell, what is it?'

'It's nothing.'

'Well, it's not nothing. You suddenly look like you want to murder me.'

'I'm fine,' she says, as firmly as she can, given that she really is shivering now.

But she's not cold, she's *furious*.

Callum is so startled that she manages to walk around him this time, but he grabs her wrist.

The shock of it – of his bare skin against her own – makes her gasp and snatch her arm away.

'I'm sorry.' He holds his hands up, his cheeks flushed. 'I'm sorry. I just want to know what I did to upset you.'

When she doesn't say anything, just shakes her head, he frowns again.

'Is it Liam? I honestly didn't mean to pry.'

'Actually you did.' The words snap off her tongue before she can bite down on them. 'Who I am seeing or no longer seeing is none of your business. Just as whoever *you*'re seeing is none of *mine*.'

Right on cue, Louise stumbles out of the French windows onto the patio then, calling his name. 'Come here,' he whispers, reaching for Shell's elbow and tugging her back into the darkness.

'Get off,' she spits, shrugging him off.

'I'm sorry.' He holds his hands up again. 'I just don't want Louise to see me.'

'Getting too complicated for you, is it?'

Callum doesn't understand what she's hinting at, though, as he exhales through his nose and mock-shudders. 'It isn't remotely complicated, actually. Louise is just drunk and keeps coming at me with the mistletoe.'

'Not in public, eh?' Shell finally says, shaking with the effort of keeping it in.

That gets his attention.

When he stops looking across the lawn at Louise and looks at her instead, it's like a door slamming shut, a cloud of cold filling the space between them.

'Excuse me?' he asks, with a look that makes her take a step back.

When Louise gives up and goes inside, Shell glances across the garden, calculating how many steps there are between her and the French windows. If she took off her heels, she could make it in fifteen seconds, she reckons. She can hear 'Cut to the Feeling' playing now and imagines Denise behind the decks with Ricky, her arms in the air, and wishes she was in there with them.

'Shell?' Callum pushes, and the way he looks at her leaves her in no doubt that if she doesn't answer him soon, his patience will falter. 'What do you mean?'

It startles her so much that she just blurts it out. 'You and Louise.'

'Me and Louise?'

All Shell can manage is a nod.

'What about me and Louise?'

She doesn't answer, but then she doesn't have to.

He already knows.

Oh, shit, she thinks, as she watches him take a step back.

Callum's face hardens and Shell knows in that moment. She knows it's not true.

Louise lied.

'Let me get this straight,' he says, and Shell doesn't know what scares her most, that she's just accused him of shagging a member of staff or that he's trying to control his temper in a way she's never seen him have to before.

'Let me get this straight,' Callum says again. 'You think that Louise Larson and I are together?'

Shell nods.

'Why?'

'Because she told me.'

'Louise Larson *told* you that we were together?'

She nods again.

'When?'

'After the carol concert. We bumped into her outside the store as we were leaving.'

'We?'

'Me, Ricky and Denise.'

The muscles in Callum's jaw twitch. 'What did Louise say?'

She hesitates because *oh God, oh God, oh God* what has she done?

'Shell, what did Louise say?'

'She said she was waiting for you to pick her up. That you were going back to your place.'

'*My* place?'

'She knew where you lived. Your car. Everything.'

Callum considers that for a moment or two, then asks, 'What else did she say?'

'Nothing.'

Callum doesn't let it go, though. 'Everyone knows what car I drive and where I live. I've hardly made a secret of either. Louise must have said *something* to make you this sure.' He frowns and takes another step towards her. 'Shell? What did she say?'

'She had this paint chart.' She curses herself as soon as she says it out loud.

'A paint chart?'

'She pulled it out when we said we didn't believe her.'

'And what precisely does a paint chart prove?'

'Nothing, I suppose. Now I think about it. But she said . . .' She shrugs, then looks down at her shoes, too ashamed to meet his eyes. 'She said you'd asked her to help you pick a colour for your bedroom.'

When he doesn't say anything, Shell starts babbling to fill the silence.

'It was just so ordinary, I guess. That's why I believed her. It wasn't a big elaborate story about how you were whisking her away to New York for Christmas, or something. It was just a paint chart.'

He tucks the cigar into the inside pocket of his tuxedo jacket. 'Thank you, Shell.'

'Callum, I—' she starts, but he strides off.

Before she can go after him, he stops and turns to face her again.

'For the record,' he says tightly, 'Louise Larson and I are *not* together.' He looks her in the eye. 'I need you to know that, Shell.'

When she nods, he nods back.

Then he's gone.

Chapter Twenty-Five

'Last one in?' Gary says, checking his watch when he sees Shell approaching Duke & Sons. 'That's not like you. Here was me thinking you left early last night so you could be tucked up in bed by eleven.'

'I wish.' Shell forces a smile. 'Did you have a good one?'

Before he can answer, the revolving door turns and Ricky marches outside.

'Where *the hell* have you been?' he snaps, taking her by the sleeve of her coat and pulling her inside.

He doesn't say anything, just drags her through the Beauty Hall and out into the back of house. Shell thinks he's taking her to the break room, but he tugs her into the supply cupboard where Denise is waiting, her foot tapping.

'Where *the hell* have you been?' she barks, as Ricky closes the door.

'I know. I'm sorry. I overslept.'

That's not true.

Oversleeping implies that she slept, which she didn't. How could she after her conversation with Callum? She spent most of the night cursing herself for believing Louise when she knew – *she knew* – she was lying.

Now she's messed everything up.

Louise is probably going to lose her job and Callum, well, poor Callum probably feels awful that Shell thinks he'd do something like that when he's been nothing but nice to her. He suggested her for the MUA job on the film with Verity. He's letting her take two months off to work on her new one in Paris. He sent her flowers. Let her have yesterday off for all her hard work on the first annual Duke & Son's White Christmas and how does she repay him?

By spreading a rumour that he's shagging one of his staff with *no proof*.

She's a terrible, terrible person.

'Anyway,' Denise says, adjusting the collar of her shirt, 'after you kissed Liam and ran last night, which,' Denise raises a finger – and an eyebrow – to her, 'was very rude by the way . . .'

'I had to.' Shell cringes. 'Callum caught us. I wanted to die.'

'Poor Liam.' Ricky pouts. 'He probably thinks you hate him.'

'He doesn't. I texted him from the cab.'

They perk up at that.

'And I invited him to join us at the Anchor after work,' Shell adds with a small shrug.

'Well, that's something,' Denise says, clearly thrilled at this new development. 'Anyway—'

Ricky doesn't let her finish. 'You would not believe what you missed after you left last night!'

Shell braces herself as he grabs her arm and shakes her.

'Callum sacked Louise!'

'What?' Shell gasps, the back of her neck burning.

But it's less *oh, no, what happened?* and more *Oh, no, what have I done?*

'Louise was a *mess,*' Ricky tells her. 'Shell, you saw the state of her, but she got even worse after you left. It was awful. She was going from table to table, finishing off people's drinks, *and then,* I put on "Toxic". She was dancing so much, one of her boobs popped out of her dress.'

Shell presses her hands to her cheeks. 'No!'

'*Then,*' he goes on, 'she *threw* herself at Callum. She had mistletoe and tried to kiss him—'

'They're not together,' Denise interrupts. 'Louise made the whole thing up.'

Shell stares at them, hands still pressed to her face. She knows that, but how do *they* know it?

'I felt so bad for her, Shell,' Denise says, closing her eyes. 'It was *mortifying.*'

'Mor-ti-fying!' Ricky concurs. 'Callum was *livid.* He had to put Louise into a cab. David from Furniture said she was so drunk, Callum had to give the driver a hundred quid to take her.'

Denise shakes her head. 'Mess.'

Ricky does the same. 'Mess.'

Shell doesn't know what to say and just stares at them.

'Then,' Denise lowers her voice as Shell finally takes her hands away from her face, 'after Louise left, I found Camilla crying in the loos and as I was comforting her she let rip and told me *everything.*'

'Told you *what?*' Shell asks.

'You can't tell anyone, though. This isn't silly shop-floor gossip. It's serious.'

'I swear.' Shell crosses her chest with her finger. 'I won't tell a soul.'

'Louise had to call off her engagement.'

'Because of Callum?' Shell asks, the words out before she can swallow them back.

'Of course not!' She looks disgusted. 'It was ages ago. Like, in October. Way before Callum started.'

'*October?*'

'Her fiancé cheated on her with some woman from his office.'

'Den, that's *awful.*'

'I know. But she's in complete denial. That's why she's still wearing her engagement ring.'

'She's not considering taking him back, is she?'

They nod in unison.

'Why?'

'Because she's *miserable*,' Ricky says, with a sad frown.

Denise lowers her voice to a whisper. 'Camilla says Louise would rather be with him than be on her own.'

'No,' Shell says. 'That's so sad.'

'It is sad,' Ricky agrees. 'She's smoking because she says it kills her appetite and she's doing all of these absurd juice cleanses to fit into a wedding dress for a wedding that isn't even happening. It's tragic.'

'Poor Louise,' she murmurs, looking down at the empty bucket and mop by her feet.

Denise glances at the door to the supply cupboard. 'That's why she's so obsessed with Callum.'

Shell arches an eyebrow at *obsessed*.

'He was nice to her, like, one time.'

Ricky interjects to nudge Shell. 'After the Christmas Changeover meeting, remember? She stormed out.'

'She came back,' Shell says, trying not to shout as she remembers. 'After I'd taken the float to the safe.'

Denise nods furiously. 'It was *that* night. He took her to the new Thai place in Church Cabham.'

That was the night before her first date with Nick, wasn't it? Shell thinks.

Callum said that he'd just been, which was why he told them to steer clear of the Pad Thai.

So Louise hadn't lied about that.

It wasn't honest of her to imply it was a date, of course, but she and Callum had gone there together.

'Camilla says nothing happened. They just talked,' Denise adds.

But there's no need. Shell can picture it. Callum chatting away about restoring his house, about the steam shower and the wine fridge, while Louise picked at her curry and tried not to cry about her fiancé. She knows how easy those conversations with Callum are. How intoxicating it is to have a few moments of his attention. Shell shakes her head. 'Poor Louise.'

'Poor Callum, more like,' Ricky says, and there's a hint of defensiveness that lets her know he's decided to re-stan. 'He was just trying to be nice to her and Louise turned it into this whole other thing in her head.'

'Yeah, but we all do stuff when we're sad, Ricky.' Shell

wrinkles her nose at him. 'Stupid stuff to make it hurt less. Some people drink too much or fall face first into a tub of Ben & Jerry's. Louise created this world in her head where she and Callum were together.' She lets out a small groan. 'We've all done it, haven't we? Seen stuff that isn't there. I mean look at me and Nick.'

Denise doesn't hesitate. 'That is not the same!'

'Yeah.' Ricky reaches out to squeeze her arm. 'Louise and Callum went for *one* dinner.'

'And it wasn't in your head,' Denise adds, before Shell can think it. 'Because you got together, didn't you?'

Before Shell can agree, the door to the supply cupboard swings open.

The three turn to see who it is then jump back when they realise it's Callum.

'Forgive me for breaking up this mothers' meeting.' He taps his watch. 'But it's nine thirty.'

'Did you fire Louise Larson?'

Shell doesn't realise she's said it until she hears Ricky and Denise gasp.

Her cheeks burn as Callum's whole face changes and he steps inside, closing the door behind him. 'I did not fire Louise Larson.' He makes sure he looks Shell in the eye. 'She's taken a sabbatical.'

Ricky's gaze narrows. 'Is that a posh word for sacked?'

'Of course not,' Callum says. 'Louise has some personal issues so I've given her some time off. When she's ready, she'll be back. In the meantime, we still have a store to run.'

He turns to open the door and the three of them scurry out.

After the morning meeting, Callum says he hopes the day isn't too difficult for everyone with their hangovers, promising coffee and bacon butties at lunch. He thanks them, clapping his hands, and as they join in, Ricky nudges Shell, then nods at Camilla, who is waving at them, looking slightly panicked. She's in charge of the Gaulin counter now that Louise is 'on sabbatical' and obviously has no idea what she's doing.

'I'll go,' Ricky offers.

And that's how it is for the rest of the day, the pair of them running back and forth, helping Camilla between clients. Louise used to do everything, it seems. She wouldn't let the other girls do anything so Camilla barely knows how to use the till and Shell has to show her how to cash up at the end of the day.

It takes so long that she barely has time to change into her mustard yellow jumper before her date/not date with Liam. She's clutching her coat and bag and rushing back into the Beauty Hall, hoping she has time at least to refresh her lipstick, and *almost* makes it back to the counter when she hears someone call her name.

She turns on her heel to find it's Callum and the shock makes her drop everything she's carrying.

'Sorry!' he says. 'I didn't mean to startle you.'

She hasn't seen him since the morning meeting, which isn't like him at all. He usually does a circuit of each floor at least three times a day, chatting to customers and asking staff if they're all right, but he hasn't today.

But here he is.

'It's okay,' she says, trying to sound casual and not like she's about to cringe her skin clean off her bones.

'Let me help.' He closes the few steps to where she is crouched, picking up her stuff.

He squats next to her, grabbing a can of hairspray before it rolls under the Gaulin counter.

'About last night,' he says quickly, his eyes on Ricky and Denise, who are watching, but in no rush to help.

'Yes?' she whispers, her heart thundering as she peeks at him from under her fringe.

'Can we talk?' he whispers back, his blue eyes brighter than she's ever seen them. 'Please,' he adds, and when she watches them bloom from blue to black, she almost drops the hairspray as he hands it back.

He's not mad.

She thought he'd be mad.

Before she can respond, though, she's aware of a shadow over them and looks up.

'You alright, Shell?' Liam asks, with a smile.

'It's okay, thanks. I've got it,' she says, her smile less eager as she stands up and stuffs everything back into her canvas tote.

Callum stands as well, running his finger under the collar of his shirt as he nods at Liam.

'Hey, Mr Duke,' Liam says, a little sheepishly, no doubt recalling the horror of him catching them kissing.

'Liam.' Callum's whole demeanour changes when he

realises he's there to meet Shell. 'Well,' he says, with a practised smile. 'Don't let me detain the two of you. Shell, we can catch up tomorrow.'

Chapter Twenty-Six

They don't catch up the next day. They don't speak for the rest of the week. They just orbit around one another, like a couple of planets, Callum careful to keep out of her way in case they collide.

Shell can hardly blame him after what will now be referred to as the Louise Incident.

Callum is there, but he's not. He checks in, but doesn't linger, and is careful to keep his distance when someone tries to engage him in conversation. Even then he keeps it brief.

Light.

Professional.

And again, after what happened with Louise, Shell can't blame him for that, either.

So when Callum strides into the community centre on Sunday morning, she almost spills her coffee.

Her mother doesn't notice, too busy trying to wrap a plastic dinosaur as they discuss Shell's first date with Liam. Or, at least, their first date just the two of them. Given that they've already kissed – not just at the Christmas party, but the night after as well, when they went to the pub after that excruciating exchange with

303

Callum in the Beauty Hall when she dropped all her stuff – Eleanor is somewhat bemused by the whole thing, saying that it's not a real first date unless you spend the whole night asking yourself if they're going to kiss you.

As much as it pains Shell to admit it, she's right. The date was nice. Dinner and a movie. A classic. But there was no thrill. No anticipation. And while Liam is sweet, he's too fond of beer and rugby for Shell's interest in him to blossom much further than a breathless snog outside the Anchor.

'Stop overthinking it, Shell. Just have some fun before you go to Paris,' her mother tells her, as she grapples with a piece of Sellotape, oblivious of Callum, who is now standing in front of the folding table they're behind. 'I wish I had a Liam to learn a few tricks from before your father got me knocked up.'

Eleanor Smith's timing, as always, is impeccable.

'MUM!' Shell shrieks, her whole face burning.

Her mother looks up then and gasps. 'Oh, *Jesus*.'

'Please, call me Callum,' he says, with a wicked smile.

'What are you doing here?' Shell puts down the mug she's holding, scared that she'll drop it if she doesn't.

'This is a toy drive, right?' He holds up the Duke & Sons bags in his hands. 'I brought toys.'

'Callum!' Her mother is thrilled. 'That's so nice!'

'Where would you like me to put them?'

'Over there.' She points towards the other side of the hall where Shell has organised the donations into neat piles – soft toys, books, Lego, action figures – waiting to be wrapped. 'I'll be right with you.'

When he strides off, her mother arches an eyebrow at her. 'Am I sensing some tension, Shell?'

Shell is so shaken he's there that her scalp is sweating.

Eleanor elbows her in the ribs. 'Tell me.'

'I *might have* confronted him about the Louise Larson thing at the Christmas party.'

Her mother closes her eyes. When she opens them again, she winces. 'I take it it didn't go well.'

'No, it did not,' Shell huffs. 'Turns out Louise made the whole thing up.'

Eleanor points at her. 'I knew it!'

'Yes. Well. We've barely spoken since, which is why I'm so surprised he's here.'

'I have to say,' her mother admits, as she looks at Callum, who's waiting patiently on the other side of the hall with the bags of toys. 'I feel much better. That whole thing with Louise didn't sit right with me at all, Shell. He's not like that. I know I've only met him once, but I'm rarely wrong about these things.'

'Are you ever wrong about *anything*?' Shell mutters, sipping her coffee.

Eleanor ignores her. 'The flowers, yes. That was a very Callum thing to do. Louise Larson? Absolutely not.'

'Well, you can take comfort from the fact that your flawless record of always being right remains intact.'

'Go talk to him.'

'No.' Shell tries not to pout. 'He's here for you, not me.'

Her mother puts down the Sellotape when she sees that Shell isn't going to leave the safety of the table, obviously feeling bad that they've left Callum on the other side of the hall by himself.

'Don't let him leave,' she warns. 'Now's a good time. You're on neutral territory here.'

'Fine,' Shell says, through her teeth, snatching the half-wrapped dinosaur off the table.

She decides to distract herself with finishing it, as her mother walks over to greet Callum, in an effort to avoid watching them. But she does, of course, trying not to stare as her mother helps him unpack the bags, admiring each thing before putting it into the relevant pile. By the time they're done, they're laughing, Callum in a plastic tiara, her mother delighted. Utterly, uncontainably *delighted* in a way Shell's only ever seen at home, when she's dancing around the kitchen with Shaun or when one of the kids say something funny.

She looks so happy that Shell has to look away as she feels the scratch of something that makes her cheeks warm. She secures the last piece of Sellotape to the dinosaur, and when she holds it up, Callum is in front of her. He nods towards the door. 'I'd better go.'

'Okay.' Shell gestures at his head. He frowns, then laughs when he realises he's still wearing the plastic tiara. He takes it off and sweeps his fingers through his hair.

'Sorry.' He hands it to her. When she doesn't say anything, just looks down at the sparkly pink plastic tiara, he says, 'Okay, then. I'll see you back on set later. I guess that's the last time I'll say that.'

He turns to wave goodbye to Eleanor, who glares across the hall at Shell as he leaves.

Go, her mother mouths, and Shell shakes her head. But when the steady tap of his shoes on the scuffed floor fades away, something kicks at her and she runs after him before she even knows what she's going to say.

She gets out of the community centre as he's opening his car door and calls his name. He stops, standing behind it, watching as she runs across the small car park towards him.

'Callum,' she says, out of breath as she stops in front of him, the car door between them.

'Shell?'

She can't catch her breath and it's all so needlessly dramatic. The running. The way her hands are shaking so much that she has to cross her arms so he doesn't see.

It's no big deal, is it?

All she needs to do is say sorry.

Maybe if she'd apologised immediately – as soon as she saw him the next morning instead of accusing him of sacking Louise – it would have been done and they could have gone back to how things were before.

She misses that, she realises then.

She misses him. Their small, quiet conversations on Sundays while Verity's doing her thing and Shell's organising her station for her next scene. The first, when he was helping her pack up the counter. The one they had in his office, that *horrifyingly* expensive bottle of whisky between them.

Now he doesn't even look at her when he passes through the Beauty Hall.

'I'm sorry,' she says at last, because it's too much – it's too many words – and that's all she has.

Callum just looks at her, and she feels wretched because that's not enough, is it?

Maybe it's enough to make things more pleasant at work, but not if she wants more than that.

It doesn't even occur to Shell to ask herself why she does.

'I'm sorry.' She tries again. 'For the Louise thing. For all of it. I shouldn't have told you.'

'I'm glad you did, actually,' he says, when she stops to catch her breath.

'Yeah, but you shouldn't have found out like that. I feel awful.'

'It's okay,' he says kindly. 'You weren't to know that what Louise was saying wasn't true.'

'Yes. Well.' Shell's cheeks are stinging with shame. 'I'm sorry about that as well.'

'For what, Shell?'

'For believing her.' Shell lifts her left shoulder then lets it drop again. 'For believing that you'd do something like that. Not just with a colleague, but with someone who was engaged. Or, at least, someone I *thought* was engaged.'

'Thank you, Shell,' Callum says, his voice noticeably softer.

So soft that it gives her the courage to look at him again, and when she does, he's smiling.

'I mean that,' she insists, because she wants him to know.

She wants him to know that she was wrong.

That she shouldn't have assumed the worst when he has never given her a reason to.

She can't find the courage to say that, though.

So she just says, 'Are we good?'

'We're always good,' he tells her, with a wink.

Then he's gone, out of the car park and around the corner.

She watches him go, then lets out a satisfied sigh when she hears the sound of his car fade.

When she turns to head back into the community centre, she almost walks into someone.

'Sorry!' she says. 'Didn't see you there.'

But when she looks up, it's Nick.

Chapter Twenty-Seven

Shell steps back. 'Nick.'

He steps forward. 'Shell.'

She stares at him for a moment, not entirely convinced that he's actually there.

There's a long, painful moment when they don't know what to do. She raises her arms as he does, then immediately drops them again. They do it a few times – arms up, arms down, arms up, arms down – before they just keep them in the air as they look at one another. Then Nick laughs and they give into it, embracing each other tightly before stepping back to look at each other.

'Nick Wallace,' she says, and she can hear the relief in her voice.

'Shell Smith.' He grins, tugging his black knitted hat over his ears. 'You look amazing. Your hair is full on Princess Jasmine today.'

'Oh, thanks. I'm using this new serum.' She tells herself to shut up. He's not here to talk about her new serum. 'You look great as well,' she tells him. *Much better than the last time I saw you* is left unsaid as she takes him in.

His hair is longer – and clean, thank you very much, Denise Varina-Williams – his blue eyes clearer and his cheeks a healthy shade of pink. It even looks like he's put on weight in the two weeks since she's seen him, his cheekbones not as sharp.

He looks like Nick again.

'Thanks. Remarkable what a hot meal and more than three hours of sleep will do.'

'What are you doing here? I assumed you went back to London.'

'I did. I'm back to sort out Mum's house. I managed to sell it. I just handed over the keys.'

'You okay?'

He just shrugs because how can he be okay? 'I'm glad it's sorted and a new family get to live there. It was a shame to just leave it sitting empty. I was never going to live there, was I?'

'So what's the plan?'

'Goa.' He exhales heavily. 'I know, I know. I'm such a cliché.'

So that's the second boyfriend she's lost to Goa. What is it with Goa? It's like a lost-and-found for confused middle-class white men.

'Don't worry.' Nick laughs lightly. 'I promise not to get dreadlocks and a hamsa hand tattoo.'

She gives him a look that lets him know he'd better not.

That's when she sees it: the first snowflake. It lands on the tip of his nose, melting immediately. Then there's another and another, until they look up at the big white sky as the snow starts falling around them, soft and silent and so cold that each flake stings her cheeks.

When their chins drop and they look at one another again, she grins.

Nick doesn't.

'Listen,' he says, with a tender sigh, and the joy of seeing the snow is instantly forgotten. 'You're right,' he admits, bringing his hand up to his hair and fisting it. 'I'm not okay about Mum dying.'

'I don't think you're supposed to be okay about it, Nick.'

He relaxes a little, managing a faint smile. 'I found this grief counsellor in Walthamstow. She's a bit incense-and-crystals,' he says, taking his fingers out of his hair and stuffing his hands into the pockets of his leather jacket. 'But she's great *and*,' he says, brown eyes wide as he tilts his head at her, 'as you'll no doubt be shocked to hear, you were right about the stages of grief as well.'

Shell tries not to look smug as he tells her about them.

'I did denial when Mum died. Then anger, with you, which was a fun time for everyone involved, I think you'll agree. And now I'm in depression.'

She pulls a face as if to say, *Yikes!*

'Which,' Nick says, with mock solemnity, 'I can already tell, is going to be an absolute *riot*.'

'Yeah, good luck with that.'

'And once I'm done with depression, I move on to bargaining.'

'What does that involve?'

'I'm not entirely sure, to be honest. I think it's like denial, except you try to make a deal with God or the Universe to get back whoever you've lost. That's when I could potentially go full Norman Bates. But Mum was cremated and I've sold the house.' He takes his hand out of his pocket to cross his fingers and hold them up. 'After that, it's acceptance, which is the final stage and, I imagine, a bit like achieving nirvana. That's why I'm off to Goa, because I want that to happen on a beach at sunrise, not in the little Tesco on Shoreditch High Street.'

'Nick, that's great!' she says, giddy with relief. 'I'm so proud of you.'

'Yeah. I'm kind of proud of me too.' He's smiling to himself, but then the corners of his mouth droop. 'What I'm not proud of is how I treated you. Back then and now.'

'Nick—'

'Don't,' he says, before she can finish. 'Don't say you understand. Just let me say this, okay?'

She nods.

'I'm sorry. I know that's not enough. Maybe when I'm done with counselling and I've found a way of articulating my feelings that doesn't involve getting drunk and aggressively listening to Bon Iver, I'll be give you the apology you deserve, but until then, it's all I've got.'

'It's okay, Nick.'

'Actually, it's not. It's not okay at all. You are, honest to God, the best thing that ever happened to me, Shell, and I will never forgive myself for fucking this up so royally.'

'You didn't—' He arches an eyebrow at her and she adds, 'Yeah. Okay. Maybe a bit.'

He laughs, the deep dimples in his cheeks that she hasn't seen for weeks reappearing.

'Seriously, though,' she tells him. 'You and I, we were always better as friends.'

He nods. 'You were right about that, as well.' He makes sure he looks her in the eye when he says it. 'I really do need a friend right now.'

'Well, you know me, Nick. I never leave home,' she says, with a smirk that makes him full-body cringe, his teeth clenched. 'So I'm not going anywhere. I'll always be here.'

They look at one another for a moment, before he turns towards the road.

'I'd better go before I get stuck on the A12.'

'You going back to London now?'

He nods, but he doesn't say, *There's no reason for me to stay*.

'Take care of yourself, Shell,' he says, hugging her tightly again and suggesting they go for a coffee the next time she's in London before he walks away.

He takes a few steps, then turns back to her with a reluctant sigh.

'Okay,' he says, sliding his hands back into the pockets of his leather jacket. 'In my attempt to be a better person, or whatever.' He stops to roll his eyes. 'That guy from Duke's. Kevin, is it?'

'Callum,' she reminds him, even though he knows full well what his name is.

Nick laughs unrepentantly. 'I saw you two talking when I walked into the car park earlier.'

'Yeah?' she says suspiciously.

'I know I said you like them broken, but look how well

that turned out.' He tilts his head at her. 'So maybe it's time for you to try something new. Someone unbroken.'

Before she can ask him what he means, he walks away.

But as he reaches the road, he stops and turns back to her one last time. 'Shell,' he calls, with a clumsy smile, 'it was kind of fun being seventeen again, wasn't it?'

It kind of was.

There's a spring in Shell's step as she heads to Duke & Sons for the last day of filming. She's apologised to Callum and Nick's apologised to her. So when Liam calls, she decides to go three for three and thanks him for last night, but declines his offer to join him in the pub to watch the rugby. She tells him she'll see him at work tomorrow, and it takes a moment, but when he says, 'Oh. Okay. No worries,' she's pretty sure he understands what she's getting at.

After that she feels lighter and actually holds her arms out to do a small twirl in the middle of the street.

The snow is settling now so everything is white and feels brand new.

Like a fresh start, she thinks, when she gets to Duke & Sons. She takes a deep breath before pushing through the revolving door, but it's eerily quiet on the other side.

She knew it would be. After all, they're shooting the last scene today, and with Verity on her way back from Salford after attending the *Coronation Street* Christmas party last night (spoiler alert: she's going to be in *Coronation Street*), they haven't started yet. That's why

Shell could stay longer at her mother's toy drive than she'd intended.

'Hey, Luke,' she says, nodding at one of the runners as he approaches. 'Where is everyone?'

'Verity's stuck on a train outside Manchester. Not much we can do until she gets here.'

'Thanks,' she says, as he continues towards the revolving door, a roll-up between his fingers.

She hears her phone ringing in her bag and takes it out to find it's Verity.

'Oh, my God! Help!' she wails, before Shell can even say hello.

'Vee, where are you?'

'I just got kicked off a train in the arse end of *God knows where*. Hang on. Heaton Chapel. Where *the fuck* is Heaton Chapel?'

'No idea.'

'Mike's trying to get me a car but he says it's snowing there as well. Is it?'

'Yeah.' Shell turns to look out of the revolving door. 'It's coming down pretty heavily now.'

'Bollocks. I'll be lucky to get back to civilisation today, let alone Ostley.'

'You're assuming Ostley *is* civilisation.'

Verity laughs, the big, bright laugh that always makes Shell laugh, too.

'Argh. This sucks.' Shell can actually hear her pouting. 'Mike says that if I don't get back soon, he's calling it a wrap on Duke & Sons. He says we'll have to film the last scene on set in London.'

'Oh, no! Does that mean I'm not going to see you again before Christmas?'

'I don't think I'll have time.'

Now Shell is pouting.

'Listen. I've got to go. Mike's calling. You're coming to the wrap party in the new year, right?'

'You know it.'

'You'd better bring that beautiful boy.'

'Which beautiful boy?' Shell asks, wondering how Verity knew that she'd just seen Nick.

'Callum, obviously!'

Shell laughs. 'Sure, Vee. *Okay*. Call me when you find your way back to civilisation.'

Shell lingers in the Beauty Hall, unsure what to do with herself while she waits. So she adjusts the candy canes hanging from the ribbons around the counters and pats the polar bears at the foot of the stairs. She doesn't know where she's going, just that she's wandering.

Or, at least, she *thinks* she's wandering until she finds herself outside the door to Old Mr Duke's office. She tells herself not to knock – that he's probably busy – but does anyway, holding her breath as she waits. When she hears Callum say, 'Come in,' she exhales and opens the door, poking her head around it with a smile. 'Hey.'

'Shell Smith.' His face lights up, and he gestures her in. 'Thank goodness. I had an awful feeling it was my grandfather. How we've managed to get away with this for *seven Sundays*, I don't know.'

'It's quite honestly a miracle,' she says, as she steps in, closing the door behind her.

'A Christmas one!'

'Did you hear about Verity?' she asks, walking towards the desk and stopping in front of it.

'Yeah. I thought Mike was getting her a car?'

'I don't think that'll be happening.' Shell points at the window and he turns to look outside. It's clad in thick black security bars, but they're far enough apart for them to see the snow coming down in the car park.

'When did that start?'

'A couple of hours ago.'

He taps his laptop. 'I've been so busy with these figures, I didn't notice.'

'She's been kicked off a train in Heaton Chapel.'

'Where the hell is Heaton Chapel?'

'I have no idea, but far enough away that I don't think she's going to make it back today.'

'That's a shame,' Callum says. 'As stressful as this has been, I've actually quite enjoyed it. And . . .' he points at the screen '. . . I've worked it out. What they've paid us to film here is enough to restore the staircase and that death trap of an elevator.'

'I *knew* it was a death-trap! '

He pats the arms of Old Mr Duke's leather swivel chair. 'You want the big chair?'

'I'm good.' She goes to grab the plastic fold-up one from beside the water-cooler and puts it down opposite his desk. 'Plus,' she says, when she sits down, 'it'll be nice to go back to a more manageable six-day week, won't it?'

'Don't forget we're opening on Sundays in the new year.'

Shell groans theatrically as she unbuttons her coat. She'd forgotten about that. 'Still, it's been fun, hasn't it? Working on a film.'

Old Mr Duke's chair creaks as he sits back.

'I saw a Heart in Hand film the other day,' she tells him, as she takes off her coat.

'Yeah?'

'It was really cute. It was about this woman who inherits a vineyard in Provence.'

'Don't tell me, she falls in love with the rugged handyman?'

Shell snorts. 'Something like that.'

'What was it called? Something awful like *The Grapes of Love*, I suppose.'

'*Say You'll Be Wine*,' she corrects, as if that's any better. It's his turn to groan.

'Did the rugged handyman stand in the rain at the end of the film saying, "Pick me?" Get it?' He waggles his eyebrows, unreasonably proud of himself. 'Pick me. Because it's set in a vineyard.'

'Oh, don't be so cynical,' she tells him. 'There's nothing wrong with a happy ending.'

'I didn't say there was. *When Harry Met Sally* . . . Now *that*'s a happy ending.'

'Ah, but where are you on the impossibility of male-female friendships, then?'

'Undecided,' he says, with a smile, then swiftly changes the subject. 'How was the rest of the toy drive?'

'Very loud. You left at the perfect time.'

'Well, your mother made a lot of children very happy today.'

'As did you. Thanks for the toys.'

'Oh, it was nothing. As soon as I told my grandfather about it, he dragged me around the toy department and insisted I pretty much take one of everything.'

'The store is going broke, you say?' Shell says, with mock disbelief. 'I can't think why.'

Callum throws back his head and laughs. 'God, I love him, but he'll be the death of me.'

This should be weird, Shell thinks. They should still be in that excruciating post-apology transition where everything's awkward and a bit painful.

But it's not at all. It's like putting on her favourite hoodie.

'Was that the vegan I saw walking into the car park at the community centre as I was leaving?'

Ah, there it is.

'Yeah,' she says, fussing over her fringe with her fingers so she doesn't have to meet his gaze.

'Well, your mascara is intact so I guess it went well.'

He says *mascara*, but Shell hears *lipstick*.

'It was good,' she says. 'He's good. He's seeing a grief counsellor.'

'That's brilliant, good for him.' Callum says, and she believes him.

'So I'm firmly Team Harry now. The male-female friendship thing? Impossible.'

'Harry changed his mind, though.'

When Shell looks up, Callum is watching her, his head cocked.

'Well, I won't,' she says. 'Then I politely declined Liam's request to go out again, so it's been quite a day.'

Callum seems confused. 'What's wrong with Liam?'

'Nothing. There's absolutely nothing wrong with him. We just don't have anything in common. He likes playing rugby and surfing and camping. Can you imagine me camping?'

The look he gives her tells her he cannot.

'Denise suggested it once, but Ricky said that the nearest he'd ever get to camping is passing out on the beach at Brighton Pride. I mean, it might not be *that* bad, but I'd really rather not.'

'God didn't invent the Four Seasons for us to sleep on the ground, Shell.'

'It's not Liam's fault. I've always had this *type*, you know. I've always gone for creative, arty guys. And, yeah, I admit that I'm partial to a guy with long hair in skinny jeans, but I don't care if they're an accountant, or whatever, as long as they're passionate about something, you know?'

'But not camping?'

She sniggers and shakes her head.

'I take it Liam wasn't your type, then?'

'No, but that's the point. I've been so obsessed with finding *my type*,' she emphasises the words with her fingers, 'for so long because I thought that's what made you compatible with someone. Having stuff in common. Liking the same music and books and films.'

Callum doesn't say anything, but when she looks up at him again, he's listening intently.

So she goes on. 'I keep thinking about the guys I've dismissed over the years because they were too much of a lad or because they weren't into Bon Iver. Because . . .' *Sod it,* she thinks, when she stops herself. *If I'm being honest, I may as well just say it.* 'Because they weren't Nick, basically. But look at my parents. They had nothing in common when they met. And they've been together for *twenty-eight years.* I want *that.*' She realises at last. 'I want what they have. Because, in twenty-eight years, it won't matter if he wears skinny jeans or likes Bon Iver, will it? What matters is if he makes me laugh and if he gets me. Gets that I love my family, not just my parents and the twins, but the one I've made for myself, Emma and Ricky and Denise, whom I love and need just as much. Gets how much my job means to me and doesn't make me feel bad if I'm late home for dinner. Doesn't just get me, but *sees* me, you know?'

She presses her hands to her chest. 'Really *sees* me. Sees all that I am and all that I'm trying to be, even if I'm not quite there yet. I just want to be with someone and *know.* For them to just fit. Slot into my life without me noticing, without having to change who I am or make space for them, like with my parents. And Emma.' She points at him over the desk. 'The first day of school, she came up to me in the playground and said she liked my Sonic the Hedgehog backpack and we've been best friends ever since. Why can't I have that with a guy? Why can't it be that easy with a guy?'

She's aware that she's whining and stops. But when she looks up, Callum looks down, and her cheeks flush as she asks herself if she's said too much. If she's crossed some unseen line between them. He's not her boss, but he will be. As easy as it is to talk to him about these things, that doesn't mean she should.

But then he smiles. 'It will happen, Shell.'

'How do you know?'

'Because you're *trying*. With Nick and Liam and the mortician, who I still think you were rather hasty with, by the way. I think you were just scared that he'd be better at makeup than you.'

Shell laughs – actually, it's more of a splutter – and tilts her head at him as if to say, *Come on!*

'Seriously, though. At least you're putting yourself out there. I have no idea how you find the time, given how much you work. That's always been my excuse. You're showing me up.'

There's a knock on the door then and Callum says, 'Come in.'

It's Mike, who marches in, clearly flustered. 'Sorry, Cal.'

'No problem. What's up?'

'I'm calling it. Verity's not gonna make it so we'll pack up and load out.'

'You're not going to hang around for a drink?'

'Nah. Everyone's worried about getting back to London in the snow.'

'Good point. I may well leave my car here. It's very pretty, but it's not really built for snow.'

323

Mike strides over to the desk and extends his hand. 'Thanks so much for letting us use the store, Cal.'

'It was a pleasure.' He stands up and they shake. 'Can't wait to see the finished film.'

'There's already talk of a sequel so we'll be in touch.' Mike turns to Shell, squeezing her shoulder with his hand. 'Thanks for stepping in at the last minute. You're an absolute angel. I'll email you about Paris, okay?'

She watches him stride out, closing the door behind him, then turns to Callum with a frown.

'That's a shame. If I'd known last Sunday was going to be our last day I would have . . . I don't know.' Shell shrugs as he sits down. 'Enjoyed it more, I guess. At least said goodbye to everyone.'

'I know,' Callum agrees.

'Plus, I was looking forward to our unofficial wrap party tonight. Even if it was in the Anchor.'

'We can still go. Or, if you're hungry, maybe we can grab an early dinner, or something.'

'It's alright. I'm knackered. I just want to go home, put on my pyjamas and watch *New Girl*. The only Nick I want in my life is Nick Miller. TV boyfriends only from now on, I've decided. It's much safer.'

'Fair enough,' Callum says, with a small smile, standing up as she pulls her coat back on.

'See you in the morning,' she sings, heading out of his office with a wave.

She's halfway down it when she stops.

Wait. Did Callum Duke just ask me out?

★

She gets home just as her father is about to serve up Sunday dinner and it's just what she needs.

After, while the kids are in the living room counting who has the most presents under the tree and Shell is at the kitchen table, ignoring the washing-up, with her parents who are letting her ignore the washing-up, she fills them in on her day. About Nick and the movie coming to such an abrupt end and her conversation with Callum.

'It was so *weird*,' Shell says, scratching her head. 'Maybe he wasn't asking me *out* out.'

Eleanor leans forward. 'What did he say exactly?'

'Something like, *Maybe we can grab an early dinner, or something.*'

Her mother perks up at *or something*, turning to her father, eyebrows raised hopefully.

'Mum, calm down,' Shell tells her.

'He's a very handsome man, Shell. And an eligible bachelor.'

'An *eligible bachelor*? Okay, Jane Austen.'

'Fine. He's peng.'

'*Peng?* Mum, you're *so cringe* sometimes!'

When Shell gets up and finally starts stacking the dishwasher, her mother laughs. 'Anything to avoid the subject, eh?'

Chapter Twenty-Eight

Shell is coming down the stairs as her mother is heading to work. They collide at the bottom, her mum in such a rush that she whacks Shell's hip with her handbag when she hugs her, then charges for the door.

'Wish me luck!' Eleanor calls, over her shoulder, as she opens it.

'Luck!' Shell calls back, but before she can ask why, her mother is gone.

So she asks her father, who is in the kitchen, whisking what looks like pancake batter in a plastic jug.

'What am I wishing Mum luck for?' she asks, kissing him on the cheek.

'She's interviewing for Robert's replacement today. He starts his new job in London in the new year.'

'Of course,' Shell says, snatching the kettle from the counter and going over to the sink to fill it.

'I hope she finds someone. She's so stressed.'

'Speaking of stressed, where are the twins?'

He snorts as he bends down to get a frying pan out of the cupboard next to the stove. 'In their rooms.'

'How come? Shouldn't they be getting ready for school? They're suspiciously quiet.'

'School's done for Christmas. Four more sleeps,' he reminds her, putting it down and lighting the gas.

'Oh, God.' She throws her head back, groaning at the ceiling. 'Work is going to be *hectic*.'

'Tired?' he asks, as she opens the bag of coffee on the counter and tries to stick her face into it.

'I didn't sleep much,' she mutters, contemplating dumping the whole lot into the cafetière.

'Your mother not the only one stressing, then?'

She groans again.

'Listen, Shell,' he says, as he holds his hand over the frying pan. 'I know there's a lot going on right now with work and this app thing you're doing with Mia. And I'm sure Nick coming back didn't help.'

'What do you mean?' she asks, leaning against the counter with her arms crossed.

'It must have made you reassess a lot of things. The path not taken, you know,' he says, as he brushes the pan with a piece of oiled kitchen towel, then pours in a circle of batter. 'What might have happened if you'd stood up for yourself and gone to art school, like you wanted to.'

'I guess.'

'But look at you,' he says proudly, as the kettle boils and she turns to pour the water into the cafetière. The kitchen immediately fills with the smell of coffee. 'You may have flailed for a bit when you dropped out of uni, but you're doing *so well* now. You're looking for a place with Ricky and Denise in the new year. You're killing it at work. You're about to go to Paris, *then* Mexico. And it's all on your own terms. You should be very proud of that.'

'Thanks, Dad.' She smiles, suddenly feeling lighter and stronger, all at once.

'Can you imagine if you'd persisted at uni and become a lawyer?'

She pretends to shudder at the thought as she puts the lid on the cafetière.

'No.' He flips the pancake. 'You're exactly where you need to be, Shell.'

As soon as Shell pushes through the concealed door in the Beauty Hall into the back of house, she hears raised voices coming from Old Mr Duke's office at the end of the corridor. It's him and Callum, she's sure, although she can't make out what they're saying. She manages to duck into the break room as the door to Old Mr Duke's office swings open and she hears Callum say, 'This is happening, Pops. Whether you like it or not. January fifth. It's happening.'

'Maybe when you go home to California for Christmas, you shouldn't come back!' Old Mr Duke counters.

The door slams and she hears Callum stride past, muttering furiously to himself.

Shell has no idea what's happening on January the fifth, but whatever they were arguing about spills onto the shop floor.

They're perfectly professional, of course. Not that they have much choice, given that, as it's the week leading to Christmas, Callum has revived the Duke & Sons tradition of greeting the customers as they arrive, directing the children towards the queue for Father Christmas and the customers to whatever floor they need.

It was supposed to be just him, but Old Mr Duke is insisting on doing it as well. Callum keeps telling him that he doesn't have to, especially with his bad hip, which isn't helping the mood between them in the slightest.

Still, they've been nothing but warm smiles in their black suits, white shirts and red tartan ties with matching pocket squares. As busy as she's been, though, Shell's been paying attention, and they haven't spoken all day.

Whatever they're arguing about must be bad because it goes on for three days.

Then it's Old Mr Duke's birthday, and although Callum makes a lovely speech and cheers when his grandfather cuts his cake, they walk away from one another as soon as the gentle hum of chatter resumes in the Beauty Hall.

Fifteen minutes later Old Mr Duke leaves, and Bella from Handbags & Accessories hurries over to where Shell, Ricky, Denise, Becca and Soph are huddled, discussing Ricky's nail bar (which they're all calling it now). He and Callum have been trialling nail techs today so they've all taken full advantage of the free manicures. Ricky's are the best, they've concluded. They're white with tiny coloured-crystal Christmas lights that are strung together with a green line connecting all five of his nails. They're so distracted by them that Bella has to say, *Hey!* to get their attention.

When she does, she smiles and arches an eyebrow at them.

'You know what they're arguing about, right? Callum and Old Mr Duke?'

Here we go, Shell thinks, as Ricky's Drama Detector goes off.

'What?' he asks, almost spilling his prosecco as he leans in.

Bella glances around the Beauty Hall to make sure there's no one nearby, then leans in. 'Last night, I went to my fiancé Jack's dad's fiftieth birthday party.' It's quite a mouthful so she has to stop and take a breath before she carries on. 'It was at that fancy golf club in Church Cabham.'

'Nice.' Soph nods, looking at Becca who does the same.

'I know, right? Free bar. Anyway.' She glances around the Beauty Hall again. 'Jack's dad plays golf with that creepy Kevin Costley. The dude who owns Costley's of Ostley.'

They all nod.

'Well, he was there and telling anyone who would listen that he's bought Duke & Sons.'

There's a collective gasp, but Shell laughs. 'Yeah. Right.'

'It's true!' Bella insists, annoyed that she doesn't believe her.

'Come on. Didn't we *just* do this when Callum started?' She gestures at Becca and Soph with her glass. 'We saw Old Mr Duke in that café in Bridge Street with Callum and all assumed the worst, remember?' Shell looks around at the others and they shrug, then go back to admiring Ricky's nails.

'Why would Kevin Costley lie, Shell?' Bella arches her eyebrow even higher.

It was obviously not the reaction she was hoping for. Maybe she thought they'd be more hysterical. That they'd cry and rend their clothing. But they just stand there, staring at her blankly.

'I don't know why he'd lie,' Ricky says. 'Was he drunk?'

'He said he's hired an architect.'

That gets Denise's attention. 'An architect?'

'Yeah.' Bella turns to her, pleased that someone is finally listening to her. 'Apparently, his plan is to keep the café in the basement and turn the Beauty Hall into a Costley's. Then he's converting the rest into luxury apartments.'

'Luxury apartments?' Shell snorts. 'Luxury apartments over a Costley's?'

The others titter, which makes Bella's cheeks flush.

'We're not laughing at you, Bells, I promise.' Shell is quick to clarify. 'It's just so ridiculous.'

'Is it?'

'*Yes.* You know rumours like this do the rounds every few months. It's nothing.'

'It's not a rumour, Shell. I *spoke* to Kevin Costley last night.' She points at her mouth. 'No one told me. I didn't overhear anything. He came to my table because he heard I work here.'

'To say what?'

'What I just said. That he's bought Duke & Sons and he's looking forward to working with me. Which,' she points at Shell this time, 'I don't believe for a moment. He won't keep any of us on. And if he does, we'll be moved onto zero-hours contracts and dropped to minimum wage before you can say, *Welcome to Costley's of Ostley.*'

'I'm not wearing that awful green and yellow uniform,' Soph pipes up then, looking genuinely worried.

Becca, on the other hand, is appalled. 'I don't want to work somewhere that sells Blueberry handbags.'

'Guys, calm down,' Shell tells them, as Becca and Soph start chatting nervously. 'It's not happening.'

Bella doesn't calm down, though. 'How do you know, Shell?'

'Because Callum told me. Kevin Costley has been trying to woo him since he started here.'

'And you trust him?'

Shell doesn't flinch. '*Yes*. Plus, it's Callum. He's spent a fortune since he started, of his own money, I might add, on the Christmas decorations and the new stock and the nail bar.'

'True.' Ricky backs her up.

'Speaking of,' Shell continues, 'look at all the new brands we're getting in the Beauty Hall in the new year. It's gonna keep us on our toes, isn't it? Maybe we won't be the ART weirdos any more.'

'We'll always be the weirdos, sister,' he reminds her, with a wink.

'She's right,' Denise says then, tilting her head at Bella. 'Why do all of that if he's going to sell?'

Bella huffs. 'Well, Jack says that all of it, the new decorations and the Duke & Sons White Christmas, was to get more people into the store so it *looks* busy and Callum can inflate the price.'

Jack's wrong.

The new Christmas decorations and the Duke & Sons White Christmas were for the film.

Ricky and Denise know that as well.

But they can't tell Bella, can they?

'Kevin Costley was winding you up, Bells,' Shell says instead.

'Why, though?'

'I don't know,' Shell says, and she honestly doesn't. 'But it's not true. It can't be.'

'Well, we'll see, won't we?' Bella says, glaring at each of them in turn. 'Here's hoping we still have jobs in the New Year. Kevin Costley said he's signing the contracts on January the fifth.'

Shell almost drops her glass.

They're not the only ones Bella tells, though. Within an hour, *everyone*'s talking about it. But from what Shell's heard, they're siding with her, saying that Callum isn't capable of masterminding a Machiavellian plan to sell Duke & Sons from under his grandfather and flee to the Cayman Islands. Ricky and Denise obviously agree because by the time they leave to meet Emma they've moved on to bickering about where to go for dinner.

Shell can't stop thinking about the argument she overhead on Monday morning, though.

This is happening, Pops. Whether you like it or not. January fifth. It's happening.

'Babe.' Emma nudges her in the ribs.

'Huh?'

'Noodles?' she asks, when Shell looks at her.

'I don't care,' she mutters, no longer hungry.

'If Shell won't choose,' Emma turns to Ricky, 'you're the deciding vote. Curry or noodles?'

'Well,' he says, as he tries to compromise, 'pumpkin katsu is bit like curry, isn't it?'

She sighs. '*Et tu*, O'Neill?'

He pouts and when he kisses her, it's forgotten, the pair of them skipping ahead, giggling and stopping to peer into the shop windows. They look so happy, silly on fizz and the promise of Christmas.

Even Emma's in a good mood, banging *on and on* about a new kitchen refit she's starting in the new year.

'Shell.' She stops suddenly and glares at her. 'Are you even listening to me?'

'I'm not. Sorry,' she admits, stopping as well. 'I'm thinking about this rumour I just heard.'

'What now?'

'It's nothing.'

'It must be something.' Emma immediately switches from irritated at being ignored to concerned. 'You look like you're about to puke.'

She might. She's wound herself up so much she feels lightheaded.

'Shell?' Emma pushes.

'It's nothing, Em.'

It *is* nothing.

Isn't it?

Shell lifts her left shoulder, then lets it drop. 'The same

old rumour about Old Mr Duke selling Duke & Sons. Except, this time, it's Callum selling to Kevin Costley.'

Emma laughs. 'He's definitely not.'

She sounds so sure that Shell finally looks up.

'If you'd been *listening* to me,' Emma explains, before she can ask, 'you'd know Callum just hired my company to redo his kitchen in the new year. I've seen the budget and, *trust me*, he's not going anywhere.'

Of course he isn't, Shell thinks, cursing herself for even entertaining the idea. She still has no idea why Kevin Costley would lie, but whatever's happening on the fifth of January, it can't be *that*.

There's a spring in her step now as they continue to Bridge Street.

When they turn the corner, Denise huffs. 'This place is cash only, isn't it?'

'I've got some,' Shell tells her, patting her bag.

'It's okay. I owe my mum twenty quid, anyway.'

'I need some as well, actually,' Ricky says, admiring his nails again. 'Plus, I can protect you from muggers.'

'My hero,' Denise says, giving him a quick kiss and stroking his Christmas-tree green wig.

'You guys go to the cashpoint while we grab a table.' Shell can see a queue outside the noodle place, so she and Emma take their time.

'Wait.' Emma stops suddenly. 'The rumour's about *this* Kevin Costley?'

She cackles and Shell turns to see what she's looking across the street at.

There it is.

Costley's of Ostley.

While it takes up one whole corner, it couldn't be more different from Duke & Sons. It's flat and drab with posters in the window advertising 2-for-1 Christmas decorations with a long, red *FURTHER REDUCTIONS* poster above them. It's gone nine, but the lights are still on so even from across the road Shell can see that it's cluttered with stock. Racks and racks of handbags on the right and shelves cluttered with beauty products on the left. Nothing seems to be in any particular order, though, just crowded together in a way that makes Shell's head hurt.

'The guy who owns *this* place wants to buy Duke & Sons?' Emma thumbs over the road at it and looks at Shell as if to say, *Come on*. 'What's he going to do? Sell out-of-date makeup from the Beauty Hall?'

She laughs at that. 'Apparently, the plan is to turn downstairs into a Costley's and convert the rest into flats.'

Emma looks even less convinced. 'Who'd want to live above a Costley's?'

True.

Still, Duke & Sons is in a prime spot on Ostley High Street. It's three minutes' walk from the station and surrounded by glossy bars and restaurants, even if they forgo them in favour of the Anchor and cheap noodles.

Plus, Old Mr Duke owns Duke & Sons outright, doesn't he? So Kevin Costley wouldn't be at the mercy of a landlord who puts his rent up every year, like he is now, Shell assumes. And the store is *huge*. Even if he kept the café in the basement, and turned the Beauty Hall into a Costley's, there's still another four floors. That's a lot of luxury apartments. Especially if he keeps all the old features, like the lifts and the staircase. People love that stuff.

'Yeah, that's bollocks.' Emma snorts. 'There's *no way* the guy who owns this can afford Duke & Sons.'

'It's doing really well, actually. They're popping up all over Somerset.'

'Still,' Emma says. 'I just can't see it.'

Me either, Shell thinks, as they carry on towards the noodle place to join the queue. But as they reach the corner, something catches Shell's eye and she turns to look over her shoulder as Callum strides out of Costley's.

'No!' Emma hisses, as Shell pulls her into the doorway of McDonald's. 'We agreed! Noodles!'

Shell presses her finger to her lips, then stares across the street.

When Emma follows her gaze, her dark eyes widen. 'Wait. Is that Callum Duke?'

It sure is.

Callum Duke on the pavement outside Costley's, buttoning his heavy wool coat.

'Who's that?' Emma shout-whispers, pointing as a man walks out to join him.

'I don't know,' Shell says, and she doesn't. She's never seen him before.

But when they smile at one another and shake hands, Emma says it before she can even think it. 'Is that Kevin Costley?'

Chapter Twenty-Nine

Emma googles him on her phone and, sure enough, it's him.

'Shit,' she mutters, when she shows Shell the photo. 'So the rumour's true, then?'

She shakes her head. 'No.'

That's all she says.

'What happened to noodles?' Denise asks, when she finds them lurking in the doorway of McDonald's.

Ricky doesn't look bothered. 'I could go for a Filet-O-Fish.'

'I needed a wee,' Shell says, squeezing Emma's arm before she can tell them what they just saw.

Mercifully, she takes the hint, for once.

Denise frowns at her. 'Couldn't you go at the noodle place?'

'Queue.'

When Denise looks up the road and sees it, she keeps walking. 'Fair enough.'

'Are you not going to tell them?' Emma says, from the corner of her mouth as they follow.

'Not until I know for sure. I don't want to worry them.'

'You gonna talk to Callum tomorrow?'

'I have to,' she says, her legs not as steady as she and Emma join the end of the queue outside the noodle place.

After another sleepless night, Shell finds herself fussing over the foundations so she has something to do while she waits for the morning meeting to start, straightening the boxes then restraightening them, fingers fidgeting as she vacillates back and forth.

Callum wouldn't.

But he has.

He wouldn't. Shell knows he wouldn't. But while she supposes it could all be a coincidence – the argument she overheard on Monday morning, Callum telling Old Mr Duke that it, whatever *it* is, is happening on January the fifth, whether he likes it or not, Callum outside Costley's shaking Kevin's hand – she keeps circling back to the same thing.

Why would Kevin Costley lie to Bella?

Shell can't think of a single reason why.

If Kevin Costley is telling everyone he's bought Duke & Sons and he hasn't, he's going to look a fool.

Who knows? Maybe he is a fool. But given how well Costley's is doing, he can't be *that* daft.

Either way, she's furious. Tired and confused and furious because *she*'s the one who is going to have to ask Callum if it's true, isn't she? After the Louise Incident it's a conversation she'd really rather not have. She could ignore it, she knows. Let it play out and see what happens.

But she can't take another minute of this.

Shell doesn't know what it is, if it's anger or fear or some combination of the two, but when Callum glides into the Beauty Hall in a Santa hat without a care in the world, she can't even pretend to hide it.

It must be obvious, because Ricky leans in and whispers. 'You alright?'

'Yeah,' she says, without taking her eyes off Callum. 'Fine.'

'"Twas the day before Christmas when all through the store,' he says quietly, his blue eyes bright, and he's so excited that he looks like a little kid, 'not a creature was stirring, not even one of Ricky's wigs.'

There's a roar of laughter, loudest of all from Ricky, who jumps up and down next to her.

'Christmas Eve, guys!' Callum holds up his hands. 'We made it!'

There's another raucous roar.

'As of five o'clock, we get to go home, eat, drink and be merry. Until January fifth, anyway.'

Shell's heart drops to her feet as everyone boos and hisses.

'I'm going to California for Christmas. So please,' he presses both hands to his chest, 'if you need anything before I go, let me know now because I'm leaving shortly. Otherwise, I just want to wish you all a very happy Christmas and the very best for the new year.' His eyes are even brighter as he looks around at all of them. 'You've all been so wonderful and worked so hard this year and I just wanted to let you know how much I appreciate it.'

There's a smattering of applause as Shell wonders if this is the speech he's given to every floor.

'So, good luck today, guys. And here's to next year!'

The applause is louder now. Shell doesn't join in, as Callum thanks them again and glides from counter to counter, saying goodbye. He seems genuinely startled by the reception, if uncomfortable with the hugs he's receiving.

Shell can't watch, looking down to tie her toolbelt around her waist, then plucks out a powder brush. As she looks up again to check her makeup in the magnifying-mirror on the counter, she jumps.

'Callum,' she says, so startled that she almost drops the brush.

He frowns at her. 'Is everything okay, Shell?'

'Yes,' she says coolly, pushing her shoulders back. 'Everything's fine.'

He picks up on it immediately, pushing his shoulders back as well. 'Well, it obviously isn't.'

Shell just stares at him because she can't ask him now, can she?

On the shop floor.

When she doesn't say anything, he gestures at her to go on. 'I leave for the airport in half an hour so . . .'

Half an hour?

Shell thought she had until the end of the day, at least. She hasn't even decided what she's going to say.

'Fine,' Callum says, with a sharp sigh. 'If you decide to tell me what's bothering you, I'll be in my office.'

Then he's gone and— *Shit. Shit.*

'Shell, are you okay?' Ricky asks again, as she stands there, panic pinning her to the spot.

Just leave it, she tells herself. *Just leave it until the new year when there's time to talk about it properly. Not like this.*

But the thought of agonising about it over Christmas brings tears to her eyes.

'Where are you going?' Ricky calls after her.

But it's too late.

She's already gone.

Shell tells herself to calm down as she charges into the back of house. But with each step down the corridor, she gets angrier and angrier. Then she's telling herself not to cry because she will not cry in front of Callum Duke.

She will not.

He must have been expecting her, because he's left the door to his office open, which he never does.

Stay calm, she tells herself one more time, but she's furious. So maddeningly, inconsolably furious. And maybe if he was just a tiny bit concerned she could stay calm, but he's looking at her as if to say, *What now, Shell?*

It's hard to pull off sanctimonious in a Santa hat, but somehow, he manages it.

He must read her mind, because there's a quick crackle of static as he tugs it off and tosses it onto the desk in front of him. Now his hair isn't as perfect, sticking up in places, and weirdly, it calms her down a bit.

'Shell,' he says, in a way that makes her wonder if he's trying to stay calm as well. 'Can we please shorthand this? I have,' he stops to check his watch, 'twenty-six minutes before my car arrives for the airport so please . . .' He gestures at her to hurry up, like she's wasting his time.

He's never made her feel like she's wasting his time and she hates how tiny it makes her feel.

'I'm honestly not trying to be cruel, Shell,' he says, and she believes him. 'But I'm already tired and I'm about to get on not one but *two* flights home.' He holds up two fingers then tucks one of them into the knot of his tartan tie and tugs it loose. 'Because you can't fly direct to LAX from Bristol, which means I have to go via Amsterdam so the whole ordeal is going to take over fourteen hours. Forgive me for wanting to get this over with,' he says, pulling the knot in his tie down low enough to be able to get it over his head, then tossing it onto the desk.

'Get what over with?' she asks, testing him to see if he'll just come clean and tell her.

'*This*,' he says, undoing the top two buttons of his white shirt and fixing the collar. 'You're obviously livid with me about something so, please, just say it.'

'I know, okay? I overheard you arguing with your grand-father on Monday morning.'

If she'd hoped that would prompt a reaction, it doesn't.

Old Mr Duke's chair bobs back and forth as he nods. 'You did?'

'Yes. I heard you telling him about January the fifth. How it was happening whether he liked it or not.'

Callum doesn't respond, just cocks his head at her as he waits for her to go on.

'And then I saw you last night, outside Costley's, shaking Kevin Costley's hand.'

'And once again, you've put two and two together and got *Callum's a jerk*.'

That makes her falter for the first time.

'No. I just—'

'Yes. You hear something, like with Louise Larson, then assume the worst about me.'

She crosses her arms across her chest. 'I'm not *assuming* anything, Callum.'

'Oh, that's right. You *know* this time, don't you, Shell?'

'I *do* know.' She's trying to maintain her composure, but it's becoming increasingly difficult. 'I *know* that Kevin Costley has bought Duke & Sons. He's signing the contracts on January the fifth.'

'Is he now?' Callum doesn't flinch. 'And how do you know that?'

'Because he's been telling anyone who will listen, apparently.'

He pounces on the *apparently*. 'But he didn't tell *you*?'

'Not *directly*,' Shell admits, her arms still crossed. 'He told Bella in Handbags & Accessories.'

'Ah. That reliable source. Bella in Handbags & Accessories.'

'Stop it!' she snaps, taking the two steps to his desk and standing over him. 'Don't you dare!'

He just tips his chin up to look at her. 'Don't I dare what, Shell?'

'Make fun of me!'

He doesn't say anything at all then, just looks at her,

and when their gaze finally meets for the first time since she stormed in, that makes her falter as well because he's not angry or confused.

He's not even being sanctimonious any more.

It's something else.

Something that makes each of the hairs on her arms stand up at once.

'Don't make fun of me,' she tells him again. 'Don't make fun of me for caring what happens to this place.'

'I'm not.'

'You are, and I don't understand because I defended you last night, Callum! I had your back!'

'You did? It certainly doesn't feel like it.'

'Well, I don't any more! Not if you're going to lie to me!'

And here they come.

The tears.

She swats the first away as quickly as she can and says it again, 'You lied to me.'

'I did?'

'Yes.' She uncrosses her arms to point at the door. 'The night the hot-air balloon almost fell. Out there. In the corridor. You told me that Kevin Costley was trying to woo you, remember?'

He nods.

'You told me that he was trying to woo you, but you would never sell this place to him.'

'I did.'

'So why are you?'

Callum doesn't say anything, just continues to look at

her, and she knows then – right in that moment as his jaw clenches and his chin shivers – that she's got it wrong again.

That she's got *him* wrong again.

'You know what?' he says. 'I give up.' He stops to close his eyes. When he opens them, they're wet, and Shell would run out of the office if she could move. 'Here you are again with the flimsiest piece of proof and you've used it to come to the worst possible conclusion about me when I've done everything I can to show you the best of me.'

She can't look at him, her chin dropping as a tear spills off her nose.

'Why do you only ever see the worst in me, Shell?'

She forces herself to look at him, her whole face burning. 'I don't!'

'How can it be that after all this, after everything, you still don't know me at all?'

'I do know you.'

'I'm not so sure you do,' he says, under his breath, and something pinches at her.

'I do know you, Callum! I know you and I like you!'

'Do you? Because you have a funny way of show-ing it.'

Then her heart is thumping for a whole other reason.

'Of course I like you!' she says again. Shouts it this time. 'That's why I got so mad at you!'

'Why didn't you just *ask* me, then? All you had to do was *ask* me.'

'I'm sorry,' she says, but it's not enough this time, is it? It's not like in the car park at the community centre the other week. He's not going to wink at her and say, *We're always good, Shell Smith* this time.

'It's fine,' he says, checking his watch again. 'I have twelve minutes until my car arrives for the airport so I'll keep this brief. Why I still feel the need to explain myself to you, though, I don't know. Maybe that's something I'll take time to consider when I'm over the Atlantic in a few hours. In the meantime.' He finally looks up and the shock of it makes her take a step back. 'I met with Mr Costley last night to return a set of golf clubs he sent me. A bottle of whisky is one thing, but golf clubs are quite another. Especially if it means I feel obliged to play a round of golf with the man.'

Shell swipes away another tear with her fingers.

'As for the argument with my grandfather you overheard on Monday morning, which, *again*, I don't know why I feel the need to explain because it's none of your business, was over a glaucoma test he's due to have at Ostley Royal Infirmary in the new year. On January fifth, to be precise. He's refusing to go because he hates the drops they put in his eyes. I was cross with him because he told my grandmother *I* was the reason he couldn't go, because the store was too busy. So, yes, I concede, I was rather harsh on him, but it's only because if he doesn't get his eyes checked, he'll go blind.'

Shell catches another tear with the back of her right hand.

'As for Mr Costley, I have no earthly idea why he's saying what he's saying.' Callum hesitates, and Shell wonders if he's asking himself why Kevin's doing it. 'But I'm not CEO yet so I couldn't sell to him, even if I wanted to. So *there*.' He holds his hands up. 'Happy? I have not sold Duke & Sons.'

'He hasn't,' Shell hears someone say behind her.

She turns to find Old Mr Duke standing in the doorway of his office, hand on his cane.

'It was me.' He looks at Callum, then at her. 'I sold Duke & Sons to Kevin Costley.'

Chapter Thirty

S hell and Callum look at one another, then at Old Mr Duke as he closes the door behind him.

'Pops?' Callum says, standing up to face his grandfather.

He suddenly looks like a little boy, like Patrick when he wakes up in the middle of the night after he's had a nightmare.

Old Mr Duke smiles politely. 'Shell, can you give us a moment, please?'

When she moves to leave, Callum holds up his hand. 'No, she stays.'

Old Mr Duke raises an eyebrow at him, but Callum stands his ground.

'No, *she stays*. Shell deserves an explanation, considering the bollocking I just gave her when . . .' he stops to meet her gaze across the desk '. . . it would appear she was right all along.'

Not about you, she wants to say, but then Old Mr Duke starts hobbling towards them.

'Fine,' he says, clearly in pain, his cane tapping unsteadily on the lino as he makes his way to the desk.

Callum doesn't hesitate, stepping out of the way as he walks around to his side of the desk.

Old Mr Duke accepts the chair with a gruff 'Thank you,' the leather creaking as he sits down.

But it's not an angry gruff, it's an exhausted one. Standing at the revolving door all week, greeting customers, has clearly taken it out of him.

'Well?' Callum says, coming to stand on the other side of the desk next to Shell.

'Well,' Old Mr Duke says, leaning forward to rest his wrists on the desk, 'I was going to discuss this with you in the new year, but Mr Costley is unable to keep his mouth shut, it seems. I'd rather not, given you've a mere . . .' he stops to take his pocket watch out of his waistcoat, his white furry eyebrows meeting as he peers at it '. . . *nine minutes* before your car is here to take you to the airport, but I suppose I don't have much choice.'

When Shell sneaks a glance at Callum, his expression should let his grandfather know he does not.

'*Why*, Pops?'

'Several reasons. First and foremost, and forgive me for saying this in front of Miss Smith, but you did insist she stay,' he says, and the back of her neck burns, 'your mother and I have discussed it.'

'My mother?' Callum says, but it's more of a splutter.

'We think it would be best that when you go home to California for Christmas you don't return.'

The silence that follows is like white noise as Shell steps back to avoid any flying shrapnel.

Callum is perfectly still, though. So still that she wonders if he heard what Old Mr Duke said, his lips parted for an agonisingly long time before he inhales a sharp breath through his nose.

Shell tenses, waiting for the fallout. *Don't say anything,* she tells herself. *Don't say anything. This is none of your business. You shouldn't even be here.*

She waits for Callum to defend himself, but he doesn't.

He doesn't shout or yell or charge at him, like Shell would have done if it was her.

He just says, 'Why?'

'This was always a trial, Callum.'

That's obviously news to him, judging by the look on his face. 'Was it?'

Old Mr Duke nods firmly. 'That's why we agreed it would be a year before I retired.'

'Yes, so I could get to know the staff and the store.'

'Callum, listen, son.' The chair creaks again as Old Mr Duke sits back with a weary sigh. 'You're clearly a very bright boy.'

Don't say anything, Shell tells herself again, as she notes the *boy.*

Callum must as well because his voice is noticeably cooler when he says, 'But?'

'And I love you dearly. I will be for ever grateful to you for your help.'

'But?'

'*But* you clearly don't have the maturity to handle managing a store like this.'

Shell feels Callum tense next to her. 'Maturity?'

Don't say anything, Shell.

'Yes.' Old Mr Duke doesn't look at him. 'The incident with Louise Larson proves that.'

It sounds as though Callum's been punched. Shell's sure she hears the air *oof* right out of him.

Don't say anything, Shell tells herself again, but the words are already lined up on her tongue. 'That's not fair!'

'It's okay, Shell,' Callum says, and touches her arm.

'It's not okay!' She stares Old Mr Duke right in the eye. 'Callum is an excellent manager.'

He doesn't flinch, though.

'He is,' she insists. 'Callum cares about Duke & Sons and he cares about *us.*'

'Oh, he does, does he? How so?'

That makes Shell falter for a second. *What does he want? Examples.*

Old Mr Duke motions at her to go on with his hand, letting her know that he does.

'Okay,' she says. 'Okay. Denise Varina-Williams.' She's aware that she sounds like an attorney, defending her client to a curmudgeonly judge. 'Callum saw her potential straight away and he was right because the lingerie brand she suggested sold out on the first day.'

'Hmm,' he murmurs.

'And Ricky O'Neill. I've worked with him for *five years* and I've never seen him so engaged about his work. And that's because Callum listened to him about the nail bar. It's booked up until the middle of January because Ricky's been banging on about it to every customer who comes to the counter, getting them to book in. It's been like working with a secondhand-car salesman.'

Old Mr Duke just nods.

'As for . . .' Shell hesitates '. . . Louise Larson, I know how it looks, but it wasn't Callum's fault. She mistook his concern for something other than him being a nice, kind, decent man. A nice, kind, decent man,' she points at him over the desk, 'you should be proud to say is your grandson because Louise clearly has issues. Issues that, if you choose to look at it this way, she's now dealing with, thanks to Callum. And when she does, Callum has been gracious enough to make sure that her job is waiting for her when she's ready. A job I hope will still be here for her when she is.'

'Is that it, Miss Smith?' Old Mr Duke asks, the chair creaking again as he sits back.

Actually, it's not, but Shell thinks it best to shut up while she's ahead, for once.

So she just nods politely.

'That's very kind of you to say, Miss Smith. And I'm sure Callum appreciates it.'

'I do.'

She turns to find him watching her, his cheeks pink, and has to bite down on a smile.

'I appreciate your enthusiasm, but I do believe my grandson has a car arriving imminently.' He stops to check his pocket watch again. 'In just five minutes. So we will have to end this here.'

'Absolutely not,' Callum tells him. 'I want to know what's going on, Pops.'

Old Mr Duke's eyes light up at the challenge.

'What is this really about, Pops?' Callum pushes. 'I

know it's not Louise Larson and I know it's not because I'm doing a bad job because we've had the best November in *five years*. If we keep going the way we are, we'll be out of the red and turning a profit again in three years.'

'And that's wonderful, Callum.'

'So why are you selling to Kevin Costley?'

Old Mr Duke just smiles. 'Because he made me an offer I couldn't refuse.'

'Yeah? So you're going to be happy with him flogging garden hoses and cheap suitcases here?'

'Mr Costley can do whatever he pleases. At least you and I will be free.'

'Free?' Callum frowns. 'Since when did you want to be free of Duke & Sons?'

Old Mr Duke taps his pocket watch. 'Four minutes.'

'I don't care about the car. Forget the car. I'll catch the next flight.'

'On Christmas Eve? I very much doubt that.'

'Pops, I'm not going anywhere until you tell me what this is about.'

'Oh, yes, good,' he says, under his breath. 'Miss your flight and waste more money.'

'Is *that* what this is about, Pops? The money?'

Old Mr Duke won't look at him. 'You can't keep bailing us out. You'll have nothing left.'

'So? I'm young. I can earn more money. This is the only chance we'll get to save Duke & Sons.'

'No.' Old Mr Duke shakes his head firmly. 'That's *your* money. You earned it.'

'I only *earned* it because *you* gave me the money to

start Hannah Banana. Without you, I wouldn't have it, Pops.'

Old Mr Duke doesn't say anything, just continues shaking his head.

'I assure you, Pops, whatever I invest in the store, I will get back, if that's why you're worried. But you've got to give me a chance. Otherwise I may as well have taken what I've spent and given it straight to Kevin Costley.'

'You *will* get it back, Callum. Every penny. From the sale of the store. Now.' He nods at the suitcase by the door that Shell hadn't even noticed was there when she ran in. 'You'd better get going.'

'Pops, I told you, I'm not going anywhere until we sort this out.'

'Sort what out? It's done, Callum.'

'Until Kevin Costley signs the contracts, there's still everything to play for.'

'Play for?' Old Mr Duke's mood suddenly darkens. 'This isn't a game, Callum.'

'I know it's not. I'm fully aware of what's at stake here, which is why I'm willing to fight for it.'

'Are you? Because I don't think you are. This is the fun part, Callum. Making changes. Stocking new brands. Bringing in new customers. But what are you going to do when the money's gone, huh?' He jabs the desk with his finger. 'When the roof is leaking or a customer falls down the stairs and threatens to sue, or the electricity company is going to switch the lights off because you can't pay the bill? I've been keeping this store going for nearly *fifty* years. I've kept it going because I love it, but also because I'm stubborn and I'm proud and I didn't want to admit that it's a burden.'

Old Mr Duke shakes his head when Callum tries to interrupt. 'No, Callum. I look at you and I see me when I took this place over in the seventies. Working all hours. The first one in and the last one out. I know you, Callum. You're as stubborn as I am and you will not let this place fail, but at what cost? And I don't just mean money, but at what cost to *you*? I will not let you do what I did!' He raises his voice, pounding his hand on the table this time. 'I will not. I want you to live a long, happy life. See the world. Get married and have children.'

'I can still do all of those things, Pops. You did.'

'I did. A wife and family I only saw on Sundays because I was always here. Do you want that? Do you want to drop dead one day in the middle of the Beauty Hall because you didn't have time to get that pain in your chest checked out? I don't want that for you, Callum. I thought I did,' he admits, with a sad sigh. 'All I wanted was to hand this place over to you on my eighty-fifth birthday and watch it flourish. But I see you, striding around the store, and you're so alive. So full of energy and ideas and potential, like I was. Shell's right, you love this store as much as I do, but it is a burden. A back-breaking, heart-breaking burden. And it's not fair to expect you to shoulder it while I waltz off and retire.'

'First of all,' Callum says, when his grandfather finally stops to heave in a breath. 'You're not waltzing off anywhere. What are you going to do? Play golf? No, you're going to be here every day, aren't you?'

Old Mr Duke almost manages a smile.

'So I'm not on my own, am I? Because I have you. And I have the staff.' He turns to Shell, who blushes when she realises that she's been staring at him. 'Look how much Shell cares about this job. She started as a Saturday girl and she's still here, yelling at me because she thought I'd sold this place from under you. And Denise, this was just supposed to be a casual thing when she graduated from uni and now she's going to overhaul our womens-wear department. So, yes, you're right. I can't handle the responsibility of this place on my own, but I don't have to. Which means I will see the world and get married and have a houseload of kids, because I have *them*.'

He thumbs at Shell. 'And, yes, you're right, this is the fun bit, but *God*.' He balls his hands into fists and holds them up. 'Isn't that why we do this? It makes worrying about leaking roofs and awful customers and paying the bills worthwhile. I'm here because I want to be here. Because I love it.'

Old Mr Duke considers that, but then Callum's phone beeps on the desk. He glances at the screen. 'Your car is here.'

'It can wait. This can't.'

Old Mr Duke huffs.

Shell's sure that's it – he's not going to give in – but then he lifts his chin to look at Callum. 'Did I ever tell you about the time I almost blew this place up?'

'What?' he gasps. 'No! When?'

'I was eighteen.' Old Mr Duke chuckles to himself at the memory. 'I had the bright idea to distil Duke & Sons whisky in a corner of the warehouse. Then there was the soda fountain I bought for the café – the first in Ostley, I might add – that almost flooded the basement.'

'Oh, Pops. No.' Callum covers his mouth with his hand as he swallows a laugh.

'The point is. I'm *eighty-four*. Eighty-four and one day and I've spent so long worrying about leaking roofs and awful customers and paying the bills that I've forgotten what a *joy* this place is. And now you're here and it feels alive again and . . . I don't want it to do to you what it did to me. I don't want it to break you, Callum.'

'It won't, Pops.' He presses both hands to his chest. 'I swear.'

They're interrupted by Callum's phone again.

Old Mr Duke glances at the screen. 'Your car will leave if you don't go soon.'

'Let it.' Callum takes a step towards the desk. 'Give me a chance, Pops.'

'You'll miss your flight,' Old Mr Duke warns.

'I don't care. Give me a chance, Pops.'

'It's Christmas Eve, Callum. You're cutting it fine as it is. If you miss this flight, you won't make it home for Christmas and all of this will be moot because your mother will kill me.'

'I don't care. Give me a chance, Pops.'

Callum's phone beeps again.

'Your cab's going to leave and you'll struggle to get another. It's snowing.'

'I don't care. Give me a chance, Pops.'

'If I give you a chance, will you get in that blasted cab?'

Callum breaks out into a grin. 'Yes!'

'Fine.' He holds up his hands in mock surrender. 'She's all yours.'

'So you're not going to sell to Kevin Costley?'

'How could I? Not when she's in such good hands,' he says, with a wicked smile, his cheeks apple red again. 'Now go! Go! Go! Get into that cab. Your mother already hates me for stealing you away from her. I fear she may never forgive me if you miss Christmas as well.'

Callum runs around to the other side of the desk and hugs him, kissing his cheek.

For a moment, she thinks he's going to run past her, but he reaches for her, scooping her into a hug so tight, the soles of her DMs leave the floor. He kisses her cheek and in that moment, in the brief bloom of heat as his mouth grazes her cheek and passes as quickly as it comes, she knows.

And with that, a door in her heart she didn't know was there opens and there he is.

Callum.

Her heart hiccups as she reaches for the lapels of his suit jacket, the tips of her fingers skimming the black wool for just a moment. But before she can reach for him, he's gone. He lets go of her and she spins, heart hammering now as she watches him grab his suitcase from by the door. She doesn't hear what he says, just registers that he's gone. The absence of him. Then all she can hear is his shoes slapping loudly in the corridor until they stop abruptly.

Then nothing.

Absolutely nothing.

If Shell had just realised a minute – a second – earlier, she could have stopped him.

'No,' she hears herself.

It's a loss she's never felt before. Just as foolish – and as careless – as all the others who went before, but, this time, she didn't even know she'd lost it until it was gone.

Shell has forgotten Old Mr Duke is there until he's standing next to her.

'Well, aren't you going to go after him, my dear?' he asks, with a slow smile.

Then she's running.

Down the corridor, past Gladys's desk and the door to the warehouse and the break room and the supply cupboard that smells of bleach and mouldy mops and out into the light of the Beauty Hall.

'Shell, do you have a clean foundation brush?' she hears Ricky call as she tears past the ART counter. But she doesn't stop, pushing through the revolving door and out into the snow.

But there's no cab.

No Callum.

Just a wall of harassed shoppers, brushing past her to get into the store.

Her eyes dart up and down the high street, and she's wondering if she's *just* missed him.

But there are no cabs.

The high street is unusually empty, except for a bus pulling up across the street.

So she pushes back through the revolving door, looking for Gary.

He sees her before she sees him, though, reaching for her arm. 'Shell? You all right?'

'Cab,' she pants, grasping for his shirt sleeve to steady herself. 'Callum. Did I miss him?'

'Yeah.' Gary nods towards the back of the store. 'It picked him up in the warehouse car park.'

Chapter Thirty-One

Shell waits until the store is closed to cry. Until the last customer has been gently ushered out, laden with so many Duke & Sons bags that Gary has to help or they wouldn't get through the revolving door. Until Ricky and Denise have left, giggling, blissfully unaware of what Shell is trying so hard to hold in as they tell her they'll meet her in the Anchor. Until she can hear the squeak of Gary's shoes and his keys jangling with each step, and Anna, the cleaner, humming happily somewhere above her as she starts on the top floor and works her way down.

Only then does she go to the break room to get her coat and bag and shut her locker for the last time this year. When she comes back, she puts them on the counter she's just spent ten minutes polishing, then stands in the middle of her big, beautiful Beauty Hall, with its glossy floors and neat rows of perfume bottles.

It's perfect. Always perfect. But no more so than tonight, on Christmas Eve, with the tree and the red and white lights. It still smells like peppermint. Although it probably doesn't. Not after two months. But isn't it just like Shell to smell something that isn't there, but not see something that's right in front of her?

She lets herself cry then.

God, it's ridiculous. Callum's only gone home for Christmas. He'll be back, won't he? He'll just be gone a couple of weeks and one morning he'll be here again, striding through the Beauty Hall with a smile for everyone.

But she won't be back in the new year, will she? She'll be in Paris, working on Verity's new film. Then she'll be in Mexico, and after that? Who knows? And just like that, a couple of weeks becomes a couple of months and a couple of months becomes a lifetime. This whole life they might have had if she'd realised when Callum was here.

Not when he was gone.

So she cries. Cries and cries until she feels like she might be able to go to the Anchor. Like she can sit with Ricky and Denise while she drinks white wine and pretends that everything is okay.

That she'll be okay.

That she hasn't lost anything.

Because you can't lose something you didn't have in the first place.

She turns to walk over to the counter to grab her coat and bag, then stops.

'Hey,' Callum says, with a smile that's just for her this time.

Shell stares at him, wondering if her mind – or her heart – is playing tricks on her.

So she squeezes her eyes shut and wishes on every candy cane, on every lipstick and bottle of perfume that it isn't the quiet magic of the Beauty Hall that has conjured him out of her sheer need to see him again.

She holds her breath as she opens them again and he's still there. Definitely there, leaning against the ART counter with his arms crossed, snowflakes melting into the shoulders of his heavy wool coat, his suitcase at his feet.

'Callum.'

His name sounds different when she hears herself say it.

Like she's saying it for the first time.

He unfolds his arms and stands up to face her, watching her across the Beauty Hall.

No one has ever looked at her like that before. Like he sees her. Really *sees* her. Things even she can't see. Things that, someday, she thinks, if she's lucky and she doesn't do anything to mess this up again, he'll tell her about. Or at least see reflected back at her in the mirror of his heart.

'You missed your flight,' she says, which is a terrible waste of words, given all the others she should be saying.

'I did miss my flight. Would you like to know why?'

She would.

'So I get to the airport,' he says, slipping out of his coat and tossing it next to hers on the counter. 'And my flight's delayed because of the snow. It's Christmas Eve so the airport's a mess, of course. All the flights are delayed and I can't even check in. So I figured I'd get a drink. Wait it out.'

He takes a step towards her.

'So there I am, sitting in this sad little hotel bar, next to the airport, listening to Bing Crosby and drinking a martini. And I decide to toast myself.' He stops, pretending to raise a glass. 'Because I won a great battle today, Shell

Smith. I, little Callum Duke, who used to steal jelly beans from the sweetshop on the children's floor, got the great Charles Duke to stand down.'

She watches the patch of parquet floor between them get smaller as he takes another step towards her.

'So, I'm feeling pretty good about myself. But something's not right. Because that wasn't the great battle I was supposed to win today.' He waits for her to meet his gaze. 'Don't get me wrong, it was great, but it wasn't it. The trouble is,' he says, 'I didn't know that. And I might never have known that if it hadn't been for the aforementioned great Charles Duke. Who, great as he is, has yet to master the art of charging his phone, but managed to send me a little text message. In all caps, of course. Do you want to know what it said?'

She does.

He reaches into the inside pocket of his jacket and pulls out his phone.

He taps on the screen, peers at it for a moment, then says, '*Did she find you?*'

Callum looks up at her and her heart hiccups.

'It took a few more texts.' He slips his phone back into the inside pocket of his jacket. 'And a phone call to decipher who was trying to find me and, from what I gather, it was you, Shell Smith.'

It was.

'So,' he says, taking the last step towards her, so close that she can feel the heat of him. 'I abandoned my drink and came back because I'm curious to hear what you were going to say when you found me.'

He looks down at her with a slow smile and this is it, she knows.

It's her turn.

'I just—' She has to stop, suddenly, painfully aware of the weight of each word, scared that if she says them wrong or puts them in the wrong order, like she has so many times with him, he's going to take his suitcase and go.

'I just—' she tries again, then stops again, shaking her head.

Just say it, Shell.

'Just say it, Shell,' he says, like it's that easy.

Like there's no right order, she just has to say it.

So she does.

'You're not my type.'

'Excellent start, Shell.'

'Well, you're not. You're far too pretty and I'm almost certain that you have no idea who Bon Iver is.'

'I don't.'

'But I didn't want you to leave thinking that I only see the worst in you, because I don't. I see you. All of you. The best of you. I see your heart.' She wants to reach out and press her palm to his chest, but she doesn't dare. Scared that if she touches him, he'll disappear in a puff of smoke. 'And I see how much you love this place and your grandfather and how you will do *exactly* what he says and let this place kill you, if I let you.'

His pupils blow black at that. 'If you let me?'

'Yes.' She nods with a certainty she hasn't felt in a very long time. 'But you'd *never* tell your grandfather that because you want him to spend whatever time he has left falling in love with this place again, because you know he lost that and he really needs it back. And I see that you will sink *every penny* you have into this place to make sure that happens because you don't care about the money, you care about him. And us. All of us. Even Louise Larson, who doesn't even deserve you to care about her,' she says, with a sigh. 'But she does, of course, because if you don't care about her, no one else will, apparently, and I don't like *that* about you, actually.'

'What?'

'That you made me feel sorry for Louise Larson. But I like everything else about you.' She peers at him from under her fringe. 'And I'm so sorry if I ever made you feel like I only ever see the worst in you. And *that*,' she takes a deep breath and pushes it back out through her lips, 'is what I would have said to you this morning, if I'd gone through the warehouse instead.'

'Is it now?'

'Yes. And I probably would have said it wrong and I definitely would have yelled at you, like it was your fault. Which it kind of is, when you think about it. And all of it would have been dramatic and unnecessary because there was only one thing I really wanted to say.'

'What's that?'

She makes sure she looks him in the eye when she says it. 'There you are.'

'Where am I, Shell?'

'There.' She shrugs. 'Just *there*. You slotted into my life and I didn't even notice or have to change who I am or make space for you. You're just there and when you left this morning, I knew.'

'Knew what?'

'That I didn't want you to go. That I wanted you to always be there.'

Then everything is still.

Still in a way it only is at night, when the doors are locked and it's just her, wandering around the Beauty Hall, straightening the perfume bottles and wiping the smudges from the glass countertops with the sleeve of her coat.

It goes on and on and on until finally – *finally* – he smiles.

The smile that's just for her.

'Well, I'm here. So what now, Shell Smith?'

'I think this is the part where you kiss me.'

'Is it?' he says, his smile sharpening to a smirk. 'Well, okay, then.'

Callum reaches for her, her heart knocking into her ribs as he pulls her to him. He tilts his head and when their mouths meet and he kisses her, it's exactly what she wanted, but it still feels sudden.

So sudden that she's sure she can hear the perfume bottles shivering.

ONE YEAR LATER

'Hello, stranger,' Gary says, as Shell pushes through the revolving doors into Duke & Sons.

'Hey Gary! How's it going?'

'I was about to lock up and head to the Anchor. You coming?'

Before she can tell him that she'd love to, but can't, she hears Ricky shriek from the ART counter.

'Shell Smith! Get your fabulous arse over here right now!'

She gives Gary a quick kiss on the cheek, then does as she's told, waving at the chorus of *Hey, Shell* as she passes through the Beauty Hall.

It looks exactly the same. Same hot-air balloon hanging from the ceiling. Same polar bears in Christmas jumpers at the foot of the stairs. Same smell of peppermint candy canes and Gaulin perfume.

It's like coming home.

Ricky runs around the counter to greet her, almost knocking her over as he hugs her. 'How was New York?' he asks, when he finally lets go.

'Good. Cold. Where's Louise?'

'I let her go to the Anchor with Becca and Soph while I waited for you.'

'How's she doing?'

'Still *wanging on* about her year in Goa *constantly*.' He rolls his eyes. 'But she's so much happier. She's dyed her hair pink and is dating a stupidly hot barista called Jackson.'

Shell arches an eyebrow at that. 'Free coffee?'

'You know it. *Anyway*.' He holds his hands out with an eager smile. 'What'd you bring me?'

She gives him the Sephora bag she's holding, which makes him shriek again. 'You have to share that with Denise,' she tells him sternly.

As if on cue, Shell hears her running towards her, heels clacking furiously on the parquet floor, her arms open.

'Shell!'

'Denise!'

They hug so tightly, it knocks the air clean out of them as they sway from side to side, giggling.

'How was New York?' Denise asks, when she steps back. 'What's the real Reese Witherspoon like?'

'So sweet. She has the most incredible skin, Den. Seriously. Doing her makeup was a dream.'

'Did you tell her?' Ricky tugs on the sleeve of her coat. 'Did you tell her about Wreath Witherspoon?'

'Of course! And showed her photos. She was delighted.'

He does a little wiggle. 'You have to do a film with Emily Blunt next.'

Why? Shell almost asks, but thinks better of it.

She's about to show them the photo she took with

Reese when she hears Callum say, 'Shell Smith,' and her heart starts hiccuping in that way it does when he says her name. She scans the Beauty Hall for him and there he is, striding towards her in an immaculate black suit, the top three buttons of his white shirt undone. He smiles, scooping her up into a kiss that makes the soles of her DMs leave the floor.

'Get a room,' she hears Ricky mutter, but Shell doesn't care, fingers curled into the lapels of Callum's jacket.

'Forgive me for the shameless display of public affection,' Callum says, a little breathless as he stands back and gazes at her. 'But I haven't seen my fiancée for twenty-two days. Not that I've been counting.'

'You ready?' she asks, tugging on his lapels.

'Always.' He kisses her quickly, then turns to Ricky and Denise. 'We're off for a Smith Christmas Eve.'

'Have fun,' Denise grins, waving at them. 'We're still coming to yours on Boxing Day for dinner, right?'

'Absolutely,' Callum assures her. 'We promise anything but turkey.'

'Thank God,' Ricky mutters, checking his white glitter acrylics. 'You know I'm a vegan now, right?'

Callum blinks at him. 'Since when?'

'*Yesterday*.' Denise says. 'He's only doing it to wind his parents up because they won't buy him a car.'

'Okay, then. Have a wonderful Christmas, guys.' Callum turns to wave at the rest of the Beauty Hall, wishing everyone else the same as they wave back. 'Let me know what you think of the film tonight, guys!'

'Oh, yes! It's the premiere, isn't it?' Shell says.

With the trauma of almost not being able to fly out of JFK last night because of the snow, she'd forgotten.

'Don't say that word.' He groans, taking her hand and leading her through the Beauty Hall.

'What word?'

'Premiere.' He mock-shudders.

'Old Mr Duke still driving you mad?'

'We did the whole red-carpet thing with Verity at the beginning of the month for the trailer.'

'I was there,' Shell says soothingly, squeezing his hand. 'It was very exciting.'

'Then we did the whole big eighty-fifth birthday-party thing for him last night, with the ceremonial handing over of the Duke & Sons keys to me. The mayor was here, for goodness' sake, and he's *still* mad at me because he can't have *another* party for the film premiere tonight? *No one* wants to sit in a store for two hours watching a film. On Christmas Eve, no less. People have families.'

'I know.' She pats his arm. 'But at least he has the launch party for Mia's and my app to look forward to in the New Year. He's trying to source a peacock, apparently.'

'A peacock? We can't have a peacock strutting around the Beauty Hall!'

Shell just shakes her head.

'I know what this is *really* about,' Callum hisses, as they head out into the back of house. 'Pops isn't mad at me for not telling him about the film. He's mad because *he's* not in it.'

'Oh, for sure.'

'Unbelievable. The store is in profit,' he holds up two

fingers, '*two years* ahead of schedule. We've been approached to franchise, and *this* is all he cares about.'

Shell shrugs. 'It's his legacy, apparently.'

'He spoke to you about it?'

'Of course he did. He called me in New York last week, demanding that I come home and talk some sense into you when you wouldn't let him have the premiere party tonight.'

'Legacy,' Callum mutters, under his breath. 'I thought Duke & Sons was his legacy.'

'No, a made-for-TV Christmas film is his legacy, apparently.'

Callum slows as they walk through the warehouse.

'What?' she asks, when he peers around a pile of cardboard boxes.

'You never know. Liam might still be harbouring feelings for you.'

'We went on *one* proper date *a year* ago. I think he'll get over it.'

'That's a relief. He's a big dude.'

'Don't worry,' Shell assures him. 'I'll protect you.'

'Hey!' Callum squeaks. 'I do Bikram yoga. I'm stronger than I look.'

'When did you start doing Bikram yoga?'

'Last week. With your mum.'

'Where?'

'The community centre. They put the heating up and we have to wear, like, fourteen sweaters.'

She laughs and when she squeezes his hand again, he grins. 'What?' she asks.

'Nothing.' He brings her hand up to his mouth and kisses it. 'I've just missed you.'

'Yeah?'

He stops and pulls her to him with a growl, pretending to chomp on her neck, like a vampire.

'Get off!' she tells him, squealing with delight because, *God*, she loves this Callum.

Shell wriggles away, but Callum grabs her, picking her up and peppering her face with kisses. She holds onto him and squeals again, telling him to put her down, but he doesn't, just swings her around until she's dizzy.

When he finally does, she whacks his arm, but he just laughs, wild and bright.

They hear someone clear their throat and turn to find Mick, who runs the warehouse, watching.

'Mick.' Callum nods politely, running a hand through his hair. 'How are you this fine Christmas Eve?'

'Good, Mr Duke.'

'Great.' Callum fusses with his coat collar. 'Excellent.'

'Merry Christmas, Mr Duke,' Mick says, trying to fight a smile. 'You too, Shell.'

'Have a good one,' she tells him, with a small wave as he saunters off.

As soon as he does, Callum and Shell burst out laughing.

'Very professional,' Shell says, as they continue to the door.

'Always.' He grins, waiting for her to go out first then following.

'So,' she says, 'are you ready for Christmas Eve with the Smiths?'

'I've had dinner with the Smiths. Several times.'

'I know,' she says, when he slips his arm around her waist and pulls her to him as they trudge through the snow to his car. 'But you've not had Christmas Eve dinner with the Smiths. It's a very different thing.'

'I think I'll manage,' he says, with a sweet smile, as he opens the car door for her.

She glances over her shoulder when she gets in, then glares at him as he jumps into the driver's seat.

'Callum,' she hisses, waving at all the presents on the back seat. 'I told you not to get the twins anything.'

He pulls a face as he puts on his seatbelt. 'How am I going to get them to like me if I don't bribe them?'

'You don't *have* to bribe them. You'll win them over with your charming, slightly awkward personality.'

He looks horrified. 'Kids who don't need to be bribed? What sort of family are your parents trying to raise?'

When they pull up outside her house, Shell takes her seatbelt off and turns to him with a frown. 'Ready?'

'Ready.'

'Okay. Let's do this.'

'Shell, we're having supper with your family. Why are you acting like we're about to go to war?' he asks, then tuts when she doesn't wait for him to come around and open her car door.

'Callum,' she says, joining him on the pavement as he leans in to retrieve the presents from the back. 'I know you've been to my house before, but you have *no idea* what you're about to walk into.'

'Hmm.' He hands her a stack of boxes wrapped in red tartan paper, each with a green ribbon bow.

'It's six o'clock on *Christmas Eve*,' she reminds him. 'The twins are going to be *feral*.'

'I saw them earlier when they came into the store to meet Santa. They were fine.'

'Do you have any idea how much sugar they've had since then?' she asks, as he adds more presents to the pile she's holding. She can no longer see him and has to lift her chin to peer over them. 'It's going to be *so loud*.'

'I think I can cope.' He takes the stack from her and hands her a canvas bag.

'Fine.' She stomps through the snow towards the house. 'Don't say I didn't warn you.'

She can hear them – the twins – before she's even reached the doorstep and gives Callum a smug smile as she hooks the handle of the canvas bag into the crook of her arm and reaches into her handbag for her keys.

'It's fine,' he says, but takes a deep breath as she opens the front door.

It swings open and there's Kitty, rolling towards them with her arms out.

She crashes into Shell as soon as she steps inside, and it's somewhere between a fall and a hug.

'I thought you weren't allowed to wear those in the house?' Shell asks, nodding down at her Heelys.

Kitty shrugs. 'Dad won't let me wear them in the street so when can I wear them?'

Fair enough.

Kitty spots the pile of presents Callum is holding, her eyes wide. 'Are they for us?'

It would be nice if she acknowledged him before the presents, but as she's nine years old and it's Christmas Eve, Shell lets her off.

'You were so well behaved earlier at the store,' Callum tells her, 'that Santa sent them.'

Kitty whispers. 'I know Santa isn't real.'

'Of course he's real,' Callum says, with such conviction that Shell wonders if he really does believe it.

'He's not,' Kitty says. 'Mark Fitzburg at school told me, but I'm just going along with it cos—'

Shell arches an eyebrow at her. 'More presents?'

Kitty sighs, as if to say, *Of course*. 'And for Sim. She still believes, bless her young heart.'

'You are *literally* three minutes older than her.'

'Three minutes is a long time when you're nine.'

Shell supposes it is.

Then Kitty's gone, turning and rolling back up the hallway.

'Aren't you going to say hello to Callum?' Shell asks.

'Hey, Callum!' Kitty says, over her shoulder, raising her arm as she rolls into the kitchen.

'Are they trainers with wheels on?' Callum asks, as he watches her go.

'Oh, yeah.'

Shell starts to lead him into the living room, but before she can, Arun runs out. 'Presents!'

'Also *Callum*,' she says, but it's futile. She doesn't know who takes what, but they're attacked by several pairs of little hands and then the presents are gone as she and Callum wander into the kitchen empty-handed.

'What's going on out there? I thought you lot had calmed down,' Eleanor calls, then beams when she sees Shell and Callum walking into the kitchen. 'You've arrived! When did you guys get here?'

'Good evening, Eleanor. How are you?'

'Mad at *you*, actually. You know I love you, Callum Duke, but *why* did you buy my daughters a drum kit *and* a bass guitar for their birthday? Are you trying to kill me?'

'Hey, Mum,' Shell says, with a small wave.

'There's my baby girl. I've missed this face.' She kisses Shell's cheek then steps back. 'What'd you bring me?'

Shell pulls a pair of KLM earplugs out of her bag.

Her mother cackles maniacally. 'Thank God you're home, Shell.' She hugs her again. 'Well, not *home* home,' she says, with a pantomime pout, when she steps back. 'But at least back in Ostley.'

Eleanor playfully slaps Callum's arm. 'Reason number two why you're on my list, Duke. Taking my daughter away, so Shaun and I aren't just outnumbered, we don't stand a chance.'

'Would this help?' he asks, taking the tote bag from Shell and pulling out a bottle of champagne.

Eleanor studies the label. 'Veuve Clicquot.' She smiles. 'You're forgiven.'

'Where's Dad?' Shell asks, suddenly suspicious that she can't smell roast potatoes. 'What's for dinner? I'm *so sick* of room-service chicken tenders and craft-table Twizzlers.'

'It's your mother's turn to cook this year,' Shaun says, wandering in with a mug of tea.

'So, Chinese?' Shell says, giving him a huge hug.

'On its way.' He winks as the doorbell rings. 'There it is, in fact! Don't you dare,' Shaun warns, as Callum goes to answer it. 'I'm paying this time.'

They return a few minutes later with two bags of food, the smell of beef chow mein and warm, vinegary sweet and sour sauce making Shell feel positively giddy. Patrick must smell it too, because he tears into the kitchen.

'Living-room picnic!' he yells, arms in the air.

All hell breaks loose as the whole house thunders with the sound of three pairs of feet on the stairs.

'No one take my spring roll!' Eleanor warns, the kitchen suddenly full, everyone talking at once.

'Can someone put a blanket down on the living-room floor, please?' Shaun asks, as he grabs a tea towel and takes the plates out of the oven, but is roundly ignored as the twins oversee the equal distribution of *everything*.

'Sim has one more prawn cracker than everyone else,' Arun wails, counting each one meticulously.

'There,' Eleanor says, resolving the dispute by snatching it off Sim's plate and biting into it.

'Blanket. Floor. Please,' Shaun tries again.

Shell and Callum decide to leave them to it, standing by the kettle as he pours them each a glass of white wine. As soon as they clink, Eleanor spins around, holding out her hand. She immediately realises her mistake and spins back to face the table. 'No one touch my spring roll!'

'How come *you* get an extra spring roll?' Kitty huffs.

'Because I paid for it. You got spring-roll money? No? Get a job!'

'We need some help in the warehouse,' Callum tells Kitty, as she storms out of the kitchen with her plate.

'Hey!' Arun frowns as Eleanor picks up two plates. 'Who's the extra one for?'

But she ignores him, looking over her shoulder. 'Callum, can you bring the wine, darling?'

'Of course,' he says, snatching the bottle off the counter and heading after her.

Shell follows, grabbing the only two plates left when everyone else pads out of the kitchen. As she's approaching the living room, she hears Callum gasp and walks in to find him, beaming.

'Pops!'

There he is, Old Mr Duke, sitting in the armchair in the living room.

Callum stoops down to kiss his cheek. 'I didn't know you were here!'

'Well, it wouldn't have been a surprise if you did, would it?' He chuckles merrily.

'I invited him,' Eleanor says, handing Old Mr Duke the other plate she's holding. 'It's not quite the red-carpet premiere you were hoping for, Mr Duke, but I hope you don't mind making do with us.'

'Making do?' Old Mr Duke snorts as the kids grin up at him from the floor where someone – Shell's father, probably – has spread a blanket. 'A living-room picnic with these monkeys. What could be better?'

'How's the retired life treating you, Charles?' Shaun asks.

He huffs. 'It's been twenty-four hours and I don't care for it much, I have to say.'

Callum closes his eyes and takes a deep breath as Shell rubs his back.

'What are you up to?' Shaun asks, as Eleanor sits on the floor.

'Just spending time with my darling children.'

'So, not waiting to eat what they don't finish, then?'

Her shoulders slump. 'Arun picks the prawns out of his prawn balls and only eats the batter. It's a waste.'

'Here, Mum,' he says, with an angelic smile, handing her one.

'Thank you, baby boy,' she says, kissing his cheek and taking the prawn from him.

'Wait!' Callum says, checking his watch when he and Shell sit on the sofa. 'It's seven o'clock.'

'Quick!' Shaun says, to no one in particular. 'Turn it to the film! Turn it to the film!'

Someone does so as an ad for toilet roll is ending.

'Oh, good. We didn't miss anything,' Old Mr Duke says, settling back into the armchair with his plate.

As soon as he does, the channel's Christmas logo appears and the screen fades to black.

When it lights up again, everyone cheers.

'There she is!' Old Mr Duke squeals, when the snowy scene of Duke & Sons appears.

'We were there today!' Patrick says, waving at the television and looking at Old Mr Duke. 'Meeting Santa!'

Old Mr Duke leans down to stroke his head. 'You certainly were, young man.'

Christmas music starts playing and they all giggle eagerly. Then there she is, Verity Appleton, running through the snow towards Duke & Sons.

'I did her contour!' Shell says, arm in the air.

'I don't know what that is,' Old Mr Duke says, utterly beside himself. 'But I'm very proud!'

Everyone cheers and Callum takes advantage of the situation to nick one of Shell's prawn balls.

'Um.' She almost stabs him with her fork. 'I love you, Callum Duke, but don't even think about it.'

'But your mum didn't give me any.' He pouts.

'Liar!' Eleanor says, from the living-room floor. 'I am firm, but fair.'

'Callum.' Shell blinks at him. 'I just saw you stuff them into your gob.'

'Yeah, but I was hungry and they looked *so* good.'

'Hush, Callum. You can have one of mine.' Old Mr Duke points his fork at the television screen. 'Look at the Beauty Hall! It's so beautiful! Look at the decorations! The hot-air balloon! The polar bears!'

'She looks all right, doesn't she?' Callum smiles.

'Look! Look! Look!' Old Mr Duke sits forward in the armchair so suddenly that a piece of crispy shredded beef falls off the edge of his plate. Luckily Patrick catches it in his mouth, like a dog, much to Eleanor's horror.

'You happy, Pops?'

'Of course. But do you know what's missing?' He points his fork at his chest. 'Me!'

'Oh, good,' Callum says, under his breath. 'Glad he's letting that go, then.'

'Hey. How about you, Mr Duke?' Shell nudges Callum while everyone sings along and shoulder-dances to 'Rocking Around the Christmas Tree' as *Someday at Christmas* comes up on the screen. 'Are you happy?'

'Blissfully.' He kisses her on the mouth. 'But I'd be happier if you let me have one of your prawn balls.'

She pulls her plate away. 'Forget it.'

'In six months we're going to be married,' Callum reminds her. 'What's yours is mine, and all that.'

Shell just smiles. 'Ask me again in six months, then.'

Acknowledgements

First and foremost, I have to express my endless gratitude to my editor, Melissa Cox, who gave me an opportunity to write a book about a brown fat girl living her best life who falls in love without having to change a thing about herself. Melissa not only understood the story I was trying to tell but cheered me on every step – or word – along the way. We were determined to make this book as joyful as we could so if, like me, you've ever asked yourself if you take up too much space, I hope you read this and know that you deserve to take up every inch.

To my friends Suzie, Angela, Catherine, Tracy and Duncan, thank you for making sure I ate and distracting Frida so I could write this.

To Holly and Sara for telling me that I could write this book and reminding me of that fact every time I insisted that I couldn't. I love you.

To everyone at Space NK Brighton, thank you for indulging my weakness for skincare I can't afford and letting me try all the Diptyque perfumes even though you know I'm going to buy Figuier.

Finally, all the love to my wonderful agent, Claire

Wilson, without whom this book wouldn't be in your hands right now. I don't even know how to begin thanking her for everything she has done – and put up with! – these last nine years, but these few meager words will have to do for now.